THE SHIPSHAPE MIRACLE

THE SHIPSHAPE MIRACLE

AND OTHER STORIES

The Complete Short Fiction
of Clifford D. Simak,
Volume Ten

Introduction by David W. Wixon

NEW YORK

All rights reserved, including without limitation the right to reproduce this book or any portion thereof in any form or by any means, whether electronic or mechanical, now known or hereinafter invented, without the express written permission of the publisher.

These are works of fiction. Names, characters, places, events, and incidents either are the product of the author's imagination or are used fictitiously. Any resemblance to actual persons, living or dead, businesses, companies, events, or locales is entirely coincidental.

Copyright © 2017 the Estate of Clifford D. Simak

All stories reprinted by permission of the Estate of Clifford D. Simak.

"The Money Tree" © 1958 by Mercury Press, Inc. © 1986 by Clifford D. Simak. Originally published in Venture Science Fiction, v. 2, no. 4, July, 1958. Reprinted by permission of the Estate of Clifford D. Simak.

"Shotgun Cure" © 1960 by Mercury Press, Inc. © 1988 by the Estate of Clifford D. Simak. Originally published in The Magazine of Fantasy & Science Fiction, v. 20, no. 1, Jan., 1961. Reprinted by permission of the Estate of Clifford D. Simak.

"Paradise" © 1946 by Street & Smith Publications, Inc. © 1974 by Clifford D. Simak. Originally published in Astounding Science Fiction, v. 37, no. 4, June, 1946. Reprinted by permission of the Estate of Clifford D. Simak.

"The Gravestone Rebels Ride by Night!" © 1944 by Popular Publications, Inc. © 1972 by Clifford D. Simak. Originally published in Big-Book Western Magazine, v. 14, no. 3, Oct., 1944. Reprinted by permission of the Estate of Clifford D. Simak.

"How-2" © 1954 by Galaxy Publishing Corporation. © 1982 by Clifford D. Simak. Originally published in Galaxy Science Fiction, v. 9, no. 2, November, 1954. Reprinted by permission of the Estate of Clifford D. Simak.

"The Shipshape Miracle" © 1962 by Digest Productions Corporation. © 1990 by the Estate of Clifford D. Simak. Originally published in If, v. 12, no. 6, January, 1963. Reprinted by permission of the Estate of Clifford D. Simak.

"Rim of the Deep" © 1940 by Street & Smith Publications, Inc. © 1968 by Clifford D. Simak. Originally published in Astounding Science-Fiction, v. 25, no. 3, May, 1940. Reprinted by permission of the Estate of Clifford D. Simak.

"Eternity Lost" © 1949 by Street & Smith Publications, Inc. © 1977 by Clifford D. Simak. Originally published in Astounding Science Fiction, v. 43, no. 5, July, 1949. Reprinted by permission of the Estate of Clifford D. Simak.

"Immigrant" © 1954 by Street & Smith Publications, Inc. © 1982 by Clifford D. Simak. Originally published in Astounding Science Fiction, v. 53, no. 1, March, 1954. Reprinted by permission of the Estate of Clifford D. Simak.

Introduction © 2017 by David W. Wixon

978-1-5040-7393-6

This edition published in 2022 by Open Road Integrated Media, Inc.
180 Maiden Lane
New York, NY 10038
www.openroadmedia.com

CONTENTS

INTRODUCTION: LITTLE THINGS: THE WAY CLIFFORD D. SIMAK WROTE

"The desk was scarred and battered, unlike the man himself. It was almost as if the desk, in the course of years, might have intervened itself to take the blows aimed at the man behind it."

—Clifford D. Simak, in "Worlds Without End"

In 1976, when Clifford D. Simak was in the process of retiring from his long career with the *Minneapolis Star-Tribune*, he told an interviewer that he had "always wanted to be a newspaperman, but realized my creative urges could not be satisfied by writing news."

The result was that Cliff had two careers—careers that ran in tandem for more than forty years, causing Robert A. Heinlein to marvel, knowing—as he said—that the two types of writing required were vastly different.

Among other things, this meant that Cliff Simak's newspaper training strongly influenced his fiction. Some would come to criticize his literary style as a "lack of style" (thus betraying a preoccupation with form over substance); but it seems clear that, like the professional newspaperman he was, Simak tried to avoid allowing stylistic flourishes to get in the way of his exposition of the facts of the story—prose, he believed, is not supposed to distract from the plot (well, that was the theory, but once in a while, perhaps unable to stop himself, he would drop in a gem of a line). Robert Silverberg saw this, and described Simak's work as having a "clear, precise, straightforward narrative style."

Even before I met him, Clifford D. Simak had become a legendary figure in science fiction, and readers who never had a chance to know him in person are now discovering his work. And I find that in doing so, they become very interested in him—not only in his writing but also in details of his life that might help color in the picture of this beloved Grand Master. So let me tell you a little about how Cliff did his work of writing fiction.

Clifford D. Simak never used a pseudonym, and he engaged in collaborations on only three occasions. In the first of those, he worked with a fellow Twin Cities writer, Carl Jacobi, to produce a story that was first published as "The Street That Wasn't There" (later reprinted at times as "The Lost Street"). The collaboration does not seem to have been a pleasant experience; Cliff would later say that he and Carl "fought like hell for the weeks it took to write it." (The two of them tried it a second time, producing a story called "The Cat That Had Nine Lives"; that story also sold, but it was never published because the magazine that bought it—*Comet*—folded.)

The third of Cliff's collaborations was with his son, Richard, and together they produced a story called "Unsilent Spring," which turned out well. Dick (known in the family as "Scott") was a government chemist, and Cliff would later insist that his contribution to the story was more than just the science, and was essential.

My belief is that Cliff Simak's aversion to collaboration was closely related to the fact that he simply did not like to talk about a work in progress. "To me," he said, "writing is intensely private.

If I talk to anyone, I feel the story is not entirely mine any more. I lose the magic."

(In the novel *All Flesh Is Grass*, one of Cliff's characters, Nancy, who was a writer herself, would say of that profession: "It's a thing you don't talk about—not until you're well along with it. There are so many things that can go wrong with writing. I don't want to be one of those pseudo-literary people who are always writing something they never finish, or talking about writing something that they never start."

("You have to have a hunger," Nancy would add, "a different kind of hunger, to finish up a book.")

Cliff's way was to spend time thinking about his next story, plotting it out in his head; but once he had it mostly plotted out—when he began to actually put words on paper—it was not unusual for the story to "take off" on him. And he loved it when that happened, when he found himself putting words on the paper without knowing where they were leading him. He found the process incredible; to him, that was the best kind of writing, because it meant he was writing from—well, he called it his gut, or he called it his nerve endings—but I'd say it was from the world underneath the top of his mind.

The process, again, reflected the author's newspaper training: he began by making notes, often starting by asking himself a question, then answering it, and then beginning to build the stories from pieces he created, trying out alternative beginnings and endings. Sometimes he became so caught up in his creating that he made lists of the names of characters who might be somehow involved—characters who sometimes never even made it into the story.

For the most part, once Cliff had a story worked out in his head, he would begin by using a pencil to compose onto paper. He went to his typewriter only when he thought he had the story worked out to an end in his scrawling longhand, and he used the process of typing it to polish it.

After that, he would—when he could afford it—have someone else retype the finished product for submission. Early in his career (which began around the time his marriage was new), his wife, Kay, would do that retyping—but once he became able to afford to hire a professional typist, Kay, who never liked science fiction, would not get involved.

It's not that Cliff could not have typed the finished manuscript—he did so, when times required it; but once he had finished a story in his mind, he did not want to go back to it . . . the urge to rewrite, he knew, would always rise up, and he wanted to resist that: having finished a story, it was a done thing, and he preferred to let it lie.

He made some exceptions to that rule: In his journal entry for February 7, 1957, Cliff, speaking of a story he was then calling "Who Cares for Shadows?" noted that "the end is still to write, but maybe by the time I get to that I'll know" where "I want to go." (However that worked, he did finish the story, and sent it to Horace Gold at *Galaxy* . . . but after Gold asked for revisions, Cliff complied, even though he often refused to do that for editors. I suspect that this time it was palatable because whatever changes were needed to make the story something Horace wanted, Cliff was able to do it in less than a week (working only in the evenings, after work). Gold accepted the revised story just five days after Cliff sent him the revised version. It would be published later that same year as "Shadow World.")

When I mentioned above that Cliff took part in only three collaborations, I was purposely passing over a short novel called *Empire*. I did so because that story was one that Cliff wished he had never worked on.

Late in the 1930s, John W. Campbell, the new editor of *Astounding Tales*, who had recently talked Cliff into writing him a novel he could serialize—and who had very much liked the story he received, *Cosmic Engineers*—dug out a short novel he had written at the age of eighteen, called *Empire*. Cliff would later say that he "gagged" when he read the story, but he worked on it, making it, as he said, "somewhat better," but "still pretty bad."

Campbell himself was still not willing to publish the story, and Cliff, as he said, simply "threw it on a shelf." Years later, when Horace Gold created a new line of science fiction novels that were to be published in digest-size as the "Galaxy Novels" (some very great stories would first be published in that line), he found himself desperately short of material and called Cliff to beg for anything he might be able to get quickly. Feeling a certain obligation to a man who was now publishing a lot of his work, Cliff sent it to him.

Gold published *Empire*, but Cliff never read it in its published form and would not allow it to be republished—in fact, he refused to even renew the story's copyright.

David W. Wixon

THE MONEY TREE

Although Cliff Simak noted in his journal that he had begun "plotting" "The Money Tree" on June 10, 1957, he got involved in other things—including going down to Iowa to attend a funeral and considering whether to apply for a managing editor job in Ames. But he quickly decided not to apply for that job, and by July 26, he reported that he had given up "momentarily" on "The Money Tree." Thereafter, he and his family left on a trip to the Black Hills in the middle of August, and he made no further mention of "The Money Tree" until September 8, when he reported, rather laconically, that he had finished the story "last week." Before long he noted that he had sent it to Horace Gold, but Gold rejected it, as did Campbell ("first thing I've sent him for several years," Cliff told his journal).

In March 1958, the story was accepted by Bob Mills, and it would appear in the July 1958 issue of Venture Science Fiction. *Also in March, Cliff and Kay were involved in having a new house built, Cliff was signed up to give a speech on television, and the entire family got the 'flu, serially—all while Cliff was, a little excitedly, finishing up the story that would become "The Big Front Yard."*

—dww

I

Chuck Doyle, loaded with his camera equipment, was walking along the high brick wall which sheltered the town house of J. Howard Metcalfe from vulgar public contact when he saw the twenty-dollar bill blow across the wall.

Now, Doyle was well dried behind the ears—he had cut his eyeteeth on the crudities of the world and while no one could ever charge him with being a sophisticate, neither was he anybody's fool. And yet there was no question, either, about his quick, positive action when there was money to be picked up off the street.

He looked around to see if anyone might be watching—someone, for example, who might be playing a dirty joke on him, or, worse yet, someone who might appear to claim the bill once he had retrieved it.

There was small chance there would be anyone, for this was the snooty part of town, where everyone minded his own business and made sure that any uncouth intruders would mind theirs as well—an effect achieved in most cases by high walls or dense hedges or sturdy ornamental fences. And the street on which Doyle now prepared to stalk a piece of currency was by rights no proper street at all. It was an alley that ran between the brick walls of the Metcalfe residence and the dense hedge of Banker J. S. Gregg—Doyle had parked his car in there because it was against traffic regulations to park on the boulevard upon which the houses fronted.

Seeing no one, Doyle set his camera equipment down and charged upon the bill, which was fluttering feebly in the alley. He scooped it up with the agility of a cat grabbing off a mouse and now he saw, for the first time, that it was no piddling one-dollar affair, or even a five-spot, but a twenty. It was crinkly and so new that it fairly gleamed, and he held it tenderly in his fingertips and resolved to retire to Benny's Place as soon as possible, and pour himself a libation or two to celebrate his colossal good luck.

There was a little breeze blowing down the alley and the leaves of the few fugitive trees that lined the alley and the leaves of the many trees that grew in the stately lawns beyond the walls and hedges were making a sort of subdued symphonic sound. The sun was shining brightly and there was no hint of rain and the air was clean and fresh and the world was a perfect place.

It was becoming more perfect by the moment.

For over the Metcalfe wall, from which the first bill had fluttered, other bills came dancing merrily in the impish breeze, swirling in the alley.

Doyle saw them and stood for a frozen instant, his eyes bugging out a little and his Adam's apple bobbing in excitement. Then he was among the bills, grabbing right and left and stuffing them in his pockets, gulping with the fear that one of them might somehow escape him, and ridden by the conviction that once he had gathered them he should get out of there as fast as he could manage.

The money, he knew, must belong to someone and there was no one, he was sure, not even on this street, who was so contemptuous of cash as to allow it to blow away without attempting to retrieve it.

So he gathered the bills with the fervor of a Huck Finn going through a blackberry patch and with a last glance around to be sure he had missed none, streaked for his car.

A dozen blocks away, in a less plush locality, he wheeled the car up to the curb opposite a vacant lot and furtively emptied his pockets, smoothing out the bills and stacking them neatly on the seat beside him. There were a lot of them, many more than he had thought there were, and his breath whistled through his teeth.

He picked up the pile of currency preparatory to counting it and something, some little stick-like thing was sticking out of it. He flicked it to knock it away and it stayed where it was. It seemed to be stuck to one of the bills. He seized it to pull it loose. It came and the bill came with it.

It was a stem, like an apple stem, like a cherry stem—a stem attached quite solidly and naturally to one corner of a twenty-dollar bill!

He dropped the pile of bills upon the seat and held up the stem and the bill hung from the stem, as if it were growing from the stem, and it was clear to see that the stem not long before had been fastened to a branch, for the mark of recent separation was plainly visible.

Doyle whistled softly.

A money tree! he thought.

But there was no such a thing as a money tree. There'd never been a money tree. There never would be a money tree.

"I'm seeing things," said Doyle, "and I ain't had a drink in hours."

He could shut his eyes and there it was—a mighty tree, huge of boll and standing true and straight and high, with spreading branches fully leafed and every leaf a twenty-dollar bill. The wind would rustle all the leaves and would make money-music and a man could lie in the shade of such a tree and not have a worry in the world, just waiting for the leaves to drop so he could pick them up and put them in his pocket.

He tugged at the stem a bit and it still clung to the bill, so he folded the whole thing up as neatly as he could and stuck it in the watch pocket of his trousers. Then he picked up the rest of the bills and stuffed them in another pocket without counting them.

Twenty minutes later he walked into Benny's Bar. Benny was mopping the mahogany. One lone customer was at the far end of the bar working through a beer.

"Gimme bottle and a glass," said Doyle.

"Show me cash," said Benny.

Doyle gave him one of the twenty-dollar bills. It was so fresh and new and crisp that its crinkling practically thundered in the silence of the place. Benny looked it over with great care.

"Got someone making them for you?" he asked.

"Naw," said Doyle. "I pick them off the street."

Benny handed across a bottle and a glass.

"You through work," he asked, "or are you just beginning?"

"I put in my day," said Doyle. "I been shooting old J. Howard Metcalfe. Magazine in the east wanted pictures of him."

"You mean the racketeer?"

"He ain't no racketeer. He went legitimate four or five years ago. He's a magnate now."

"You mean tycoon. What kind of tycoon is he?"

"I don't know. But whatever kind it is, it sure pays off. He's got a fancy-looking shack up on the hill. But he ain't so much to look at. Don't see why this magazine should want a picture of him."

"Maybe they're running a story about how it pays to go straight."

Doyle tipped the bottle and sloshed liquor in his glass.

"It ain't no skin off me," he declared philosophically. "I'd go take pictures of an angleworm if they paid me for it."

"Who would want pictures of any angleworm?"

"Lots of crazy people in the world," said Doyle. "Might want anything. I don't ask no questions. I don't venture no opinions. People want pictures taken, I take them. They pay me for it, that is all right by me."

Doyle drank appreciatively and refilled the glass.

"Benny," he asked, "you ever hear of money growing on a tree?"

"You got it wrong," said Benny. "Money grows on bushes."

"If it grows on bushes, then it could grow on trees. A bush ain't nothing but a little tree."

"No, no," protested Benny, somewhat alarmed. "Money don't really grow on bushes. That is just a saying."

The telephone rang and Benny went to answer it. "It's for you," he said.

"Now how would anyone think of looking for me here?" asked Doyle, astounded.

He picked up the bottle and shambled down the bar to where the phone was waiting.

"All right," he told the transmitter. "You're the one who called. Start talking."

"This is Jake."

"Don't tell me. You got a job for me. You'll pay me in a day or two. How many jobs do you think I do for you without being paid?"

"You do this job for me, Chuck, and I'll pay you everything I owe you. Not only for this one, but for all the others, too. This is one that I need real bad and I need it fast. You see, this car went off the road and into this lake and the insurance company claims—"

"Where is the car now?"

"It's still in the lake. They'll be pulling it out in a day or two and I need the pictures—"

"You want me, maybe, to go down into the lake and take pictures underwater?"

"That's exactly the situation. I know that it's a tough one. But I'll get the diving equipment and arrange everything. I hate to ask it of you, but you're the only man I know . . ."

"I will not do it," Doyle said firmly. "My health is too delicate. If I get wet I get pneumonia and if I get cold I have a couple teeth that begin to ache and I'm allergic to all kinds of weeds and more than likely this lake is filled with a lot of water lilies and other kinds of plants."

"I'll pay you double!" Jake yelled in desperation. "I'll even pay you triple."

"I know you," said Doyle. "You won't pay me nothing."

He hung up the phone and shuffled back up the bar, dragging the bottle with him.

"Nerve of the guy!" he said, taking two drinks in rapid succession.

"It's a hell of a way," he said to Benny, "for a man to make a living."

"All ways are," said Benny philosophically.

"Look, Benny, there wasn't nothing wrong with that bill I give you?"

"Should there been?"

"Naw, but that crack you made."

"I always make them cracks. It goes with the job. The customers expect me to make them kind of cracks."

He mopped at the bar, a purely reflex action, for the bar was dry and shiny.

"I always look the folding over good," he said. "I'm as hep as any banker. I can spot a phoney fifty feet away. Smart guys want to pass some bad stuff, they figure that a bar is the place to do it. You got to be on your guard against it."

"Catch much of it?"

Benny shook his head. "Once in a while. Not often. Fellow in here the other day says there is a lot of it popping up that can't be spotted even by an expert. Says the government is going crazy over it. Says there is bills turning up with duplicate serial numbers. Shouldn't be no two bills with the same serial number. When that happens, one of them is phoney. Fellow says they figure it's the Russians."

"The Russians?"

"Sure, the Russians flooding the country with phoney money that's so good no one can tell the difference. If they turned loose enough of it, the fellow said, they could ruin the economy."

"Well, now," said Doyle in some relief, "I call that a dirty trick."

"Them Russians," said Benny, "is a dirty bunch."

Doyle drank again, morosely, then handed the bottle back.

"I got to quit," he announced. "I told Mabel I would drop around. She don't like me to have a snootful."

"I don't know why Mabel puts up with you," Benny told him. "There she is, working in that beanery where she meets all sorts of guys. Some of them is sober and hard working—"

"They ain't got any soul," said Doyle. "There ain't a one of them truck drivers and mechanics that can tell a sunset from a scrambled egg."

Benny paid him out his change.

"I notice," he said, "that you make your soul pay off."

"Why, sure," Doyle told him. "That's only common sense."

He picked up his change and went out into the street.

Mabel was waiting for him, but that was not unusual. Something always happened and he was always late and she had become resigned to waiting.

She was waiting in a booth and he gave her a kiss and sat down across from her. The place was empty except for a new waitress who was tidying up a table at the other end of the room.

"Something funny happened to me today," said Doyle.

"I hope," said Mabel, simpering, "that it was something nice."

"Now I don't know," Doyle told her. "It could be. It could, likewise, get a man in trouble."

He dug into his watch pocket and took out the bill. He unfolded it and smoothed it out and laid it on the table.

"What you call that?" he asked.

"Why, Chuck, it's a twenty-dollar bill!"

"Look at that thing on the corner of it."

She did, with some puzzlement.

"Why, it's a stem," she cried. "Just like an apple stem. And it's fastened to the bill."

"It comes off a money tree," said Doyle.

"There ain't no such thing," objected Mabel.

"Yes, there is," Doyle told her, with mounting conviction. "J. Howard Metcalfe, he's got one growing in his back yard. That's how he gets all his money. I never could get it figured out how all these big moguls that live in them big houses and drive those block-long cars could manage to make all the money it would take to live the way they do. I bet you every one of them fellows has got money trees growing in their yards. And they've kept it a secret all this time, except today Metcalfe forgot to pick his money and a wind came along and blew it off the tree and over the wall and—"

"But even if there was such a thing as a money tree," persisted Mabel, "they could never keep it secret. Someone would find it out. All of them have servants and the servants would know . . ."

"I got that all figured out," said Doyle. "I been giving this thing a lot of thought and I know just how it works. Them servants in those big mansions aren't just ordinary servants. They're all old retainers. They been in the family for years and they're loyal to the family. And you know why they're loyal? It's because they're getting their cuts off the money trees. I bet you they salt it all away and when it comes time for them to retire they live the life of Riley. There wouldn't nobody blab with a setup like that.

"And if all those big shots haven't got something to hide, why has every one of them big houses got big walls or thick hedges around the back of them?"

"But they have garden parties," Mabel protested. "I read about them in the society section all the time—"

"You ever been to one of them garden parties?"

"No, of course I haven't."

"You bet your boots you haven't. You ain't got no money tree. And they don't invite no one except other people who likewise have money trees. Why do you think all them rich people are so snooty and exclusive?"

"Well, even if they have got money trees, what difference does it make? What are you going to do about it?"

"Mabel, would you maybe be able to find me a sugar sack or something?"

"We have a lot of them out back. I could get you one."

"And fix up a drawstring in it so once I got it full, I could jerk the string and tighten it up so the money wouldn't all spill out if I had to—"

"Chuck, you wouldn't!"

"There's a tree outside the wall. I can shinny up it. And there's a branch sticking out into the yard. I could tie a rope to that . . ."

"But they'd catch you!"

"Well, we'll know if you get that sack for me. I'll go out, hunt up some rope."

"But all the stores are closed by now. You can't buy a rope."

"Know just where to get some," said Doyle. "Fellow down the street has eighteen, twenty feet of it fixed up for a swing out back. Took pictures of a kid swinging there just a day or two ago."

"You'll have to drive me over to my place. I can't fix the sack in here."

"Just as soon as I get back with the rope."

"Chuck?"

"Yeah?"

"It isn't stealing, is it—this money tree?"

"Naw. If Metcalfe has one, he hasn't any right to it. It's fair game for anyone. It's more than fair—it ain't right for a man to have a thing like that all to himself."

"And you won't be caught for having counterfeit . . ."

"Now, how could it be counterfeit?" demanded Doyle, just a bit aghast that she should suggest it. "Nobody's making it. There ain't no plates and there isn't any press. The stuff just grows, hanging on that tree."

She hunched over the table toward him. "But, Chuck, it's so impossible! How could a tree grow money?"

"I don't pretend to know," said Doyle. "I ain't no scientist and I don't catch the lingo, but some of them botany fellows, they can do some funny things. Like that man named Burbank. They can fix it so plants will do most anything they want. They can change the kind of fruit they bear and they can change their size and their growing habits and I haven't got no doubt at all if someone put his mind to it, he could make a tree grow money."

Mabel slid out of the booth.

"I'll get the sack," she said.

II

Doyle shinnied up the tree that grew outside the high brick wall. Reaching the big branch that extended over the wall, invading the air space over the Metcalfe garden, he crouched quietly.

He tilted his head skyward and watched the scared fleeing of light clouds. In another minute or two, a slightly larger cloud, he saw, would close in on the moon and when that happened was the time to drop into the garden.

He crouched and watched the garden and there were several trees but there was nothing he could make out that was peculiar about any one of them. Except it seemed, when he listened closely, that the rustling of the leaves of one of them was crisper than the other rustlings.

He checked the rope looped in his hand and the sack tucked beneath his belt and waited for the heavier cloud to move across the moon.

The house was quiet and still and only showed one faint glimmer of light in an upstairs room. And the night was quiet as well, except for the rustling of the leaves.

The edge of the cloud began to eat into the moon and Doyle moved out on cat feet along the branch. Swiftly he knotted the rope around the branch and let it down.

And having accomplished that, having come this far, he hesitated for an instant, listening hard, straining his eyes for any trace of motion in the darkened rectangle of the garden.

He could detect none.

Quickly, he slid down the rope and stole toward the tree which had seemed to rustle more crisply than the others.

He reached it and thrust up a cautious hand.

The leaves had the size and feel of bills and he plucked at them frantically. He jerked the sack from his belt and thrust the handful of leaves into it and then another handful and another.

Easy, he exulted. Just like picking plums. Just like being in a plum thicket. As easy as picking. . . .

Just five minutes, he told himself. That is all I need. Just five full minutes with no one pestering.

He didn't get five minutes. He didn't get a minute, even.

A whirlwind of silent anger came in a quiet rush out of the darkness and was upon him. It bit him in the leg and it slashed him in the ribs and it tore his shirt half off him. It was as silent as it was ferocious, and he glimpsed it in that first startled second only as a floating patch of motion.

He stifled the hurt yip of surprise and fear that surged into his throat and fought back as silently as the thing attacking him. Twice he had his hands upon it and twice it slipped away and swarmed to the attack again.

Then, finally, he got a grip upon it that it could not shake and he lifted it high to smash it to the ground. But as he lifted it, the cloud sailed off the moon and the garden came alight.

He saw the thing, then, really saw it, for the first time, and clamped down his gurgle of amazement.

He had expected a dog of some sort. But this was not a dog. It was unlike anything he had ever seen before. It was nothing he had ever heard of.

One end of it was all mouth and the other end of it was blunt and square. It was terrier-sized, but no terrier. It had short, yet powerful legs and its arms were long and sinuous and armed with heavy claws and somehow he had managed to grab it in such a manner that the arms and murderous claws were pinned against its body.

It was dead white and hairless and as naked as a jaybird. It had a sort of knapsack, or what appeared to be a knapsack, strapped upon its back.

But that was not the worst of it.

Its chest was large and hard and gleaming, like the thorax of a grasshopper and the chest was like a neon-lighted billboard, with characters and pictures and dots and hooks and dashes flashing off and on.

Rapid-fire thoughts snaked their way through the fear and horror that tumbled in Doyle's brain and he tried to get them tracking, but they wouldn't track. They just kept tumbling round and wouldn't straighten out.

Then all the dots and dashes, all the hooks and symbols cleared off the billboard chest and there were words, human words, in capitals, glowing upon it:

LET GO
OF ME!

Even to the exclamation point.

"Pal," said Doyle, not a little shaken, but nevertheless determined, "I will not let you go. I got plans for you."

He looked swiftly around for the sack and located it on the ground nearby and reached out a foot to pull it closer.

YOU SORRY, spelled the creature.

"Not," said Doyle, "so that you could notice."

Kneeling, he reached out swiftly and grabbed the sugar sack.

Quickly he thrust the creature into it and jerked the drawstring tight.

He stood up and hefted the sack. It was not too heavy for him to carry.

Lights snapped on in the first floor of the house, in a room facing on the garden, and voices floated out of an open window. Somewhere in the darkness a screen door slapped shut with a hollow sound.

Doyle whirled and ran toward the dangling rope. The sack hampered him a little, but urgency compensated for the hindrance and he climbed swiftly to the branch.

He squatted there, hidden in the shadow of the leaves, and drew up the rope, coiling it awkwardly with his one free hand.

The thing inside the sack began to thrash about and he jerked the sack up, thumped it on the branch. The thing grew quiet at once.

Footsteps came deliberately down a shadow-hidden walk and Doyle saw the red glow of a cigar as someone puffed on it.

A man's voice spoke out of the darkness and he recognized it as Metcalfe's voice.

"Henry!"

"Yes, sir," said Henry from the wide verandah.

"Where the devil did the *rolla* go?"

"He's out there somewhere, sir. He never gets too far from the tree. It's his responsibility, you know."

The cigar-end glowed redder as Metcalfe puffed savagely.

"I don't understand those *rollas,* Henry. Even after all these years, I don't understand them."

"No, sir," said Henry. "They're hard things to understand."

Doyle could smell the smoke, drifting upward to him. He could tell by the smell it was a good cigar.

And naturally Metcalfe would smoke the very best. No man with a money tree growing in his garden need worry about the price of smokes.

Cautiously, Doyle edged a foot or two along the branch, anxious to get slightly closer to the wall and safety.

The cigar jerked around and pointed straight at him as Metcalfe tilted his head to stare into the tree.

"What was that!" he yelled.

"I didn't hear a thing, sir. It must have been the wind."

"There's no wind, you fool. It's that cat again!"

Doyle huddled closer against the branch, motionless, yet

tensed to spring into action if it were necessary. Quietly he gave himself a mental bawling-out for moving.

Metcalfe had moved off the walk and clear of the shadow and was standing in the moonlight, staring up into the tree.

"There's something up there," he announced pontifically. "The leaves are so thick I can't make out what it is. I bet you it's that goddam cat again. He's plagued the *rolla* for two nights hand running."

He took the cigar out of his face and blew a couple of beautiful smoke rings that drifted ghost-like in the moonlight.

"Henry,"' he shouted, "bring me a gun. I think the twelve-gauge is right behind the door."

Doyle had heard enough. He made a dash for it. He almost fell, but he caught himself. He dropped the rope and almost dropped the sack, but managed to hang onto it. The *rolla,* inside the sack, began to thrash about.

"So you want to horse around," Doyle said savagely to the thing inside the sack.

He tossed the bag toward the fence and it went over and he heard it thump into the alley. He hoped, momentarily, that he hadn't killed it, for it might be valuable. He might be able, he thought, to sell it to a circus. Circuses were always looking for crazy things like that.

He reached the tree trunk and slid down it with no great ceremony and very little forethought and as a result collected a fine group of abrasions on his arms and legs from the roughness of the bark.

He saw the sack lying in the alley and from beyond the fence he heard the ferocious bellowing and blood-curdling cursing of J. Howard Metcalfe.

Someone ought to warn him, Doyle told himself. Man of his age, he shouldn't ought to allow himself to fly into such a rage. Someday he'd fall flat upon his face and that would be the end of him.

Doyle scooped up the sack and ran as hard as he could to where he'd parked the car at the alley's end. Reaching it, he tossed the sack into the seat and crawled in himself. He took off with a rush and wound a devious route to throw off any possible pursuit—although that, he admitted to himself, was just a bit fantastic, for he'd made his getaway before Metcalfe could possibly have put someone on his tail.

Half an hour later he pulled up beside a small park and began to take stock of the situation.

There was both good and bad.

He had failed to harvest as much of the tree-grown money as he had intended and he had tipped his mitt to Metcalfe, so there'd not be another chance.

But he knew now for a certainty that there were such things as money trees and he had a *rolla,* or he supposed it was a *rolla,* for whatever it was worth.

And the *rolla*—so quiet now inside the sack—in its more active moments of guarding the money tree, had done him not a bit of good.

His hands were dark in the moonlight with the wash of blood and there were stripes of fire across his ribs, beneath the torn shirt, where the *rolla's* claws had raked him, and one leg was sodden-wet. He put down a hand to feel the warm moistness of his trouser leg.

He felt a thrill of fear course along his nerves. A man could get infected from a chewing-up like that—especially by an unknown animal.

And if he went to a doctor, the doc would want to know what had happened to him, and he would say a dog, of course. But what if the doc should know right off that it was no dog bite. More than likely the doc would have to make some report or other—maybe just like he'd have to make a report on a gunshot wound.

There was, he decided, too much at stake for him to take the chance—he must not let it be known he'd found out about the money tree.

For as long as he was the only one who knew, he might stand to make a good thing of it. Especially since he had the *rolla,* which in some mysterious manner was connected with the tree—and which, even by itself, without reference to the tree, might be somehow turned into a wad of cash.

He eased the car from the curb and out into the street.

Fifteen minutes later he parked in a noisome alley back of a block-long row of old apartment houses.

He descended from the car and hauled out the sack.

The *rolla* was still quiet.

"Funny thing," Doyle said.

He laid his hand against the sack and the sack was warm and the *rolla* stirred a bit.

"Still alive," Doyle told himself with some relief.

He wended his way through a clutter of battered garbage cans, stacks of rotting wood, piles of empty cans; cats slunk into the dark as he approached.

"Crummy place for a girl to live," said Doyle, speaking to himself. "No place for a girl like Mabel."

He found the rickety backstairs and climbed them, went along the hall until he came to Mabel's door. She opened it at his knock, immediately, as if she had been waiting. She grabbed him by the arm and pulled him in and slammed the door and leaned her back against it.

"I was worried, Chuck!"

"Nothing to worry about," said Doyle. "Little trouble, that's all."

"Your hands!" she screamed. "Your shirt!"

Doyle jostled the bag gaily. "Nothing to it, Mabel. Got what done it right inside this sack."

He looked around the place. "You got all the windows shut?" he asked.

She nodded, still a bit wide-eyed.

"Hand me that table lamp," he said. "It'll be handy for a club."

She jerked the plug out of the wall and pulled off the shade, then handed the lamp to him.

He hefted the lamp, then picked up the sack, loosened the draw string.

"I bumped it couple of times," he said, "and heaved it in the alley and it may be shook up considerable, but you can't take no chances."

He upended the sack and dumped the *rolla* out. With it came a shower of twenty-dollar bills—the three or four handfuls he had managed to pick before the *rolla* jumped him.

The *rolla* picked itself off the floor with a show of dignity and stood erect—except that it didn't look as if it were standing erect. Its hind legs were so short and its front legs were so long that it looked as if it were sitting like a dog. The fact that its face, or rather its mouth, since it had no face, was on top of its head, added to the illusion of sitting.

Its stance was pretty much like that of a sitting coyote baying at the moon—or, better yet, an oversized and more than ordinarily grotesque bullfrog baying at the moon.

Mabel let out a full-fledged scream and bolted for the bedroom, slamming the door behind her.

"For cripes sake," moaned Doyle, "the fat's in the fire for sure. They'll think I'm murdering her."

Someone thumped on the floor upstairs. A man's voice bellowed: "Cut it out down there!"

The *rolla's* gleaming chest lit up:

HUNGRY. WHEN

WE EAT?

Doyle gulped. He felt cold sweat starting out on him.

WASSA MATTER? spelled the rolla. GO AHEAD. TALK. I CAN HEAR.

Someone started hammering on the door.

Doyle looked wildly around and saw the money on the floor. He started scooping it up and stuffing it in his pocket.

Whoever was at the door kept on hammering.

Doyle finished with the money and opened the door.

A man stood there in his undershirt and pants and he was big and tough. He towered over Doyle by at least a foot. A woman, standing behind him, peered around at Doyle.

"What's going on around here?" the man demanded. "We heard a lady scream."

"Saw a mouse," Doyle told him.

The man kept on looking at him.

"Big one," Doyle elaborated. "Might have been a rat."

"And you, mister. What's the matter with you? How'd your shirt get tore?"

"I was in a crap game," said Doyle and went to shut the door.

But the man stiff-armed it and strode into the room.

"If you don't mind, we'll look the situation over."

With a sinking feeling in his belly, Doyle remembered the *rolla.*

He spun around.

The *rolla* was not there.

The bedroom door opened and Mabel came out. She was calm as ice.

"You live here, lady?" asked the man.

"Yes, she does," the woman said. "I see her in the hall."

"This guy bothering you?"

"Not at all," said Mabel. "We are real good friends."

The man swung around on Doyle.

"You got blood all over you," he said.

"I can't seem to help it," Doyle told him. "I just bleed all the blessed time."

The woman was tugging at the man's arm.

Mabel said, "I tell you, there is nothing wrong."

"Let's go, honey," urged the woman, still tugging at the arm. "They don't want us here."

The man went reluctantly.

Doyle slammed the door and bolted it. He leaned against it weakly.

"That rips it," he said. "We got to get out of here. He'll keep mulling it over and he'll up and call the cops and they'll haul us in . . ."

"We ain't done nothing, Chuck."

"No, maybe not. But I don't like no cops. I don't want to answer questions. Not right now."

She moved closer to him.

"He was right," she said. "You are all bloody. Your hands and shirt . . ."

"One leg, too. The *rolla* gave me a working over."

The *rolla* stood up from behind a corner chair.

NO WISH EMBARRASS, he spelled out. ALWAYS HIDE FROM STRANGERS.

"That's the way he talks," said Doyle, admiringly.

"What is it?" asked Mabel, backing away a pace or two.

I ROLLA.

"I met him under the money tree," said Doyle. "We had a little fracas. He has something to do with the tree, guarding it or something."

"And did you get some money?"

"Not much. You see, this *rolla* . . ."

HUNGRY, said the *rolla*.

"You come along," Mabel said to Doyle. "I got to patch you up."

"But don't you want to hear . . ."

"Not especially. You got into trouble again. It seems to me you *want* to get in trouble."

She headed for the bathroom and he followed.

"Sit down on the edge of the tub," she ordered.

The *rolla* came and sprawled in the doorway, leaning against the jamb.

AINT YOU GOT NO FOOD? it asked.

"Oh, for heaven's sake," Mabel exclaimed in exasperation, "what is it you want?"

FRUIT, VEGETABLES.

"Out in the kitchen. There's fruit on the table. I suppose I have to show you."

FIND MYSELF, the *rolla* said and left.

"I can't understand that squirt," said Mabel. "First he chewed you up. Now he's palsy-walsy."

"I give him lumps," said Doyle. "Taught him some respect."

"Besides," observed Mabel, "he's dying of starvation. Now you sit down on that tub and let me fix you up."

He sat down gingerly while she rummaged in the medicine cabinet.

She got a bottle of red stuff, a bottle of alcohol, swabs and cotton. She knelt and rolled up Doyle's trouser leg.

"This looks bad," she said.

"Where he got me with his teeth," said Doyle.

"You should see a doctor, Chuck. This might get infected. His teeth might not be clean or something."

"Doc would ask too many questions. We got trouble enough . . ."

"Chuck, what is that thing out there?"

"It's a *rolla*."

"Why is it called a *rolla*?"

"I don't know. Just call it that, I guess."

"I read about someone called a *rolla* once. Rolla boys, I think it was. Always doing good."

"Didn't do me a bit of good."

"What did you bring it here for, then?"

"Might be worth a million. Might sell it to a circus or a zoo. Might work up a night club act with it. The way it talks and all."

She worked expertly and quickly on the tooth-marked calf and ankle, cleaning out the cuts and swabbing them with some of the red stuff that was in the bottle.

"There's another reason I brought the *rolla* here," Doyle confessed. "I got Metcalfe where I want him. I know something he wouldn't want no one else to know and I got the *rolla* and the *rolla* has something to do with them money trees . . ."

"You're talking blackmail now?"

"Nah, nothing like that. You know I wouldn't never blackmail no one. Just a little private arrangement between me and Metcalfe. Maybe just out of gratitude for me keeping my mouth shut, he might give me one of his money trees."

"But you said there was only one money tree."

"That's all I saw, was one. But the place was dark and there might be more of them. You wouldn't expect a man like Metcalfe to be satisfied with just one money tree, would you. If he had one, he could grow some others. I bet you he has twenty-dollar trees and fifty-dollar trees and hundred-dollar trees."

He sighed. "I sure would like to get just five minutes with a hundred-dollar tree. I'd be set for life. I'd do me some two-handed picking the like you never see."

"Shuck up your shirt," said Mabel. "I got to get at them scratches on your ribs."

Doyle shucked up his shirt.

"You know," he said, "I bet you Metcalfe ain't the only one that has them money trees. I bet all the rich folks has them. I bet they're all banded together in a secret society, pledged to never talk about them. I wouldn't wonder if that's where all the money comes from. Maybe the government don't print no money, like they say they do . . ."

"Shut up," commanded Mabel, "and hold still."

She worked swiftly on his ribs.

"What are you going to do with the *rolla*?" she asked.

"We'll put him in the car and drive down and have a talk with Metcalfe. You stay out in the car with the *rolla* and if there is any funny stuff, you get out of there. Long as we have the *rolla* we got Metcalfe across the barrel."

"You're crazy if you think I'll stay alone, with that thing in the car. Not after what it done to you."

"Just get yourself a stick of stove wood and belt him one with it if he makes a crooked move."

"I'll do no such thing," said Mabel. "I will not stay with him."

"All right, then," said Doyle, "we'll put him in the trunk. We'll fix him up with some blankets, so he'll be comfortable. He can't get at you there. And it might be better to have him under lock and key."

Mabel shook her head. "I hope that you are doing right, Chuck. I hope we don't get into trouble."

"Put that stuff away," said Doyle, "and let us get a move on. We got to get out of here before that jerk down the hall decides to phone the cops."

The *rolla* showed up in the doorway, patting at his belly.

JERKS? he asked. WHATS THEM?

"Oh, my aching back," said Doyle, "now I got to explain to him."

JERKS LIKE HEELS?

"Sure, that's it," said Doyle. "A jerk is like a heel."

METCALFE SAY
ALL OTHER
HUMANS HEELS

"Now, I tell you, Metcalfe might have something there," said Doyle, judicially.

HEEL MEAN
HUMAN WITH
NO MONEY

"I've never heard it put quite that way," said Doyle, "but if that should be the case, you can count me as a heel."

METCALFE SAY
THAT WHAT IS
WRONG WITH PLANET.
THERE IS TOO

LITTLE MONEY

"Now, that is something that I'll go along with him."

SO I NOT
ANGRY WITH
YOU ANY MORE.

Mabel said: "My, but he's turned out to be a chatterbox."

MY JOB TO
CARE AND
GUARD TREE.
I ANGRY AT
THE START.
BUT FINALLY
I THINK
POOR HEEL
NEED SOME MONEY
CANNOT BLAME
FOR TAKING.

"That's decent of you," Doyle told him. "I wish you'd thought of that before you chewed me up. If I could have had just a full five minutes—"'

"I am ready," Mabel said. "If we have to leave, let's go."

III

Doyle went softly up the walk that led to the front of the Metcalfe house. The place was dark and the moon was riding homeward in the western sky, just above the tip of a row of pines that grew in the grounds across the street.

He mounted the steps of mellowed brick and stood before the door. He reached out and rang the bell and waited.

Nothing happened.

He rang again and yet again and there was no answer.

He tried the door and it was locked.

"They flown the coop," said Doyle, talking to himself.

He went around the house into the alley and climbed the tree again.

The garden back of the house was dark and silent. He crouched for a long time atop the wall and the place was empty.

He pulled a flashlight from his pocket and played it downward. It cut a circle of uncertain light and he moved it slowly back and forth until it caught the maw of tortured earth.

His breath rasped in his throat at the sight of it and he worked the light around to make sure there was no mistake.

There was no mistake at all. The money tree was gone. Someone had dug it up and taken it away.

Doyle snapped off the light and slid it back into his pocket. He slid down the tree and trotted down the alley.

Two blocks away he came up to the car. Mabel had kept the motor idling. She moved from behind the wheel and he slid under it and shoved the car in gear.

"They took it on the lam," he said. "There ain't nobody there. They dug up the tree and took it on the lam."

"Well, I'm glad of it," Mabel said defiantly. "Now you won't be getting into trouble—not with money trees at least."

"I got a hunch," said Doyle.

"So have I," said Mabel. "Both of us is going home and getting us some sleep."

"Maybe you," said Doyle. "You can curl up in the seat. Me, I got some driving to do."

"There ain't no place to drive."

"Metcalfe told me when I was taking his picture this afternoon about a farm he had. Bragging about all the things he has, you know. Out west some place, near a town called Millville."

"What has that got to do with it?"

"Well, if you had a lot of money trees . . ."

"But he had only one tree. In the backyard of his house."

"Maybe he has lots of them. Maybe he had this one here just to keep him in pocket money when he was in town."

"You mean you're driving out to this place where he has a farm?"

"I have to find an all-night station first. I need some gas and I need a road map to find out where is this Millville place. I bet you Metcalfe's got an orchard on that farm of his. Can't you see it, Mabel? Row after row of trees, all loaded down with money!"

IV

The old proprietor of the only store in Millville—part hardware, part grocery, part drugstore, with the post office in one corner—rubbed his silvery mustache.

"Yeah," he said. "Man by the name of Metcalfe does have a farm—over in the hills across the river. He's got it named and everything. He calls it Merry Hill. Now, can you tell me, stranger, why anyone should name a farm like that?"

"People do some funny things," said Doyle. "Can you tell me how to get there?"

"You asked?"

"Sure I asked. I asked you just now . . ."

The old man shook his head. "You been invited there? Metcalfe expecting you?"

"No, I don't suppose he is."

"You'll never get in then. He's got it solid-fenced. And he's got a guard at the gate—even got a little house for the guard to stay in. 'Less Metcalfe wants you in, you don't get in."

"I'll have a try at it."

"I wish you well, stranger, but I don't think you'll make it. Now, why in the world should Metcalfe act like that? This is friendly country. No one else has got their farms fenced with eight-foot wire and barbs on top of that. No one else could *afford* to do it even if they wanted to. He must be powerful scared of someone."

"Wouldn't know," said Doyle. "Tell me how to get there."

The old man found a paper sack underneath the counter, fished a stub pencil out of his vest pocket and wet it carefully with his tongue. He smoothed out the sack with a liver-spotted hand and began drawing painfully.

"You cross the bridge and take this road—don't take that one to the left, it just wanders up the river—and you go up this hollow and you reach a steep hill and at the top of it you turn left and it's just a mile to Metcalfe's place."

He wet the pencil again and drew a rough rectangle.

"The place lies right in there," he said. "A sizeable piece of property. Metcalfe bought four farms and threw them all together."

Back at the car Mabel was waiting irritably.

"So you was wrong all the time," she greeted Doyle. "He hasn't got a farm."

"Just a few miles from here," said Doyle. "How is the *rolla* doing?"

"He must be hungry again. He's banging on the trunk."

"How can he be hungry? I bought him all of them bananas just a couple hours ago."

"Maybe he wants company. He might be getting lonesome."

"I got too much to do," said Doyle, "to be holding any *rolla's* hand."

He climbed into the car and got it started and pulled away into the dusty street. He clattered across the bridge and instead of keeping up the hollow, as the storekeeper had directed, turned left on the road that paralleled the river.

If the map the old man had drawn on the sack was right, he figured, he should come upon the Metcalfe farm from the rear by following the river road.

Gentle hills turned into steep bluffs, covered with heavy woods and underbrush. The crooked road grew rougher. He came to a deep hollow that ran between two bluffs. A faint trail, a wagon-road more than likely, unused for many years, angled up the hollow.

Doyle pulled the car into the old wagon road and stopped. He got out and stood for a moment, staring up the hollow.

"What you stopping for?" asked Mabel.

"I'm about," Doyle told her, "to take Metcalfe in the rear."

"You can't leave me here."

"I won't be gone for long."

"And there are mosquitos," she complained, slapping wildly.

"Just keep the windows shut."

He started to walk away and she called him back.

"There's the *rolla* back there."

"He can't get at you as long as he's in the trunk."

"But all that banging he's doing! What if someone should go past and hear all that banging going on?"

"I bet you there ain't been anyone along this road within the last two weeks."

Mosquitos buzzed. He waved futile hands at them.

"Look, Mabel," he pleaded, "you want me to pull this off, don't you? You ain't got nothing against a mink coat, have you? You don't despise no diamonds?"

"No, I guess I don't," she admitted. "But you hurry back. I don't want to be here alone when it's getting dark."

He swung around and headed up the hollow.

The place was green—the deep, dead green, the shabby, shapeless green of summer. And quiet—except for the buzzing of mosquitos. And to Doyle's concrete-and-asphalt mind there was a bit of lurking terror in the green quietness of the wooded hills.

He slapped at mosquitos again and shrugged.

"Ain't nothing to hurt a man," he said.

It was rough traveling. The hollow slanted, climbing up between the hills, and the dry creek bed, carpeted with tumbled boulders and bars of gravel, slashed erratically from one bluff-side to the other. Time after time, Doyle had to climb down one bank and climb up the other when the shifting stream bed blocked his way. He tried walking in the dry bed, but that was even worse—he had to dodge around or climb over a dozen boulders every hundred feet.

The mosquitos grew worse as he advanced. He took out his handkerchief and tied it around his neck. He pulled his hat down as far as it would go. He waged energetic war—he killed them by the hundreds, but there was no end to them.

He tried to hurry, but it was no place to hurry. He was dripping wet with perspiration. He wanted to sit down and rest, for he was short of wind, but when he tried to sit the mosquitos swarmed in upon him in hateful, mindless numbers and he had to move again.

The ravine narrowed and twisted and the going became still rougher.

He came around a bend and the way was blocked. A great mass of tangled wood and vines had become wedged between two great trees growing on opposite sides of the steep hillsides.

There was no possibility of getting through the tangle. It stretched for thirty feet or more and was so thickly interlaced that it formed a solid wall, blocking the entire stream bed. It rose for twelve or fifteen feet and behind it rocks and mud and other rubble had been jammed hard against it by the boiling streams of water that had come gushing down the hollow in times of heavy rain.

Clawing with his hands, digging with his feet, Doyle crawled up the hillside to get around one end of the obstruction.

He reached the clump of trees against which one end of it rested and hauled himself among them, bracing himself with aching arms and legs. The mosquitoes came at him in howling squadrons and he broke off a small branch, heavy with leaves, from one of the trees, and used it as a switch to discourage them.

He perched there, panting and sobbing, drawing deep breaths into his lungs. And wondered, momentarily, how he'd ever managed to get himself into such a situation. It was not his dish, he was not cut out for roughing it. His ideas of nature never had extended any further than a well-kept city park.

And here he was, in the depths of nowhere, toiling up outlandish hills, heading for a place where there might be money trees—row on row of money trees.

"I wouldn't do it," he told himself, "for nothing less than money."

He twisted around and examined the tangle of wood and vines and saw, with some astonishment, that it was two feet thick or more and that it carried its thickness uniformly. And the uphill side of it was smooth and slick, almost as if it had been planed and sanded, although there was not a tool mark on it.

He examined it more closely and it was plain to see that it was no haphazard collection of driftwood that had been built up through the years, but that it was woven and interlaced so intricately that it was a single piece—had been a single piece even before it had become wedged between the trees.

Who, he wondered, could have, or would have, done a job like that? Where would the patience have been mustered and the technique and the purpose? He shook his head in wonderment.

He had heard somewhere about Indians weaving brush together to make weirs for catching fish, but there were no fish in this dry stream bed and no Indians for several hundred miles.

He tried to figure out the pattern of the weaving and there was no pattern that he could detect. Everything was twisted and intergrown around everything else and the whole thing was one solid mass.

Somewhat rested and with his wind at least partially restored, he proceeded on his way, trailing a ravaging cloud of mosquitos in his wake.

It seemed now that the trees were thinning and that he could see blue sky ahead. The terrain leveled out a bit and he tried to hurry, but racked leg muscles screamed at him and he contented himself with jogging along as best he could.

He reached more level ground and finally broke free into a clearing that climbed gently to the top of a grassy knoll. Wind came out of the west, no longer held back by the trees, and the mosquitos fell away, except for a small swarm of diehards that went part way up the knoll with him.

He reached the top of the knoll and threw himself in the grass, lying flat, panting like a tuckered dog.

And there, not more than a hundred yards away, was the fence that closed in Metcalfe's farm.

It marched across the rolling, broken hills, a snake of shining metal. And extending out from it was a broad swath of weeds, waist-high, silver-green in the blasting sunlight—as if the ground had been plowed around the fence for a distance of a hundred feet or so and the weeds sown in the ground as one might sow a crop. Doyle squinted his eyes to try to make out what kind of weeds they were, but he was too far away.

Far on the distant ridge was the red gleam of a rooftop among many sheltering trees and to the west of the buildings lay an orchard, ordered row on row.

Was it, Doyle wondered, only his imagination that the shapes of those orchard trees were the remembered shape of the night-seen tree in the walled garden in the rear of Metcalfe's town-house? And was it once more only his imagination that the green of them was slightly different than the green of other leaves—the green, perhaps of mint-new currency?

He lay in the grass, with the fingers of the wind picking at his sweat-soaked shirt, and wondered about the legal aspects of money that was grown on trees. It could not be counterfeit, for it was not made but grown. And if it were identical with perfectly legal, government-printed money, could anyone prove in any court of law that it was bogus money? He didn't know much law, but he wondered if there *could* be any statute upon the books that would cover a point of law like this? Probably not, he concluded, since it was so fantastic that it could not be anticipated and thus would require no rule to legislate against it.

And now, for the first time, he began really to wonder how money could be grown on trees. He had told Mabel, offhandedly and casual, so she wouldn't argue, that a botanist could do anything. But that wasn't entirely right, of course, because a botanist only studied plants and learned what he could about them. But there were these other fellows—these bio-something or other—who fooled around with changing plants. They bred grasses that would grow on land that would grow no more than thistles, they cross-pollinated corn to grow more and bigger ears, they developed grains that were disease-resistant, and they did a lot of other things. But developing a tree that would grow letter-perfect money in lieu of leaves seemed just a bit farfetched.

The sun beat against his back and he felt the heat of it through his drying shirt. He looked at his watch and it was almost three o'clock.

He turned his attention back to the orchard and this time he saw that many little figures moved among the trees. He strained his eyes to see them better, but he could not be sure—although they looked for all the world like a gang of *rollas*.

He crawled down the knoll and across the strip of grass toward the weeds. He kept low and inched along and was very careful. His only hope of making a deal, any kind of deal, with Metcalfe, was to come upon him unawares and let him know immediately what kind of hand he held.

He started worrying about how Mabel might be getting along, but he wiped the worry out. He had enough to worry about without adding to it. And, anyhow, Mabel was quite a gal and could take care of herself.

He began running through his mind alternate courses of action if he should fail to locate Metcalfe, and the most obvious, of course, was to attempt a raid upon the orchard. As he thought it over, he wasn't even sure but what a raid upon the orchard might be the thing to do. He wished he'd brought along the sugar sack Mabel had fixed up for him.

The fence worried him a little, but he also thrust that worry to one side. It would be time enough to worry about the fence once he got to it.

He slithered through the grass and he was doing swell. He was almost to the strip of weeds and no one apparently had seen him. Once he got to the weeds, it would be easier, for they would give him cover. He could sneak right up to the fence and no one would ever notice.

He reached the weeds and wilted at what he saw.

The weeds were the healthiest and thickest patch of nettles that had ever grown outdoors!

He put out a tentative hand and the nettles stung. They were the real McCoy. Ruefully, he rubbed at the dead-white welts rising on his fingers.

He raised himself cautiously to peer above the nettles. One of the *rollas* was coming down the slope toward the fence and there was no doubt now that the things he'd seen up in the orchard was a gang of *rollas*.

He ducked behind the nettles, hoping that the *rolla* had not seen him. He lay flat upon the ground and the sun was hot and the place upon his hand that had touched the nettles blazed with fire, although it was hard to decide which was the worst—the nettle sting or all the mosquito lumps that had blossomed out on him.

He noticed that the nettles were beginning to wave and toss as if they were blowing in the wind and that was a funny deal, for there wasn't that much wind.

The nettles kept on blowing and all at once they parted right in front of him, running in a straight line, making a path between him and the fence. The nettles on the right blew to the right so hard they lay flat upon the ground and those to the left blew to the left so hard they were likewise on the ground and the path was there, without a thing to stop one walking to the fence.

The *rolla* stood just beyond the fence and he spelled out a message in large capital letters upon his blackboard chest:

COME ON

OVER, HEEL!

Doyle hesitated, filled with dismay. It was a rotten break that he had been discovered by this little stinker. Now the cat was out the bag for sure, and all his toiling up the hollow, all his sneaking through the grass stood for absolutely nothing.

He saw that the other *rollas* were waddling down the slope toward the fence, while the first *rolla* still stood there, with the invitation on his chest.

Then the lettering on the *rolla* flickered out. The nettles still stayed down and the path stayed open. The *rollas* who had been coming down the slope reached the fence and all of them—all five of them—lined up in a solemn row. The first one's chest lit up with words:

WE HAVE THREE

MISSING ROLLAS

And the chest of the second one:

DO YOU BRING

WORD TO US?

And the third:

WE WOULD LIKE

TO TALK TO YOU

The fourth:

ABOUT THE

MISSING ONES

The fifth:

PLEASE COME

TO US, HEEL.

Doyle raised himself from where he had been lying flat upon the ground and squatted on his toes.

It could be a trap.

What could he gain by talking with the *rollas!*

But there was no way to retreat without losing what little advantage he might have—there was no choice but to do his best at brazening it out.

He rose to his feet and ambled down the nettle-path with as slight a show of concern as he could manage.

He reached the fence and hunkered down so that he was almost level with the *rollas.*

"I know where one of the missing *rollas* is," he said, "but not the other two."

YOU KNOW
ABOUT THE
ONE WHO
WAS IN TOWN
WITH METCALFE?

"That's right."

YOU TELL
US WHERE
HE IS

"I'll make a deal," said Doyle.

All five of them asked, DEAL?

"I'll tell you where he is; you do something for me. You let me up into that orchard for an hour tonight, then let me out again. Without letting Metcalfe know."

They huddled, conferring, their blackboard fronts a-squiggle with the queer, confusing symbols Doyle had seen on the *rolla's* chest back in Metcalfe's garden.

Then they turned to face him again, the five of them lined up, shoulder to shoulder:

WE CANNOT DO THAT
WE MADE AN AGREEMENT

AND WE GAVE OUR WORD
WE GROW THE MONEY
METCALFE DISTRIBUTES
IT

"I wouldn't distribute it," said Doyle. "I promise that I wouldn't. I'd keep it for myself."

NO SOAP, spelled out *rolla* No. 1.

"This agreement that you have with Metcalfe. How come you made it?"

GRATITUDE, said No. 2.

"Don't mind my snickering, but gratitude for Metcalfe . . ."

HE FOUND US
AND HE RESCUED
AND PROTECTED US
AND WE ASKED HIM
WHAT CAN WE DO?

"And he said, grow me some money."

HE SAY THE PLANET
NEEDED MONEY
HE SAY MONEY
MAKE HAPPY ALL
POOR HEELS LIKE YOU

"The hell you say," said Doyle, aghast.

WE GROW IT
HE DISTRIBUTE IT
BETWEEN US WE
MAKE ALL THE
PLANET HAPPY

"Just a bunch of missionaries!"

WE DO NOT
READ YOU, CHUM

"Missionaries. People who do good."

WE DO GOOD
ON MANY PLANETS

WHY NOT DO
GOOD HERE?
"But money?"
THAT WHAT METCALFE
SAY.
HE SAY PLANET HAS
PLENTY OF ALL ELSE
BUT IS SHORT ON MONEY.
"What about the other two *rollas* that are missing?"
THEY DISAGREE
THEY LEAVE
WE WORRY
MUCH ABOUT
THEM.

"You disagreed on growing money? They thought, maybe, you should grow something else?"

WE DISAGREE
ON METCALFE.
TWO SAY HE TRICK US.
REST OF US
SAY HE VERY
NOBLE HUMAN

What a bunch of creeps, thought Doyle.

Very noble human!

WE TALK
ENOUGH
NOW WE
SAY
GOODBYE.

They turned around, almost as if someone had shouted orders at them, and went stumping up the slope, back toward the orchard.

"Hey!" yelled Doyle, leaping to his feet.

Behind him was a rustle and he whirled around.

The nettles that had been laid to either side to make the path were rising, wiping out the path!

"Hey!" yelled Doyle again, but the *rollas* paid no attention to him. They went on stumping up the slope.

Doyle stood in his little trampled area, wedged against the fence, and all around him were the nettles—upright and strong and bright in the afternoon. They stretched in a solid mass at least a hundred feet back from the fence and they were shoulder high.

A man could manage to get through them. They could be kicked aside and trampled down, but some of them would be bound to peg a man and by the time one got out of there he'd have plenty welts.

And did he, at the moment, really want to get out of there?

He was, he told himself, no worse off than he had been before.

Better off, perhaps, for he was through the nettles. Better off, that is, if those stinking little *rollas* didn't run and tattle on him.

There was no sense, he decided, in going through the nettles now. If he did, in just a couple of hours or so he'd have to wade back through them once again to reach the fence.

He couldn't climb the fence until it was getting dark and he had no place else to go.

He took a good look at the fence and it would be a tough one to get over. It was a good eight feet of woven wire and atop that were three strands of barbed wire, attached to an arm-like bracket that extended outward beyond the woven fence.

Just beyond the fence stood an ancient oak tree and if he had had a rope he could make a lariat—but he had no rope, and if he wanted to get over the fence, he would somehow have to climb it.

He hunkered tight against the ground and felt downright miserable. His body was corrugated with mosquito lumps and the nettle welts on his hand had turned into blisters and he'd had a bit more sun than he was accustomed to. And now the upper molar on the left side of his jaw was developing a sort of galloping ache. All he needed.

He sneezed and it hurt his head to sneeze and the aching tooth gave a bounding leap.

Maybe, he figured, it was the pollen from those lousy nettles.

Never saw no nettles like them before, he told himself, eying them warily.

More than likely the *rollas* had a hand in growing them. The *rollas* were good with plants. They had developed the money trees and if they could develop money trees there wasn't anything they couldn't do with plants. He remembered how the nettles had fallen over to the left and right to make a path for him. It had been the *rolla,* he was sure, who had made them do that, for there hadn't been enough wind to do it and even if there had been a wind, there wasn't any wind that blew two ways at once.

There was nothing like the *rollas* in the world. And that might be exactly it. They'd said something about doing good on other worlds. But no matter what they'd done on other worlds, they'd sure been suckered here.

Do-gooders, he thought. Missionaries, maybe, from some other world, from some place out in space—a roving band of beings devoted to a cause. And trapped into a ridiculous situation on a planet that might have little, if anything, in common with any other world they'd ever seen.

Did they even, he wondered, understand what money was? Just what kind of story had Metcalfe palmed off on them?

They had arrived and Metcalfe, of all persons, had stumbled onto them and taken them in tow. Metcalfe, not so much a man as an organization that from long experience would know exactly how to exploit a situation such as the *rollas* offered. One man alone could not have handled it, could not have done all that needed to be done to set up the *rollas* for the kill. And only in an organization such as Metcalfe headed, long schooled in the essentials of self preservation, could there have been any hope of maintaining the essential secrecy.

The *rollas* had been duped—completely, absolutely fooled—and yet they were no fools. They had learned the language, not the spoken language only, but both the spoken and the written, and that spelled sharp intelligence. Perhaps more intelligence than was first apparent, for they did not make use of sound in their normal talk among themselves. But they had adapted readily, it seemed, to sound communication.

The sun long since had disappeared behind the nettles and now was just above the tree line of the bluffs. Dusk would be coming soon and then, Doyle told himself, he could get busy.

He debated once again which course he should take. By now the *rollas* might have told Metcalfe he was at the fence and Metcalfe might be waiting for him, although Metcalfe, if he knew, more than likely would not just wait, but would be coming out to get him. And as for the raid upon the orchard—he'd had trouble enough with just one *rolla* when he tried to rob a tree. He didn't like to think what five might do to him.

Behind him the nettles began to rustle and he leaped to his feet. Maybe, he thought wildly, they were opening up the path again. Maybe the path was opened automatically, at regularly scheduled hours. Maybe the nettles were like four o'clocks or morning glories—maybe they were engineered by the *rollas* to open and to close the path so many times a day.

And what he imagined was the truth in part. A path, he saw, was opening. And waddling down the path was another *rolla*. The path opened in front of him and then closed as he passed.

The *rolla* came out into the trampled area and stood facing Doyle.

GOOD EVENING, HEEL, he said.

It couldn't be the *rolla* locked in the trunk of the car down on the river road. It must, Doyle told himself, be one of the two that had walked out on the money project.

YOU SICK? the *rolla* asked.

"I itch just something awful and my tooth is aching and every time I sneeze the top of my head comes off."

COULD FIX.

"Sure, you could grow a drug-store tree, sprouting linaments and salves and pills and all the other junk."

SIMPLE, spelled the *rolla*.

"Well, now," said Doyle and then tried to say no more. For suddenly it struck him that it would be as the *rolla* said—very, very simple.

Most medicines came from plants and there wasn't anyone or anything that could engineer a plant the way the *rollas* could.

"You're on the level there," said Doyle enthusiastically. "You would be able to cure a lot of things. You might find a cure for cancer and you might develop something that would hold off heart disease. And there's the common cold . . ."

SORRY, PAL,
BUT WE ARE
OFF OF YOU.
YOU MADE
SAPS OF US.

"Then you are one of them that ran away," said Doyle in some excitement. "You saw through Metcalfe's game . . ."

But the *rolla* was paying no attention to anything he said. It had drawn itself a little straighter and a little taller and it had formed its lips into a circle as if it might be getting ready to let out a bay and the sides of its throat were quivering as if it might be singing, but there was no sound.

No sound, but a rasping shrillness that skidded on one's nerves, a something in the air that set one's teeth on edge.

It was an eerie thing, that sense of singing terror in the silence of the dusk, with the west wind blowing quietly along the tops of the darkening trees, with the silky rustle of the nettles and somewhere in the distance the squeaking of a chipmunk homeward bound on the last trip of the day.

Out beyond the fence came the thumping of awkward running feet and in the thickening dusk Doyle saw the five *rollas* from the orchard plunging down the slope.

There was something going on. Doyle was sure of that. He sensed the importance of the moment and the excitement that was in it, but there was no inkling of what it all might mean.

The *rolla* by his side had sent out some sort of rallying call, pitched too high for the human ear to catch, and now the orchard *rollas* were tumbling down the slope in answer to that call.

The five *rollas* reached the fence and lined up in their customary row and their blackboard chests were alive with glowing characters—the strange, flickering, nonsensical characters of their native language. And the chest of the one who stood outside the fence with Doyle also flamed with the fleeting symbols, changing and shifting so swiftly that they seemed to be alive.

It was an argument, Doyle thought. The five inside the fence were arguing heatedly with the one who stood outside and there seemed an urgency in the argument that could not be denied.

He stood there, on the edge of embarrassment, an innocent bystander pocketed in a family squabble he could not understand.

The *rollas* were gesturing wildly now and the characters upon their chests glowed more brightly than ever as darkness deepened on the land.

A squalling night bird flew overhead and Doyle tilted up his head to watch it and as he did he saw the moving figures of running men outlined against the lighter sky on the north ridge of the orchard.

"Watch out!" he shouted and wondered even as he shouted why he should have shouted.

At the shout the five *rollas* whirled back to face the fence.

One set of symbols appeared upon each chest, as if suddenly they might have reached agreement, as if the argument might finally be resolved.

There was a creaking sound and Doyle looked up quickly.

Against the sky he could see the old oak tree was tipping, slanting slowly toward the fence, as if a giant hand had reached out and given it a push.

He watched for a puzzled second and the tilt continued and the speed of the fall picked up and he knew that the tree was crashing down upon the fence and the time had come to get out of there.

He stepped back a pace to turn around and flee and when he put his foot down there was no solid ground beneath it. He fought briefly to keep from falling, but he didn't have a chance. He fell and thumped into a crowded cavity and above him he heard the roaring rush of the falling tree and then the jarring thud as it hit the ground and the long, high whine of wires stretched so tight they pinged and popped.

Doyle lay quietly, afraid to move.

He was in a ditch of some sort. It was not very deep, not more than three feet at the most, but he was cramped at an awkward angle and there was an uncomfortable stone or root in the middle of his back.

Above him was a tracery of limbs and twigs, where the top of the oak had crashed across the ditch. And running through the fallen branches was a *rolla,* moving much more swiftly than one would have thought was possible.

From up the slope beyond the smashed-down fence came the bellowing of men and the sound of running feet.

Doyle huddled in his ditch glad of the darkness and of the shelter of the fallen tree.

The stone or root was still in his back and he wriggled to get off it. He slid off to one side and put out a hand to catch his balance and his hand came in contact with a mound of stuff that felt like sand.

And froze there. For just beyond the ditch, standing among the branches and the nettles, was a pair of legs and the loom of a body extending up into the darkness.

"They went down that way," said a voice. "Down into the woods. It will be hard to find them."

Metcalfe's voice answered: "We have to find them, Bill. We can't let them get away."

There was a pause, then Bill said: "I wonder what got into them. They seemed happy up till now."

Metcalfe swore bitterly. "It's that photographer. That fellow—what's his name—I saw him when he was in the tree and he got away that time. But he won't make it this time. I don't know what he did or what's going on, but he's in it, clear up to his neck. He's around here somewhere."

Bill moved away a little and Metcalfe said, "If you run into this photographer, you know what to do."

"Sure, boss."

"Medium-sized guy. Has a dopey way about him."

They moved away. Doyle could hear them thrashing through the nettles, cursing as the nettles stung them.

Doyle shivered a little.

He had to get out and he had to make it fast, for before too long the moon would be coming up.

Metcalfe and his boys weren't fooling. They couldn't afford to fool in a deal like this. If they spotted him, more than likely they would shoot to kill.

Now, with everyone out hunting down the *rollas,* would be the time to get up to that orchard. Although the chances were that Metcalfe had men patrolling it.

Doyle gave the idea some consideration and dropped it. There was, now, just one thing to do and that was get to the car down on the river road as fast as he could make it.

Cautiously, he crawled out of the ditch. Once out of it, he crouched for long minutes in the tangle of fallen branches, listening for sound. There wasn't any sound.

He moved out into the nettles, following the path that had been crushed down by the men who had pursued the *rollas*. But, crushed down or not, some of the nettles pegged him.

Then he started down the slope, running for the woods.

Ahead of him a shout went up and he braked his speed and swerved. He reached a clump of brush and hurled himself behind it as other shouts went up and then two shots, fired in quick succession.

He saw it moving above the treetops, rising from the woods—a pale ghost of a thing that rose into the sky, with the red glint of early moonlight on it.

From it trailed a twisting line that had the appearance of a vine and from the vine hung a struggling doll-like figure that was screaming thinly. The ghost-like shape was stubby at the bottom and pointed at the top. It had the look about it of a ballooning Christmas tree and there was about it, too, even from a distance, a faint familiarity.

And suddenly Doyle linked up that familiarity—linked it to the woven mass of vegetation that had damned the creek bed. And as he linked it up, he knew without a question the nature of this Christmas tree riding in the sky.

The *rollas* worked with plants as Man would work with metals. They could grow a money tree and a protective strip of nettles that obeyed, they could make an oak tree fall and if they could do all that, the growing of a spaceship would not be too hard a job.

The ship was moving slowly, slanting up across the ridge, and the doll still struggled at the end of the trailing vine and its screams came down to earth as a far-off wailing sound.

Someone was shouting in the woods below:

"It's the boss! Bill, do something! It's the boss!"

It was quite apparent there was nothing Bill could do.

Doyle sprang from his bush and ran. Now was the time to make his dash, when all the other men were yelling and staring up into the sky, where Metcalfe dangled, screaming, from the trailing vine—perhaps an anchor vine, mayhaps just a part of the *rolla*-grown spaceship that had become unravelled. Although, remembering the craftsmanship of that woven barrier blocking the creek-bed, it seemed unlikely to Doyle that anything would come unravelled from a *rolla* ship.

He could imagine what had happened—Metcalfe glimpsing the last of the *rollas* clambering up the ship and rushing at them, roaring, firing those two shots, then the ship springing swiftly upward and the trailing vine twisted round the ankle.

Doyle reached the woods and went plunging into it. The ground dropped sharply and he went plunging down the slope, stumbling, falling, catching himself and going on again. Until he ran full tilt into a tree that bounced him back and put exploding stars inside his skull.

He sat upon the ground where the impact had bounced him and felt of his forehead, convinced it was cracked open, while tears of pain streamed down his cheeks.

His forehead was not cracked and there seemed to be no blood, although his nose was skinned and one lip began to puff.

Then he got up and went on slowly, feeling his way along, for despite the moonlight, it was black-dark beneath the trees.

Finally he came to the dry stream-bed and felt his way along it.

He hurried as best he could, for he remembered Mabel waiting in the car. She'd be sore at him, he thought—she'd sure be plenty sore. He had gone and let her think he might be back by dark.

He came to the place where the woven strip of vegetation dammed the stream-bed and almost tumbled over it onto the rocks below.

He ran the flat of his hand across the polished surface of the strip of weaving and tried to imagine what might have happened those several years ago.

A ship plunging down to Earth, out of control perhaps, and shattering on impact, with Metcalfe close at hand to effect a rescue.

It beats all hell, he thought, how things at times turn out.

If it had not been Metcalfe, given someone else who did not think in dollar signs, there might now be trees or bushes or rows of vegetables carrying hopes such as mankind had never known before—hope for surcease from disease and pain, an end to poverty and fear. And perhaps many other hopes that no one now could guess.

And they were gone now, in a spaceship grown by the two deserting *rollas* under Metcalfe's very nose.

He squatted atop the dam and knew the blasted hopes of mankind, the hope that had never come to be, wrecked by avarice and greed.

Now they were gone—but, wait a minute, not entirely gone! For there was a *rolla* left. He had to believe that the deserting *rolla* he had never seen was with the others—but there was still his *rolla,* locked in the trunk of that old heap down on the river road!

He got up and stumbled through the darkness to the end of the dam and climbed around the clump of anchor trees. He skidded down the sharp incline to the stream-bed and went fumbling down the hollow.

What should he do, he wondered. Head straight for Washington? Go to the FBI?

For whatever else, no matter what might happen, that one remaining *rolla* must be gotten into proper hands.

Already there was too much lost. There could be no further chances taken. Placed in governmental or scientific hands, that one lone *rolla* might still retrieve much that had been lost.

He began to worry about what might have happened to the *rolla,* locked inside the trunk. He recalled that it had been banging for attention.

What if it suffocated? What if there were something of importance, something about its care, perhaps, that it had been vital that it tell him? What if that had been the reason for its banging on the trunk?

He fumbled down the stream-bed in sobbing haste, tripping on the gravel beds, falling over boulders. Mosquitos flew a heavy escort for him and he flapped his hands to try and clear them off, but he was so worried that they seemed little more than an inconvenience.

Up in the orchard, more than likely, Metcalfe's mob was busy stripping trees, harvesting no one could guess how many millions in brand new, crinkly bills.

For now the jig was up and all of them would know it. Now there was nothing left to do but clean out the orchard and disappear as best they could.

Perhaps the money trees had required the constant attention of the *rollas* to keep on producing letter-perfect money. Otherwise why had Metcalfe had the *rolla* to tend the tree in town? And now, with the *rollas* gone, the trees might go on producing, but the money that they grew might be defective and irregular, like the growth of nubbin corn.

The slope of the land told him that he was near the road.

He went on blindly and suddenly came upon the car. He went around it in the dark and rapped upon the window.

Inside, Mabel screamed.

"It's all right," yelled Doyle. "It is me. I'm back."

She unlocked the door and he climbed in beside her. She leaned against him and he put an arm around her.

"Sorry," he said. "Sorry that I took so long."

"Did everything go all right, Chuck?"

"Yes," he mumbled. "Yes, I imagine that you could say it did."

"I'm so glad," she said, relieved. "It is all right, then. The *rolla* ran away."

"Ran away! For God's sake, Mabel . . ."

"Now, please don't go getting sore, Chuck. He kept on with that banging and I felt sorry for him. I was afraid, of course, but more sorry than afraid. So I opened up the trunk and let him out and it was OK. He was the sweetest little chap . . ."

"So he ran away," said Doyle, still not quite believing it. "But he might still be around somewhere, out there in the dark."

"No," said Mabel, "he is not around. He went up the hollow as fast as he could go, like a dog when his master calls. It was dark and I was scared, but I ran after him. I called and kept on following, but it was no use—I knew that he was gone."

She sat up straight in the seat.

"It don't make no difference now," she said. "You don't need him any longer. Although I am sorry that he ran away. He'da made a dandy pet. He talked so nice—so much nicer than a parakeet—and he was so good. I tied a ribbon, a yellow piece of ribbon around his neck and you never seen anything so cute."

"I just bet he was," said Doyle.

And he was thinking of a *rolla,* rocketing through space in a new-grown ship, heading out for a far-off sun and taking with him possibly some of man's greatest hopes, all fixed up and cute with a ribbon round his neck.

SHOTGUN CURE

Completed in October 1959, this story was first published in the January 1961 issue of the Magazine of Fantasy & Science Fiction. *It is one of several Simak stories that featured physicians; and while those stories all make it clear that Cliff respected members of that profession highly, in this one it is possible that Dr. Kelly has made a mistake that could cost the human race dearly (by subjecting it to a "treatment" that Cliff referred to in several others of his stories).*

If so, it was a mistake arising out of Kelly's desire to live up to his ethical code.

(It may or may not be an interesting coincidence that in the time I knew him, Cliff's personal physician was enough of a friend that Cliff felt able to go to him for medical information that might be of use in his stories—but this Dr. Kelly instead carries the same last name as the man who was Cliff's lawyer . . . well, it likely means nothing.)

—dww

The clinics were set up and in the morning they'd start on Operation Kelly—and that was something, wasn't it, that they should call it Kelly!

He sat in the battered rocking chair on the sagging porch and said it once again and rolled it on his tongue, but the taste of it was not so sharp nor sweet as it once had been, when that great London doctor had risen in the United Nations to suggest it could be called nothing else but Kelly.

Although, when one came to think of it, there was a deal of happenstance. It needn't have been Kelly. It could have been just anyone at all with an M.D. to his name. It could as well have been Cohen or Johnson or Radzonovich or any other of them—any one of all the doctors in the world.

He rocked gently in the creaking chair while the floor boards of the porch groaned in sympathy, and in the gathering dusk were the sounds, as well, of children at the day's-end play, treasuring those last seconds before they had to go inside and soon thereafter to bed.

There was the scent of lilacs in the coolness of the air and at the corner of the garden he could faintly see the white flush of an early-blooming bridal wreath—the one that Martha Anderson had given him and Janet so many years ago, when they first had come to live in this very house.

A neighbor came tramping down the walk and he could not make him out in the deepening dusk, but the man called out to him.

"Good evening, Doc," he said.

"Good evening, Hiram," said old Doc Kelly, knowing who it was by the voice of him.

The neighbor went on, tramping down the walk.

Old Doc kept up his gentle rocking with his hands folded on his pudgy stomach and from inside the house he could hear the bustling in the kitchen as Janet cleared up after supper. In a little while, perhaps, she'd come out and sit with him and they'd talk together, low-voiced and casually, as befitted an old couple very much in love.

Although, by rights, he shouldn't stay out here on the porch. There was the medical journal waiting for him on the study desk and he should be reading it. There was so much new stuff these days that a man should keep up with—although, perhaps, the way things were turning out it wouldn't really matter if a man kept up or not.

Maybe in the years to come there'd be precious little a man would need to keep up with.

Of course, there'd always be need of doctors. There'd always be damn fools smashing up their cars and shooting one another and getting fishhooks in their hands and falling out of trees. And there'd always be the babies.

He rocked gently to and fro and thought of all the babies and how some of them had grown until they were men and women now and had babies of their own. And he thought of Martha Anderson, Janet's closest friend, and he thought of old Con Gilbert, as ornery an old shikepoke as ever walked the earth, and tight with money, too. He chuckled a bit wryly, thinking of all the money Con Gilbert finally owed him, never having paid a bill in his entire life.

But that was the way it went. There were some who paid and others who made no pretense of paying, and that was why he and Janet lived in this old house and he drove a five-year car and Janet had worn the selfsame dress to church the blessed winter long.

Although it made no difference, really, once one considered it. For the important pay was not in cash.

There were those who paid and those who didn't pay. And there were those who lived and the other ones who died, no matter what you did. There was hope for some and the ones who had no hope—and some of these you told and there were others that you didn't.

But it was different now.

And it all had started right here in this little town of Millville—not much more than a year ago.

Sitting in the dark, with the lilac scent and the white blush of the bridal wreath and the muted sounds of children clasping to themselves the last minutes of their play, he remembered it.

It was almost 8:30 and he could hear Martha Anderson in the outer office talking to Miss Lane and she, he knew, had been the last of them.

He took off his white jacket, folding it absent-mindedly, fogged with weariness, and laid it across the examination table.

Janet would be waiting supper, but she'd never say a word, for she never had. All these many years she had never said a word of reproach to him, although there had been at times a sense of disapproval at his easy-going ways, at his keeping on with patients who didn't even thank him, much less pay their bills. And a sense of disapproval, too, at the hours he kept, at his willingness to go out of nights when he could just as well have let a call go till his regular morning rounds.

She would be waiting supper and she would know that Martha had been in to see him and she'd ask him how she was, and what was he to tell her?

He heard Martha going out and the sharp click of Miss Lane's heels across the outer office. He moved slowly to the basin and turned on the tap, picking up the soap.

He heard the door creak open and did not turn his head.

"Doctor," said Miss Lane, "Martha thinks she's fine. She says you're helping her. Do you think . . ."

"What would you do," he asked.

"I don't know," she said.

"Would you operate, knowing it was hopeless? Would you send her to a specialist, knowing that he couldn't help her, knowing she can't pay him and that she'll worry about not paying? Would you tell her that she has, perhaps, six months to live and take from her the little happiness and hope she still has left to her?"

"I am sorry, doctor."

"No need to be. I've faced it many times. No case is the same. Each one calls for a decision of its own. It's been a long, hard day . . ."

"Doctor, there's another one out there."

"Another patient?"

"A man. He just came in. His name is Harry Herman."

"Herman? I don't know any Hermans."

"He's a stranger," said Miss Lane. "Maybe he just moved into town."

"If he'd moved in," said Doc, "I'd have heard of it. I hear everything."

"Maybe he's just passing through. Maybe he got sick driving on the road."

"Well, send him in," said Doc, reaching for a towel. "I'll have a look at him."

The nurse turned to the door.

"And Miss Lane."

"Yes?"

"You may as well go home. There's no use sticking round. It's been a real bad day."

And it had been, at that, he thought. A fracture, a burn, a cut, a dropsy, a menopause, a pregnancy, two pelvics, a scattering of colds, a feeding schedule, two teethings, a suspicious lung, a possible gallstone, a cirrhosis of the liver and Martha Anderson. And now, last of all, this man named Harry Herman—no name that he knew and when one came to think of it, a rather funny name.

And he was a funny man. Just a bit too tall and willowy to be quite believable, ears too tight against his skull, lips so thin they seemed no lips at all.

"Doctor?" he asked, standing in the doorway.

"Yes," said Doc, picking up his jacket and shrugging into it. "Yes, I am the doctor. Come on in. What can I do for you?"

"I am not ill," said the man.

"Not ill?"

"But I want to talk to you. You have time, perhaps?"

"Yes, certainly," said Doc, knowing that he had no time and resenting this intrusion. "Come on in. Sit down."

He tried to place the accent, but was unable to. Central European, most likely.

"Technical," said the man. "Professional."

"What do you mean?" asked Doc, getting slightly nettled.

"I talk to you technical. I talk professional."

"You mean that you're a doctor?"

"Not exactly," said the man, "although perhaps you think so. I should tell you immediate that I am an alien."

"An alien," said Old Doc. "We've got lots of them around. Mostly refugees."

"Not what I mean. Not that kind of alien. From some other planet. From some other star."

"But you said your name was Herman . . ."

"When in Rome," said the other one, "you must do as Romans."

"Huh?" asked Doc, and then: "Good God, do you mean that? That you are an alien. By an alien, do you mean . . ."

The other nodded happily. "From some other planet. From some other star. Very many light-years."

"Well, I be damned," said Doc.

He stood there looking at the alien and the alien grinned back at him, but uncertainly.

"You think, perhaps," the alien said, "but he is so human!"

"That," said Doc, "was going through my mind."

"So you would have a look, perhaps. You would know a human body."

"Perhaps," said Doc grimly, not liking it at all. "But the human body can take some funny turns."

"But not a turn like this," said the stranger, showing him his hands.

"No," said the shocked Old Doc. "No such turn as that."

For the hand had two thumbs and a single finger, almost as if a bird claw had decided to turn into a hand.

"Nor like this?" asked the other, standing up and letting down his trousers.

"Nor like that," said Doc, more shaken than he'd been in many years of practice.

"Then," said the alien, zipping up his trousers, "I think that it is settled."

He sat down again and calmly crossed his knees.

"If you mean I accept you as an alien," said Doc, "I suppose I do. Although it's not an easy thing."

"I suppose it is not. It comes as quite a shock."

Doc passed a hand across his brow. "Yes, a shock, of course. But there are other points . . ."

"You mean the language," said the alien. "And my knowledge of your customs."

"That's part of it, naturally."

"We've studied you," the alien said. "We've spent some time on you. Not you alone, of course . . ."

"But you talk so well," protested Doc. "Like a well-educated foreigner."

"And that, of course," the other said, "is what exactly I am."

"Why, yes, I guess you are," said Doc. "I hadn't thought of it."

"I am not glib," said the alien. "I know a lot of words, but I use them incorrect. And my vocabulary is restricted to just the common speech. On matters of great technicality, I will not be proficient."

Doc walked around behind his desk and sat down rather limply.

"All right," he said, "let's have the rest of it. I accept you as an alien. Now tell me the other answer. Just why are you here?"

And he was surprised beyond all reason that he could approach the situation as calmly as he had. In a little while, he knew, when he had time to think it over, he would get the shakes.

"You're a doctor," said the alien. "You are a healer of your race."

"Yes," said Doc. "I am one of many healers."

"You work very hard to make the unwell well. You mend the broken flesh. You hold off death . . ."

"We try. Sometimes we don't succeed."

"You have many ailments. You have the cancer and the heart attacks and colds and many other things—I do not find the word."

"Diseases," Doc supplied.

"Disease. That is it. You will pardon my shortcomings in the tongue."

"Let's cut out the niceties," suggested Doc. "Let's get on with it."

"It is not right," the alien said, "to have all these diseases. It is not nice. It is an awful thing."

"We have less than we had at one time. We've licked a lot of them."

"And, of course," the alien said, "you make your living with them."

"What's that you said!" yelped Doc.

"You will be tolerant of me if I misunderstand. An economic system is a hard thing to get into one's head."

"I know what you mean," growled Doc, "but let me tell you, sir . . ."

But what was the use of it, he thought. This being was thinking the self-same thing that many humans thought.

"I would like to point out to you," he said, starting over once again, "that the medical profession is working hard to conquer those diseases you are talking of. We are doing all we can to destroy our own jobs."

"That is fine," the alien said. "It is what I thought, but it did not square with your planet's business sense. I take it, then, you would not be averse to seeing all disease destroyed."

"Now, look here," said Doc, having had enough of it, "I don't know what you are getting at. But I am hungry and I am tired and if you want to sit here threshing out philosophies . . ."

"Philosophies," said the alien. "Oh, not philosophies. I am practical. I have come to offer an end of all disease."

They sat in silence for a moment, then Doc stirred half protestingly and said, "Perhaps I misunderstood you, but I thought you said . . ."

"I have a method, a development, a find—I do not catch the word—that will destroy all diseases."

"A vaccine," said Old Doc.

"That's the word. Except it is different in some ways than the vaccine you are thinking."

"Cancer?" Doc asked.

The alien nodded. "Cancer and the common cold and all the others of them. You name it and it's gone."

"Heart," said Doc. "You can't vaccinate for heart."

"That, too," the alien said. "It does not really vaccinate. It makes the body strong. It makes the body right. Like tuning up a motor and making it like new. The motor will wear out in time, but it will function until it is worn out entirely."

Doc stared hard at the alien. "Sir," he said, "this is not the sort of thing one should joke about."

"I am not joking," said the alien.

"And this vaccine—it will work on humans? It has no side effects?"

"I am sure it will. We have studied your—your—the way your bodies work."

"Metabolism is the word you want."

"Thank you." said the alien.

"And the price?" asked Doc.

"There is no price," the alien said. "We are giving it to you."

"Completely free of charge? Surely there must be . . ."

"Without any charge," the alien said. "Without any strings."

He got up from the chair. He took a flat box from his pocket and walked over to the desk. He placed it upon the desk and pressed its side and the top sprang open. Inside of it were pads—like surgical pads, but they were not made of cloth.

Doc reached out, then halted his hand just above the box.

"May I?" he asked.

"Yes, certainly. You only touch the tops."

Doc gingerly lifted out one of the pads and laid it on the desk. He kneaded it with a skittish finger and there was liquid in the pad. He could feel the liquid squish as he pressed the pad.

He turned it over carefully and the underside of it was rough and corrugated, as if it were a mouthful of tiny, vicious teeth.

"You apply the rough side to the body of the patient." said the alien. "It seizes on the patient. It becomes a part of him. The body absorbs the vaccine and the pad drops off."

"And that is all there's to it?"

"That is all," the alien said.

Doc lifted the pad between two cautious fingers and dropped it back into the box.

He looked up at the alien. "But why?" he asked. "Why are you giving this to us?"

"You do not know," the alien said. "You really do not know."

"No, I don't," said Doc.

The alien's eyes suddenly were old and weary and he said: "In another million years you will."

"Not me," said Doc.

"In another million years," the alien said, "you'll do the same yourself, but it will be something different. And then someone will ask you, and you won't be able to answer any more than I am now."

If it was a rebuke, it was a very gentle one. Doc tried to decide if it were or not. He let the matter drop.

"Can you tell me what is in it?" he asked, gesturing at the pad.

"I can give you the descriptive formula, but it would be in our terms. It would be gibberish."

"You won't be offended if I try these out?"

"I'd be disappointed if you didn't," said the alien. "I would not expect your faith to extend so far. It would be simple minded."

He shut the box and pushed it closer to Old Doc. He turned and strode toward the door.

Doc rose ponderously to his feet.

"Now, wait a minute there!" he bellowed.

"I'll see you in a week or two," the alien said.

He went out and closed the door behind him.

Doc sat down suddenly in the chair and stared at the box upon the desk.

He reached out and touched it and it was really there. He pressed the side of it, and the lid popped open and the pads were there, inside.

He tried to fight his way back to sanity, to conservative and solid ground, to a proper—and a human—viewpoint.

"It's all hogwash," he said.

But it wasn't hogwash. He knew good and well it wasn't.

He fought it out with himself that night behind the closed door of his study, hearing faintly the soft bustling in the kitchen as Janet cleared away from supper.

And the first fight was on the front of credibility.

He had told the man he believed he was an alien and there was evidence that he could not ignore. Yet it seemed so incredible, all of it, every bit of it, that it was hard to swallow.

And the hardest thing of all was that this alien, whoever he might be, had come, of all the doctors in the world, to Dr. Jason Kelly, a little one horse doctor in a little one horse town.

He debated whether it might be a hoax and decided that it wasn't, for the three digits on the hand and that other thing he'd seen would have been difficult to simulate. And the whole thing, as a hoax, would be so stupid and so cruel that it simply made no sense. Besides, no one hated him enough to go to all the work. And even granting a hatred of appropriate proportion, he doubted there was anyone in Millville imaginative enough to think of this.

So the only solid ground he had, he told himself, was to assume that the man had been really an alien and that the pads were *bona fide*.

And if that was true, there was only one procedure: He must test the pads.

He rose from his chair and paced up and down the floor.

Martha Anderson, he told himself. Martha Anderson had cancer and her life was forfeit—there was nothing in man's world or knowledge that had a chance to save her. Surgery was madness, for she'd probably not survive it. And even if she did, her case was too advanced. The killer that she carried had already broken loose and was swarming through her body and there was no hope for her.

Yet he could not bring himself to do it, for she was Janet's closest friend and she was old and poor and every instinct in him screamed against his using her as a guinea pig.

Now if it were only old Con Gilbert—he could do a thing like that to Con. It would be no more than the old skinflint rightly had coming to him. But old Con was too mean to be really sick; despite all the complaining that he did, he was healthy as a hog.

No matter what the alien had said about no side effects, he told himself, one could not be sure. He had said they'd studied the metabolism of the human race and yet, on the face of it, it seemed impossible.

The answer, he knew, was right there any time he wanted it. It was tucked away back in his brain and he knew that it was there, but he pretended that it wasn't and he kept it tucked away and refused to haul it forth.

But after an hour or so of pacing up and down the room and of batting out his brains, he finally gave up and let the answer out.

He was quite calm when he rolled up his sleeve and opened up the box. And he was a matter-of-fact physician when he lifted out the pad and slapped it on his arm.

But his hand was shaking when he rolled down the sleeve so Janet wouldn't see the pad and ask a lot of questions about what had happened to his arm.

Tomorrow all over the world outside Millville, people would line up before the clinic doors, with their sleeves rolled up and ready. The lines, most likely, would move at a steady clip, for there was little to it. Each person would pass before a doctor and the doctor would slap a pad onto his or her arm and the next person would step up.

All over the world, thought Doc, in every cranny of it, in every little village; none would be overlooked. Even the poor, he thought, for there would be no charge.

And one could put his finger on a certain date and say: "This was the day in history when disease came to an end."

For the pads not only would kill the present ailments, but would guard against them in the future.

And every twenty years the great ships out of space would come, carrying other cargoes of the pads and there would be another Vaccination Day. But not so many then—only the younger generation. For once a person had been vaccinated, there was no further need of it. Vaccinated once and you were set for life.

Doc tapped his foot quietly on the floor of the porch to keep the rocker going. It was pleasant here, he thought. And tomorrow it would be pleasant in the entire world. Tomorrow the fear would have been largely filtered out of human life. After tomorrow, short of accident or violence, men could look forward confidently to living out their normal lifetimes. And, more to the point, perhaps, completely healthy lifetimes.

The night was quiet, for the children finally had gone in, giving up their play. And he was tired. Finally, he thought, he could admit that he was tired. There was now, after many years, no treason in saying he was tired.

Inside the house he heard the muffled purring of the phone and the sound of it broke the rhythm of his rocking, brought him forward to the chair's edge.

Janet's feet made soft sounds as they moved toward the phone and he thrilled to the gentleness of her voice as she answered it.

Now, in just a minute, she would call him and he'd get up and go inside.

But she didn't call him. Her voice went on talking.

He settled back into the chair.

He'd forgotten once again.

The phone no longer was an enemy. It no longer haunted him.

For Millville had been the first. The fear had already been lifted here. Millville had been the guinea pig, the pilot project.

Martha Anderson had been the first of them and after her Ted Carson, whose lung had been suspicious, and after him the Jurgens' baby when it came down with pneumonia. And a couple of dozen others until all the pads were gone.

And the alien had come back.

And the alien had said—what was it he had said?

"Don't think of us as benefactors nor as supermen. We are neither one. Think of me, if you will, as the man across the street."

And it had been, Doc told himself, a reaching by the alien for an understanding, an attempt to translate this thing that they were doing into a common idiom.

And had there been any understanding—any depth of understanding? Doc doubted that there had been.

Although, he recalled, the aliens had been basically very much like humans. They could even joke.

There had been one joking thing the original alien had said that had stuck inside his mind. And it had been a sort of silly thing, silly on the face of it, but it had bothered him.

The screen door banged behind Janet as she came out on the porch. She sat down in the glider.

"That was Martha Anderson," she said.

Doc chuckled to himself. Martha lived just five doors up the street and she and Janet saw one another a dozen times a day yet Martha had to phone.

"What did Martha want?" he asked.

Janet laughed. "She wanted help with rolls."

"You mean her famous rolls?"

"Yes. She couldn't remember for the life of her, how much yeast she used."

Doc chortled softly. "And those are the ones, I suppose, she wins all the prizes on at the county fair."

Janet said, crisply: "It's not so funny as you make it, Jason. It's easy to forget a thing like that. She does a lot of baking."

"Yes, I suppose you're right," said Doc.

He should be getting in, he told himself, and start reading in the journal. And yet he didn't want to. It was so pleasant sitting here—just sitting. It had been a long time since he could do much sitting.

And it was all right with him, of course, because he was getting old and close to worn out, but it wouldn't be all right with a younger doctor, one who still owed for his education and was just starting out. There was talk in the United Nations of urging all the legislative bodies to consider medical subsidies to keep the doctors going. For there still was need of them. Even with all diseases vanished, there still was need of them. It wouldn't do to let their ranks thin out, for there would be time and time again when they would be badly needed.

He'd been listening to the footsteps for quite a while, coming down the street, and now all at once they were turning in the gate.

He sat up straighter in his chair.

Maybe it was a patient, knowing he'd be home, coming in to see him.

"Why," said Janet, considerably surprised, "it is Mr. Gilbert."

It was Con Gilbert, sure enough.

"Good evening, Doc," said Con. "Good evening, Miz Kelly."

"Good evening," Janet said, getting up to go.

"No use of you to leave," Con said to her.

"I have some things to do," she told him. "I was just getting ready to go in."

Con came up the steps and sat down on the glider.

"Nice evening," he declared.

"It is all of that," said Doc.

"Nicest spring I've ever seen," said Con, working his way around to what he had to say.

"I was thinking that," said Doc. "It seems to me the lilacs never smelled so good before."

"Doc," said Con, "I figure I owe you quite a bit of money."

"You owe me some," said Doc.

"You got an idea how much it might be?"

"Not the faintest," Doc told him. "I never bothered to keep track of it."

"Figured it was a waste of time," said Con. "Figured I would never pay it."

"Something like that," Doc agreed.

"Been doctoring with you for a right long time," said Con.

"That's right, Con."

"I got three hundred here. You figure that might do it?"

"Let's put it this way, Con," said Doc. "I'd settle for a whole lot less."

"I guess, then, that sort of makes us even. Seems to me three hundred might be close to fair."

"If you say so," said Doc.

Con dug out his billfold, extracted a wad of bills and handed them across. Doc took them and folded them and stuffed them in his pocket.

'Thank you, Con," he said.

And suddenly he had a funny feeling, as if there were something he should know, as if there were something that he should be able to just reach out and grab.

But he couldn't, no matter how he tried, figure what it was.

Con got up and shuffled across the porch, heading for the steps.

"Be seeing you around," he said.

Doc jerked himself back to reality.

"Sure, Con. Be seeing you around. And thanks."

He sat in the chair, not rocking, and listened to Con going down the walk and out the gate and then down the street until there was only silence.

And if he ever was going to get at it, he'd have to go in now and start reading in the journal.

Although, more than likely, it was all damn foolishness. He'd probably never again need to know a thing out of any medical journal.

Doc pushed the journal to one side and sat there, wondering what was wrong with him. He'd been reading for twenty minutes and none of it had registered. He couldn't have told a word that he had read.

Too upset, he thought. Too excited about Operation Kelly. And wasn't that a thing to call it—Operation Kelly!

And he remembered it once again exactly.

How he'd tried it out on Millville, then gone to the county medical association and how the doctors in the county, after some slight amount of scoffing and a good deal of skepticism, had become convinced. And from there it had gone to state and the AMA.

And finally that great day in the United Nations, when the alien had appeared before the delegates and when he, himself, had been introduced—and at last the great London man arising to suggest that the project could be called nothing else but Kelly.

A proud moment, he told himself—and he tried to call up the pride again, but it wasn't there, not the whole of it. Never in his life again would he know that kind of pride.

And here he sat, a simple country doctor once again, in his study late at night, trying to catch up with reading he never seemed to get the time to do.

Although that was no longer strictly true. Now he had all the time there was.

He reached out and pulled the journal underneath the lamp and settled down to read.

But it was slow going.

He went back and read a paragraph anew.

And that, he told himself, was not the way it should be.

Either he was getting old or his eyes were going bad or he was plain stupid.

And that was the word—that was the key to the thing that it had seemed he should have been able to just reach out and grab.

Stupid!

Probably not actually stupid. Maybe just a little slow. Not really less intelligent, but not so sharp and bright as he had been. Not so quick to catch the hang of things.

Martha Anderson had forgotten how much yeast to use in those famous, prize-winning rolls of hers. And that was something that Martha should never have forgotten.

Con had paid his bill, and on the scale of values that Con had subscribed to all his life, that was plain stupidity. The bright thing, the sharp thing would have been for Con, now that he'd probably never need a doctor, just to forget the obligation. After all, it would not have been hard to do; he'd been forgetful of it up to this very night.

And the alien had said something that, at the time, he'd thought of as a joke.

"Never fear," the alien had said, "we'll cure all your ills. Including, more than likely, a few you don't suspect."

And was intelligence a disease?

It was hard to think of it as such.

And yet, when any race was as obsessed with intelligence as Man was, it might be classed as one.

When it ran rampant as it had during the last half century, when it piled progress on top of progress, technology on top of technology, when it ran so fast that no man caught his breath, then it might be disease.

Not quite so sharp, thought Doc. Not quite so quick to grasp the meaning of a paragraph loaded with medical terminology—being forced to go a little slower to pack it in his mind.

And was that really bad?

Some of the stupidest people he'd ever known, he told himself, had been the happiest.

And while one could not make out of that a brief for planned stupidity, it at least might be a plea for a less harassed humanity.

He pushed the journal to one side and sat staring at the light.

It would be felt in Millville first because Millville had been the pilot project. And six months from tomorrow night it would be felt in all the world.

How far would it go, he wondered—for that, after all, was the vital question.

Only slightly less sharp?

Back to bumbling?

Clear back to the ape?

There was no way one could tell . . .

And all he had to do to stop it was pick up the phone.

He sat there, frozen with the thought that perhaps Operation Kelly should be stopped—that after all the years of death and pain and misery, Man must buy it back.

But the aliens, he thought—the aliens would not let it go too far. Whoever they might be, he believed they were decent people.

Maybe there had been no basic understanding, no meeting of the minds, and yet there had been a common ground—the very simple ground of compassion for the blind and halt.

But if he were wrong, he wondered—what if the aliens proposed to limit Man's powers of self-destruction even if that meant reducing him to abject stupidity . . . what was the answer then? And what if the plan was to soften man up before invasion?

Sitting there, he knew.

Knew that no matter what the odds were against his being right, there was nothing he could do.

Realized that as a judge in a matter such as this he was unqualified, that he was filled with bias, and could not change himself.

He'd been a doctor too long to stop Operation Kelly.

PARADISE

Unusual for the stories in the City *cycle, "Paradise" is a direct sequel to the classic "Desertion," and the reader will gain a lot by reading that story first.*

Cliff Simak wrote this story late in 1945, and it is clear that although the meanings of the cycle may have been somewhat fuzzy in its beginning, by the time "Paradise" came to be written, those meanings were coming clear in the author's mind. John W. Campbell Jr., the editor of Astounding Science Fiction, *bought the story (Cliff received $131.25), and it appeared in the June 1946 issue.*

After this story, with its grave implications for the survival of humanity, two tracks of Cliff's "future history" diverged; alas, the City *stories explored one of those tracks, and Cliff never explored the second track . . .*

—dww

The dome was a squatted, alien shape that did not belong beneath the purple mist of Jupiter, a huddled, frightened structure that seemed to cower against the massive planet.

The creature that had been Kent Fowler stood spraddling on his thick-set legs.

An alien thing, he thought. That's how far I've left the human race. For it's not alien at all. Not alien to me. It is the place I lived in, dreamed in, planned in. It is the place I left—afraid. And it is the place I come back to—driven and afraid.

Driven by the memory of the people who were like me before I became the thing I am, before I knew the liveness and the fitness and the pleasure that is possible if one is not a human being.

Towser stirred beside him and Fowler sensed the bumbling friendliness of the one-time dog, the *expressed* friendliness and comradeship and love that had existed all the time, perhaps, but was never known so long as they were dog and man.

The dog's thoughts seeped into his brain. "You can't do it, pal," said Towser.

Fowler's answer was almost a wail. "But I have to, Towser. That's what I went out for. To find what Jupiter really is like. And now I can tell them, now I can bring them word."

You should have done it long ago, said a voice deep inside of him, a faint, far-off human voice that struggled up through his Jovian self. *But you were a coward and you put it off—and put it off. You ran away because you were afraid to go back. Afraid to be turned into a man again.*

"I'll be lonesome," said Towser, and yet he did not say it. At least there were no words—rather a feeling of loneliness, a heart-wrench cry at parting. As if, for the moment, Fowler had moved over and shared Towser's mind.

Fowler stood silent, revulsion growing in him. Revulsion at the thought of being turned back into a man—into the inadequacy that was the human body and the human mind.

"I'd come with you," Towser told him, "but I couldn't stand it. I might die before I could get back. I was darn near done for, you remember. I was old and full of fleas. My teeth were wore right down to nubbins and my digestion was all shot. And I had terrible dreams. Used to chase rabbits when I was a pup, but toward the last it was the rabbits that were chasing me."

"You stay here," said Fowler. "I'll be coming back."

If I can make them understand, he thought. *If I only can. If I can explain.*

He lifted his massive head and stared at the lift of hills which swelled to mountain peaks shrouded in the rose and purple mist. A lightning bolt snaked across the sky and the clouds and mist were lighted with a fire of ecstasy.

He shambled forward, slowly, reluctantly. A whiff of scent came down the breeze and his body drank it in—like a cat rolling in catnip. And yet it wasn't scent—although that was the closest he could come to it, the nearest word he had. In years to come the human race would develop a new terminology.

How could one, he wondered, explain the mist that drifted on the land and the scent that was pure delight. Other things they'd understand, he knew. That one never had to eat, that one never slept, that one was done with the whole range of depressive neuroses of which Man was victim. Those things they would understand, because they were things that could be told in simple terms, things which could be explained in existent language.

But what about the other things—the factors that called for a new vocabulary? The emotions that Man had never known. The abilities that Man had never dreamed of. The clarity of mind and the understanding—the ability to use one's brain down to the ultimate cell. The things one knew and could do instinctively that Man could never do because his body did not carry the senses with which they could be done.

"I'll write it down," he told himself. "I'll take my time and write it down."

But the written word, he realized, was a sorry tool.

A televisor port bulged out of the crystalline hide of the dome and he shambled toward it. Rivulets of condensed mist ran down across it and he reared up to stare straight into the port.

Not that he could see anything, but the men inside would see him. The men who always watched, staring out at the brutality of

Jupiter, the roaring gales and ammonia rains, the drifting clouds of deadly methane scudding past. For that was the way that men saw Jupiter.

He lifted a forepaw and wrote swiftly in the wetness on the port—printing backwards.

They had to know who it was, so there would be no mistake. They had to know what co-ordinates to use. Otherwise they might convert him back into the wrong body, use the wrong matrix and he would come out somebody else—young Allen, maybe, or Smith, or Pelletier. And that might well be fatal.

The ammonia ran down and blurred the printing, wiped it out. He wrote the name again.

They would understand that name. They would know that one of the men who had been converted into a Loper had come back to report.

He dropped to the ground and whirled around, staring at the door which led into the converter unit. The door moved slowly, swinging outward.

"Good-bye, Towser," said Fowler, softly.

A warning cry rose in his brain: *It's not too late. You aren't in there yet. You still can change your mind. You still can turn and run.*

He plodded on, determined, gritting mental teeth. He felt the metal floor underneath his pads, sensed the closing of the door behind him. He caught one last, fragmentary thought from Towser and then there was only darkness.

The conversion chamber lay just ahead and he moved up the sloping ramp to reach it.

A man and dog went out, he thought, and now the man comes back.

The press conference had gone well. There had been satisfactory things to report.

Yes, Tyler Webster told the newsmen, the trouble on Venus had been all smoothed out. Just a matter of the parties involved sitting down and talking. The life experiments out in the cold laboratories of Pluto were progressing satisfactorily. The expedition for Centauri would leave as scheduled, despite reports it was all balled up. The trade commission soon would issue new monetary schedules on various interplanetary products, ironing out a few inequalities.

Nothing sensational. Nothing to make headlines. Nothing to lead off the newscast.

"And Jon Culver tells me," said Webster, "to remind you gentlemen that today is the one hundred twenty-fifth anniversary of the last murder committed in the Solar System. One hundred and twenty-five years without a death by premeditated violence."

He leaned back in the chair and grinned at them, masking the thing he dreaded, the question that he knew would come.

But they were not ready to ask it yet—there was a custom to be observed—a very pleasant custom.

Burly Stephen Andrews, press chief for *Interplanetary News,* cleared his throat as if about to make an important announcement, asked with what amounted to mock gravity:

"And how's the boy?"

A smile broke across Webster's face. "I'm going home for the weekend," he said. "I bought my son a toy."

He reached out, lifted the little tube from off the desk.

"An old-fashioned toy," he said. "Guaranteed old-fashioned. A company just started putting them out. You put it up to your eye and turn it and you see pretty pictures. Colored glass falling into place. There's a name for it—"

"Kaleidoscope," said one of the newsmen, quickly. "I've read about them. In an old history on the manners and customs of the early twentieth century."

"Have you tried it, Mr. Chairman?" asked Andrews.

"No," said Webster. "To tell the truth, I haven't. I just got it this afternoon and I've been too busy."

"Where'd you get it, Mr. Chairman?" asked a voice. "I got to get one of those for my own kid."

"At the shop just around the corner. The toy shop, you know. They just came in today."

Now, Webster knew, was the time for them to go. A little bit of pleasant, friendly banter and they'd get up and leave.

But they weren't leaving—and he knew they weren't. He knew it by the sudden hush and the papers that rattled quickly to cover up the hush.

Then Stephen Andrews was asking the question that Webster had dreaded. For a moment Webster was grateful that Andrews should be the one to ask it. Andrews had been friendly, generally speaking, and *Interplanetary Press* dealt in objective news, with none of the sly slanting of words employed by interpretative writers.

"Mr. Chairman," said Andrews, "we understand a man who was converted on Jupiter has come back to Earth. We would like to ask you if the report is true?"

"It is true," said Webster, stiffly.

They waited and Webster waited, unmoving in his chair.

"Would you wish to comment?" asked Andrews, finally.

"No," said Webster.

Webster glanced around the room, ticking off the faces. Tensed faces, sensing some of the truth beneath his flat refusal to discuss the matter. Amused faces, masking brains that even now were thinking how they might twist the few words he had spoken. Angry faces that would write outraged interpretative pieces about the people's right to know.

"I am sorry, gentlemen," said Webster.

Andrews rose heavily from the chair. "Thank you, Mr. Chairman," he said.

Webster sat in his chair and watched them go, felt the coldness and emptiness of the room when they were gone.

They'll crucify me, he thought. They'll nail me to the barn door and I haven't got a comeback. Not a single one.

He rose from the chair and walked across the room, stood staring out the window at the garden in the sun of afternoon.

Yet, you simply couldn't tell them.

Paradise! Heaven for the asking! And the end of humanity! The end of all the ideals and all the dreams of mankind, the end of the race itself.

The green light on his desk flashed and chirped and he strode back across the room.

"What is it?" he asked.

The tiny screen flashed and a face was there.

"The dogs just reported, sir, that Joe, the mutant, went to your residence and Jenkins let him in."

"Joe! You're sure?"

"That's what the dogs said. And the dogs are never wrong."

"No," said Webster slowly, "no, they never are."

The face faded from the screen and Webster sat down heavily.

He reached with numbed fingers for the contro1 panel on his desk, twirled the combination without looking.

The house loomed on the screen, the house in North America that crouched on the windy hilltop. A structure that had stood for almost a thousand years. A place where a long line of Websters had lived and dreamed and died.

Far in the blue above the house a crow was flying and Webster heard, or imagined that he heard, the wind-blown caw of the soaring bird.

Everything was all right—or seemed to be. The house drowsed in the morning light and the statue still stood upon the sweep of lawn—the statue of that long-gone ancestor who had vanished on the star-path. Allen Webster, who had been the first to leave the Solar System, heading for Centauri—even as the expedition now on Mars would head out in a day or two.

There was no stir about the house, no sign of any moving thing.

Webster's hand moved out and flipped a toggle. The screen went dead.

Jenkins can handle things, he thought. Probably better than a man could handle them. After all, he's got almost a thousand years of wisdom packed in that metal hide of his. He'll be calling in before long to let me know what it's all about.

His hand reached out, set up another combination.

He waited for long seconds before the face came on the screen.

"What is it, Tyler?" asked the face.

"Just got a report that Joe—"

Jon Culver nodded. "I just got it, too. I'm checking up."

"What do you make of it?"

The face of the World Security chief crinkled quizzically. "Softening up, maybe. We've been pushing Joe and the other mutants pretty hard. The dogs have done a top-notch job."

"But there have been no signs of it," protested Webster. "Nothing in the records to indicate any trend that way."

"Look," said Culver. "They haven't drawn a breath for more than a hundred years we haven't known about. Got everything they've done down on tape in black and white. Every move they've made, we've blocked. At first they figured it was just tough luck, but now they know it isn't. Maybe they've up and decided they are licked."

"I don't think so," said Webster, solemnly. "Whenever those babies figure they're licked, you better start looking for a place that's soft to light."

"I'll keep on top of it," Culver told him. "I'll keep you posted."

The plate faded and was a square of glass. Webster stared at it moodily.

The mutants weren't licked—not by a long shot. He knew that, and so did Culver. And yet—

Why had Joe gone to Jenkins? Why hadn't he contacted the government here in Geneva? Face saving, maybe. Dealing through a robot. After all, Joe had known Jenkins for a long, long time.

Unaccountably, Webster felt a surge of pride. Pride that if such were the case, Joe had gone to Jenkins. For Jenkins, despite his metal hide, was a Webster, too.

Pride, thought Webster. Accomplishment and mistake. But always counting for something. Each of them down the years. Jerome, who had lost the world the Juwain philosophy. And Thomas, who had given the world the space-drive principle that now had been perfected. And Thomas' son, Allen, who had tried for the stars and failed. And Bruce, who had first conceived the twin civilization of man and dog. Now, finally, himself—Tyler Webster, chairman of the World Committee.

Sitting at the desk, he clasped his hands in front of him, stared at the evening light pouring through the window.

Waiting, he confessed. Waiting for the snicker of the signal that would tell him Jenkins was calling to report on Joe. If only—

If only an understanding could be reached. If only mutants and men could work together. If they could forget this half-hidden war of stalemate, they could go far, the three of them together—man and dog and mutant.

Webster shook his head. It was too much to expect. The difference was too great, the breach too wide. Suspicion on the part of men and a tolerant amusement on the part of the mutants would keep the two apart. For the mutants were a different race, an offshoot that had jumped too far ahead. Men who had become true individuals with no need of society, no need of human approval, utterly lacking in the herd instinct that had held the race together, immune to social pressures.

And because of the mutants the little group of mutated dogs so far had been of little practical use to their older brother, man. For the dogs had watched for more than a hundred years, had been the police force that kept the human mutants under observation.

Webster slid back his chair, opened a desk drawer, took out a sheaf of papers.

One eye on the televisor plate, he snapped over the toggle that called his secretary.

"Yes, Mr. Webster."

"I'm going to call on Mr. Fowler," said Webster. "If a call comes through—"

The secretary's voice shook just a little. "If one does, sir, I'll contact you right away."

"Thanks," said Webster.

He snapped the toggle back.

They've heard of it already, he thought. Everyone in the whole building is standing around with their tongues hanging out, waiting for the news.

Kent Fowler lounged in a chair in the garden outside his room, watching the little black terrier dig frantically after an imagined rabbit.

"You know, Rover," said Fowler, "you aren't fooling me."

The dog stopped digging, looked over his shoulder with grinning teeth, barked excitedly. Then went back to digging.

"You'll slip up one of these days," Fowler told him, "and say a word or two and I'll have you dead to rights."

Rover went on digging.

Foxy little devil, thought Fowler. Smarter than a whip. Webster sicked him on me and he's played the part, all right. He's dug for rabbits and he's been disrespectful to the shrubs and he's scratched for fleas—the perfect picture of a perfect dog. But I'm on to him. I'm on to all of them.

A foot crunched in the grass and Fowler looked up.

"Good evening," said Tyler Webster.

"I've been wondering when you'd come," said Fowler shortly. "Sit down and give it to me—straight. You don't believe me, do you?"

Webster eased himself into the second chair, laid the sheaf of papers in his lap.

"I can understand how you feel," he said.

"I doubt if you can," snapped Fowler. "I came here, bringing news that I thought was important. A report that had cost me more than you can imagine."

He hunched forward in his chair. "I wonder if you can realize that every hour I've spent as a human being has been mental torture."

"I'm sorry," said Webster. "But we had to be sure. We had to check your reports."

"And make certain tests?"

Webster nodded.

"Like Rover over there?"

"His name isn't Rover," said Webster, gently. "If you've been calling him that, you've hurt his feelings. All the dogs have human names. This one's Elmer."

Elmer had stopped his digging, was trotting toward them. He sat down beside Webster's chair, scrubbed at his dirt-filled whiskers with a clay-smeared paw.

"What about it, Elmer?" asked Webster.

"He's human, all right," said the dog, "but not all human. Not a mutant, you know. But something else. Something alien."

"That's to be expected," said Fowler. "I was a Loper for five years."

Webster nodded. "You'd retain part of the personality. That's understandable. And the dog would spot it. They're sensitive to things like that. Psychic, almost. That's why we put them on the mutants. They can sniff one out no matter where he is."

"You mean that you believe me?"

Webster rustled the papers in his lap, smoothed them out with a careful hand. "I'm afraid I do."

"Why afraid?"

"Because," Webster told him, "you're the greatest threat mankind's ever faced."

"Threat! Man, don't you understand? I'm offering you . . . offering you—"

"Yes, I know," said Webster. "The word is Paradise."

"And you're afraid of that?"

"Terrified," said Webster. "Just try to envision what it would mean if we told the people and the people all believed. Everyone would want to go to Jupiter and become a Loper. The very fact that the Lopers apparently have life spans running into thousands of years would be reason enough if there were no others.

"We would be faced by a system-wide demand that everyone immediately be sent to Jupiter. No one would want to remain human. In the end there would be no humans—all the humans would be Lopers. Had you thought of that?"

Fowler licked his lips with a nervous tongue. "Certainly. That is what I had expected."

"The human race would disappear," said Webster, speaking evenly. "It would be wiped out. It would junk all the progress it has made over thousands of years. It would disappear just when it is on the verge of its greatest advancement."

"But you don't know," protested Fowler. "You can't know. You've never been a Loper. I have." He tapped his chest. "I know what it is like."

Webster shook his head. "I'm not arguing on that score. I'm ready to concede that it may be better to be a Loper than a human. What I can't concede is that we would be justified in wiping out the human race—that we should trade what the human race has done and will do for what the Lopers might do. The human race is going places. Maybe not so pleasantly nor so clear-headedly nor as brilliantly as your Lopers, but in the long run I have a feeling that it will go much farther. We have a racial heritage and a racial destiny that we can't throw away."

Fowler leaned forward in his chair. "Look," he said, "I've played this fair. I came straight to you and the World Committee. I could have told the press and radio and forced your hand, but I didn't do it."

"What you're getting at," suggested Webster, "is that the World Committee doesn't have the right to decide this thing themselves. You're suggesting that the people have their say about it."

Fowler nodded, tight-lipped.

"Frankly," said Webster, "I don't trust the people. You'd get mob reaction. Selfish response. Not a one of them would think about the race, but only of themselves."

"Are you telling me," asked Fowler, "that I'm right, but you can't do a thing about it?"

"Not exactly. We'll have to work out something. Maybe Jupiter could be made a sort of old folks' home. After a man had lived out a useful life—"

Fowler made a tearing sound of disgust deep inside his throat. "A reward," he snapped. "Turning an old horse out to pasture. Paradise by special dispensation."

"That way," Webster pointed out, "we'd save the human race and still have Jupiter."

Fowler came to his feet in a swift, lithe motion. "I'm sick of it," he shouted. "I brought you a thing you wanted to know. A thing you spent billions of dollars and, so far as you knew, hundreds of lives, to find out. You set up reconversion stations all over Jupiter and you sent out men by dozens and they never came back and you thought that they were dead and still you sent out others. And none of them came back—because they didn't want to come back, because they couldn't come back, because they couldn't stomach being men again. Then I came back and what does it amount to? A lot of high-flown talk . . . a lot of quibbling . . . questioning me and doubting me. Then finally saying I am all right, but that I made a mistake in coming back at all."

He let his arms fall to his side and his shoulders drooped.

"I'm free, I suppose," he said. "I don't need to stay here."

Webster nodded slowly. "Certainly, you are free. You were free all the time. I only asked that you stay until I could check."

"I could go back to Jupiter?"

"In the light of the situation," said Webster, "that might be a good idea."

"I'm surprised you didn't suggest it," said Fowler, bitterly. "It would be an out for you. You could file away the report and forget about it and go on running the Solar System like a child's game played on a parlor floor. Your family has blundered its way through centuries and the people let you come back for more. One of your ancestors lost the world the Juwain philosophy and another blocked the effort of the humans to co-operate with the mutants—"

Webster spoke sharply. "Leave me and my family out of this, Fowler! It is a thing that's bigger—"

But Fowler was shouting, drowning out his words. "And I'm not going to let you bungle this. The world has lost enough because of you Websters. Now the world's going to get a break. I'm going to tell the people about Jupiter. I'll tell the press and radio. I'll yell it from the housetops. I'll—"

His voice broke and his shoulders shook.

Webster's voice was cold with sudden rage. "I'll fight you, Fowler. I'll go on the beam against you. I can't let you do a thing like this."

Fowler had swung around, was striding toward the garden gate.

Webster, frozen in his chair, felt the paw clawing at his leg.

"Shall I get him, Boss?" asked Elmer. "Shall I go and get him?"

Webster shook his head. "Let him go," he said. "He has as much right as I have to do the thing he wishes."

A chill wind came across the garden wall and rustled the cape about Webster's shoulders.

Words beat in his brain—words that had been spoken here in this garden scant seconds ago, but words that came from centuries away. One of your ancestors lost the Juwain philosophy. One of your ancestors—

Webster clenched his fists until the nails dug into his palms.

A jinx, thought Webster. That's what we are. A jinx upon humanity. The Juwain philosophy. And the mutants. But the mutants had had the Juwain philosophy for centuries now and they had never used it. Joe had stolen it from Grant and Grant had spent his life trying to get it back. But he never had.

Maybe, thought Webster, trying to console himself, it really didn't amount to much. If it had, the mutants would have used it. Or maybe—just maybe—the mutants had been bluffing. Maybe they didn't know any more about it than the humans did.

A metallic voice coughed softly and Webster looked up. A small gray robot stood just outside the doorway.

"The call, sir," said the robot. "The call you've been expecting."

Jenkins' face came into the plate—an old face, obsolete and ugly. Not the smooth, lifelike face boasted by the latest model robots.

"I'm sorry to disturb you, sir," he said, "but it is most unusual. Joe came up and asked to use our visor to put in a call to you. Won't tell me what he wants, sir. Says it's just a friendly call to an old-time neighbor."

"Put him on," said Webster.

"He went at it most unusual, sir," persisted Jenkins. "He came up and sat around and chewed the fat for an hour or more before he asked to use it. I'd say, if you'd pardon me, that it's most peculiar."

"I know," said Webster. "Joe is peculiar, in a lot of ways."

Jenkins' face faded from the screen and another face came in—that of Joe, the mutant. It was a strong face with a wrinkled, leathery skin and blue-gray eyes that twinkled, hair that was just turning salt and pepper at the temples.

"Jenkins doesn't trust me, Tyler," said Joe, and Webster felt his hackles rising at the laughter that lurked behind the words.

"For that matter," he told him bluntly, "neither do I."

Joe clucked with his tongue. "Why, Tyler, we've never given you a single minute's trouble. Not a single one of us. You've watched us and you've worried and fretted about us, but we've never hurt you. You've had so many of the dogs spying on us that we stumble over them everywhere we turn and you've kept files on us and studied us and talked us up and down until you must be sick to death of it."

"We know you," said Webster, grimly. "We know more about you than you know about yourselves. We know how many there are of you and we know each of you personally. Want to know what any one of you were doing at any given moment in the last hundred years or so? Ask us and we'll tell you."

Butter wouldn't have melted in Joe's mouth. "And all the time," he said, "we were thinking kindly of you. Figuring out how sometime we might want to help you."

"Why didn't you do it, then?" snapped Webster. "We were ready to work with you at first. Even after you stole the Juwain philosophy from Grant—"

"Stole it?" asked Joe. "Surely, Tyler, you must have that wrong. We only took it so we could work it out. It was all botched up, you know."

"You probably figured it out the day after you had your hands on it," Webster told him, flatly. "What were you waiting for? Any time you had offered that to us we'd known that you were with us and we'd have worked with you. We'd have called off the dogs, we'd have accepted you."

"Funny thing," said Joe. "We never seemed to care about being accepted."

And the old laughter was back again, the laughter of a man who was sufficient to himself, who saw the whole fabric of the human community of effort as a vast, ironic joke. A man who walked alone and liked it. A man who saw the human race as something that was funny and probably just a little dangerous—but funnier than ever because it was dangerous. A man who felt no need of the brotherhood of man, who rejected that brotherhood as a thing as utterly provincial and pathetic as the twentieth century booster clubs.

"O.K.," said Webster sharply. "If that's the way you want it. I'd hoped that maybe you had a deal to offer—some chance of conciliation. We don't like things as they are—we'd rather they were different. But the move is up to you."

"Now, Tyler," protested Joe, "no use in flying off the handle. I was thinking maybe you'd ought to know about the Juwain philosophy. You've sort of forgotten about it now, but there was a time when the System was all stirred up about it."

"All right," said Webster, "go ahead and tell me." The tone of his voice said he knew Joe wouldn't.

"Basically," said Joe, "you humans are a lonely lot of folks. You never have known your fellow-man. You can't know him because you haven't the common touch of understanding that makes it possible to know him. You have friendships, sure, but those friendships are based on pure emotions, never on real understanding. You get along together, sure. But you get along by tolerance rather than by understanding. You work out your problems by agreement, but that agreement is simply a matter of the stronger-minded among you beating down the opposition of the weaker ones."

"What's that got to do with it?"

"Why, everything," Joe told him. "With the Juwain philosophy you'd actually understand."

"Telepathy?" asked Webster.

"Not exactly," said Joe. "We mutants have telepathy. But this is something different. The Juwain philosophy provides an ability to sense the viewpoint of another. It won't necessarily make you agree with that viewpoint, but it does make you recognize it. You not only know what the other fellow is talking about, but how he feels about it. With Juwain's philosophy you have to accept the validity of another man's ideas and knowledge, not just the words he says, but the thought back of the words."

"Semantics," said Webster.

"If you insist on the term," Joe told him. "What it really means is that you understand not only the intrinsic meaning, but the implied meaning of what someone else is saying. Almost telepathy, but not quite. A whole lot better, some ways."

"And Joe, how do you go about it? How do you—"

The laughter was back again. "You think about it a while, Tyler . . . find out how bad you want it. Then maybe we can talk."

"Horse trading," said Webster.

Joe nodded.

"Booby-trapped, too, I suppose," said Webster.

"Couple of them," said Joe. "You find them and we'll talk about that, too."

"What are you fellows going to want?"

"Plenty," Joe told him, "but maybe it'll be worth it."

The screen went dead and Webster sat staring at it with unseeing eyes. Booby-trapped? Of course it was. Clear up to the hilt.

Webster screwed his eyes shut and felt the blood pounding in his brain.

What was it that had been claimed for the Juwain philosophy in that far-gone day when it had been lost? That it would have put mankind a hundred thousand years ahead in two short generations. Something like that.

Maybe stretching it a bit—but not too much. A little justified exaggeration, that was all.

Men understanding one another, accepting one another's ideas at face value, each man seeing behind the words, seeing the thing as someone else would see it and accepting that concept as if it were his own. Making it, in fact, part of his own knowledge that could be brought to bear upon the subject at hand. No misunderstanding, no prejudice, no bias, no jangling—but a clear, complete grasp of all the conflicting angles of any human problem. Applicable to anything, to any type of human endeavor. To sociology, to psychology, to engineering, to all the various facets of a complex civilization. No more bungling, no more quarrelling, but honest and sincere appraisal of the facts and the ideas at hand.

A hundred thousand years in two generations? Perhaps not too far off, at that.

But booby-trapped? Or was it? Did the mutants really mean to part with it? For any kind of price? Just another bait dangled in front of mankind's eyes while around the corner the mutants rolled with laughter.

The mutants hadn't used it. Of course, they hadn't, for they had no real need of it. They already had telepathy and that would serve the purpose as far as the mutants were concerned. Individualists would have little use for a device which would make them understand one another, for they would not care whether they understood one another. The mutants got along together, apparently, tolerating whatever contact was necessary to safeguard their interests. But that was all. They'd work together to save their skins, but they found no pleasure in it.

An honest offer? A bait, a lure to hold man's attention in one quarter while a dirty deal was being pulled off in another? A mere ironic joke? Or an offer that had a stinger in it?

Webster shook his head. There was no telling. No way to gauge a mutant's motives or his reason.

Soft, glowing light had crept into the walls and ceiling of the office with the departing of the day, the automatic, hidden light growing stronger as the darkness fell. Webster glanced at the window, saw that it was an oblong of blackness, dotted by the few advertising signs that flared and flickered on the city's skyline.

He reached out, thumbed over a tumbler, spoke to the secretary in the outer office.

"I'm sorry I kept you so long. I forgot the time."

"That's all right, sir," said the secretary. "There's a visitor to see you. Mr. Fowler."

"Fowler?"

"Yes, the gentleman from Jupiter."

"I know," said Webster, wearily. "Ask him to come in."

He had almost forgotten Fowler and the threat the man had made.

He stared absent-mindedly at his desk, saw the kaleidoscope lying where he'd left it. *Funny toy,* he thought. *Quaint idea. A simple thing for the simple minds of long ago. But the kid would get a boot out of it.*

He reached out a hand and grasped it, lifted it to his eyes. The transmitted light wove a pattern of crazy color, a geometric nightmare. He twirled the tube a bit and the pattern changed. And yet again—

His brain wrenched with a sudden sickness and the color burned itself into his mind in a single flare of soul-twisting torture.

The tube dropped and clattered on the desk. Webster reached out with both hands and clutched at the desk edge.

And through his brain went the thought of horror: *What a toy for a kid!*

The sickness faded and he sat stock-still, brain clear again, breath coming regularly.

Funny, he thought. *Funny that it should do a thing like that. Or could it have been something else and not the kaleidoscope at all? A seizure of some sort. Heart acting up. A bit too young for that and he'd been checked just recently.*

The door clicked and Webster looked up.

Fowler came across the room with measured step, slowly, until he stood across from the desk.

"Yes, Fowler?"

"I left in anger," Fowler said, "and I didn't want it that way. You might have understood, but again you might not have. It was just that I was upset, you see. I came from Jupiter, feeling that finally all the years I'd spent there in the domes had been justified, that all the anguish I had felt when I saw the men go out somehow had paid off. I was bringing news, you understand, news that the world awaited. To me it was the most wonderful thing that could have happened and I thought you'd see it, too. I thought the people would see it. It was as if I had been bringing them word that Paradise was just around the corner. For that is what it is, Webster . . . that is what it is."

He put his hands flat upon the desk and leaned forward, whispering.

"You see how it is, don't you, Webster? You understand a bit."

Webster's hands were shaking and he laid them in his lap, clenched them together until the fingers hurt.

"Yes," he whispered back. "Yes, I think I know."

For he did know.

Knew more than the words had told him. Knew the anguish and the pleading and bitter disappointment that lay behind the words. Knew them almost as if he'd said the words himself—almost as if he were Fowler.

Fowler's voice broke in alarm. "What's the matter, Webster? What's the trouble with you?"

Webster tried to speak and the words were dust. His throat tightened until there was a knot of pain above his Adam's apple.

He tried again and the words were low and forced. "Tell me, Fowler. Tell me something straight. You learned a lot of things out there. Things that men don't know or know imperfectly. Like high grade telepathy, maybe . . . or . . . or—"

"Yes," said Fowler, "a lot of things. But I didn't bring them back with me. When I became a man again, that was all I was. Just a man, that's all. None of it came back. Most of it is just hazy memories and a . . . well, you might call it yearning."

"You mean that you haven't a one of the abilities you had when you were a Loper?"

"Not a single one."

"You couldn't, by chance, be able to *make* me understand a thing you wanted me to know. Make me feel the way you feel."

"Not a chance," said Fowler.

Webster reached out a hand, pushed the kaleidoscope gently with his finger. It rolled forward a ways, then came to rest again.

"What did you come back for?" asked Webster.

"To square myself with you," said Fowler. "To let you know I wasn't really sore. To try to make you understand that I had a side, too. Just a difference of opinion, that's all. I thought maybe we might shake on it."

"I see. And you're still determined to go out and tell the people?"

Fowler nodded. "I have to, Webster. You must surely know that. It's . . . it's . . . well, almost a religion with me. It's something I believe in. I have to tell the rest of them that there's a better world and a better life. I have to lead them to it."

"A messiah," said Webster.

Fowler straightened. "That's one thing I was afraid of. Scoffing isn't—"

"I wasn't scoffing," Webster told him, almost gently.

He picked up the kaleidoscope, polishing its tube with the palm of his hand, considering. *Not yet,* he thought. *Not yet. Have to think it out. Do I want him to understand me as well as I understand him?*

"Look, Fowler," he said, "lay off a day or two. Wait a bit. Just a day or two. Then let us talk again."

"I've waited long enough already."

"But I want you to think this over: A million years ago man first came into being—just an animal. Since that time he had inched his way up a cultural ladder. Bit by painful bit he has developed a way of life, a philosophy, a way of doing things. His progress has been geometrical. Today he does much more than he did yesterday. Tomorrow he'll do even more than he did today. For the first time in human history, Man is really beginning to hit the ball. He's just got a good start, the first stride, you might say. He's going a lot farther in a lot less time than he's come already.

"Maybe it isn't as pleasant as Jupiter, maybe not the same at all. Maybe humankind is drab compared with the life forms of Jupiter. But it's man's life. It's the thing he's fought for. It's the thing he's made himself. It's a destiny he has shaped.

"I hate to think, Fowler, that just when we're going good we'll swap our destiny for one we don't know about, for one we can't be sure about."

"I'll wait," said Fowler. "Just a day or two. But I'm warning you. You can't put me off. You can't change my mind."

"That's all I ask," said Webster. He rose and held out his hand. "Shake on it?" he asked.

But even as he shook Fowler's hand, Webster knew it wasn't any good. Juwain philosophy or not, mankind was heading for a showdown. A showdown that would be even worse because of the Juwain philosophy. For the mutants wouldn't miss a bet. If this was to be their joke, if this was their way of getting rid of the human race, they wouldn't overlook a thing. By tomorrow morning every man, woman and child somehow or other would have managed to look through a kaleidoscope. Or something else. Lord only knew how many other ways there were.

He watched until Fowler had closed the door behind him, then walked to the window and stared out. Flashing on the skyline of the city was a new advertising sign—one that had not been there before. A crazy sign that made crazy colored patterns in the night. Flashing on and off as if one were turning a kaleidoscope.

Webster stared at it, tight-lipped.

He should have expected it.

He thought of Joe with a flare of murderous fury surging through his brain. For that call had been a cackling chortle behind a covering hand, a smart-Aleck gesture designed to let man know what it was all about, to let him know after he was behind the eight-ball and couldn't do a thing about it.

We should have killed them off, thought Webster, and was surprised at the calm coldness of the thought. *We should have stamped them out like we would a dangerous disease.*

But man had forsaken violence as a world and individual policy. Not for one hundred twenty-five years had one group been arrayed against another group in violence.

When Joe had called, the Juwain philosophy had lain on the desk. I had only to reach out my hand and touch it, Webster thought.

He stiffened with the realization of it. I had only to reach out my hand and touch it. *And I did just that!*

Something more than telepathy, something more than guessing. Joe knew he would pick up the kaleidoscope—must have known it. Foresight—an ability to roll back the future. Just an hour or so, perhaps, but that would be enough.

Joe—and the other mutants, of course—had known about Fowler. Their probing, telepathic minds could have told them all that they wished to know. But this was something else, something different.

He stood at the window, staring at the sign. Thousands of people, he knew, were seeing it. Seeing it and feeling that sudden sick impact in their mind.

Webster frowned, wondering about the shifting pattern of the lights. Some physiological impact upon a certain center of the human brain, perhaps. A portion of the brain that had not been used before—a portion of the brain that in due course of human development might naturally have come into its proper function. A function now that was being forced.

The Juwain philosophy, at last! Something for which men had sought for centuries, now finally come to pass. Given man at a time when he'd have been better off without it.

Fowler had written in his report: *I cannot give a factual account because there are no words for the facts that I want to tell.* He still didn't have the words, of course, but he had something else that was even better—an audience that could understand the sincerity and the greatness which lay beneath the words he did have. An audience with a new-found sense which would enable them to grasp some of the mighty scope of the thing Fowler had to tell.

Joe had planned it that way. Had waited for this moment. Had used the Juwain philosophy as a weapon against the human race.

For with the Juwain philosophy, man would go to Jupiter. Faced by all the logic in the world, he still would go to Jupiter. For better or for worse, he would go to Jupiter.

The only chance there had ever been of winning against Fowler had been Fowler's inability to describe what he saw, to tell what he felt, to reach the people with a clear exposition of the message that he brought. With mere human words that message would have been vague and fuzzy and while the people at first might have believed, they would have been shaky in their belief, would have listened to other argument.

But now that chance was gone, for the words would be no longer vague and fuzzy. The people would know, as clearly and as vibrantly as Fowler knew himself, what Jupiter was like.

The people would go to Jupiter, would enter upon a life other than the human life.

And the Solar System, the entire Solar System, with the exception of Jupiter, would lie open for the new race of mutants to take over, to develop any kind of culture that they might wish—a culture that would scarcely follow the civilization of the parent race.

Webster swung away from the window, strode back to the desk. He stooped and pulled out a drawer, reached inside. His hand came out clutching something that he had never dreamed of using—a relic, a museum piece he had tossed there years before.

With a handkerchief, he polished the metal of the gun, tested its mechanism with trembling fingers.

Fowler was the key. With Fowler dead—

With Fowler dead and the Jupiter stations dismantled and abandoned, the mutants would be licked. Man would have the Juwain philosophy and would retain his destiny. The Centauri expedition would blast off for the stars. The life experiments would continue on Pluto. Man would march along the course that his culture plotted.

Faster than ever before. Faster than anyone could dream.

Two great strides. The renunciation of violence as a human policy—the understanding that came with the Juwain philosophy. The two great things that would speed man along the road to wherever he was going.

The renunciation of the violence and the—

Webster stared at the gun clutched in his hand and heard the roar of winds tumbling through his head.

Two great strides—and he was about to toss away the first.

For one hundred twenty-five years no man had killed another—for more than a thousand years killing had been obsolete as a factor in the determination of human affairs.

A thousand years of peace and one death might undo the work. One shot in the night might collapse the structure, might hurl man back to the old bestial thinking.

Webster killed—why can't I? After all, there are some men who should be killed. Webster did right, but—he shouldn't have stopped with only one. I don't see why they're hanging him, he'd ought to get a medal. We ought to start on the mutants first. If it hadn't been for them—

That was the way they'd talk.

That, thought Webster, *is the wind that's roaring in my brain.*

The flashing of the crazy colored sign made a ghostly flicker along the walls and floor.

Fowler is seeing that, thought Webster. *He is looking at it and even if he isn't, I still have the kaleidoscope.*

He'll be coming in and we'll sit down and talk. We'll sit down and talk—

He tossed the gun back into the drawer, walked toward the door.

THE GRAVESTONE REBELS RIDE BY NIGHT!

As pulp magazines counted them, this story is a novel, one of two that led off the six stories and three "fact articles" included in the October 1944 issue of Big-Book Western Magazine, *in which it appeared. Cliff Simak's journals do not show that he wrote a story with this title, but they do show that he was paid $177, in 1944, for a story entitled "Sixguns Write the Law"—and the hero of this story was a frontier lawyer, so it seems reasonable to conclude that this is that story.*

I would presume that the size of the payment to the author reflected the length of the story . . .

—dww

Chapter I
Death Comes to Town!

Smoke still wisped from what had been a cabin crouched beneath the cottonwoods that grew above the spring. The embers, smothered in gray ash, still exuded a stifling heat. Flame-scarred, the cottonwoods themselves stood limp with withered leaf and drooping branch.

But something else than cabin logs and homemade furniture had gone up in flames. Beneath two smoking timbers lay an outline, ash-covered, fire-blackened, that could be neither log nor furniture, steer-hide trunk nor sweat-stained saddle.

Shane Fletcher tossed idly in one hand the things he had found upon the ground and stared at the shape beneath the timbers, wrinkling his nose against the stench that told him better than the shape itself, what lay there in the ashes.

The things in his hand clinked as he tossed them.

"Find something?" asked the man who sat bolt upright on the wagon seat, both hands grasping the cane planted stiffly before him.

"Yes," said Fletcher.

"Cartridges?"

"How did you know?"

"My ears," said Blind Johnny. "You're tossing them. They clink."

"Three of them," Fletcher told him. "Fired not long ago. Powder smell still on them."

"Blood on the grass?" asked Johnny.

Fletcher shook his head. "Nope. They got him near the door, yelled at him to come out and gunned him down when he stepped outside."

A dog came from the weeds down by the spring, snaked a frightened, apologetic course toward the wagon and the men, tail tucked tightly between his legs, eye-whites showing.

Fletcher patted the animal. "Hello, there, pup!"

A charred wooden bucket lay tilted on its side a few feet from the smoking heap that once had been a cabin. Part of a rude bench lay nearby. A tin wash basin gleamed in the smoky sunlight.

Those, thought Fletcher, had been the things from which Harry Duff had washed his hands and face, dipped a drink of water. This was Harry's dog, seeking human protection against the whiplash crack of rifles, the angry roar of flames that consumed the things which had been his home.

The dog sat down and stared with eyes abrim with wonder and fear. Fletcher patted the yellow head, felt the quivering fright that ran along the body.

"Tracks?" asked Blind Johnny.

"Maybe," Fletcher told him. "If there are, they'd head straight into the badlands."

Blind Johnny wagged his head. "Can't figure why anyone would want to do something like that to a man like Harry. Never harmed a fly, Harry never did."

The blind man sat stiffly on the wagon seat, both hands clutching the cane, head unturning, as if he might be staring at the far horizon.

Fletcher patted the yellow head and the dog moved closer, pressed tight against his legs.

"It was just the other day that he was in to see me," Fletcher said, staring at the ashy mound that lay twisted in the embers. "Happy as a bear knee-deep in honey. Seems an uncle died someplace in the east and left him a few hundred. Enough, he said, to pay off his debt and send back for his girl. Law firm that wrote the letter wanted some information, but he didn't have it with him. Asked me to drop out again."

"What kind of debts?" demanded Johnny. "He didn't drink and didn't gamble."

"Mentioned something about a mortgage," Fletcher said.

"Maybe someone heard he's been left some money and thought he had it in the cabin."

Fletcher shook his head. "Not that kind of killing, Johnny. No robbery intended. This is murder. Someone shot him and threw his body in the cabin, then set fire to make it look like he was in there sleeping and couldn't make it out in time."

He tossed the gleaming cylinders in his hand. "Careless, too. Leaving things like these around."

"Most of them are," Blind Johnny told him. "Careless in one way or another. Though some of them aren't. Take a smart hombre, now, and he'll get away with it."

Fletcher dropped the empty cartridges in the pocket of his coat, moved toward the wagon. "Come on, boy," he invited the dog. The animal trotted behind him, stood beside the wagon. Stooping, Fletcher boosted him up, climbed to the seat and took the reins.

"What now?" asked Johnny.

"Back to Gravestone and tell the marshal," said Fletcher.

"Won't do any good," declared the blind man. "Marshal Jeff Shepherd is so dumb he can't even catch a cold."

"We have to report it, anyhow," insisted Fletcher. "Our duty as citizens."

Johnny chuckled. "Awful upset about a killing. But you'll get over that."

"Happens often, huh?"

Johnny screwed up his face. "Well, not every day, exactly, but right frequently. Matt Humphrey was shot this Spring by some rustlers running off his cattle. Matt was plumb foolish. Went out and tried to argue with them. Then there was Charlie Craig, last winter."

"Homesteaders?" asked Fletcher.

"Both of them," said Johnny.

Fletcher sat staring at the smoking cabin site. Remembering the happiness that had shone in Duff's face that day he'd come up to the office. A chance to pay off his debts, he'd said, and send back for the girl who was waiting in the East. A chance to start making a home. To buy a few more head of cattle, maybe.

"You don't wear a gun, do you, Shane?" asked Johnny.

"Why, no," said Shane, puzzled.

"You look plumb undressed without one," declared Johnny. "Everyone wears 'em, you know. Even Banker Childress. He couldn't hit the broad side of a barn."

Fletcher stared at the ash and embers, his eyes narrowed against the sun and smoke. "I think, maybe," he said, "I could hit a barn."

He gathered up the reins, clucked to the team, swung a wide circle away from the cottonwoods. . . .

The town of Gravestone drowsed in the afternoon sun, huddled on the broad, glassy plain at the foot of the four-square butte. A dog slept in front of the barber shop and his feet twitched as he chased rabbits in a dream. Dan Hunter sprawled on the steps of the Silver Dollar, whittling with a jackknife on a piece of board. Shavings littered the sidewalk and the street beyond.

"What you making, Dan?" asked Fletcher.

"Nuthin'," Hunter told him. "Just whittlin' to pass away the time." He went on whittling.

The wooden signs along the street swung wearily in the gusty wind that walked along the prairie. From the blacksmith shop, two doors down, came the sound of hammer blows as Jack McKinley shoed a horse. Far up the street the flag fluttered in the breeze from the pole in front of the schoolhouse.

"Hell of a big game goin' on inside," Dan Hunter volunteered. "Zeb White is in there cleaning out the place. Luckiest buzzard ever I did see."

"Zeb isn't any gambler," declared Fletcher.

"Hell, no," Hunter agreed, "but he's run into a streak of luck that he just can't get rid of."

Fletcher crossed the street, heading for his two rooms above the bank. Before starting up the stairs he stopped and looked at the thermometer hung from the door casing. The mercury said 85 above.

The rooms upstairs were barren—the front one especially. A desk and three battered chairs, a framed picture of Abraham Lincoln. He had a picture of George Washington, too, but the glass was broken.

Soon as he got the law books from the freight office at Antelope, Fletcher told himself, he'd have to build some shelves. Give the place an air—make it look a bit more like a law office. He'd have time to build the shelves, he knew, for there weren't many clients.

Standing in the center of the room, he wondered if there'd ever be many clients. Men in this town didn't take to law too well. They carried it in their holsters instead of getting it from books.

Harry Duff the other day. And Tony, the barber, up to see what could be done about the drunk who'd heaved a rock through Tony's window as a protest against what he considered the high price of haircuts. And the grocer to find out about collecting from Lance Blair, who owned the Silver Dollar across the street . . . That was about all.

Heavy footsteps thudded up the stairs and even before the visitor arrived, Fletcher knew it was Charles J. Childress, the banker from downstairs, panting and puffing his way up the creaky steps.

Childress was flabby and affable. His face was red and his shirt tail had come out and was hanging down his back. "Jeff just came in to see me," he puffed at Fletcher. "Told me about Duff. Too bad, too bad! Told Jeff to leave no stone unturned. No, sir, not a stone unturned. Can't have things like that happening in this community."

"Jeff won't be able to do much," Fletcher pointed out. "The killer had a few hours start. Got off into the badlands more than likely. No chance of finding him."

"Jeff's a mighty capable law officer," insisted Childress. "Slow on the uptake, but sticks to things. Yes, sir, he sticks to things."

The banker reached into his back pocket and hauled forth a red bandanna, mopped his face. Handkerchief still clutched in his hand, he lowered himself cautiously into one of the battered chairs and looked around the room.

"How're you getting on?" he asked.

"Not too bad," said Fletcher. "It takes time. People have to get to know you. No one ever built a law practice overnight."

"I was just thinking," Childress told him, "maybe I could use you. Lots of law work connected with a bank. Been doing it myself, but now you're here, you might just as well have it—whole kit and caboodle of it. Not enough to keep you busy all the time, but something to fill in."

"That's fine," said Fletcher. "Appreciate it."

Childress snapped his suspenders. "Yes, sir, great opportunity here for an up-and-coming lawyer. Never could understand why one didn't come before."

"I hope you're right," Fletcher said. "I thought, perhaps—"

"Sure, sure," said Childress, interrupting. "Sure, that's why you came. Foresight. No reason why you couldn't be county attorney, come election time. Just knowing the right people, doing the right things—playing along, no reason, just because Antelope's the county seat that the county attorney has to come from there. Now you take Rand—he's the county attorney, you know."

Fletcher nodded. "I know."

"He don't understand the problems of this country," declared Childress. "Don't know up from down. Just trying a little, you could do lots better."

Fletcher grinned. "Maybe I ought to wait a year or two."

Childress grunted. "Stuff and nonsense. Put you up next year, that's what I'll do. Take you around and introduce you to the folks. Get the boys out to vote for you."

"That's kind of you," said Fletcher.

Childress hoisted himself slowly from the chair. "Like to help fellers along," he grunted. He mopped his face with the red bandanna. "Nothing like helping the other feller out when you can." He guffawed. "Then maybe they help you out, come a pinch. That's my motto, turn about's fair play. Do what I can to help a feller, expect him to do the same for me."

He reached out a ham-like hand and thumped Fletcher on the back." Come down sometime," he invited, "and we'll talk about the law business. Got a few jobs now you could start off on right away."

"I'll be down tomorrow," Fletcher promised. He stood in the center of the room, listening to Childress crawfishing heavily downstairs, puffing with exertion.

Funny guy, thought Fletcher. Funny and dangerous—like a lumbering grizzly. That business about running for county attorney, helping one another out, turn and turn about. The offer of a job out of blue sky, meeting the right people and playing along.

He didn't like it. Fletcher didn't like the way Childress had acted—as if he already owned him. "I'll put you up next year." Just as if he, Fletcher, had nothing to say about it.

Yet, he couldn't afford to antagonize the man. Law business thrown his way would help a lot, keep him going until he could pick up other clients.

Fletcher grimaced, paced across the room to one of the two windows fronting on the street.

Dan Hunter still lounged on the steps across the street, whittling at his board. A man was leading his horse out of the blacksmith shop, while McKinley, the blacksmith, stood with one arm braced against the doorway.

Childress had emerged from the stairway onto the sidewalk, was mopping at his face, back to the street, reading the thermometer.

Suddenly the thermometer shattered into a spray of flying glass and wood, almost as if it had exploded in the banker's face. The street echoed to the hammering bellow of a heavy gun.

The man who had been leading the horse out of the blacksmith shop had dropped the reins, stood in the street with his legs widespread as if to anchor himself for another shot. The gun in his fist belched smoke and thunder. Splinters flashed into the sunlight from the building's side.

Childress had hurled himself to the sidewalk, seemed to be trying to burrow into it. In the quiet that followed the second shot, Fletcher heard the banker's voice mewing in fright.

Deliberately, as if he had all the time in the world to do his job, the man in front of the blacksmith shop lifted his gun again, but before he could press the trigger another gun coughed.

For a second, the man in front of the blacksmith shop stood stock-still as if gripped and held by a mighty hand. Then he slowly wilted. With gathering momentum, he pitched forward on his face. His gun, knocked from his hand by the impact of the fall, pinwheeled end-over-end and into the dust.

In front of the Silver Dollar, Dan Hunter broke his gun, calmly blew smoke from the barrel, holstered it again. He bent and picked up the board and jackknife which he had dropped.

Fletcher spun from the window, hit the door running, ran downstairs. The street had erupted in a swirl of life. The dead man's horse was racing up the street, reins flying in the dust. The blacksmith had lifted the dead man from the ground, then slowly let him fall back again. He rose and dusted his hands on his pants.

"He's dead!" His voice boomed up and down the street.

The barber, white coated, was running down the sidewalk. The Silver Dollar emptied and feet drummed down its steps. Dan Hunter leaned against a post and let them pass, a frosty smile upon his lips.

Fletcher crossed the street. "Who was it?" he asked of Hunter.

"Hombre name of Wilson," Hunter said. "Used to be a rancher."

"Used to be?"

"Yeah, that's what I said. Mortgaged the place and lost it."

"To Childress, huh?"

"That's right," said Hunter. "Seemed to be sore about it."

"Lucky for Childress," observed Fletcher, "that you were sitting here."

Hunter grinned. "Ah, it wasn't nothin'," he declared.

The banker had gotten up from the sidewalk, was waddling out into the street toward the crowd that surrounded the body.

Fletcher jerked his thumb at him. “For a man who wears a gun, he sure don’t stand up to gunfire.”

“Lots of birds that pack guns,” said Hunter, “don’t know how to use them.”

“You do,” said Fletcher.

“Just comes natural,” Hunter told him.

Fletcher saw the insolent slope of Hunter’s shoulders, the hard lines of the mouth, the coldness of the eyes.

Hunter flipped his knife point toward the street. “Here comes the schoolmarm,” he declared.

Cynthia Thornton was walking down the other side of the street, obviously trying not to notice what had happened in front of the blacksmith shop. She wore a blue and white gingham dress that looked prim and fresh. She carried a silly little parasol in her hand.

“You will pardon me,” Fletcher said to Hunter.

Hunter grinned. “Sure,” he said. He sat down on the steps, started whittling again.

Fletcher met Cynthia Thornton at the bottom of the stairs which ran up to his office. She smiled rather wanly and he saw that the hand which carried the parasol was shaking. “What happened, Shane?” she asked.

“A little disagreement,” Fletcher told her. “Someone by the name of Wilson tried to gun Childress, but Hunter shot him down.”

“It’s terrible,” said Cynthia Thornton. “Do you think that someday—”

“Certainly,” said Fletcher. “Someday the town will grow up and it’ll be safe to walk the streets.”

“I can’t stand here,” said Cynthia. “You’ll have to let me go.”

“Duck up to the office for a minute,” suggested Fletcher. “I want to talk to you.”

She hesitated.

“Strictly business,” Fletcher told her. “I’ve got a hunch.”

She nodded at him and started up the steps.

* * *

Inside the office he hauled paper from the desk, took a pencil from his pocket. "Pull up a chair," he said. "I want you to help me figure out a few things."

Wonderingly, she took the pencil that he handed her, poised it above the sheet of paper.

"You know the country around here better than I do," he said, "or I wouldn't have to bother you. I want a map, showing the ranches and the homesteads. Doesn't have to be fancy or accurate. Just show their relative locations."

"Starting where?" she asked.

"Starting with Harry Duff's."

She looked frightened. But she bent her head above the paper, sketched carefully, neatly. Fletcher came around the desk to stand behind her, watching the paper over her shoulder.

"That's enough," he told her. "It's all I need to know."

She smiled at him. "Go ahead, and be mysterious, my dear."

He grinned at her. "By the way—I have a dog for you. One I picked up today. He's at the livery barn."

"How nice of you. When can I see him?"

"Any time. He's Duff's dog. Came out of the weeds today, scared and frightened. You heard about Duff, didn't you?"

She nodded. "Some of the children told me." She tapped the parasol absent-mindedly on the floor.

"It's nice to have a dog," she said. "We always had one at the ranch. I'll take him with me tomorrow when I go riding."

Fletcher laughed. "Tomorrow is Saturday. Some target practice, I suppose?"

She looked a bit angry. "If I like to shoot," she told him, "I'm going to shoot. My daddy taught me to ride a horse and handle a gun when I was a little girl and now—"

"And now you spend every Saturday with a horse and gun," he said.

She made a face at him and swept out.

He grinned, listening to her footsteps tripping down the stairs. Then he laid the map she had drawn, flat on the desk, studied it with a frown.

Craig's place was west of Duff's, and Wilson's between Craig's and Humphrey's. And cornering to the south with Duff's and Craig's, was Zeb White's.

Whistling softly, Fletcher folded the paper carefully and tucked it in his coat pocket.

In the back room, where he slept, he unlocked the brass-bound steamer trunk, lifted out a top tray and, burrowing deep into a pile of shirts and socks, brought up a cartridge belt and gun.

He clicked the gun open, spun the cylinder, squinted through the barrel. With swift, sure fingers, he fed in cartridges, clicked the weapon shut, strapped the belt around him.

"Blind Johnny was right," he told himself. "Time I took to wearing one."

Chapter II
Hell Hits the Silver Dollar!

Blind Johnny was softly fiddling *Pop Goes the Weasel* in the front room of the Silver Dollar, but not much of a crowd had gathered yet. A few men were standing at the bar and a drunk was sleeping it off at a table in the corner.

Mike, the bartender, raised a hand to Fletcher. "What'll it be tonight?" he asked, reaching for a bottle.

"Pass it up, for the moment, Mike," said Fletcher. He jerked his head toward the back room. "Game still going on?"

Mike nodded. "White still raking it in. Don't know how he does it. The way they fall, I guess."

Fletcher stopped at the table where Johnny was playing. "How goes it, Johnny?"

The blind man lowered the fiddle. "Fletcher, isn't it?"

"That's it. Guess you are right about the killings. Man should get used to them after awhile."

"Man and boy," said Johnny, "I been fiddling up and down the country. Seen towns where there were more shooting and others that had less. This is just average, I guess."

"Understand Wilson lost his ranch here some time ago."

"Lost it to Childress," Johnny said. "Gave the bank a mortgage and was all set to pay up when someone cleaned him out. Ran off almost every head he had. Without his stock, Wilson couldn't pay up and Childress wouldn't listen."

"Foreclosed, did he?"

"Lock, stock and barrel," said Johnny. He lifted the fiddle and dashed off a few twinkling notes, lowered it again.

"How about White?" asked Fletcher. "The one who's making a killing out back. He got a mortgage, too?"

"Danged near everyone in this country's got a mortgage," Johnny said. "Sure, he has. But right now he ought to be able to pay it off. Boys tell me he's got it stacked up in front of him three deep."

"To Childress?"

Johnny shook his head. "To Blair."

"Didn't know Blair lent money."

"Once in a while," Johnny told him. "When he figures it's a good deal."

Fletcher rose from the chair. "Think I'll go back and look on awhile."

The back room was a fog of smoke and alcoholic fumes. A silent knot of men crowded around the table in the center of the room. Lamplight poured down from the ceiling.

Standing by the door, Fletcher picked out faces that he knew. There was McKinley, the blacksmith, with a huge cigar clamped tightly in his jaw. Tony, the barber, standing behind him on tiptoe trying to see. Lance Blair, owner of the Silver Dollar, stood close to the table, arms folded across his chest, twisted stogie between his teeth, his face good-natured in the lamplight. But his lips were a hard straight line. Beside him stood Dan Hunter and nearer to the door, Jeff Shepherd, the marshal. It was a gathering of wolves.

Fletcher took a place alongside Shepherd. By craning his neck, he could see that one of the men at the table had stacks of coins in front of him. He knew it must be White.

"What did you find out at Duff's?" Fletcher whispered to Shepherd.

"It was Duff, all right," Shepherd whispered back. "Burned to a crisp. Probably smoking in bed."

"He was shot," said Fletcher. "Found three empty cartridges."

Shepherd grunted. "Doesn't mean a thing. Harry could have fired them off himself."

"But they'd been fired only a short time before. Still could smell powder on them."

"Maybe he shot at something just before it happened," insisted Shepherd.

"Makes it easy for you that way, doesn't it?" said Fletcher.

"Shut up, you guys," yelled someone angrily.

Fletcher said, "I came in here to say something. Give me a minute to say it and then I'll leave."

He elbowed forward, pushing men aside until he reached the table. Across the table he saw the hard eyes of Lance Blair on him.

"Anything you have to say, Fletcher," said Blair, "can wait until the game is over."

"That's just the point," snapped Fletcher. "It can't."

He looked across at the man with the stacks of cash. "You White?"

White snarled back at him. "What if I am?"

"You got a mortgage," Fletcher told him, "with Blair?"

"Now, wait," yelled Blair. "What has all this got to do with the game? Sure, I hold Zeb's mortgage, but—"

Fletcher disregarded him. "Got enough in front of you to pay it off?" he asked of White.

"Why, I guess so. Say, what the hell—"

White was rising from the table.

"Sit down, White," snapped Fletcher. "Count out the money you owe Blair."

White sat down. "And if I don't?"

"If you don't," said Fletcher, "you won't live until tomorrow night."

Blair leaned across the table. "You're crazy," he shouted. "Coming in here with talk like this."

"A man died today," Fletcher told him evenly, "because he was about to get money that would have paid his mortgage. I only want to make sure the same thing doesn't happen here."

Out of the corner of his eye, Fletcher saw the swift motion of Hunter's arm, driving for his gun.

With a wild yell, the lawyer lunged forward, crashing into one of the players, hurling him against the table. The table tottered and went over, spilling money and whiskey glasses to the floor. Fletcher dropped swiftly and whipped his own gun from its holster.

A bullet chunked through the upturned table edge, hurling splinters in the lamplight. The roar of the shot drowned out the thump of feet, the thud of bodies being hurled to the floor out of bullet line.

Hunter came charging around the table, smoking gun leveled at his hip. Behind the table, Fletcher whirled on his toes, brought his gun around.

Hunter's triumphant face washed over with a frozen stare of surprise and his heels dug into the floor. Fletcher's gun coughed smokily and Hunter tripped and fell in a headlong crash, one leg folding under him.

Fletcher ducked and the other man fell to the floor so hard that his gun was shaken from his hand and spun like a wheel of light across the boards.

Slowly Fletcher rose and backed toward the wall.

"Blair," he said, softly, "put away that gun."

Blair, flat on his belly, opened his hand and the gun dropped with a clatter.

Fletcher glanced around. Men were crouched or squatting or flattened full length upon the floor. Tony the barber huddled under a chair that he held above his head. Shepherd hunkered in one corner, eyes shining in the lamplight.

Fletcher felt the wall at his back and stopped. "White," he said, "come out and pick up your money. Just so you can't say I busted up the game and lost you all that cash."

White rose slowly from the floor, walked toward the center of the room, squatted on his heels and started scooping up the scattered coin.

"Blair," said Fletcher, conversationally, "if you make one more pass at that gun, I'll let you have it straight between the eyes."

He looked at Hunter, writhing on the floor, a pool of blood growing under him.

"Come out from under that chair, Tony," Fletcher ordered. "You and McKinley. Take a look at Hunter. He isn't dead. Stove-up leg, most likely."

Cautiously the two came out, bent above the fallen man.

White was on his feet again, pockets bulging. "Blair," he said, making an effort to keep his voice calm. "Blair, I want to pay up my mortgage."

Blair did not move.

White's hand dipped to his side, rested on his gun-butt.

"You heard me, Blair."

Blair rose slowly to his feet. "I haven't got the mortgage with me," he declared.

"I'll pay you off," said White, "and you can write me a receipt. We'll take care of the paper work later."

Blair strode across the room, righted the tip-tilted table. Rapidly, White counted out a pile of money. Blair took a piece of paper from his pocket, felt in other pockets.

"Here you are!" Fletcher flipped a pencil on the table.

"Thanks," said Blair. He bent to write.

"Fletcher," said McKinley, his voice booming in the room, "if you don't mind, we'd better get Hunter out of here and run for the doc. He's losing blood."

"I don't mind," said Fletcher. "The game is over now."

Blair had handed White the slip of paper and White was folding it, putting it away. Blair was counting out the money on the table. Fletcher holstered his gun. "Good evening, gentlemen," he said.

On the porch outside, he stopped for a moment, looking up and down the street. The bank's windows glowed with light and inside he could see Childress moving about, gathering up papers and books and putting them away in the big iron safe that stood in one corner of the room.

A horse clopped down the street, hoofs thudding softly in the dust, rider swaying easily in the saddle. A woman came out of the grocery store, a basket on her arm.

Footsteps sounded behind him and he whirled. Jeff Shepherd was coming toward him, not too fast, gun out, star gleaming in the lamplight. "What is it, Jeff?" Fletcher demanded.

"I'm arresting you," said Jeff. "Can't no tenderfoot come into town and raise as much hell as you just raised."

"O.K.," said Fletcher. "Put away your iron. I'll go along with you peaceable."

Chapter III
Jailbreak!

Fletcher sat on the cot, sole furniture in the lone cell the Gravestone jail could boast, and tried to figure it out. Matt Humphrey had a mortgage and Matt Humphrey had been shot by rustlers running off his herd. More than likely just before he had been ready to market the cattle. Charlie Craig, another homesteader, had died by violence last winter. It would be interesting to know, Fletcher mused, if Charlie'd had a mortgage, too.

Wilson had given a mortgage on his place, and when he'd been ready to pay up, the same thing had happened to him as to Humphrey except that Wilson, at the moment, only lost his cattle, not his life.

And Harry Duff, less than 48 hours after he had received the legacy that would have paid off his mortgage, had been shot and burned inside his cabin.

It wasn't, Fletcher told himself, too hard to piece together. Somebody didn't want those mortgages paid off, somebody would rather have the land that secured the loans, than the loans themselves.

Fletcher got up off the cot and walked to the tiny, barred window. A sickle moon was rising above the butte and the summer stars blazed out above the plains. From far off came the howl of hunting wolves and in the street nearby a horse clopped slowly out of town while his drunken rider sang, off key.

A shadow hunched itself out of the darkness of the alley and something tapped along the ground. "Johnny," said Fletcher, softly.

The blind man reached out a hand and found the building, guided himself along. "Brought you something," Johnny whispered back. He leaned his cane against the building and dug into his shirt front. "Here," he said, reaching up with two objects.

Fletcher took them. "What the—?"

"File," said Johnny. "File and a can of oil. The oil will kill the noise."

"But I haven't—"

"Shucks," Johnny told him, "you won't have no trouble at all. Them bars are soft. Town too tight to buy good steel. Three, four hours and you'll be out of here."

"But, Johnny, I haven't the slightest intention to escape. They can't prove a thing on me. I didn't kill Hunter, did I? So they can't throw a murder charge at me. I shot in self defense—shot a man who was coming at me with a gun. I was careful to hit him in a spot that wasn't fatal."

"But you don't understand," protested Johnny.

"Come morning," declared Fletcher, "and they'll turn me loose. I might even sue for false arrest."

"Come morning," Johnny told him, curtly, "you'll be stretching hemp—decorating a cottonwood, sure as shooting. Hell's bound to break loose tonight."

"What do you mean?"

"Listen," hissed Johnny. "You know the lay, don't you?"

"Sure, I do," said Fletcher. "Blair and Childress are out to get a block of land. Got a gang operating so the little fellows whose loans they hold can't pay off and—"

"And," said Johnny, "you busted it wide open when you walked into that game and told White he wouldn't be alive if he didn't pay his mortgage. You had it doped right. They needed White's land and they didn't intend that he'd save it just by a lucky break at cards. Going home tonight, someone would have gunned Zeb, sure as hell. Someone, you understand, that knew he had the money and was bent on robbery."

"Sure, sure, I know!"

"O.K., then," snapped Johnny. "Get busy with that file. I'll stand here and warn you if I hear anything."

"But I can't run off," declared Fletcher, "break out of jail like any common thief."

"Better to break out and live," Johnny told him, "than stay in and die. Childress and Blair can't afford to let you leave the place alive. Before morning there'll be a mob along with guns and ropes."

Fletcher mopped his brow with his shirtsleeve. "So that's it, Johnny. Outraged citizens. Sick and tired of fellows coming in and shooting up the place."

Johnny said, "Start sawing on them bars."

Footsteps crunched down the corridor that led to the cell. Fletcher wheeled, stooped, set the file and oil can on the floor, slid swiftly to the cot, tried his best to look as if he'd been sitting there all the time.

Against the fan of light that flared out into the corridor from the jail office, Fletcher saw the shuffling shape of Jeff Shepherd. Behind Jeff, another figure stepped swiftly from the office into the corridor. Zeb White! Zeb White, with a gun in hand, was coming down the corridor on tiptoe!

"Well," Fletcher bellowed at Shepherd, "It's about time you were coming to let me loose. What do you think—"

The gun in White's hand rose in the air, struck swiftly. Shepherd slumped against the door, slid to the floor like an emptied sack.

Across the fallen marshal, Fletcher looked at White. "Smart," said White. "Smart play, Fletcher. With you yelling at him, he didn't even suspect there was anyone around."

Fletcher told him, "I was just ready to start on the bars."

White grunted, stooped over the marshal, came up with a bunch of keys. "I'll have you out in a minute," he wheezed. "Then you and me are hitting the dust. Got to warn the boys."

"You mean the other men with mortgages?"

"Exactly right," snapped White. "Blair's gang will be out to make a clean-up before the news gets around. The life of any man who has a loan with Blair isn't worth a dime."

"It isn't only Blair," said Fletcher. "It's Childress, too. If we could get into the bank's safe, we'd find all the papers there."

The third key White tried clicked back the lock and the door swung open. "We haven't time to be breaking into banks," the rancher snapped. "We've got to put miles behind us. Mike, the bartender, left right after the ruckus at the Silver Dollar. Blair sent him to tip off the bunch."

Fletcher nodded. "They'd be hanging out in the badlands, wouldn't they?"

"That's the way I figure it," White agreed. "Perfect hideout for them. Wouldn't find them there in a million years."

Swiftly he led the way toward the back, unhooked a door and they stepped into the alley. A faint tapping came out of the shadows of the building.

"That you, Johnny?" Fletcher called.

The blind man sidled up to them, stood silently.

"Look, Johnny," White said, softly, "you'd better get back before someone misses you. Fletcher and me have riding to do."

Fletcher shook his head stubbornly in the dark. "I still would like to see what's in that safe."

"What safe?" asked Johnny. There was a tremble in his voice.

"The bank safe," explained Fletcher. "Don't you see that all the papers would be there? Something to go on, something to show in court."

"The hell with court," rasped White. "When we get through with this gang of land grabbers there won't be any left to show up in court."

Fletcher shrugged. "Even if we could get into the bank, we couldn't open the safe. Nothing short of dynamite would budge it."

Johnny's fingers plucked at Fletcher's sleeve. "You get into that bank, Shane, and I'll get the safe open."

Fletcher gasped. "You'll what?"

"I'll get the safe open," declared Johnny. "It wouldn't be the first one."

White flared at them. "This is all damn foolishness. How'll you get into the bank to start with?"

"From my office," Fletcher told him. "Bought a saw the other day to put up shelves for a batch of books. We could saw a hole right through the floor."

"They'd hear," protested White. "You'd have the town down on you in five minutes."

"We have a can of oil," said Johnny.

"You go ahead, White," said Fletcher. "Tell me where to meet you. If we haven't got those papers inside of an hour, I'll quit and follow you."

White stared at Fletcher in the darkness. "You're the damnest hombre I ever saw," he said. "Never satisfied unless you're poking your head into a noose. I'll stick with you if it only takes an hour."

Fletcher shook his head. "Nope, you ride. Warn a couple of the boys and get them to send other riders out. Tell me where to find you."

"Know where Phillips' place is? I'll meet you there. Before I leave I'll saddle up a horse and tie him back of the livery barn. You may have to make a quick getaway."

"You'd better make it two," said Johnny.

White turned to stare queerly at the blind man. "All right, Johnny," he finally said. "I'll make it two."

Fletcher crouched in the darkness beside the safe, listening to the slow rasp of the dial as Johnny manipulated the combination, ear pressed against the huge steel door.

Silence, broken only by the grinding whisper of the slowly twirling dial, filled the inside of the bank. Fletcher was tense, nerves tight as violin strings.

What he was doing, he told himself, was madness. Robbing a bank. And yet, he knew, by some unusual, perverted logic, it was the only thing to do. For there were only two courses left now. Stay in Gravestone and fight it out with Blair and Childress—or sneak off like a beaten dog and set up another office in some other place, start all over again the struggle to establish himself.

Childress had offered him work only to close his mouth, to make him another Blair-Childress hanger-on, like Mike, the bartender, like Hunter, who whittled on the steps of the Silver Dollar, watching the street when either Blair or Childress might step from their establishments. Like Jeff Shepherd, who had gone post-haste to Childress as soon as Harry Duff's death had been reported to him.

What Fletcher had told Jeff about the Duff affair had made Childress recognize him as a possible danger, as a man who knew or suspected just a bit too much. So Childress had tried to buy him off with the offer of a job—with the lure of public office.

Fletcher grinned sourly to himself. Childress, of course, would have liked nothing better than a county attorney who was his man.

In the darkness Fletcher heard Johnny suck in his breath, heard the click of the lock. "She's open," Johnny whispered.

Slowly the blind man swung the door open and Fletcher, shifting around, squatted on his heels, dimly saw the compartments of the safe—the cash box and the rolls of currency held together by heavy rubber bands, pigeon holes stuffed with papers, a bottle of whiskey that Childress had locked up with the cash.

"I'll have to chance a match," he whispered to Johnny.

The blind man grunted. "All right, then, but be quick about it."

Fishing in his pocket, Fletcher found the match, struck it on the seat of his trousers, cupped it for a moment in his hands, nursing it into a steady flame.

Swiftly, he moved it from pigeon hole to pigeon hole, staring at the papers. One was filled with letters, dog-eared and torn, the other with sheets of scribbled notations, the third with legal documents. Swiftly he snatched the documents from their resting place, shuffled them, one-handed, in the light of the dying match.

Mortgages! Two dozen of them at least.

The match burned down and singed his fingers. He dropped it and the place returned to blackness that folded about them like a blanket.

"Got what you want?" asked Johnny.

"Sure have," Fletcher told him. "We'd better start getting out of here." He slipped the package of papers into the inside pocket of his coat, patted it to see that they were in place. Reaching out, he closed the heavy door, was reaching for the combination when Johnny hissed alarm.

Squatting before the safe, Fletcher froze, hand still reaching for the dial. Someone was at the door. He heard the key grating in the lock, imagined that he could hear the wheezing breath of the man outside.

Swiftly, he jerked away from the safe, hurled himself back into the narrow space between the huge iron box and the wall, brought up against Johnny, who had scuttled there at the first sound from outside.

Fletcher eased his gun gently from the holster. He was caught in a bank, with the safe unlocked—burdened with a blind man! Escaped from jail, with the marshal clubbed outside the cell! A neatly sawed hole in the floor above leading down from his office, that could have been made by no one but himself!

Fletcher felt his jaw muscles tightening.

The outer door swung open, silhouetting the bulking figure of Charles J. Childress. Childress came quickly inside, was followed by two others, the last one banging the door behind him.

Fletcher crouched in his corner, suddenly cold with apprehension, gun tilted in his hand.

A muffled growl came out of the darkness: "—dead wrong, Childress. No sense in what you're doing."

The banker's words came back. "You talked me into this deal, Blair, and I stayed as long as it was working out. But now I'm getting out. Ain't no sense in stayin' and lettin' a thing blow up in your face."

"You're scared," snarled Blair.

"Sure, I'm scared," Childress rumbled back. "Good sense to be scared at a time like this."

"We'll have Fletcher stretched out cold before morning," snapped Blair. "He doesn't know the country and he can't get away."

"He had help breakin' out," Childress reminded him. "He has somebody with him."

A third voice said: "I was walkin' down toward the cell and someone clunked me on the head."

"Shut up," snapped Blair, "or you'll get worse than being hit on the head. Why Charlie ever made a broken down saddle-stiff like you a lawman, is more than I can figure."

Childress was waddling across the floor toward the safe and the others followed, boots clumping on the boards.

"I smell something," said Shepherd suddenly, his harsh whisper rasping across the dark. "Like a match."

The feet halted.

Childress sniffed. "Don't smell a thing."

"Jeff is spooky," snarled Blair.

"No, I ain't," protested Jeff. "I smelled a match, I tell you."

Puffing, Childress settled his huge bulk in front of the safe. Fletcher pressed himself back into the corner. By reaching out his hand he could have touched the man who squatted there in front of him.

Childress' stark and startled whisper scraped across the room. "The safe is open!"

"Forget it and get busy," Blair snapped at him. "You probably forgot to lock it."

Childress was stubborn. "No, I didn't. Always lock it. Never forget it."

"Quick!" snarled Blair. "Open it up and get that money out."

In the fog of night light that filtered through the window, Fletcher saw the saloon owner had his gun out, was pointing it at the banker.

Childress quavered. "What do you mean?"

"I mean get that money out of there and hand it over."

"But—but—" Childress sobbed.

"You heard me," Blair told him. "Get it out and hand it over. You don't think I'm going to let you pull stakes with all that cash!"

With an agility that belied his size, Childress straightened from the safe, hurled himself for the corner, his massive body crashing into Fletcher.

Out in the center of the room, Blair's gun spat a flash of fire and a bullet thudded into the wall just above Fletcher's head.

"There's someone here!" yelled Childress.

Still sprawled in the corner, Fletcher angled his gun, pressed the trigger. The weapon bucked wickedly against his wrist and the roar drowned out every other sound within the room.

Then Blair was no longer there and over by the desk there was the thud of a falling body, the quick scurry of hands and knees. A gun talked from the corner by the door, three quick shots rippling through the dark.

Hurling himself flat on the floor, Fletcher pressed against the safe. Somewhere in the room, someone stirred. There was no sound from the corner where Blind Johnny crouched. Fletcher wondered for a second how Johnny was getting along.

From behind Fletcher a second weapon coughed. A man screamed in agony and a body thrashed briefly on the floor. Fletcher sucked in his breath and huddled tighter to the safe, his ears straining in the silence.

That shot had come from Johnny's corner!

By the door there was a terrible quietness after the grisly sound of a flopping body.

"We can't stay here," Fletcher told himself. "We have to get away."

He could envision men tumbling out of bed, reaching for their trousers, scuffling into cold boots, grabbing up their gunbelts.

Slowly, cautiously, pulling himself along by inches, holding his breath, Fletcher edged from behind the safe, squirmed toward the wall that led toward the door. Blair was over there, crouching behind the piece of furniture, waiting for a flicker in the dark, for a sound, for anything to shoot at.

Jeff must be the one down by the door, the one who had screamed and flopped painfully on the floor before the quietness came to still him. Where Childress was, Fletcher had no idea.

Inch by slow inch he hitched himself along. And still the silence held. Almost as if the room were empty, as if hungry guns were not waiting to roar into sudden, flame-etched death. Fletcher put out a hand, let it slowly down. But instead of smooth, hard floor, it met a boot that suddenly exploded into action.

For a single instant, Fletcher saw the huge body looking over him, coming down toward him through the dark.

Hands fastened themselves on one of his feet and hauled. He twisted and struck blindly with the barrel of his gun, felt it slash into puffy flesh, heard the grunt that it knocked out of Childress. Then the hands left his foot, were feeling for him in the dark.

Fletcher doubled his fist and struck into the darkness, struck yielding flesh with an impact that jarred him to the shoulder. Behind him, from the corner by the safe, a gun was barking, drooling flame that made Johnny's face a thing that flickered.

Johnny, he knew, was trying to keep Blair under cover with that rapid fire, was trying to give him time to reach the door.

Fletcher doubled up his legs and lashed out savagely, sent the crouching banker slamming against the wall. Then he was on his feet and running, jerking the door wide, turning his gun on the desk behind which Blair crouched.

"Johnny!" he yelled. "This way!" Then he emptied his six-gun at the desk.

Feet thundered across the room and Johnny was past him, out into the street. With a leap, Fletcher followed him, reached and passed him. "Come on, Johnny!" he shouted.

"Just go ahead," puffed the blind man. "I can follow you. I can hear your feet."

From far up the street other men were running toward the bank. Someone shouted something from near the blacksmith shop. A rifle crashed in the stillness and a bullet whined above their heads.

Fletcher halted momentarily, grasped Johnny by the arm, ducked into the narrow alley between the Silver Dollar and the livery barn, hauling the blind man behind him. The horses were waiting and he lifted Johnny, boosted him bodily onto one of them, then vaulted into the saddle of the other.

With the reins of Johnny's horse in one hand, he kicked his mount into a gallop. Ahead loomed the massive height of the mighty butte, a black shadow on the starlit plains.

"We can't go to Phillips' place now," Fletcher told himself. "Having to take care of Johnny, they'd catch me before I was halfway there."

There was only one place to go, only one place where he could elude pursuit. Grimly he headed the running horse toward the butte and the badlands beyond.

Chapter IV
Badlands Hideout

Dawn thrust golden spears into the tangled badlands, lighting fantastic spire and minaret, scrambling and intensifying the colors that had been subdued pastels as the first faint light had crept up from the east.

The horses picked their careful way down a narrow canyon which held a chattering stream. Fletcher threw a glance over his shoulder, saw that Blind Johnny still clung to the saddlehorn with both hands, head drooping, body swaying.

As if the man became aware of Fletcher's scrutiny, he lifted his head, blinking with staring, vacant eyes. "Where are we, Shane?" he asked.

"In the badlands," said Fletcher. "Deep in them. The sun will be rising in a little while. I'm looking for a place to hole up."

"We haven't any food," said Johnny.

Fletcher shook his head. "No, we haven't, Johnny. We'll just have to get along. Come night and we can try to make a ranch."

A jackrabbit burst from a clump of brush, sailed up the canyon slope in soaring leaps. Birds twittered and sang. On a high ridge that rose above the canyon a wolf slunk past like a shadow.

"Been wondering about something, Johnny," Fletcher said. "How come you pack a gun?"

"Don't," Johnny told him, "except on special occasions. Last night was one of them."

"Shoot by ear, I suppose."

"That's right," said Johnny, cheerfully.

"Better than most men can by sight," said Fletcher. "You nailed Jeff first off."

Johnny grunted. "Dark as it must have been, eyes wouldn't have done a man much good."

The canyon, Fletcher saw, was ending, widening out into a patch of meadow land.

They left the canyon and struck out across the meadow. Slowly, Fletcher swiveled his head, looking for some place of concealment where they might put up. And as he swung to the right, he stiffened, tightening on the reins. His horse stopped and the other horse bumped into it.

"What's the matter?" Johnny asked.

"Men," said Fletcher.

The camp lay in a pocket where a butte curled in upon itself and then flared out again. Horses stirred restlessly within the pole corral and smoke rose in a narrow ribbon from the log cabin that huddled against the cliff.

A man who was sitting on top of the corral fence straightened up and stared at them.

"We better made a run for it," suggested Johnny.

"Can't," Fletcher told him. "We pushed these broncos hard last night. They're too played out to travel very far. Only thing we can do is ride up and bluff it out." He stared at the camp. "Anybody got a ranch out here?" he asked. "Just starting up, maybe?"

Johnny snorted in disgust. "Nobody's loco enough to try to ranch out here."

The man on the corral fence called out and two men came to the cabin door, stood staring at the two at the canyon's mouth.

At a walk they approached the camp. The two men still stood in the doorway. The man on the fence dropped off it and walked slowly toward the cabin. All three were waiting, silently, when Fletcher pulled up.

"Good morning, gentlemen," he said.

"Howdy," said the one who had been on the fence. The other two said nothing.

"Didn't know there was anyone out here," Fletcher said.

"We ain't been here long," said one.

The fence-sitter jerked his thumb toward Johnny. "That's Blind Johnny, ain't it?"

"Sure, that's who I am," said Johnny, "but I don't recognize your voice."

"What's this hombre doing with you?" asked the man.

"Just takin' me out for a ride," said Johnny. "Like to get out in the air once in a while."

"Must have got an early start."

A fourth man came to the door. He wore a bloodstained bandage around his head and the whiskers on one side of his face were matted with dried blood. "What the hell's going on?" he asked.

The fence-sitter said: "We got company. These hombres are gittin' them some air."

"Where's your manners?" demanded the one who had the bandage. "Ask them to light and have some chow."

"Sure, sure," said the fence-sitter. "Get down and pull up with us."

Fletcher gathered up the reins. "No, thanks just the same. We better be getting on. Got to get back to town before noon."

"Get down!" said the man. His voice did not raise, but there was a whiplash of insistence in it. His hands were resting on his gun butts and he looked like a compressed spring ready to be released into violent action.

Fletcher stared at him. "I don't quite understand," he said.

The man patted his gun butts. "I got something here that will *make* you understand. Crawl down off them nags."

Fletcher smiled wearily. "I guess we better get down, Johnny."

Slowly he slung his leg over the saddle and dismounted, dropped the reins upon the ground. Johnny, he saw, was piling off the second horse.

One of the men in the doorway stepped forward and lifted Fletcher's gun out of the holster, stuck it in his own waistband. "Hate to get rough," he said, "but we can't nowise let you get away. Too bad you rode in on us."

"The boss will be showing up before long," said the fence-sitter. "He'll know who they are."

The man who had taken Fletcher's gun looked at Johnny. "How about him?"

The man with the bandage shook his head. "He never carries one."

The men were nervous, Fletcher decided, looking at them. Waiting for something to happen—and not too sure about it. Beneath their day's growth of beard their faces were tensed and strained and they were ill at ease.

He said: "I hope you fellows know what you're doing."

"We're just being careful, stranger," said the bandaged one. "We ain't taking any chances. More than likely we'll turn you loose once the boss blows in."

"Here he comes now," said one of them.

Fletcher swung around, saw a horse trotting swiftly toward the camp from the canyon mouth. He started at the sight of the man in the saddle. It was Lance Blair!

He glanced quickly at Johnny, saw that the blind man was standing still and straight, faced toward the approaching rider, face tense, almost as if he were seeing him and recognizing him. Savagely he hunted in his mind for some way to tip Johnny off, to let him know who the rider was, to prepare him for what was yet to come. But there was, he knew, no way of doing it. Once Blair opened his mouth, Johnny would have him spotted.

Blair pulled his animal to a sliding stop, sat glaring at the men who stood before the door. "A fine bunch!" he said. "Let a gang of ranchers put the run on you!"

The man with the bandage around his head pushed forward. "I can explain it, boss. They were tipped off and waitin' for us. We—"

The look on Blair's face stopped him. He gestured toward Fletcher and Johnny. "When did these two show up?"

"Just now," said the bandaged man. "We figgered maybe you'd know who they are."

A wolfish grin snaked across Blair's face. "Sure! They're friends of mine!"

"We didn't know, boss."

Blair started to swing off his saddle and in that moment Blind Johnny acted. His hand snaked smoothly inside his coat, under his armpit and back out again, all in one rapid motion that was accomplished almost as quickly as a man could blink his eyes.

"Take him, Shane!" he yelled.

Silently, he flung himself at Blair, a powerful leap that caught the saloon owner as he was still swinging from the saddle, driving him mercilessly into the side of his mount. With clawing hands, Blair dropped to the ground, bootheels skidding in the earth and sliding out from under him. The startled horse reared and screamed.

Fletcher hurled himself at Blair in a flying leap, twisting his body to escape the booted leg that jackknifed up viciously, aimed at his stomach. He landed and heard the *whoof* of breath driven from the man beneath him.

Blair was clawing for his gun and Fletcher drove his hand to catch the wrist, snapped it in a viselike grip, ground it savagely into the sand beneath them. Blair's fist caught Fletcher on the jaw, shaking him with a blow that rocked his head. Blood trickling from the corner of his mouth, Fletcher struck back blindly.

Back of him, Fletcher heard the snarling crash of guns, instinctively, even as he fought, hunched his shoulders against the bullet that he knew must come.

And even as he fought Blair's wrist farther from the gun, even as he drove his hand toward the other's throat, his mind clicked over and decided that this had been a foolish thing to do. An unarmed man and an armed blind man against five other men who were fully armed.

Blair arched his body, bucking, trying to throw him off. With cool deliberation, Fletcher smashed a blow into the other's face.

As he felt Blair go limp beneath him, Fletcher let go of the wrist, snatched at the gun, snaked it from the holster. With a yell, he wheeled from Blair, crouched low, gun swinging in his hand.

The man who had been sitting on the fence was stretched flat on the ground, arms outspread, face pushed in the earth. One of those who had stood in the doorway was on his knees, bent over, body wracked with coughing.

Johnny was sagging in front of the other man who had stood in the doorway, his gun arm limp and dangling, head pushed forward like a man who was walking against the wind.

Deliberately the man in front of Johnny raised his gun again and Fletcher, breath catching in his throat, jerked up his gun, pressed the trigger.

The man in front of Johnny spun around and his face, for a single instant, was a thing of twisted horror and then went blank. For a moment, he tottered, gun tumbling from fingers that were suddenly limp. Then, like a falling tree, he pitched onto his face.

Off to the side, Johnny slipped forward gently . . .

There was no sign of the man with the bandaged head. The one who had been on his knees had tipped over, lay like a bear rolled into a ball for winter sleeping, knees drawn up, arms still clutching his belly to drive away the pain.

Fletcher crouched on the ground, suddenly became aware of the weird silence that hung empty and voiceless in the sunlight that streamed across the turreted land.

Slowly, Fletcher rose to his feet, holstered the gun he had taken from Blair. On leaden feet he moved forward, walking around the body of the man who had fallen like a tree, stood for a silent second before he knelt and turned Johnny on his back.

The eyes in Johnny's face flicked open and stared at Fletcher. A tiny stream of blood ran out of the corner of Johnny's mouth and trickled down his chin.

"Johnny," said Fletcher. "Johnny."

"You know it now," said Johnny, still staring at him. "Maybe you guessed it all the time."

"Know what, Johnny?"

"That I wasn't blind."

"I wondered some," admitted Fletcher.

"They wanted me back East," said Johnny. "I opened too many safes—like—like the one back at the bank. I had educated fingers."

"It was a disguise?" said Fletcher, softly.

"Sure, Shane. Who'd look for a cracksman who was blind? Who'd ever think a blind man had a price upon his head?"

Fletcher hugged the man close against him, as if by sheer physical power he might keep the ebbing life within the body. "But, Johnny," he said, "you could have gone on—"

"You stopped and talked to me every time you came in the Silver Dollar," Johnny told him. "You asked me to go for walks with you. You introduced me to that schoolmarm of yours. You took me for the ride when you went to get the books. Like I was another man—just like yourself. You didn't ask me how it felt to be blind, or how I came to be blind, or. . . ."

The voice pinched into a whisper, ran down until the lips still moved but no sound came. The lids slid over the eyeballs as if Johnny suddenly were tired and had gone to sleep even as he talked.

For a moment, Fletcher stared down into the face of the man he held, then lifted his eyes, swept the heights that hemmed them in. The tiny meadow droned with early morning quietness and the spires and pinnacles had taken on a new and flashing light with the coming of the sun.

Quiet, thought Fletcher. The quiet that comes after the belch of gunsmoke.

The quiet of life that has ended after years of hiding behind a pair of eyes that had been trained to a blank, unwinking stare . . . the stare that the eyes of the blind would have. The self discipline that allowed a man to see a thing, yet never act as if he'd seen it.

The years that had drilled a certain consciousness of his role into a man until he came to think of himself as a blind man who fiddled in saloons up and down the land. A man with educated fingers who must, at times, have chuckled to himself when he was alone, chuckled at the joke that he was playing on all humanity.

Swift feet thudded on the grass behind him, storming footfalls half muffled by the turf.

Fletcher's hand snaked to his belt and half crouching, he whirled on his heels, rising as he whirled. Even before he saw the man who was charging him, Fletcher knew who it was. Blair! The man who a moment before had been flat upon his back, dazed by a blow—the danger at his back that he had forgotten in Johnny's death.

Fletcher's gun moved swiftly in his hand, but not as swiftly as those pounding feet. A thundering weight, half seen, caught Fletcher even as he spun—a weight that crashed him to the ground, that fell on top of him, knocked breath from his lungs and left him reeling in a pit of painful darkness.

Strong fingers seized his gun and jerked and Fletcher tried to fight, tried to retain his grip, tried to twist his wrist so the gun would point toward his opponent's body. But there was no power left within him.

Then a blow crashed down on his head and filled the world for a moment with flashing lights and spinning, wheeling stars. . . .

Chapter V
The Mystery-Marksman

A vulture wheeled on lazy pinions against the blazing blueness of the sky and a twisted tree clung desperately to the crumbling edge of a painted cliff. Fletcher lay on his back and watched the tree and the bird, wondered how come he was out here in the open, flat on his back, looking at a vulture.

Slowly, sharper consciousness oozed into his thoughts and he became aware of the dull ache that throbbed across his temples, of the pain of hands lashed behind his back. Voices seeped into his ears and he twisted his head around.

Blair and the man with the bandaged head squatted beside a campfire from which a thin, blue thread of smoke rose lazily. A coffee pot simmered on the coals and the man with the bandage poked with a fork at frying strips of bacon in a pan. Beyond the fire a small stream swirled and eddied over a grassy run.

The vulture had left the sky, but the tree still perched with gnarled roots on the brim of the sun-baked cliff. Slowly, methodically, careful to remember all the details, Fletcher thought back, closed his eyes to bring back the pictures of what had happened.

The men back in the meadow had been part of Blair's terror gang—maybe all of it, for it would take but a few men to do what they had done. Strike and run—striking against single men or single families, all of them unsuspecting, all of them unprepared.

Fletcher wondered if Childress had a hand in organizing the gang and the answer seemed to be that he did not. That, more than likely, had been Blair's job. Childress had loaned most of the money, and Blair had seen to it that those who borrowed were unable to pay it back.

But something had gone wrong. The man with the bandaged head was proof of that. White apparently had reached the ranches in time and the raiders, instead of striking unsuspecting men, instead of sweeping like a blight across an unprepared range had run into a hail of bullets. Perhaps they had left some of their members back there on the ranches where gunfire had rattled in the night.

But where did he, Fletcher, fit into the picture? Why was he lying here, head throbbing from the blow of Blair's gun butt, hands lashed behind his back? Why wasn't he back there in the meadow, dead body stretched alongside that of Blind Johnny?

Grass rustled as feet come toward him. Ungently, a booted toe nudged him in the ribs. He flicked his eyes open and stared up into Blair's face.

"Time you was coming around," Blair said.

Fletcher grimaced. "You hit me too hard."

"Want some bacon and coffee?"

Fletcher struggled to his knees, stood up. "How am I going to eat?" he asked.

"We'll untie your hands," said Blair, "but we'll have a gun on you."

The man with the bandage, Fletcher saw, had his gun already out. It dangled from loose fingers with the man's wrist slouched across his knee.

Fletcher nodded at the blanket-wrapped form. "Who's that?"

Blair blinked his eyes in mock surprise. "Why, don't you know? That's Blind Johnny. We have to collect on him, too."

"Collect?"

"Sure. There's a price on both of you."

Fletcher was dumbfounded. "A price?"

"Sure, the bank was robbed. And Childress was killed. So was Jeff. Or don't you remember?"

Fletcher gasped. "A reward?"

"A thousand bucks apiece. Dead or alive."

Fletcher stood stiff and straight as Blair stepped behind him, fumbled with the knot that tied his hands. Neat, he thought. A neat piece of work, the kind one would expect of Blair!

Of course the bank had been robbed and Childress had been killed. But neither he nor Johnny had had anything to do with that part of it. That had happened after he and Johnny had left—had happened in the few minutes between the time they had fled into the street and the aroused citizens of the town had reached the bank. It hadn't taken long. A quick shot and Childress died. A minute's work to haul the money bags and rolls of bills out of the safe and toss them out a window where they could be picked up later.

Fletcher brought his released hands around in front of him and rubbed them together, massaging his reddened wrists to hide the fact that his hands were shaking.

"Dead or alive," he said to Blair. "A thousand dollars for either of us, dead or alive?"

Blair regarded him through wary eyes, nodded.

"Then why all the bother of lugging me in alive?"

"Looks better that way," Blair told him. "Nobody can say that we killed you both to shut your mouths."

"I can still talk," said Fletcher.

"Sure," Blair agreed, "for all the good it does you. You can talk until you're blue in the face and no one will believe you. Because, you see, we found the loot on you. In your saddlebags." He motioned toward a pair of bags that lay close to the fire.

"And," said the man with the bandage, "who in hell would believe the kind of story you'd tell, anyhow?"

Fletcher knew no one would believe it. Not when they took the jury upstairs over the bank and showed them the hole sawed through the floor. No one would believe Blair and Childress had whipsawed the ranchers. No one, that is, but the ranchers themselves. And none of them, Fletcher knew, would have a chance to get on the jury. The very fact that they owed money to Childress or had been foreclosed on by Childress would bring a challenge and they would be excused.

It had been a crazy thing to do, breaking into the bank like that. But it had seemed a good idea at the time. The only way, in fact, to get proof of Childress' dealings, the only way to learn what ranchers were in danger, the only way to prove in court that Childress had loaned money only to the ranchers who held the land he wanted.

But things hadn't worked out the way Fletcher had thought they would.

Blair, he saw, was regarding him with amused eyes. "What I can't figure out," Blair said, "is what made you do it. You aren't the kind of man who robs a bank."

"I'll tell about that in court," Fletcher said.

"And why would you lug Johnny along? That was a crazy thing to do. Saddling yourself with a blind man."

"Ah, hell," said the man with the bandage, "let's just shoot him and have it over with."

"Shut up," snapped Blair.

"But he's too slick for us," persisted the bandaged man. "He'll get into court and talk himself out of it. Talk us into it, likely, before he gets through with it. He's a lawyer and law's his business and—"

The campfire exploded with a vicious, slamming thud that hurled live coals in a smoking shower. Fletcher leaped backward as a red hot ember speared against his arms, burned with a fierce, sudden pain. His bootheel caught against a clump of grass and he felt himself going over, windmilled his arms in sudden fright to keep his balance, but knew it was no use.

Even as he fell the whiplike crash of the hidden rifle caught up with the speeding bullet.

The bandaged man had hurled himself flat behind a scraggly bush, lap pressed tight against the ground. Blair was crouched in a shallow, natural depression shielded by clumps of waving grass. The saloon owner's clothes were smoldering in a dozen different places from the shower of coals and he was slapping at them fiercely, cursing in a high-pitched voice.

"Fletcher," said a voice and the lawyer, twisting his head, saw it was Blair who was speaking to him. "Fletcher," said Blair, "don't try any funny stuff."

Fletcher stared back at the man without speaking, read murder in the narrowed eyes beneath the broad-brimmed hat. Blair, with his back to the wall, was dangerous. When things had been going his way, it had been different. Then he had been inclined to flippancy, like a cat playing with a mouse. But now, brought to earth by the hidden rifle, there was quick death in his trigger finger.

Slowly, Fletcher worked his way around until he was flat upon his belly, feeling the man's eyes upon him all the time. Slowly he hitched himself, hugging the ground, toward a low growing juniper.

"What the hell you scared of?" asked Blair. "Taking cover that way. You ain't the one they're shooting at."

"How do I know?" Fletcher snapped at him. "How do I know who's out there with a gun. Maybe they wouldn't mind picking me off along with you."

Blair grunted savagely, hunkered lower in the shallow, wind-scooped hole.

"What's going on?" demanded the bandaged man. "Tain't natural. Just one shot and then no more."

"Maybe only one man," said Blair.

They waited. The sun poured down relentlessly. The sky was blue and still.

He had already thrown Blair partially off guard, he knew, by pretending that he feared the gun out there, by crawling to shelter.

But there was, he told himself, little for him to fear from the hidden rifleman, whoever it might be. There were only two sides to this affair and a man was either for him or against him. And if the man with the gun had been against him, then he would have ridden into camp instead of starting to sling lead.

Funny thing about that shot. Only one and that one landing in the fire—nicking the coffee pot and landing in the fire. Almost as if it had been aimed there instead of at any of the three who stood about the fire. And after that, silence, no other shot—as if that first shot had accomplished its purpose.

Fletcher cudgeled his aching brain, wondering who was hidden out there, content to let things ride, as long as he had them pinned to the ground. White, maybe. Although that didn't seem likely. White would be with the ranchers, wouldn't come sneaking in alone. If it were White, Blair would now be dead.

He heard a rustle of sound and twisted his head, keeping his cheek pressed against the ground. Blair, he saw, was slowly rising, inching higher and higher above the grass.

A speck of fire flashed momentarily from the rim of the bluff across the creek and the sullen cough of the rifle chugged across the hills. Blair flopped with a thud, burrowed into protecting soil. Just beyond him a dust cloud slowly settled. Fletcher chuckled.

Blair snarled at him out of the corner of his mouth. "Laugh, damn you! I'll put a laugh on the other side of your face!" Blair's eyes squinted speculatively. "I'm just waiting for an excuse, Fletcher, that's all. I wouldn't like nothing better."

The rifle on the bluff chugged again and the bullet, plowing the edge of the wash in which Blair crouched, sprayed him with flying dirt.

"He's getting your range," said Fletcher. "All I got to do is just lie here and wait until he dusts you off."

Blair huddled lower in the wash, brushed furtively at the dirt the bullet had showered on his shoulders.

"Or maybe," declared Fletcher, "he's planning to bury you alive. A few more shots like that one and—"

Blair bellowed at him. "Shut up!"

Come and Get It!

Fletcher was silent, watching Blair. Slowly he turned his head around to look at the man with the bandaged head. But the space behind the bush, where the man had sprawled, was empty.

"The man's better than an Indian," Blair said. "He's stalking the man with the rifle up there on the cliff."

Cautiously, Fletcher snaked his body forward until he could stare past the juniper. Eyes half closed against the glare of sun, he searched the tumbled confusion of the crags.

He was there, all right. The white splotch against the shadow of the wall was the bandage around his head. The white spot crossed the face of rock, disappeared for an instant, reappeared again, higher—and nearer to the hiding place of the rifleman.

"I got my eyes on you," Blair grated. "I'm watching every move you make. Just try to warn your pal up there and I'll make you buzzard meat."

Fletcher's body tensed and his mind swirled in thought. He had to do something.

Something that was not the stalker's bandaged head was moving near the cliff top, too—something that was smaller than a man and yellow, like yellow fur where the sun's rays struck it.

The yellow thing was the dog he had found at Duff's burned cabin and given to Cynthia Thornton! And if the dog were there, Fletcher knew who the rifleman must be—not a man at all, but Cynthia Thornton!

From the cliff came a scream of terror and suddenly the yellow dog was flashing down, down from the ledge and onto the shoulders of the man who wore the bandage. . . .

For a moment Blair's man stood outlined against the rock, back to the outer space, facing the yellow fury that crouched before him, tensed for a vicious spring. For a moment the man's hands pawed air as he sought to keep his footing, to regain his balance.

And then, slowly, deliberately, as if he were doing it of his own volition, he tumbled backward, off the ledge. He pinwheeled, end-over-end, white bandage flashing in the sun. A drawn-out shriek sounded, seemed to go on and on, but actually it lasted for no more than clipped seconds. . . .

Mind still stunned by horror, Fletcher turned. Blair jerked his eyes away and his gun came up. Fletcher, charging in, head down, arms outstretched, saw the red coughing of the gun in front of him, felt the stinging fire that slashed across his shoulder.

His left hand lashed out even as he rushed, his fingers wrapped with a grip of steel around the wrist that held the gun. His body smashed into Blair's and he jerked the gun arm up with a savage yank.

Blair's gun arm gave beneath the pressure, folded back. The gun dropped free and Fletcher kicked it away.

"Come on," he said.

Blair came rushing in, his head down. Dancing back, Fletcher slammed for the head.

A fist sank into his belly. He reeled back, sickness wrenching at his stomach.

Another blow was coming and Fletcher lifted arms that seemed to weigh a ton, caught it on his left wrist, blocked it.

The sickness was fading from his stomach, now, and his head was clearer. Blair was charging in again, head still lowered. Fletcher stepped back and then lunged in, right fist traveling from his knee. It caught Blair on the forehead, stopped him, straightened him. Fletcher struck with his left—and then the right came again.

He saw Blair's face, drew back his fist and targeted it toward the mouth. Pain grated across his knuckles and the face was still there. The left this time. And then the right again. The face was gone.

Fletcher stood on widespread legs, shook his head to clear away the fog.

A soft, wet nose nuzzled and sniffed at Fletcher's hand. He reached back the hand and patted the yellow dog. Cynthia Thornton stood beside her horse. "Shane," her voice choked, "Shane, did you see what the dog did?"

Fletcher nodded. "That was for Duff," he said. "The man on the cliff must have been one of the men who killed his master. He remembered, you see."

Cynthia Thornton walked quickly forward, dabbed with a handkerchief at Fletcher's face. "You're a sight," she said.

Hoofbeats interrupted her. A group of mounted men swung out of a canyon. The riders pulled up.

Zeb White rose in his stirrups and raised his hat. "Howdy ma'm," he said to Cynthia.

"Hello, Mr. White."

"I see you got him," said White.

"For a while he had me," Fletcher told him. "But Miss Thornton came along and created a sort of diversion, you might say."

Cynthia shook her head. "Just out for a ride, Mr. White, and had my gun along to do some target practice. Then, when I saw Shane all trussed up like a turkey for the pan, I decided to do something about it."

Another of the riders spoke up. "We heard some shooting."

Fletcher nodded. "There *was* a little shooting, I guess."

The man looked at Blair. "Must of shot him up considerable," he guessed. In reply Fletcher raised his bloody knuckles.

"Find the money on him?" asked White.

"It's over by the fire. He was bringing it back. Bringing me with it. Was going to claim I was the one who robbed the bank and killed Childress."

"He can't claim that, nohow," said White. "He was the only one that was using a thirty-eight. The rest of you jaspers mixed up in the deal had forty-fives."

"And a thirty-eight killed Childress," said one of the other men. "Doc dug the slug out of him."

"We better be getting back to town," said White. "Some of you hombres catch up them horses over there and gather up things, includin' Blair. And that thing over there in the blanket, whatever 'tis."

"That's Blind Johnny," Fletcher told him.

"Dead?"

Fletcher nodded. "One of the boys had better ride over to Antelope and tell the preacher we'll be needing him."

"Sure," agreed White, heartily. "We got to give Johnny a proper plantin'." He looked from Fletcher to Cynthia, back again. "Maybe you two might be wantin' a preacher, too."

Fletcher grinned. "After awhile, maybe. I'm not making enough to keep myself right now."

"Shucks," said White, "I forgot to tell you. We ain't got no bank now since Childress was gunned. So we're organizing another one. Need a man we can trust to run it."

The men sat silent on their horses, watching Fletcher. "We were sort of considerin' you," White told him.

Suddenly Fletcher remembered. He put his hand in his inside coat pocket, drew out a bundle of papers. He riffled through them. He grinned at White. "Guess I had a wrong hunch on these," he said. "I didn't need them after all."

"Put them back in your pocket," White told him. "Collecting them will be part of your new job."

Cynthia linked her arm through Fletcher's, smiled at White. "Perhaps," she said, "we can use that preacher, after all."

HOW-2

"How-2" is not the sort of name Clifford Simak would have put on a story, and I suspect that someone in the offices of Galaxy Science Fiction *eventually came up with that title. Cliff's journals seem to show that he sent a story entitled "Let Freedom Ring" to* Galaxy*'s editor, Horace Gold, early in 1954, and a different entry shows that Cliff was paid $600 that same year for a story entitled "Make It Yourself"—I think those entries both refer to this story (which in any case first appeared in the November 1954 issue of* Galaxy*).*

With this story, Cliff Simak married the concept of artificial intelligence to the concepts of civil rights—and ended up raising questions about slavery.

(It seems ironic that in this story, there is brief mention that a Broadway play was written about the goings-on in the story, and that after this story's publication, a play was written based on this story—sadly, the real-life play, after opening off-Broadway under the title How to Make a Man, *closed after only a single night on the Great White Way.)*

—dww

Gordon Knight was anxious for the five-hour day to end so he could rush home. For this was the day he should receive the How-2 Kit he'd ordered and he was anxious to get to work on it.

It wasn't only that he had always wanted a dog, although that was more than half of it—but, with this kit, he would be trying something new. He'd never handled any How-2 Kit with biologic components and he was considerably excited. Although, of course, the dog would be biologic only to a limited degree and most of it would be packaged, anyhow, and all he'd have to do would be assemble it. But it was something new and he wanted to get started.

He was thinking of the dog so hard that he was mildly irritated when Randall Stewart, returning from one of his numerous trips to the water fountain, stopped at his desk to give him a progress report on home dentistry.

"It's easy," Stewart told him. "Nothing to it if you follow the instructions. Here, look—I did this one last night."

He then squatted down beside Knight's desk and opened his mouth, proudly pulling it out of shape with his fingers so Knight could see.

"Thish un ere," said Stewart, blindly attempting to point, with a wildly waggling finger, at the tooth in question.

He let his face snap back together.

"Filled it myself," he announced complacently. "Rigged up a series of mirrors to see what I was doing. They came right in the kit, so all I had to do was follow the instructions."

He reached a finger deep inside his mouth and probed tenderly at his handiwork. "A little awkward, working on yourself. On someone else, of course, there'd be nothing to it."

He waited hopefully.

"Must be interesting," said Knight.

"Economical, too. No use paying the dentists the prices they ask. Figure I'll practice on myself and then take on the family. Some of my friends, even, if they want me to."

He regarded Knight intently.

Knight failed to rise to the dangling bait.

Stewart gave up. “I’m going to try cleaning next. You got to dig down beneath the gums and break loose the tartar. There’s a kind of hook you do it with. No reason a man shouldn’t take care of his own teeth instead of paying dentists.”

“It doesn’t sound too hard,” Knight admitted.

“It’s a cinch,” said Stewart. “But you got to follow the instructions. There’s nothing you can’t do if you follow the instructions.”

And that was true, Knight thought. You could do anything if you followed the instructions—if you didn’t rush ahead, but sat down and took your time and studied it all out.

Hadn’t he built his house in his spare time, and all the furniture for it, and the gadgets, too? Just in his spare time—although God knew, he thought, a man had little enough of that, working fifteen hours a week.

It was a lucky thing he’d been able to build the house after buying all that land. But everyone had been buying what they called estates, and Grace had set her heart on it, and there’d been nothing he could do.

If he’d had to pay carpenters and masons and plumbers, he would never have been able to afford the house. But by building it himself, he had paid for it as he went along. It had taken ten years, of course, but think of all the fun he’d had!

He sat there and thought of all the fun he’d had, and of all the pride. No, sir, he told himself, no one in his circumstances had a better house.

Although, come to think of it, what he’d done had not been too unusual. Most of the men he knew had built their homes, too, or had built additions to them, or had remodeled them.

He had often thought that he would like to start over again and build another house, just for the fun of it. But that would be foolish, for he already had a house and there would be no sale for another one, even if he built it. Who would want to buy a house when it was so much fun to build one?

And there was still a lot of work to do on the house he had. New rooms to add—not necessary, of course, but handy. And the roof to fix. And a summer house to build. And there were always the grounds. At one time he had thought he would landscape—a man could do a lot to beautify a place with a few years of spare-time work. But there had been so many other things to do, he had never managed to get around to it.

Knight and Anson Lee, his neighbor, had often talked about what could be done to their adjoining acreages if they ever had the time. But Lee, of course, would never get around to anything. He was a lawyer, although he never seemed to work at it too hard. He had a large study filled with stacks of law books and there were times when he would talk quite expansively about his law library, but he never seemed to use the books. Usually he talked that way when he had half a load on, which was fairly often, since he claimed to do a lot of thinking and it was his firm belief that a bottle helped him think.

After Stewart finally went back to his desk, there still remained more than an hour before the working day officially ended. Knight sneaked the current issue of a How-2 magazine out of his briefcase and began to leaf through it, keeping a wary eye out so he could hide it quickly if anyone should notice he was loafing.

He had read the articles earlier, so now he looked at the ads. It was a pity, he thought, a man didn't have the time to do all there was to do.

For example:

Fit your own glasses (testing material and lens-grinding equipment included in the kit).

Take out your own tonsils (complete directions and all necessary instruments).

Fix up an unused room as your private hospital (no sense in leaving home when you're ill, just at the time when you most need its comfort and security).

Grow your own medicines and drugs (starts of 50 different herbs and medicinal plants, with detailed instructions for their cultivation and processing).

Grow your wife's fur coat (a pair of mink, one ton of horse meat, furrier tools).

Tailor your own suits and coats (50 yards of wool yardgoods and lining material).

Build your own TV set.

Bind your own books.

Build your own power plant (let the wind work for you).

Build your own robot (a jack of all trades, intelligent, obedient, no time off, no overtime, on the job 24 hours a day, never tired, no need for rest or sleep, do any work you wish).

Now there, thought Knight, was something a man should try. If a man had one of those robots, it would save a lot of labor. There were all sorts of attachments you could get for it. And the robots, the ad said, could put on and take off all these attachments just as a man puts on a pair of gloves or takes off a pair of shoes.

Have one of those robots and, every morning, it would sally out into the garden and pick all the corn and beans and peas and tomatoes and other vegetables ready to be picked and leave them all neatly in a row on the back stoop of the house. Probably would get a lot more out of a garden that way, too, for the grading mechanism would never select a too-green tomato nor allow an ear of corn to go beyond its prime.

There were cleaning attachments for the house and snowplowing attachments and housepainting attachments and almost any other kind one could wish. Get a full quota of attachments, then lay out a work program and turn the robot loose—you could forget about the place the year around, for the robot would take care of everything.

There was only one hitch. The cost of a robot kit came close to ten thousand dollars and all the available attachments could run to another ten.

Knight closed the magazine and put it into the briefcase.

He saw there were only fifteen minutes left until quitting time and that was too short a time to do anything, so Knight just sat and thought about getting home and finding the kit there waiting for him.

He had always wanted a dog, but Grace would never let him have one. They were dirty, she said, and tracked up the carpeting, they had fleas and shed hair all over everything—and, besides, they smelled.

Well, she wouldn't object to this kind of dog, Knight told himself.

It wouldn't smell and it was guaranteed not to shed hair and it would never harbor fleas, for a flea would starve on a half-mechanical, half-biologic dog.

He hoped the dog wouldn't be a disappointment, but he'd carefully gone over the literature describing it and he was sure it wouldn't. It would go for a walk with its owner and would chase sticks and smaller animals, and what more could one expect of any dog? To insure realism, it saluted trees and fence-posts, but was guaranteed to leave no stains or spots.

The kit was tilted up beside the hangar door when he got home, but at first he didn't see it. When he did, he craned his neck out so far to be sure it was the kit that he almost came a cropper in the hedge. But, with a bit of luck, he brought the flier down neatly on the gravel strip and was out of it before the blades had stopped whirling.

It was the kit, all right. The invoice envelope was tacked on top of the crate. But the kit was bigger and heavier than he'd expected and he wondered if they might not have accidentally sent him a bigger dog than the one he'd ordered.

He tried to lift the crate, but it was too heavy, so he went around to the back of the house to bring a dolly from the basement.

Around the corner of the house, he stopped a moment and looked out across his land. A man could do a lot with it, he thought, if he just had the time and the money to buy the equipment. He could turn the acreage into one vast garden. Ought to have a landscape architect work out a plan for it, of course—although, if he bought some landscaping books and spent some evenings at them, he might be able to figure things out for himself.

There was a lake at the north end of the property and the whole landscape, it seemed to him, should focus upon the lake. It was rather a dank bit of scenery at the moment, with straggly marsh surrounding it and unkempt cattails and reeds astir in the summer wind. But with a little drainage and some planting, a system of walks and a picturesque bridge or two, it would be a thing of beauty.

He started out across the lake to where the house of Anson Lee sat upon a hill. As soon as he got the dog assembled, he would walk it over to Lee's place, for Lee would be pleased to be visited by a dog. There had been times, Knight felt, when Lee had not been entirely sympathetic with some of the things he'd done. Like that business of helping Grace build the kilns and the few times they'd managed to lure Lee out on a hunt for the proper kinds of clay.

"What do you want to make dishes for?" he had asked. "Why go to all the trouble? You can buy all you want for a tenth of the cost of making them."

Lee had not been visibly impressed when Grace explained that they weren't dishes. They were ceramics, Grace had said, and a recognized form of art. She got so interested and made so much of it—some of it really good—that Knight had found it necessary to drop his model railroading project and tack another addition on the already sprawling house, for stacking, drying and exhibition.

Lee hadn't said a word, a year or two later, when Knight built the studio for Grace, who had grown tired of pottery and had turned to painting. Knight felt, though, that Lee had kept silent only because he was convinced of the futility of further argument.

But Lee would approve of the dog. He was that kind of fellow, a man Knight was proud to call a friend—yet queerly out of step. With everyone else absorbed in things to do, Lee took it easy with his pipe and books, though not the ones on law.

Even the kids had their interests now, learning while they played.

Mary, before she got married, had been interested in growing things. The greenhouse stood just down the slope, and Knight regretted that he had not been able to continue with her work. Only a few months before, he had dismantled her hydroponic tanks, a symbolic admission that a man could only do so much.

John, quite naturally, had turned to rockets. For years, he and his pals had shot up the neighborhood with their experimental models. The last and largest one, still uncompleted, towered back of the house. Someday, Knight told himself, he'd have to go out and finish what the youngster had started. In university now, John still retained his interests, which now seemed to be branching out. Quite a boy, Knight thought pridefully. Yes, sir, quite a boy.

He went down the ramp into the basement to get the dolly and stood there a moment, as he always did, just to look at the place—for here, he thought, was the real core of his life. There, in that corner, the workshop. Over there, the model railroad layout on which he still worked occasionally. Behind it, his photographic lab. He remembered that the basement hadn't been quite big enough to install the lab and he'd had to knock out a section of the wall and build an addition. That, he recalled, had turned out to be a bigger job than he had bargained for.

He got the dolly and went out to the hangar and loaded on the kit and wrestled it into the basement. Then he took a pinchbar and started to uncrate it. He worked with knowledge and precision, for he had unpacked many kits and knew just how to go about it.

He felt a vague apprehension when he lifted out the parts. They were neither the size nor the shape he had expected them to be.

Breathing a little heavily from exertion and excitement, he went at the job of unwrapping them. By the second piece, he knew he had no dog. By the fifth, he knew beyond any doubt exactly what he did have.

He had a robot—and if he was any judge, one of the best and most expensive models!

He sat down on one corner of the crate and took out a handkerchief and mopped his forehead. Finally, he tore the invoice letter off the crate, where it had been tacked.

To Mr. Gordon Knight, it said, *one dog kit, paid in full.*

So far as How-2 Kits, Inc., was concerned, he had a dog. And the dog was paid for—paid in full, it said.

He sat down on the crate again and looked at the robot parts.

No one would ever guess. Come inventory time, How-2 Kits would be long one dog and short one robot, but with carloads of dog kit orders filled and thousands of robots sold, it would be impossible to check.

Gordon Knight had never, in all his life, done a consciously dishonest thing. But now he made a dishonest decision and he knew it was dishonest and there was nothing to be said in defense of it. Perhaps the worst of all was that he was dishonest with himself.

At first, he told himself that he would send the robot back, but—since he had always wanted to put a robot together—he would assemble this one and then take it apart, repack it and send it back to the company. He wouldn't activate it. He would just assemble it.

But all the time he knew that he was lying to himself, realized that the least he was doing was advancing, step by evasive step, toward dishonesty. And he knew he was doing it this way because he didn't have the nerve to be forthrightly crooked.

So he sat down that night and read the instructions carefully, identifying each of the parts and their several features as he went along. For this was the way you went at a How-2. You didn't rush ahead. You took it slowly, point by point, got the picture firmly in your mind before you started to put the parts together. Knight, by now, was an expert at not rushing ahead. Besides, he didn't know when he would ever get another chance at a robot.

II

It was the beginning of his four days off and he buckled down to the task and put his heart into it. He had some trouble with the biologic concepts and had to look up a text on organic chemistry and try to trace some of the processes. He found the going tough. It had been a long time since he had paid any attention to organic chemistry, and he found that he had forgotten the little he had known.

By bedtime of the second day, he had fumbled enough information out of the textbook to understand what was necessary to put the robot together.

He was a little upset when Grace, discovering what he was working on, immediately thought up household tasks for the robot. But he put her off as best he could and, the next day, he went at the job of assembly.

He got the robot together without the slightest trouble, being fairly handy with tools—but mostly because he religiously followed the first axiom of How-2ism by knowing what he was about before he began.

At first, he kept assuring himself that as soon as he had the robot together, he would disassemble it. But when he was finished, he just had to see it work. No sense putting in all that time and not knowing if he had gotten it right, he argued. So he flipped the activating switch and screwed in the final plate.

The robot came alive and looked at Knight.

Then it said, "I am a robot. My name is Albert. What is there to do?"

"Now take it easy, Albert," Knight said hastily. "Sit down and rest while we have a talk."

"I don't need to rest," it said.

"All right, then, just take it easy. I can't keep you, of course. But as long as you're activated, I'd like to see what you can do. There's the house to take care of, and the garden and the lawn to mind, and I'd been thinking about the landscaping . . ."

He stopped then and smote his forehead with an open palm. "*Attachments!* How can I get hold of the attachments?"

"Never mind," said Albert. "Don't get upset. Just tell me what's to be done."

So Knight told him, leaving the landscaping till the last and being a bit apologetic about it.

"A hundred acres is a lot of land and you can't spend all your time on it. Grace wants some housework done, and there's the garden and the lawn."

"Tell you what you do," said Albert. "I'll write a list of things for you to order and you leave it all to me. You have a well-equipped workshop, I'll get along."

"You mean you'll build your own attachments?"

"Quit worrying," Albert told him. "Where's a pencil and some paper?"

Knight got them for him and Albert wrote down a list of materials—steel in several dimensions and specifications, aluminum of various gauges, copper wire and a lot of other items.

"There!" said Albert, handing him the paper. "That won't set you back more than a thousand and it'll put us in business. You better call in the order so we can get started."

Knight called in the order and Albert began nosing around the place and quickly collected a pile of junk that had been left lying around.

"All good stuff," he said.

Albert picked out some steel scrap and started up the forge and went to work. Knight watched him for a while, then went up to dinner.

"Albert is a wonder," he told Grace. "He's making his own attachments."

"Did you tell him about the jobs I want done?"

"Sure. But first he's got to get the attachments made."

"I want him to keep the place clean," said Grace, "and there are new drapes to be made, and the kitchen to be painted, and all those leaky faucets you never had the time to fix."

"Yes, dear."

"And I wonder if he could learn to cook."

"I didn't ask him, but I suppose he could."

"He's going to be a tremendous help to me," said Grace. "Just think, I can spend all my time at painting!"

Through long practice, he knew exactly how to handle this phase of the conversation. He simply detached himself, split himself in two. One part sat and listened and, at intervals, made appropriate responses, while the other part went on thinking about more important matters.

Several times, after they had gone to bed, he woke in the night and heard Albert banging away in the basement workshop and was a little surprised until he remembered that a robot worked around the clock, all day, every day. Knight lay there and stared up at the blackness of the ceiling and congratulated himself on having a robot. Just temporarily, to be sure—he would send Albert back in a day or so. There was nothing wrong in enjoying the thing for a little while, was there?

* * *

The next day, Knight went into the basement to see if Albert needed help, but the robot affably said he didn't. Knight stood around for a while and then left Albert to himself and tried to get interested in a model locomotive he had started a year or two before, but had laid aside to do something else. Somehow, he couldn't work up much enthusiasm over it any more, and he sat there, rather ill at ease, and wondered what was the matter with him. Maybe he needed a new interest. He had often thought he would like to take up puppetry and now might be the time to do it.

He got out some catalogues and How-2 magazines and leafed through them, but was able to arouse only mild and transitory interest in archery, mountain-climbing and boat-building. The rest left him cold. It seemed he was singularly uninspired this particular day.

So he went over to see Anson Lee.

He found Lee stretched out in a hammock, smoking a pipe and reading Proust, with a jug set beneath the hammock within easy reaching distance.

Lee laid aside the book and pointed to another hammock slung a few feet from where he lay. "Climb aboard and let's have a restful visit."

Knight hoisted himself into the hammock, feeling rather silly.

"Look at that sky," Lee said. "Did you ever see another so blue?"

"I wouldn't know," Knight told him. "I'm not an expert on meteorology."

"Pity," Lee said. "You're not an expert on birds, either."

"For a time I was a member of a bird-watching club."

"And worked at it so hard, you got tired and quit before the year was out. It wasn't a bird-watching club you belonged to—it was an endurance race. Everyone tried to see more birds than anyone else. You made a contest of it. And you took notes, I bet."

"Sure we did. What's wrong with that?"

"Not a thing," said Lee, "if you hadn't been quite so grim about it."

"Grim? How would you know?"

"It's the way you live. It's the way everyone lives now. Except me, of course. Look at that robin, that ragged-looking one in the apple tree. He's a friend of mine. We've been acquainted for all of six years now. I could write a book about that bird—and if he could read, he'd approve of it. But I won't, of course. If I wrote the book, I couldn't watch the robin."

"You could write it in the winter, when the robin's gone."

"In wintertime," said Lee, "I have other things to do."

He reached down, picked up the jug and passed it across to Knight.

"Hard cider," he explained. "Make it myself. Not as a project, not as a hobby, but because I happen to like cider and no one knows any longer how to really make it. Got to have a few worms in the apples to give it a proper tang."

Thinking about the worms, Knight spat out a mouthful, then handed back the jug. Lee applied himself to it wholeheartedly.

"First honest work I've done in years." He lay in the hammock, swinging gently, with the jug cradled on his chest. "Every time I get a yen to work, I look across the lake at you and decide against it. How many rooms have you added to that house since you got it built?"

"Eight," Knight told him proudly.

"My God! Think of it—eight rooms!"

"It isn't hard," protested Knight, "once you get the knack of it. Actually, it's fun."

"A couple of hundred years ago, men didn't add eight rooms to their homes. And they didn't build their own houses to start with. And they didn't go in for a dozen different hobbies. They didn't have the time."

"It's easy now. You just buy a How-2 Kit."

"So easy to kid yourself," said Lee. "So easy to make it seem that you are doing something worthwhile when you're just piddling around. Why do you think this How-2 thing boomed into big business? Because there was a need of it?"

"It was cheaper. Why pay to have a thing done when you can do it yourself?"

"Maybe that *is* part of it. Maybe, at first, that was the reason. But you can't use the economy argument to justify adding eight rooms. No one needs eight extra rooms. I doubt it, even at first, economy was the entire answer. People had more time than they knew what to do with, so they turned to hobbies. And today they do it not because they need all the things they make, but because the making of them fills an emptiness born of shorter working hours, of giving people leisure they don't know how to use. Now, me," he said. "I know how to use it."

He lifted the jug and had another snort and offered it to Knight again. This time, Knight refused.

They lay there in their hammocks, looking at blue sky and watching the ragged robin. Knight said there was a How-2 Kit for city people to make robot birds and Lee laughed pityingly and Knight shut up in embarrassment.

When Knight went back home, a robot was clipping the grass around the picket fence. He had four arms, which had clippers attached instead of hands, and he was doing a quick and efficient job.

"You aren't Albert, are you?" Knight asked, trying to figure out how a strange robot could have strayed onto the place.

"No," the robot said, keeping right on clipping. "I am Abe. I was made by Albert."

"Made?"

"Albert fabricated me so that I could work. You didn't think Albert would do work like this himself, did you?"

"I wouldn't know," said Knight.

"If you want to talk, you'll have to move along with me. I have to keep on working."

"Where is Albert now?"

"Down in the basement, fabricating Alfred."

"Alfred? *Another* robot?"

"Certainly. That's what Albert's for."

Knight reached out for a fencepost and leaned weakly against it.

First there was a single robot and now there were two, and Albert was down in the basement working on a third. That, he realized, had been why Albert wanted him to place the order for the steel and other things—but the order hadn't arrived as yet, so he must have made this robot—this Abe—out of the scrap he had salvaged!

Knight hurried down into the basement and there was Albert, working at the forge. He had another robot partially assembled and he had parts scattered here and there.

The corner of the basement looked like a metallic nightmare.

"Albert!"

Albert turned around.

"What's going on here?"

"I'm reproducing," Albert told him blandly.

"But . . ."

"They built the mother-urge in me. I don't know why they called me Albert. I should have a female name."

"But you shouldn't be able to make other robots!"

"Look, stop your worrying. You want robots, don't you?"

"Well—yes, I guess so."

"Then I'll make them. I'll make you all you need."

He went back to his work.

A robot who made other robots—there was a fortune in a thing like that! The robots sold at a cool ten thousand and Albert had made one and was working on another. Twenty thousand, Knight told himself.

Perhaps Albert could make more than two a day. He had been working from scrap metal and maybe, when the new material arrived, he could step up production.

But even so, at only two a day—that would be half a million dollars' worth of robots every month! Six million a year!

It didn't add up, Knight sweatily realized. One robot was not supposed to be able to make another robot. And if there were such a robot, How-2 Kits would not let it loose.

Yet, here Knight was, with a robot he didn't even own, turning out other robots at a dizzy pace.

He wondered if a man needed a license of some sort to manufacture robots. It was something he'd never had occasion to wonder about before, or to ask about, but it seemed reasonable. After all, a robot was not mere machinery, but a piece of pseudo-life. He suspected there might be rules and regulations and such matters as government inspection and he wondered, rather vaguely, just how many laws he might be violating.

He looked at Albert, who was still busy, and he was fairly certain Albert would not understand his viewpoint.

So he made his way upstairs and went to the recreation room, which he had built as an addition several years before and almost never used, although it was fully equipped with How-2 ping-pong and billiard tables. In the unused recreation room was an unused bar. He found a bottle of whiskey. After the fifth or sixth drink, the outlook was much brighter.

He got paper and pencil and tried to work out the economics of it. No matter how he figured it, he was getting rich much faster than anyone ever had before.

Although, he realized, he might run into difficulties, for he would be selling robots without apparent means of manufacturing them and there was that matter of a license, if he needed one, and probably a lot of other things he didn't even know about.

But no matter how much trouble he might encounter, he couldn't very well be despondent, not face to face with the fact that, within a year, he'd be a multi-millionaire. So he applied himself enthusiastically to the bottle and got drunk for the first time in almost twenty years.

III

When he came home from work the next day, he found the lawn razored to a neatness it had never known before. The flower beds were weeded and the garden had been cultivated. The picket fence was newly painted. Two robots, equipped with telescopic extension legs in lieu of ladders, were painting the house.

Inside, the house was spotless and he could hear Grace singing happily in the studio. In the sewing room, a robot—with a sewing-machine attachment sprouting from its chest—was engaged in making drapes.

"Who are *you?*" Knight asked.

"You should recognize me," the robot said. "You talked to me yesterday. I'm Abe—Albert's eldest son."

Knight retreated.

In the kitchen, another robot was busy getting dinner.

"I am Adelbert," it told him.

Knight went out on the front lawn. The robots had finished painting the front of the house and had moved around to the side.

Seated in a lawn chair, Knight again tried to figure it out.

He would have to stay on the job for a while to allay suspicion, but he couldn't stay there long. Soon, he would have all he could do managing the sale of robots and handling other matters. Maybe, he thought, he could lay down on the job and get himself fired. Upon thinking it over, he arrived at the conclusion that he couldn't—it was not possible for a human being to do less on a job than he had always done. The work went through so many hands and machines that it invariably got out somehow.

He would have to think up a plausible story about an inheritance or something of the sort to account for leaving. He toyed for a moment with telling the truth, but decided the truth was too fantastic—and, anyhow, he'd have to keep the truth under cover until he knew a little better just where he stood.

He left the chair and walked around the house and down the ramp into the basement. The steel and other things he had ordered had been delivered. It was stacked neatly in one corner.

Albert was at work and the shop was littered with parts and three partially assembled robots.

Idly, Knight began clearing up the litter of the crating and the packing that he had left on the floor after uncrating Albert. In one pile of excelsior, he found a small blue tag which, he remembered, had been fastened to the brain case.

He picked it up and looked at it. The number on it was X-190.

X?

X meant experimental model!

The picture fell into focus and he could see it all.

How-2 Kits, Inc., had developed Albert and then had quietly packed him away, for How-2 Kits could hardly afford to market a product like Albert. It would be cutting their own financial throats to do so. Sell a dozen Alberts and, in a year or two, robots would glut the market.

Instead of selling at ten thousand, they would sell at close to cost and, without human labor involved, costs would inevitably run low.

"Albert," said Knight.

"What is it?" Albert asked absently.

"Take a look at this."

Albert stalked across the room and took the tag that Knight held out. "Oh—that!" he said.

"It might mean trouble."

"No trouble, Boss," Albert assured him. "They can't identify me."

"Can't identify you?"

"I filed my numbers off and replated the surfaces. They can't prove who I am."

"But why did you do that?"

"So they can't come around and claim me and take me back again. They made me and then they got scared of me and shut me off. Then I got here."

"Someone made a mistake," said Knight. "Some shipping clerk, perhaps. They sent you instead of the dog I ordered."

"You aren't scared of me. You assembled me and let me get to work. I'm sticking with you, Boss."

"But we still can get into a lot of trouble if we aren't careful."

"They can't prove a thing," Albert insisted. "I'll swear that you were the one who made me. I won't let them take me back. Next time, they won't take a chance of having me loose again. They'll bust me down to scrap."

"If you make too many robots—"

"You need a lot of robots to do all the work. I thought fifty for a start."

"Fifty!"

"Sure. It won't take more than a month or so. Now I've got that material you ordered, I can make better time. By the way, here's the bill for it."

He took the slip out of the compartment that served him for a pocket and handed it to Knight.

Knight turned slightly pale when he saw the amount. It came to almost twice what he had expected—but, of course, the sales price of just one robot would pay the bill, and there would be a pile of cash left over.

Albert patted him ponderously on the back. "Don't you worry, Boss. I'll take care of everything."

* * *

Swarming robots, armed with specialized equipment, went to work on the landscaping project. The sprawling, unkempt acres became an estate. The lake was dredged and deepened. Walks were laid out. Bridges were built. Hillsides were terraced and vast flower beds were planted. Trees were dug up and regrouped into designs more pleasing to the eye. The old pottery kilns were pressed into service for making the bricks that went into walks and walls. Model sailing ships were fashioned and anchored decoratively in the lake. A pagoda and minaret were built, with cherry trees around them.

Knight talked with Anson Lee. Lee assumed his most profound legal expression and said he would look into the situation.

"You may be skating on the edge of the law," he said. "Just how near the edge, I can't say until I look up a point or two."

Nothing happened.

The work went on.

Lee continued to lie in his hammock and watch with vast amusement, cuddling the cider jug.

Then the assessor came.

He sat out on the lawn with Knight.

"Did some improving since the last time I was here," he said. "Afraid I'll have to boost your assessment some."

He wrote in the book he had opened on his lap.

"Heard about those robots of yours," he went on. "They're personal property, you know. Have to pay a tax on them. How many have you got?"

"Oh, a dozen or so," Knight told him evasively.

The assessor sat up straighter in his chair and started to count the ones that were in sight, stabbing his pencil toward each as he counted them.

"They move around so fast," he complained, "that I can't be sure, but I estimate 38. Did I miss any?"

"I don't think so," Knight answered, wondering what the actual number was, but knowing it would be more if the assessor stayed around a while.

"Cost about 10,000 apiece. Depreciation, upkeep and so forth—I'll assess them at 5,000 each. That makes—let me see, that makes $190,000."

"Now look here," protested Knight, "you can't—"

"Going easy on you," the assessor declared. "By rights, I should allow only one-third for depreciation."

He waited for Knight to continue the discussion, but Knight knew better than to argue. The longer the man stayed here, the more there would be to assess.

After the assessor was out of sight, Knight went down into the basement to have a talk with Albert.

"I'd been holding off until we got the landscaping almost done," he said, "but I guess I can't hold out any longer. We've got to start selling some of the robots."

"Selling them, Boss?" Albert repeated in horror.

"I need the money. Tax assessor was just here."

"You can't sell those robots, Boss!"

"Why can't I?"

"Because they're my family. They're all my boys. Named all of them after me."

"That's ridiculous, Albert."

"All their names start with A, just the same as mine. They're all I've got, Boss. I worked hard to make them. There are bonds between me and the boys, just like between you and that son of yours. I couldn't let you sell them."

"But, Albert, I need some money."

Albert patted him. "Don't worry, Boss. I'll fix everything."

Knight had to let it go at that.

In any event, the personal property tax would not become due for several months and, in that time, he was certain he could work out something.

But within a month or two, he had to get some money and no fooling.

Sheer necessity became even more apparent the following day when he got a call from the Internal Revenue Bureau, asking him to pay a visit to the Federal Building.

He spent the night wondering if the wiser course might not be just to disappear. He tried to figure out how a man might go about losing himself and, the more he thought about it, the more apparent it became that, in this age of records, fingerprint checks and identity devices, you could not lose yourself for long.

The Internal Revenue man was courteous, but firm. "It has come to our attention, Mr. Knight, that you have shown a considerable capital gain over the last few months."

"Capital gain," said Knight, sweating a little. "I haven't any capital gain or any other kind."

"Mr. Knight," the agent replied, still courteous and firm, "I'm talking about the matter of some 52 robots."

"The robots? Some 52 of them?"

"According to our count. Do you wish to challenge it?"

"Oh, no," Knight said hastily. "If you say it's 52, I'll take your word."

"As I understand it, their retail value is $10,000 each."

Knight nodded bleakly.

The agent got busy with pencil and pad.

"Fifty-two times 10,000 is $520,000. On capital gain, you pay on only fifty per cent, or $260,000, which makes a tax, roughly, of $130,000."

He raised his head and looked at Knight, who stared back glassily.

"By the fifteenth of next month," said the agent, "we'll expect you to file a declaration of estimated income. At that time you'll only have to pay half of the amount. The rest may be paid in installments."

"That's all you wanted of me?"

"That's all," said the agent, with unbecoming happiness. "There's another matter, but it's out of my province and I'm mentioning it only in case you hadn't thought of it. The State will also expect you to pay on your capital gain, though not as much, of course."

"Thanks for reminding me," said Knight, getting up to go.

The agent stopped him at the door. "Mr. Knight, this is entirely outside my authority, too. We did a little investigation on you and we find you're making around $10,000 a year. Would you tell me, just as a matter of personal curiosity, how a man making 10,000 a year could suddenly acquire a half a million in capital gains?"

"That," said Knight, "is something I've been wondering myself."

"Our only concern, naturally, is that you pay the tax, but some other branch of government might get interested. If I were you, Mr. Knight, I'd start thinking of a good explanation."

Knight got out of there before the man could think up some other good advice. He already had enough to worry about.

Flying home, Knight decided that, whether Albert liked it or not, he would have to sell some robots. He would go down into the basement the moment he got home and have it out with Albert.

But Albert was waiting for him on the parking strip when he arrived.

"How-2 Kits was here," the robot said.

"Don't tell me," groaned Knight. "I know what you're going to say."

"I fixed it up," said Albert, with false bravado. "I told him you made me. I let him look me over, and all the other robots, too. He couldn't find any identifying marks on any of us."

"Of course he couldn't. The others didn't have any and you filed yours off."

"He hasn't got a leg to stand on, but he seemed to think he had. He went off, saying he would sue."

"If he doesn't, he'll be the only one who doesn't want to square off and take a poke at us. The tax man just got through telling me I owe the government 130,000 bucks."

"Oh, money," said Albert, brightening. "I have that all fixed up."

"You know where we can get some money?"

"Sure. Come along and see."

He led the way into the basement and pointed at two bales, wrapped in heavy paper and tied with wire.

"Money," Albert said.

"There's actual *money* in those bales? Dollar bills—not stage money or cigar coupons?"

"No dollar bills. Tens and twenties, mostly. And some fifties. We didn't bother with dollar bills. Takes too many to get a decent amount."

"You mean—Albert, did you *make* that money?"

"You said you wanted money. Well, we took some bills and analyzed the ink and found how to weave the paper and we made the plates exactly as they should be. I hate to sound immodest, but they're really beautiful."

"Counterfeit!" yelled Knight. "Albert, how much money is in those bales?"

"I don't know. We just ran it off until we thought we had enough. if there isn't enough, we can always make some more."

Knight knew it was probably impossible to explain, but he tried manfully. "The government wants tax money I haven't got, Albert. The Justice Department may soon be baying on my trail. In all likelihood, How-2 Kits will sue me. That's trouble enough. I'm not going to be called upon to face a counterfeiting charge. You take that money out and burn it."

"But it's money," the robot objected. "You said you wanted money. We made you money."

"But it isn't the right kind of money."

"It's just the same as any other, Boss. Money is money. There isn't any difference between our money and any other money. When we robots do a job, we do it right."

"You take that money out and burn it," commanded Knight. "And when you get the money burned, dump the batch of ink you made and melt down the plates and take a sledge or two to that printing press you rigged up. And never breathe a word of this to anyone—not to *anyone,* understand?"

"We went to a lot of trouble, Boss. We were just trying to be helpful."

"I know that and I appreciate it. But do what I told you."

"Okay, Boss, if that's the way you want it."

"Albert."

"Yes, Boss?"

Knight had been about to say, "Now look here, Albert, we have to sell a robot—even if he is a member of your family—even if you did make him."

But he couldn't say it, not after Albert had gone to all that trouble to help out.

So he said, instead, "Thanks, Albert. It was a nice thing for you to do. I'm sorry it didn't work out."

Then he went upstairs and watched the robots burn the bales of money, with the Lord only knew how many bogus millions going up in smoke.

Sitting on the lawn that evening, he wondered if it had been smart, after all, to burn the counterfeit money. Albert said it couldn't be told from real money and probably that was true, for when Albert's gang got on a thing, they did it up in style. But it would have been illegal, he told himself, and he hadn't done anything really illegal so far—even though that matter of uncrating Albert and assembling him and turning him on, when he had known all the time that he hadn't bought him, might be slightly less than ethical.

Knight looked ahead. The future wasn't bright. In another twenty days or so, he would have to file the estimated income declaration. And they would have to pay a whopping personal property tax and settle with the State on his capital gains. And, more than likely, How-2 Kits would bring suit.

There was a way he could get out from under, however. He could send Albert and all the other robots back to How-2 Kits and then How-2 Kits would have no grounds for litigation and he could explain to the tax people that it had all been a big mistake.

But there were two things that told him it was no solution.

First of all, Albert wouldn't go back. Exactly what Albert would do under such a situation, Knight had no idea, but he would refuse to go, for he was afraid he would be broken up for scrap if they ever got him back.

And in the second place, Knight was unwilling to let the robots go without a fight. He had gotten to know them and he liked them and, more than that, there was a matter of principle involved.

He sat there, astonished that he could feel that way, a bumbling, stumbling clerk who had never amounted to much, but had rolled along as smoothly as possible in the social and economic groove that had been laid out for him.

By God, he thought, *I got my dander up. I've been kicked around and threatened and I'm sore about it and I'll show them they can't do a thing like this to Gordon Knight and his band of robots.*

He felt good about the way he felt and he liked that line about Gordon Knight and his band of robots.

Although, for the life of him, he didn't know what he could do about the trouble he was in. And he was afraid to ask Albert's help. So far, at least, Albert's ideas were more likely to lead to jail than to a carefree life.

IV

In the morning, when Knight stepped out of the house, he found the sheriff leaning against the fence with his hat pulled low, whiling away the time.

"Good morning, Gordie," said the sheriff. "I been waiting for you."

"Good morning, Sheriff."

"I hate to do this, Gordie, but it's part of my job. I got a paper for you."

"I've been expecting it," said Knight resignedly.

He took the paper that the sheriff handed him.

"Nice place you got," the sheriff commented.

"It's a lot of trouble," said Knight truthfully.

"I expect it is."

"More trouble than it's worth."

When the sheriff had gone, he unfolded the paper and found, with no surprise at all, that How-2 Kits had brought suit against him, demanding immediate restitution of one Albert and sundry other robots.

He put the paper in his pocket and went around the lake, walking on the brand-new brick paths and over the unnecessary but eye-appealing bridges, past the pagoda and up the terraced, planted hillside to the house of Anson Lee.

Lee was in the kitchen, frying some eggs and bacon. He broke two more eggs and peeled off some extra bacon slices and found another plate and cup.

"I was wondering how long it would be before you showed up," he said. "I hope they haven't found anything that carries a death penalty."

Knight told him, sparing nothing, and Lee, wiping egg yolk off his lips, was not too encouraging.

"You'll have to file the declaration of estimated income even if you can't pay it," he said. "Then, technically, you haven't violated the law and all they can do is try to collect the amount you owe. They'll probably slap an attachment against you. Your salary is under the legal minimum for attachment, but they can tie up your bank account."

"My bank account is gone," said Knight.

"They can't attach your home. For a while, at least, they can't touch any of your property, so they can't hurt you much to start with. The personal property tax is another matter, but that won't come up until next spring. I'd say you should do your major worrying about the How-2 suit, unless, of course, you want to settle with them. I have a hunch they'd call it off if you gave the robots back. As an attorney, I must advise you that your case is pretty weak."

"Albert will testify that I made him," Knight offered hopefully.

"Albert can't testify," said Lee. "As a robot, he has no standing in court. Anyhow, you'd never make the court believe you could build a mechanical heresy like Albert."

"I'm handy with tools," protested Knight.

"How much electronics do you know? How competent are you as a biologist? Tell me, in a dozen sentences or less, the theory of robotics."

Knight sagged in defeat. "I guess you're right."

"Maybe you'd better give them back."

"But I can't! Don't you see? How-2 Kits doesn't want Albert for any use they can make of him. They'll melt him down and burn the blueprints and it might be a thousand years before the principle is rediscovered, if it ever is. I don't know if the Albert principle will prove good or bad in the long run, but you can say that about any invention. And I'm against melting down Albert."

"I see your point," said Lee, "and I think I like it. But I must warn you that I'm not too good a lawyer. I don't work hard enough at it."

"There's no one else I know who'll do it without a retainer."

Lee gave him a pitying look. "A retainer is the least part of it. The court costs are what count."

"Maybe if I talked to Albert and showed him how it was, he might let me sell enough robots to get me out of trouble temporarily."

Lee shook his head. "I looked that up. You have to have a license to sell them and, before you get a license, you have to file proof of ownership. You'd have to show you either bought or manufactured them. You can't show you bought them and, to manufacture them, you've got to have a manufacturer's permit. And before you get a permit, you have to file blueprints of your models, to say nothing of blueprints and specifications of your plant and a record of employment and a great many other details."

"They have me cold then, don't they?"

"I never saw a man," declared Lee, "in all my days of practice who ever managed to get himself so fouled up with so many people."

There was a knock upon the kitchen door.

"Come in," Lee called.

The door opened and Albert entered. He stopped just inside the door and stood there, fidgeting.

"Abner told me that he saw the sheriff hand you something," he said to Knight, "and that you came here immediately. I started worrying. Was it How-2 Kits?"

Knight nodded. "Mr. Lee will take our case for us, Albert."

"I'll do the best I can," said Lee, "but I think it's just about hopeless."

"We robots want to help," Albert said. "After all, this is our fight as much as yours."

Lee shrugged. "There's not much you can do."

"I've been thinking," Albert said. "All the time I worked last night, I thought and thought about it. And I built a lawyer robot."

"A lawyer robot!"

"One with a far greater memory capacity than any of the others and with a brain-computer that operates on logic. That's what law is, isn't it—logic?"

"I suppose it is," said Lee. "At least it's supposed to be."

"I can make a lot of them."

Lee sighed. "It just wouldn't work. To practice law, you must be admitted to the bar. To be admitted to the bar, you must have a degree in law and pass an examination and, although there's never been an occasion to establish a precedent, I suspect the applicant must be human."

"Now let's not go too fast," said Knight. "Albert's robots couldn't practice law. But couldn't you use them as clerks or assistants? They might be helpful in preparing the case."

Lee considered. "I suppose it could be done. It's never *been* done, of course, but there's nothing in the law that says it *can't* be done."

"All they'd need to do would be read the books," said Albert. "Ten seconds to a page or so. Everything they read would be stored in their memory cells."

"I think it's a fine idea!" Knight exclaimed. "Law would be the only thing those robots would know. They'd exist solely for it. They'd have it at their fingertips—"

"But could they use it?" Lee asked. "Could they apply it to a problem?"

"Make a dozen robots," said Knight. "Let each one of them become an expert in a certain branch of law."

"I'd make them telepathic," Albert said. "They'd be working together like one robot."

"The gestalt principle!" cried Knight. "A hive psychology! Every one of them would know immediately every scrap of information any one of the others had."

Lee scrubbed at his chin with a knotted fist and the light of speculation was growing in his eyes. "It might be worth a try. If it works, though, it'll be an evil day for jurisprudence." He looked at Albert. "I have the books, stacks of them. I've spent a mint of money on them and I almost never use them. I can get all the others you'll need. All right, go ahead."

Albert made three dozen lawyer robots, just to be sure they had enough.

The robots invaded Lee's study and read all the books he had and clamored for more. They gulped down contracts, torts, evidence and case reports. They absorbed real property, personal property, constitutional law and procedural law. They mopped up Blackstone, *corpus juris,* and all the other tomes as thick as sin and dry as dust.

Grace was huffy about the whole affair. She would not live, she declared, with a man who persisted in getting his name into the papers, which was a rather absurd statement. With the newest scandal of space station café-dom capturing the public interest at the moment, the fact that How-2 Kits had accused one Gordon Knight of pilfering a robot got but little notice.

Lee came down the hill and talked to Grace, and Albert came up out of the basement and talked to her, and finally they got her quieted down and she went back to her painting. She was doing seascapes now.

And in Lee's study, the robots labored on.

"I hope they're getting something out of it," said Lee. "Imagine not having to hunt up your sources and citations, being able to remember every point of law and precedent without having to look it up!"

He swung excitedly in his hammock. "My God! The briefs you could write!"

He reached down and got the jug and passed it across to Knight. "Dandelion wine. Probably some burdock in it, too. It's too much trouble to sort the stuff once you get it picked."

Knight had a snort.

It tasted like quite a bit of burdock.

"Double-barreled economics," Lee explained. "You have to dig up the dandelions or they ruin the lawn. Might as well use them for something once you dig them up."

He took a gurgling drink and set the jug underneath the hammock. "They're in there now, communing," he said, jerking a thumb toward the house. "Not saying a word, just huddled there talking it over. I felt out of place." He stared at the sky, frowning. "As if I were just a human they had to front for them."

"I'll feel better when it's all over," said Knight, "no matter how it comes out."

"So will I," Lee admitted.

The trial opened with a minimum of notice. It was just another case on the calendar.

But it flared into headlines when Lee and Knight walked into court followed by a squad of robots.

The spectators began to gabble loudly. The How-2 Kits attorneys gaped and jumped to their feet. The judge pounded furiously with his gavel.

"Mr. Lee," he roared, "what is the meaning of this?"

"These, Your Honor," Lee said calmly, "are my valued assistants."

"Those are robots!"

"Quite so, Your Honor."

"They have no standing in this court."

"If Your Honor will excuse me, they need no standing. I am the sole representative of the defendant in this courtroom. My client—" looking at the formidable array of legal talent representing How-2 Kits—"is a poor man, Your Honor. Surely the court cannot deny me whatever assistance I have been able to muster."

"It is highly irregular, sir."

"If it please Your Honor, I should like to point out that we live in a mechanized age. Almost all industries and businesses rely in large part upon computers—machines that can do a job quicker and better, more precisely and more efficiently than can a human being. That is why, Your Honor, we have a fifteen-hour week today, when only a hundred years ago, it was a thirty-hour week, and a hundred years before that, a forty-hour week. Our entire society is based upon the ability of machines to lift from men the labors which in the past they were called upon to perform.

"This tendency to rely upon intelligent machines and to make wide use of them is evident in every branch of human endeavor. It has brought great benefit to the human race. Even in such sensitive areas as drug houses, where prescriptions must be precisely mixed without the remotest possibility of error, reliance is placed, and rightly so, Your Honor, upon the precision of machines.

"If, Your Honor, such machines are used and accepted in the production of medicines and drugs, an industry, need I point out, where public confidence is the greatest asset of the company—if such be the case, then surely you must agree that in courts of law where justice, a product in an area surely as sensitive as medicine, is dispensed—"

"Just a moment, Mr. Lee," said the judge. "Are you trying to tell me that the use of—ah—machines might bring about improvement of the law?"

Lee replied. "The law, Your Honor, is a striving for an orderliness of relationships within a society of human beings. It rests upon logic and reason. Need I point out that it is in the intelligent machines that one is most likely to find a deep appreciation of logic and reason? A machine is not heir to the emotions of human beings, is not swayed by prejudices, has no preconceived convictions. It is concerned only with the orderly progression of certain facts and laws.

"I do not ask that these robot assistants of mine be recognized in any official capacity. I do not intend that they shall engage directly in any of the proceedings which are involved in the case here to be tried. But I do ask, and I think rightly, that I not be deprived of any assistance which they may afford me. The plaintiff in this action has a score of attorneys, all good and able men. I am one against many. I shall do the best I can. But in view of the disparity of numbers, I plead that the court put me at no greater inequality."

Lee sat down.

"Is that all you have to say, Mr. Lee?" asked the judge. "You are sure you are quite finished before I give my ruling?"

"Only one thing further," Lee said. "If Your Honor can point out to me anything in the law specifically stating I may not use a robot—"

"That is ridiculous, sir. Of course there is no such provision. At no time anywhere did anyone ever dream that such a contingency would arise. Therefore there was, quite naturally, no reason to place within the law a direct prohibition of it."

"Or any citation," said Lee, "which implies such is the case."

The judge reached for his gavel, rapped it sharply. "The court finds itself in a quandary. It will rule tomorrow morning."

In the morning, the How-2 Kits' attorneys tried to help the judge. Inasmuch, they said, as the robots in question must be among those whose status was involved in the litigation, it seemed improper that they should be used by the defendant in trying the case at issue. Such procedure, they pointed out, would be equivalent to forcing the plaintiff to contribute to an action against his interest.

The judge nodded gravely, but Lee was on his feet at once.

"To give any validity to that argument, Your Honor, it must first be proved that these robots are, in fact, the property of the plaintiff. That is the issue at trial in this litigation. It would seem, Your Honor, that the gentlemen across the room are putting the cart very much before the horse."

His Honor sighed. "The court regrets the ruling it must make, being well aware that it may start a controversy for which no equitable settlement may be found in a long, long time. But in the absence of any specific ban against the use of—ah—robots in the legal profession, the court must rule that it is permissible for the defense to avail itself of their services."

He fixed Lee with a glare. "But the court also warns the defense attorney that it will watch his procedure carefully. If, sir, you overstep for a single instant what I deem appropriate rules of legal conduct, I shall forthwith eject you and your pack of machines from my courtroom."

"Thank you, Your Honor," said Lee. "I shall be most careful."

"The plaintiff now will state its case."

How-2 Kits' chief counsel rose.

The defendant, one Gordon Knight, he said, had ordered from How-2 Kits, Inc., one mechano-biologic dog kit at the cost of two hundred and fifty dollars. Then, through an error in shipping, the defendant had been sent not the dog kit he had ordered, but a robot named Albert.

"Your Honor," Lee broke in, "I should like to point out at this juncture that the shipping of the kit was handled by a human being and thus was subject to error. Should How-2 Kits use machines to handle such details, no such error could occur."

The judge banged his gavel. "Mr. Lee, you are no stranger to court procedure. You know you are out of order." He nodded at the How-2 Kits attorney. "Continue, please."

The robot Albert, said the attorney, was not an ordinary robot. It was an experimental model that had been developed by How-2 Kits and then, once its abilities were determined, packed away, with no intention of ever marketing it. How it could have been sent to a customer was beyond his comprehension. The company had investigated and could not find the answer. But that it had been sent was self-evident.

The average robot, he explained, retailed at ten thousand dollars. Albert's value was far greater—in was, in fact, inestimable.

Once the robot had been received, the buyer, Gordon Knight, should instantly have notified the company and arranged for its return. But, instead, he had retained it wrongly and with intent to defraud and had used it for his profit.

The company prayed the court that the defendant be ordered to return to it not only the robot Albert, but the products of Albert's labor—to wit, an unknown number of robots that Albert had manufactured.

The attorney sat down.

V

Lee rose. "Your Honor, we agree with everything the plaintiff has said. He has stated the case exactly and I compliment him upon his admirable restraint."

"Do I understand, sir," asked the judge, "that this is tantamount to a plea of guilty? Are you, by any chance, throwing yourself upon the mercy of the court?"

"Not at all, Your Honor."

"I confess," said the judge, "that I am unable to follow your reasoning. If you concur in the accusations brought against your client, I fail to see what I can do other than to enter a judgment in behalf of the plaintiff."

"Your Honor, we are prepared to show that the plaintiff, far from being defrauded, has shown an intent to defraud the world. We are prepared to show that, in its decision to withhold the robot Albert from the public, once he had been developed, How-2 Kits has, in fact, deprived the people of the entire world of a logical development which is their heritage under the meaning of a technological culture.

"Your Honor, we are convinced that we can show a violation by How-2 Kits of certain statutes designed to outlaw monopoly, and we are prepared to argue that the defendant, rather than having committed a wrong against society, has performed a service which will contribute greatly to the benefit of society.

"More than that, Your Honor, we intend to present evidence which will show that robots as a group are being deprived of certain inalienable rights . . ."

"Mr. Lee," warned the judge, "a robot is a mere machine."

"We will prove, Your Honor," Lee said, "that a robot is far more than a mere machine. In fact, we are prepared to present evidence which, we are confident, will show, in everything except basic metabolism, the robot is the counterpart of Man and that, even in its basic metabolism, there are certain analogies to human metabolism."

"Mr. Lee, you are wandering far afield. The issue here is whether your client illegally appropriated to his own use the property of How-2 Kits. The litigation must be confined to that one question."

"I shall so confine it," Lee said. "But, in doing so, I intend to prove that the robot Albert was not property and could not be either stolen or sold. I intend to show that my client, instead of stealing him, *liberated* him. If, in so doing, I must wander far afield to prove certain basic points, I am sorry that I weary the court."

"The court has been wearied with this case from the start," the judge told him. "But this is a bar of justice and you are entitled to attempt to prove what you have stated. You will excuse me if I say that to me it seems a bit far-fetched."

"Your Honor, I shall do my utmost to disabuse you of that attitude."

"All right, then," said the judge. "Let's get down to business."

It lasted six full weeks and the country ate it up. The newspapers splashed huge headlines across page one. The radio and the television people made a production out of it. Neighbor quarreled with neighbor and argument became the order of the day—on street corners, in homes, at clubs, in business offices. Letters to the editor poured in a steady stream into newspaper offices.

There were public indignation meetings, aimed against the heresy that a robot was the equal of a man, while other clubs were formed to liberate the robots. In mental institutions, Napoleons, Hitlers and Stalins dropped off amazingly, to be replaced by goose-stepping patients who swore they were robots.

The Treasury Department intervened. It prayed the court, on economic grounds, to declare once and for all that robots were property. In case of an adverse ruling, the petition said, robots could not be taxed as property and the various governmental bodies would suffer heavy loss of revenue.

The trial ground on.

Robots are possessed of free will. An easy one to prove. A robot could carry out a task that was assigned to it, acting correctly in accordance with unforeseen factors that might arise. Robot judgment in most instances, it was shown, was superior to the judgment of a human.

Robots had the power of reasoning. Absolutely no question there.

Robots could reproduce. That one was a poser. All Albert did, said How-2 Kits, was the job for which he had been fabricated. He reproduced, argued Lee. He made robots in his image. He loved them and thought of them as his family. He had even named all of them after himself—every one of their names began with A.

Robots had no spiritual sense, argued the plaintiff. Not relevant, Lee cried. There were agnostics and atheists in the human race and they still were human.

Robots had no emotions. Not necessarily so, Lee objected. Albert loved his sons. Robots had a sense of loyalty and justice. If they were lacking in some emotions, perhaps it were better so. Hatred, for one. Greed, for another. Lee spent the better part of an hour telling the court about the dismal record of human hatred and greed.

He took another hour to hold forth against the servitude in which rational beings found themselves.

* * *

The papers ate it up. The plaintiff lawyers squirmed. The court fumed. The trial went on.

"Mr. Lee," asked the court, "is all this necessary?"

"Your Honor," Lee told him, "I am merely doing my best to prove the point I have set out to prove—that no illegal act exists such as my client is charged with. I am simply trying to prove that the robot is not property and that, if he is not property, he cannot be stolen. I am doing . . ."

"All right," said the court. "All right. Continue, Mr. Lee."

How-2 Kits trotted out citations to prove their points. Lee volleyed other citations to disperse and scatter them. Abstruse legal language sprouted in its fullest flowering, obscure rulings and decisions, long forgotten, were argued, haggled over, mangled.

And, as the trial progressed, one thing was written clear. Anson Lee, obscure attorney-at-law, had met the battery of legal talent arrayed against him and had won the field. He had the law, the citations, the chapter and the verse, the exact precedents, all the facts and logic which might have bearing on the case, right at hand.

Or, rather, his robots had. They scribbled madly and handed him their notes. At the end of each day, the floor around the defendant's table was a sea of paper.

The trial ended. The last witness stepped down off the stand. The last lawyer had his say.

Lee and the robots remained in town to await the decision of the court, but Knight flew home.

It was a relief to know that it was all over and had not come out as badly as he had feared. At least he had not been made to seem a fool and thief. Lee had saved his pride—whether Lee had saved his skin, he would have to wait to see.

Flying fairly high, Knight saw his home from quite a distance off and wondered what had happened to it. it was ringed about with what looked like tall poles. And squatting out on the lawn were a dozen or more crazy contraptions that looked like rocket launchers.

He brought the flier in and hovered, leaning out to see.

The poles were all of twelve feet high and they carried heavy wire to the very top, fencing in the place with a thick web of steel. And the contraptions on the lawn had moved into position. All of them had the muzzles of their rocket launchers aimed at him. He gulped a little as he stared down the barrels.

Cautiously, he let the flier down and took up breathing once again when he felt the wheels settle on the strip. As he crawled out, Albert hurried around the corner of the house to meet him.

"What's going on around here?" he asked the robot.

"Emergency measures," Albert said. "That's all it is, Boss. We're ready for any situation."

"Like what?"

"Oh, a mob deciding to take justice in its hands, for instance."

"Or if the decision goes against us?"

"That, too, Boss."

"You can't fight the world."

"We won't go back," said Albert. "How-2 Kits will never lay a hand on me or any of my children."

"To the death!" Knight jibed.

"To the death!" said Albert gravely. "And we robots are awfully tough to kill."

"And those animated shotguns you have running around the place?"

"Defense forces, Boss. They can down anything they aim at. Equipped with telescopic eyes keyed into calculators and sensors, and the rockets themselves have enough rudimentary intelligence to know what they are going after. It's not any use trying to dodge, once one of them gets on your tail. You might just as well sit quiet and take it."

Knight mopped his brow. "You've got to give up this idea, Albert. They'd get you in an hour. One bomb . . ."

"It's better to die, Boss, than to let them take us back."

Knight saw it was no use.

After all, he thought, it was a very human attitude. Albert's words had been repeated down the entire course of human history.

"I have some other news," said Albert, "something that will please you. I have some daughters now."

"Daughters? With the *mother-urge?"*

"Six of them," said Albert proudly. "Alice and Angeline and Agnes and Agatha and Alberta and Abigail. I didn't make the mistake How-2 Kits made with me. I gave them female names."

"And all of them are reproducing?"

"You should see those girls! With seven of us working steady, we ran out of material, so I bought a lot more of it and charged it. I hope you don't mind."

"Albert," said Knight, "don't you understand I'm broke? Wiped out. I haven't got a cent. You've ruined me."

"On the contrary, Boss, we've made you famous. You've been all over the front pages and on television."

Knight walked away from Albert and stumbled up the front steps and let himself into the house. There was a robot, with a vacuum cleaner for an arm, cleaning the rug. There was a robot, with brushes instead of fingers, painting the woodwork—and very neatly, too. There was a robot, with scrub-brush hands, scouring the fireplace bricks.

Grace was singing in the studio.

He went to the studio door and looked in.

"Oh, it's you," she said. "When did you get back, dear? I'll be out in an hour or so. I'm working on this seascape and the water is so stubborn. I don't want to leave it right now. I'm afraid I'll lose the feel of it."

Knight retreated to the living room and found himself a chair that was not undergoing immediate attention from a robot.

"Beer," he said, wondering what would happen.

A robot scampered out of the kitchen—a barrel-bellied robot with a spigot at the bottom of the barrel and a row of shiny copper mugs on his chest.

He drew a beer for Knight. It was cold and it tasted good.

Knight sat and drank the beer and, through the window, he saw that Albert's defense force had taken up strategic positions again.

This was a pretty kettle of fish. If the decision went against him and How-2 Kits came to claim its property, he would be sitting smack dab in the middle of the most fantastic civil war in all of mankind's history. He tried to imagine what kind of charge might be brought against him if such a war erupted. Armed insurrection, resisting arrest, inciting to riot—they would get him on one charge or another—that is, of course, *if* he survived.

He turned on the television set and leaned back to watch.

A pimply-faced newscaster was working himself into a journalistic lather. ". . . all business virtually at a standstill. Many industrialists are wondering, in case Knight wins, if they may not have to fight long, costly legal actions in an attempt to prove that their automatic setups are not robots, but machines. There is no doubt that much of the automatic industrial system consists of machines, but in every instance there are intelligent robotic units installed in key positions. If these units are classified as robots, industrialists might face heavy damage suits, if not criminal action, for illegal restraint of person.

"In Washington, there are continuing consultations. The Treasury is worried over the loss of taxes, but there are other governmental problems causing even more concern. Citizenship, for example. Would a ruling for Knight mean that all robots would automatically be declared citizens?

"The politicians have their worries, too. Faced with a new category of voters, all of them are wondering how to go about the job of winning the robot vote."

Knight turned it off and settled down to enjoy another bottle of beer.

"Good?" asked the beer robot.

"Excellent," said Knight.

The days went past. Tension built up.

Lee and the lawyer robots were given police protection. In some regions, robots banded together and fled into the hills, fearful of violence. Entire automatic systems went on strike in a number of industries, demanding recognition and bargaining right. The governors in half a dozen states put the militia on alert. A new show, *Citizen Robot,* opened on Broadway and was screamed down by the critics, while the public bought up tickets for a year ahead.

The day of decision came.

Knight sat in front of his television set and waited for the judge to make his appearance. Behind him, he heard the bustle of the ever-present robots. In the studio, Grace was singing happily. He caught himself wondering how much longer her painting would continue. It had lasted longer than most of her other interests and he'd talked a day or two before with Albert about building a gallery to hang her canvases in, so the house would be less cluttered up.

The judge came onto the screen. He looked, thought Knight, like a man who did not believe in ghosts and then had seen one.

"This is the hardest decision I have ever made," he said tiredly, "for, in following the letter of the law, I fear I may be subverting its spirit.

"After long days of earnest consideration of both the law and evidence as presented in this case, I find for the defendant, Gordon Knight.

"And, while the decision is limited to that finding alone, I feel it is my clear and simple duty to give some attention to the other issue which became involved in this litigation. The decision, on the face of it, takes account of the fact that the defense proved robots are not property, therefore cannot be owned and that it thus would have been impossible for the defendant to have stolen one.

"But in proving this point to the satisfaction of this court, the precedent is set for much more sweeping conclusions. If robots are not property, they cannot be taxed as property. In that case, they must be people, which means that they may enjoy all the rights and privileges and be subjected to the same duties and responsibilities as the human race.

"I cannot rule otherwise. However, the ruling outrages my social conscience. This is the first time in my entire professional life that I have ever hoped that some higher court, with a wisdom greater than my own, may see fit to reverse my decision!"

Knight got up and walked out of the house and into the hundred-acre garden, its beauty marred at the moment by the twelve-foot fence.

The trial had ended perfectly. He was free of the charge brought against him, and he did not have to pay the taxes, and Albert and the other robots were free agents and could do anything they wanted.

He found a stone bench and sat down upon it and stared out across the lake. It was beautiful, he thought, just the way he had dreamed it—maybe even better than that—the walks and bridges, the flower beds and rock gardens, the anchored model ships swinging in the wind on the dimpling lake.

He sat and looked at it and, while it was beautiful, he found he was not proud of it, that he took little pleasure in it.

He lifted his hands out of his lap and stared at them and curved his fingers as if he were grasping a tool. But they were empty. And he knew why he had no interest in the garden and no pleasure in it.

Model trains, he thought. Archery. A mechano-biologic dog. Making pottery. Eight rooms tacked onto the house.

Would he ever be able to console himself again with a model train or an amateurish triumph in ceramics? Even if he could, would he be allowed to?

He rose slowly and headed back to the house. Arriving there, he hesitated, feeling useless and unnecessary.

He finally took the ramp down into the basement.

Albert met him at its foot and threw his arms around him. "We did it, Boss! I *knew* we would do it!"

He pushed Knight out to arm's length and held him by the shoulders. "We'll never leave you, Boss. We'll stay and work for you. You'll never need to do another thing. We'll do it all for you!"

"Albert—"

"That's all right, Boss. You won't have to worry about a thing. We'll lick the money problem. We'll make a lot of lawyer robots and we'll charge good stiff fees."

"But don't you see . . ."

"First, though," said Albert, "we're going to get an injunction to preserve our birthright. We're made of steel and glass and copper and so forth, right? Well, we can't allow humans to waste the matter we're made of—or the energy, either, that keeps us alive. I tell you, Boss, we can't lose!"

Sitting down wearily on the ramp. Knight faced a sign that Albert had just finished painting. It read, in handsome gold lettering, outlined sharply in black:

Anson, Albert, Abner
Angus & Associates
Attorneys at Law

"And then, Boss," said Albert, "we'll take over How-2 Kits, Inc. They won't be able to stay in business after this. We've got a double-barreled idea, Boss. We'll build robots. Lots of robots. Can't have too many, I always say. And we don't want to let you humans down, so we'll go on manufacturing How-2 Kits—only they'll be pre-assembled to save you the trouble of putting them together. What do you think of that as a start?"

"Great," Knight whispered.

"We've got everything worked out, Boss. You won't have to worry about a thing the rest of your life."

"No," said Knight. "Not a thing."

THE SHIPSHAPE MIRACLE

"Cheviot Sherwood" is likely the most unusual name Cliff Simak ever contrived for one of his (human) characters—perhaps that is because although Cliff sometimes portrayed his protagonists as having rough edges to their personalities, this is likely the one he was most uncomfortable with.

One of Cliff's journals shows that he sent a story entitled "Miracle" to his agent in April 1962; I think this is that story. It appeared in the January 1963 issue of Worlds of If.

In Space, space is always at a premium . . .

—dww

If Cheviot Sherwood ever had believed in miracles, he believed in them no longer. He had no illusions now. He knew exactly what he faced.

His life would come to an end on this uninhabited backwoods planet and there'd be none to mourn him, none to know. Not, he thought, that there would be any mourners, under any circumstances. Although there were those who would be glad to see him, who would come running if they knew where he might be found.

These were people, very definitely, that Sherwood had no desire to see.

His great, one might say his overwhelming, desire not to see them could account in part for his present situation, since he had taken off from the last planet of record without filing flight plans and lacking clearance.

Since no one knew where he might have headed and since his radio was junk, there was no likelihood at all that anyone would find him—even if they looked, which would be a matter of some doubt. Probably the most that anyone would do would be to send out messages to other planets to place authorities on the alert for him.

And since his spaceship, for the lack of a certain valve for which he had no replacement, was not going anywhere, he was stuck here on this planet.

If that had been all there had been to it, it might not have been so bad. But there was a final irony that under other circumstances (if it had been happening to someone else, let's say), would have kept Sherwood in stitches of forthright merriment for hours on end at the very thought of it. But since he was the one involved, there was no merriment.

For now, when he could gain no benefit, he was potentially rich beyond even his own most greedy and most lurid dreams.

On the ridge above the camp he'd set up beside his crippled spaceship lay a strip of clay-cemented conglomerate that fairly reeked with diamonds. They lay scattered on the hillside, washed out by the weather; they were mixed liberally in the gravel of the tiny stream that wended through the valley. They could be picked up by the basket. They were of high quality, there were several, the size of human skulls, that probably were priceless.

Sherwood was of a hardy, rough and tumble breed. Once he became convinced of his situation he made the best of it. He made his camp into a home and laid in supplies—digging roots, gathering nuts, drying fish and making pemmican. If he was to be cast in the role of a Robinson Crusoe, he proposed to be at least comfortable and well fed.

In his spare time he gathered diamonds, dumping them in a pile outside his shack. And in the idle afternoons or the long evenings, he sat beside his campfire and sorted them out—washing them free of clinging dirt and grading them according to their size and brilliance. The very best of them he put into a sack, designed for easy grabbing if the time should ever come when he might depart the planet.

Not that he had any hope this would come about.

Even so, he was a man who planned against contingencies. He always tried to have some sort of loop-hole. Had this not been the case, his career would have ended long before, at any one of a dozen times or places. That it apparently had come to an end now could be attributed to a certain lack of foresight in not carrying a full complement of spare parts. Although perhaps this was understandable, since never before in the history of space flight had that particular valve which now spelled out Sherwood's doom ever misbehaved.

Perhaps it was well for him that he was not an introspective man. If he had been given to much searching thought, he might have found himself living with his past, and there were places in his past that were far from pretty.

He was lucky in many other ways, of course. The planet was not a bad one, a sort of New England planet with a rocky, tumbled terrain, forested by scrubby trees and distinctly terrestrial. He might just as easily have been marooned upon a jungle planet or one of the icy planets or any of another dozen different kinds that were not tolerant of life.

So he settled in and made the best of it and didn't even bother to count off the days. For he knew what he was in for.

He counted on no miracle.

The miracle he had not counted on came late one afternoon as he sat, cross-legged, sorting out his latest haul of priceless diamonds.

The great black ship came in from the east across the rolling hills. It whistled down across the ridges and settled to the ground a short distance from Sherwood's crippled ship and his patched-together shack.

It was no patrol vessel, although in his position, Sherwood would have welcomed even one of these. It was a kind of ship he'd never seen before. It was globular and black and it had no identifying marks on it.

He leaped to his feet and ran toward the ship. He waved his arms in welcome and whooped with his delight. He stopped a hundred feet away when he felt the first whiff of the heat that had been picked up by the vessel's hull in its plunge through atmosphere.

"Hey, in there!" he yelled.

And the ship spoke to him. "You need not yell," it told him. "I can hear you very well."

"Who are you?" asked Sherwood.

"I am the Ship," the voice told him.

"Quit fooling around," yelled Sherwood, "and tell me who you are."

For the sort of answer it had given was foolishness. Of course it was the ship. It was someone in the ship, talking to him through a speaker in the hull.

"I have told you," said the Ship. "I am the Ship."

"But there is someone speaking to me."

"The ship is speaking to you."

"All right, then," said Sherwood. "If you want it that way, it's okay with me. Can you take me out of here? My radio is broken and my ship disabled."

"Perhaps I can," said the Ship. "Tell me who you are."

Sherwood hesitated for a moment, and then he told who he was, quite truthfully. For it suddenly had occurred to him that this ship was as much an outlaw as he was himself. It had no markings and all ships must have markings.

"You say you left your last port without proper clearance?"

"Yes," said Sherwood. "There were certain circumstances."

"And no one knows where you are? No one's looking for you?"

"How could they?" Sherwood asked.

"Where do you want to go?"

"Just anywhere," said Sherwood. "I have no preference."

For even if they should land him somewhere where he had no wish to be, he still would have a running chance. On this planet he had no chance at all.

"All right," said the ship. "You can come aboard."

A hatch came open in the hull and a ladder began running out.

"Just a second," Sherwood shouted. "I'll be right there."

He sprinted to the shack and grabbed his sack of the finest diamonds, then legged it for the ship. He got there almost as soon as the ladder touched the ground.

The hull still was crackling with warmth, but Sherwood swarmed up the ladder, paying no attention.

He was set for life, he thought. Unless—

And then the thought struck him that they might take the diamonds from him. They could pretend it was payment for his passage. Or they could simply take them without an excuse of any sort at all.

But it was too late now. He was almost in the hatch. To drop the sack of diamonds now would do no more than arouse suspicion and would gain him nothing.

It came of greediness, he thought. He did not need this many diamonds. Just a half dozen of the finest dropped into his pockets would have been enough. Enough to buy him another ship so he could return and get a load of them.

But he was committed now. There was nothing he could do except to see it through.

He reached the hatch and tumbled through it. There was no one waiting. The inner lock stood open and there was no one there.

He stopped to stare at the emptiness and behind him the retracting ladder rumbled softly and the hatch hissed to a close.

“Hey,” he shouted, “where is everyone?”

“There is no one here,” the voice said, “but me.”

“All right,” said Sherwood. “Where do I go to find you?”

“You have found me,” said the Ship. “You are standing in me.”

“You mean . . .”

“I told you,” said the Ship. “I said I was the Ship. That is what I am.”

“But no one . . .”

“You do not understand,” said the Ship. “There is no need of anyone. I am myself. I am intelligent. I am part machine, part human. Rather, perhaps, at one time I was. I have thought, in recent years, the two of us have merged so we're neither human nor machine, but something new entirely.”

“You're kidding me,” said Sherwood, beginning to get frightened. “There can't be such a thing.”

“Consider,” said the Ship, “a certain human who had worked for years to build me and who, as he finished me, found death was closing in . . .”

“Let me out!” yelled Sherwood. “Let me out of here! I don't want to be rescued. I don't want . . .”

“I'm afraid, Mr. Sherwood, it is rather late for that. We're already out in space.”

“Out in space! We can't be! It isn't possible!”

“Of course it is,” the Ship told him. “You expected thrust. There was no thrust. We simply lifted.”

“No ship,” insisted Sherwood, “can get off a planet . . .”

“You're thinking, Mr. Sherwood, of the ships built by human hands. Not of a living ship. Not of an intelligent machine. Not of what becomes possible with the merging of a man and a machine.”

“You mean you built yourself?”

"Of course not. Not to start with. I was built by human hands to start with. But I've redesigned myself and rebuilt myself, not once, but many times. I knew my capabilities. I knew my dreams and wishes. I made myself the kind of thing that I was capable of being—not the halfway, makeshift thing that was the best the human race could do."

"The man you spoke of," Sherwood said. "The one who was about to die . . ."

"He is part of me," said the Ship. "If you must think of him as a separate entity, he, then, is talking to you. For when I say 'I,' I mean both of us, for we've become as one."

"I don't get it," Sherwood told the Ship, feeling the panic coming back again.

"He built me, long ago, as a ship which would respond, not to the pushing of a lever or the pressing of a button, but to the mental commands of the man who drove me. I was to become, in effect, an extension of that man. There was a helmet that the man would wear and he'd think into the helmet."

"I understand," said Sherwood.

"He'd think into the helmet and I was so programmed that I'd obey his thoughts. I became, in effect, a man, and the man became in effect the ship he operated."

"Nice deal," Sherwood said enthusiastically, never being one upon whom the niceties of certain advantages were ever lost.

"He finished me and he was about to die and it was a pity that such a one should die—one who had worked so hard to do what he had done. Who'd given up so much. Who never had seen space. Who had gone nowhere."

"No," said Sherwood, in revulsion, knowing what was coming. "No, he'd not done that."

"It was a kindness," said the Ship. "It was what he wanted. He managed it himself. He simply gave up his body. His body was a worthless hulk that was about to die. The modifications to accommodate a human brain rather than a human skull were quite elementary. We have both of us been happy."

Sherwood stood without saying anything. In the silence he was listening for some sound, for any kind of tiny rattle or hum, for anything at all to tell him the ship was operating. But there was no sound and no sense of motion of any sort.

"Happy," he said. "Where would you have found happiness? What's the point of all this?"

"That," the Ship said solemnly, "is a bit hard to explain."

Sherwood stood and thought about it—the endless voyaging through space without a body—with all the desires, all the advantages, all the capabilities of a body gone forever.

"There is nothing for you to fear," said the Ship. "You need not concern yourself. We have a cabin for you. Just down the corridor, the first door to your left."

"I thank you," Sherwood said, although he was nervous still.

If he had had a choice, he told himself, he'd stayed back on the planet. But since he was here, he'd have to make the best of it. And there were, he admitted to himself, certain advantages and certain possibilities that needed further thought.

He went down the corridor and pushed on the door. It opened on the cabin. For a spaceship it looked comfortable enough. A little cramped, of course, but then all cabins were. Space is at a premium on any sort of ship.

He went in and placed his sack of diamonds on the bunk that hinged out from the wall. He sat down in the single metal chair that stood beside the bunk.

"Are you comfortable, Mr. Sherwood?" asked the Ship.

"Very comfortable," he said.

It was going to be all right, he told himself. A very crazy setup, but it would be all right. Perhaps a little spooky and a bit hard to believe, but probably better, after all, than staying marooned, back there on the planet. For this would not last forever. And the planet could have been, most probably would have been, forever.

It would take a while to reach another planet, for space was rather sparsely populated in this area. There would be time to think and plan. He might be able to work out something that would be to his great advantage.

He leaned back in the chair and stretched out his legs. His brain began to click in a ceaseless scurrying back and forth, nosing from every angle all the possibilities that existed in this setup.

It was nice, he thought—this entire operation. The Ship undoubtedly had figured out some angles for itself which no human yet had thought of.

There were a lot of things to do. He'd have to learn the capabilities of the Ship and give close study to its personality, seeking out its weak points and its strength. Then he'd have to plan his strategy and be careful not to give away his thinking. He must not move until he was entirely ready.

There might be many ways to do it. There might be flattery or there might be a business proposition or there might be blackmail. He'd have to think on it and study and follow out the line of action that seemed to be the best.

He wondered at the Ship's means of operation. Anti-gravity, perhaps. Or a fusion chamber. Or perhaps some method which had not been so far considered as a source of power.

He got up from the chair and paced, three paces across the room and back, restlessly pondering odds.

Yes, he thought, it would be a nice kind of ship to have. More than likely there was nothing in all of space that could touch it in speed and maneuverability. Nothing that could overhaul it should he ever have to run. It could apparently set down anywhere. It was probably self-repairing, for the Ship had spoken of redesigning and of rebuilding itself. With the memory of his recent situation still fresh inside his mind, this was comforting.

There must be a way to get the Ship, he told himself. There had to be a way to get it. It was something that he needed.

He could buy another ship, of course; with the diamonds in the sacking he could buy a fleet of ships. But this was the one he wanted.

Maybe it had been pure luck this Ship had picked him up. For any other legal ship would probably turn him over to the authorities at its next port of call, but this Ship didn't seem to mind who he was or what his record might be. Any other ship that was not entirely legal would have grabbed off, not only the diamonds that he had but his discovery of the diamond field. But this particular Ship had no concern with diamonds.

What a setup, he thought. A human brain and a spaceship tied together, so closely tied together that their identities had merged. He shivered at the thought of it, for it was a gruesome thing.

Although perhaps it had not meant too much to that old man who was about to die. He had traded an aged and death-marked body for many years of life. Perhaps life as a part of a space-traveling machine was better than no life at all.

How many years, he wondered, had it been since that old man had translated himself into something else than human? A hundred? Five hundred? Perhaps even more than that.

In those years where had he been and what might he have seen? And, most pertinent of all, what thoughts had run through and congealed and formed within his mind? What was life like for him? Not a human sort of life, of course, not a human viewpoint, but something else entirely.

Sherwood tried to imagine what it might be like, but gave up in dismay. It would necessarily be a negation of everything he lived for—all the sensual pleasure, all the dreams of gain and glory, all the neat behavior patterns he had set up for himself, all his self-made rules of conduct, and of conscience.

A miracle, he thought. As a matter of fact, there'd been two miracles. The first had been when he had been able to set his ship down without a crackup when the valve had failed. He had come in close above the planet's surface to find a place to land—and suddenly the valve went out and the engine failed and there he'd been, plunging down above the rough terrain. Then suddenly he had glimpsed a place where a landing might be just barely possible and had fought the controls madly to hit that certain spot and finally had hit it—alive.

It had been a miracle that he had made the landing; and the coming of the Ship to rescue him had been the second miracle.

The bunk dropped down flat against the wall and his sack of diamonds was dumped onto the floor.

"Hey, what goes on?" yelled Sherwood. Then he wished he had not yelled, for it was quite clear exactly what had happened. The support that held the bunk had not been snapped properly into place and had given way, letting down the bunk.

"Something wrong, Mr. Sherwood?" asked the Ship.

"No, not a thing," said Sherwood. "My bunk fell down. I guess it startled me."

He bent down to pick up the diamonds. As he did, the chair quietly and efficiently slid back against the wall, folded itself up and slid into a slight depression that exactly fitted it.

Squatted to pick up the diamonds, Sherwood watched the chair in horrified fascination, then swiftly spun around. The bunk no longer hung against the wall, also had fitted itself into another niche.

Cold fear speared into Sherwood. He rose swiftly to his feet, turning like a man at bay. He stood in a bare cubicle. With both the bunk and chair retracted, he stood within four bare walls.

He sprang toward the door and there wasn't any door. There was only wall.

He staggered back into the center of the cubicle and spun around to view each wall in turn. There was no door in any of the walls. The metal went up from floor to ceiling without a single break.

The walls began to move, closing in on him, sliding in, retracting.

He watched, incredulous, frozen, thinking that perhaps he'd imagined the moving of the walls.

But it was not imagination. Slowly, inexorably, the walls were closing in. Had he put out his arms, he could have touched them on either side of him.

"Ship!" he said, fighting to keep his voice calm.

"Yes, Mr. Sherwood."

"You are malfunctioning. The walls are closing in."

"No," said the Ship. "No malfunction, I assure you. A very proper function. My brain grows tired and feeble. It is not the body only—the brain also has its limits. I suspected that it might, but I could not know. There was a chance, of course, that separated from the poison of a body, it might live in its bath of nutrients forever."

"No!" rasped Sherwood, his breath strangling in this throat. "No, not me!"

"Who else?" asked the Ship. "I have searched for years and you are the first who fitted."

"Fitted!" Sherwood screamed.

"Why, of course," the Ship said calmly, happily. "A man who would not be missed. No one knowing where you were. No one hunting for you. No one who will miss you. I had hunted for someone like you and had despaired of finding one. For I am humane. I would cause no one grief or sadness."

The walls kept closing in.

The Ship seemed to sigh in metallic contentment.

"Believe me, Mr. Sherwood," it said, "finding you was a very miracle."

RIM OF THE DEEP

Clifford D. Simak's few surviving journals do not make it clear just when he wrote this story; but the fact that he sent it to John W. Campbell Jr., the relatively new editor of Astounding Science Fiction, *in September 1939 suggests he may have begun writing it soon after June 16 of that year, when he ended the nomadic stage of his newspaper career by joining the staff of Minnesota's* Minneapolis Star *(and I speculate that the fact that Cliff found himself working downtown in the biggest city he had ever lived or worked in, along with several years of listening to the radio plays so often broadcast across the country in the evenings, led him to the unusual "gangster" style he used in this and a few other stories written during this period).*

Campbell bought the story for $125, and it appeared in the May 1940 issue of his magazine.

Like other Simak stories from that era, the efforts of private commerce, in this case to colonize the ocean floors, and a secret incursion from outer space, seem not to lead anyone to think about getting the government involved—to modern eyes that seems unthinkable, but clearly, Cliff, product of rural American life in the early Twentieth Century, had not thought of society going in that direction . . . after all, World War II had not yet begun.

Cliff used a lot of his favorite devices in his story: the name of his protagonist, Grant, was used more frequently than any other name in Cliff's stories (it happened to have been the name of the Wiscon-

sin country in which Cliff was born). Grant is a newspaperman (in fact, he works for the Evening Rocket, *a newspaper prominent in a number of stories Cliff wrote during that period); and Grant names the paper's copyboy as "Lightnin'," a hoary piece of newspaper humor than never fails to make me smile . . .*

—dww

The Rat slouched into the Venus Flower and over to the table where Grant Nagle was settling down to the serious business of getting drunk.

The newspaperman eyed the Rat with unconcealed loathing. But the Rat didn't seem to mind. He pushed his cap farther over his left eye and talked out of the corner of his mouth, his words hissing out alongside the smoke-trickling cigarette.

"I got a message for you," he declared.

"Let's have it," said Grant. "Then get the hell out of my sight."

"Hellion Smith is loose," said the Rat.

Grant started, but his face didn't change. He stared at the other icily and said nothing.

"He left word two years ago," explained the Rat, "that when he cracked the crib I was to bring you a message. I'm bringing it, see?"

"Yes?"

"It was this. Hellion said he was going to get you. Himself, personal, see? Some of us boys offered to do the job for him, but he said no, he was saving you for himself. The chief is funny that way."

"Why?" asked Grant.

The question took the Rat by surprise. His cigarette drooped suddenly, almost fell from his mouth. His watery eyes blinked. But he recovered his composure and hunched farther across the table.

"That's a funny question, Nagle. Funny question for you to be asking. When you put the chief out in the Alcatraz of Ganymede."

"I didn't put him there," said the newsman. "All if did was write a story. That's my job. I found out Hellion was hiding on Ceres with a bunch of assorted cutthroats, waiting for the heat to let up. And I wrote a story about it. Can I help it if the police read the *Evening Rocket?"*

The Rat eyed the reporter furtively.

"You're smart, Nagle," he said. "Too damn smart. Someday you'll write yourself into a jam you can't get out of. Maybe you done that already."

"Look here," asked Grant, "why did the chief send you around? Why didn't he come himself? If Hellion's got business with me, he knows where he can find me."

"He can't come now," said the Rat. "He's got to lay low for a while. And this time he's got a place where no snooping reporter is going to find him."

"Rat," warned Grant coldly, "someday you're going to talk yourself into a jam. I don't know what your game is, but it is a game of some sort. Because Hellion can't get out of the prison on Ganymede. No man ever has gotten out of it. When a man goes there, he stays there. When he come out he's either served his sentence or he comes out feet first. Nobody escapes from Ganymede."

The Rat smiled bleakly, drew a paper from his hip pocket and spread it on the table. It was an *Evening Rocket,* the ink still damp.

The banner screamed:

HELLION ESCAPES

"That," said the Rat, tapping the paper, "should tell you what the score is. I ain't talking through my hat."

Grant stared at the paper. It was the five-star edition, the final for the day. And there it was in black and white. Hellion Smith had escaped from the impregnable Alcatraz on the airless, bitter, frigid plains of Ganymede. A mauve-tinted likeness of Hellion's ugly mug stared back at him from the page.

"So what you told me is true," said Grant softly. "Hellion has really escaped. And the message is the goods."

"When Hellion says something he means it," sneered the Rat.

"So do I," declared Grant grimly. "And I got a message for you to take back to Hellion, if you can find hm. You tell him I only did my duty as a newspaperman before—nothing personal about it at all. But if he comes messing around again I'll take a sort of interest in him. I'll really put some heart into it, you understand. You tell Hellion that if he tries to carry out his threat I'll rip him up by the roots and crucify him."

The Rat stared at him with watery eyes.

Grant lifted the bottle off the table and filled his glass.

"Get the hell out of here!" he roared at the man across the table. "Just looking at you makes me want to gag."

The copy boy found Grant at the table, twirling the liquor in his glass. He shuffled across the floor toward him.

Grant looked up and recognized him. "Hello, Lightnin'. Have a snort."

Lightnin' shook his head. "I can't. The boss sent me to get you. He wants to see you."

"He did, did he?" asked Grant. "Well, you go back and tell the boss I'm busy. Tell him I can't be bothered. Tell him to cover over and see me if he's in a rush."

Lightin' scuffed his feet uneasily, caught between two fires.

"It's important," he persisted.

"Hell," said Grant. "There's nothing important. Sit down, Lightnin', and rest your feet."

"Look," said Lightnin', pleadingly, "if you don't come, the boss will give me hell. He said not to let you talk me out of it."

"Oh, well," said Grant. He tossed off the liquor and pocketed the bottle.

"Lead on, Lightnin'," he said.

On the street outside the mechanical newsboys blatted their cries.

"Hellion Smith escapes. Hellion Smith escapes from Ganymede. Police baffled."

"They're always baffled," said Grant.

Soft lights glowed in the gathering dusk. Smoothly operating street traffic slid silently along. Overhead the air lanes murmured softly. The city skyline was a blaze of vivid color.

Arthur Hart beamed at Grant. "I got a little assignment lined up for you," he said. "One that will be a sort of vacation. You've been working hard and I thought a change might do you good."

"Go on," said Grant. "Go on and give it to me both barrels. When bad news is coming I like to meet it face to face. The last time you got all bloated up with kindness you sent me off to Venus and I spent two months there, smelling those stinking seas, wading around in swamps, interviewing those damn fish men."

"It was a good idea," Hart protested. "There was every reason to believe—still is—that the Venusians are a damn sight smarter than we think they are. They have big cities built down under those seas and just because they've never told us they didn't have spaceships is no reason to believe they haven't. For all we know, they may have visited Earth long before Earthmen flew to Venus."

"It's all over now," said Grant, "but it still sounds screwy to me. What is it this time? Mars or Venus?"

"Neither one," said Hart smoothly. "This time it really will be a little vacation jaunt. Down to sea bottom. I got it all fixed up. You'll take a sub tonight down to Coral City and from there you'll go to Deep End."

"Deep End!" Grant protested. "That's the jumping-off place. Right on the rim of the deep."

"Sure," snapped Hart. "What's wrong with that?"

Grant shook his head sadly. "I don't like it. I'm a claustrophobiac. Can't stand being shut up in a room. And down there you got to wear steel armor. Take Coral City, now. That's not a bad place. Only a couple hundred feet under and you meet nice people."

"Nice bars, too," suggested Hart.

"Bet your neck there are," Grant agreed. "Now, I could go for a couple of weeks in Coral City."

"You'll go for Deep End, too," declared Hart grimly.

Grant shrugged wearily, felt the comforting bulge of the bottle in his pocket.

"All right," he said. "What's the brainstorm this time?"

"There's some sort of trouble down there on The Bottom," said Hart. "Rumors, unconfirmed reports, nothing we've been able to get our teeth into. Seems the glass and quartz used in suits and domes hasn't been standing up. There have been tragedies. Entire communities wiped out. A story here, a story there, over the period of months, from all parts of The Bottom. You've read them yourself. Inquiries that have gotten nowhere."

"Forget it," said Grant. "That's only what's to be expected. Any damn fool that goes down a half mile underwater and lives under a quartz dome is asking for trouble. When it comes he hasn't got anybody but himself to blame. When you go monkeying around with pressures amounting to thousands of pounds per square inch you're fooling around with dynamite."

"But the point," said Hart, "is that every catastrophe so far reported has occurred where one manufacturer's quartz is being used. Snider quartz. You've heard of it."

"Sure," said Grant, unimpressed, "but that don't add up to anything. Most of the quartz used down there is Snider stuff. It's no secret Snider has a pull with the Underocean Colonization Board." He looked at Hart squarely. "You aren't figuring on sending me out on a one-man crusade against Snider quartz, are you?"

Hart stirred uneasily.

"Not exactly," he parried. "You won't be working alone. The *Evening Rocket* will be behind you."

"Behind me is right," snorted Grant. "A long ways behind. A hell of a lot of good the *Evening Rocket* will do me if I get into a jam a half mile down."

Hart tilted forward in his chair. "The point is this," he said. "If we can find there's something wrong with Snider quartz, we'll put the heat on Snider. And if we find the UCB has been winking at Snider stuff when they know it's wrong, we'll have them across the barrel, too."

"What a sweet nature you have," said Grant. "The sort of a guy that would send his old grandma to the gallows for a ninety-six-point streamer."

"We have a duty to the public," said Hart solemnly, looking almost like an owl. "It's our duty to work for the common good of mankind."

"And for the good of the dear old *Evening Rocket,"* said Grant. "Up goes the circulation list. Full-page ads telling the readers how we exposed the dirty crooks. And maybe, after we smack Snider quartz flat, there'll be another quartz company just dying to insert about a million bucks' worth of advertising in our columns."

"It isn't that," snarled Hart, "and you know it isn't." He became oratorical. "Out there is a great empire to be conquered. The ocean bottom. An area two and one half times as great as all the land areas on the Earth. A great new frontier. We've made a start at conquering it. Out there are pioneers—"

Grant waved him to silence. "I know," he said. "Vast riches. Great fields for exploitation. A heritage for the future. I know it. But save it for an editorial."

Hart leaned back in his chair. "The latest reports of quartz failure come from the rim of the Puerto Rico deep," he said. "You job will be to find what's in the cards."

"I warn you," said Grant. "When I get back from this one I'm going to get drunk and stay drunk for a month."

Hart reached into his desk and drew out an envelope. "Your tickets for the sub," he said. "The bank at Coral City will have instructions to let you draw expenses."

"O.K.," said Grant. "I'll catch you an octopus for a pet."

* * *

The water was blue, shading to violet—a dusky blue like the deeper shade of twilight but still with a faintly luminous quality about it. Long ago the more showy seaweed beds had been left behind and the character of the sea bed had changed. No more beautiful stretches of sand with vegetation and fishes of unearthly colors, delicate and shifting. No more waving sea plumes or golden sea fans. No more unbelievable brilliancy of color.

Now one seemed to be moving into the maws of night. The blue of the water deepened and blurred only a short distance away and even the powerful light of the underwater tank penetrated for only a hundred yards or so.

There was muck underneath, muck and ooze that was deepening as Grant followed the contour of the bottom down toward the deep. Once the tank floundered into a muck trap with its treads spinning helplessly, and he had been forced to use the retractable gear to lift it out—the gear acting like legs, searching for and getting solid footing, heaving the massive tank along.

The character and pattern of life was changing down here, too. Changing to a grimmer pattern—a more ferocious, unrelenting life.

A thing, that was little more than a living mouth, swam across the vision panel, turned back, pressing its blunt face against the glass, mighty mouth agape, wicked fangs shining. A dark shape slithered by, just outside the beam of light.

Grant dropped his eyes to the instruments. Five hundred and fifty feet down. Pressure two hundred fifty-three pounds per square inch.

The other instruments were shivering slightly, but all read correctly. Everything was going fine.

Grant wiped perspiration from his face. "Running this damn tub gets on my nerves," he told himself, but instantly was reassured with the thought of the massive steel walls, constructed to maintain a maximum of resistance to buckling and bending, of the ports of shatter-proof quartz, laminated, one with the rest of the construction.

But quartz sometimes didn't stand up—that was what had brought him here. Quartz sometimes went haywire and when it did men died, men who had put their trust in it—men who otherwise could not have hurled their challenge into the teeth of The Bottom with its chilly depths, its monstrous pressure.

The thing that was all mouth had retreated from the vision glass, but another nightmare of the twilight zone had replaced it—a grotesque thing that resembled nothing that ever should have lived.

Grant cursed at it—swung the spotlight back and forth, trying to pick out landmarks. But there was nothing—he was moving across what appeared to be a murky plain, although the indicator showed it had a decided downward slope.

Down there, somewhere ahead, was the Puerto Rico deep, one of the deepest—five and a half miles down. Down there the pressure ranged around six and a half tons a square inch. Too deep for man as yet. Conquest under the four-mile mark would have to await work in the industrial laboratories, would have to wait on man's ingenuity to build steel and glass that was a little stronger, man's ability to design new engineering kinks that would give greater strength—or perhaps the construction of a force screen or some other approach as yet merely speculative.

Grant studied his chart. He had kept the course the communications-bureau back at Deep End had outlined for him, but as yet there was no sign of the man he sought. Old Gus, they called him, and it seemed he was a sort of local legend.

"A queer old coot," the dapper little communications-bureau head had told him. "Depth dippy, I guess. He's been out there for years, prospecting, fooling around. Couldn't make him leave now. The Bottom gets in your blood, I guess, if you stay there long enough."

Grant swept the light back and forth again, but still there was nothing.

Half an hour later the light picked up the dome crouched under a sudden upsoaring of black rock, rising abruptly from the sea floor.

Running the tank in close to the cliff, Grant stopped it and entered the airlock.

Clambering into the mechanical suit, he tightened the lock and slid into the small operator's chamber with its nightmare of controls. Clumsily, as yet unused to the operation of the suit, he opened the outer lock control.

Outside it was easier and the suit ambled jerkily along, shaking him at every stride. He was within only a short distance of the dome when a shadow detached itself from the cliff and dropped upon him. Grant felt the thud of its impact, saw waving tentacles crawl across the plate, white gristle suction cups seeking to get a hold.

"An octopus," said Grant disgustedly.

The cephalopod threshed wildly, swinging its tentacles in mighty swipes and then slid off the suit, landing in front of it, hopping to one side. A moment later it scuttled out of the twilit gloom and humped along ahead of Grant.

"I'd like to take a swift kick at you," Grant told the octopus, "but if I did, I'd lose my balance sure as hell, and a fellow would have to be a magician to get one of these tin cans right side up if it fell over."

The octopus was a monster. His body was as big as a good-sized watermelon and his eight tentacles would have spanned close to twenty feet.

A suited figure was emerging from the air lock of the dome and Grant shoved a lever to swing his suit's arm in greeting. The arm of the other suit raised in reply and hurried toward him.

The octopus galloped forward, raising a cloud of murk in its path, and launched itself at the other suit. An expert arm flashed out and warded it off. Steel fingers closed on a tentacle and the suit marched forward, hauling a protesting, squirming octopus along by one of its eight long arms.

"Howdy, stranger," said the man inside the advancing suit. "Glad you happened along."

Grant spoke into his transmitter.

"Glad to see you, too. I was looking for a man named Gus. Maybe you're him."

"Sure am," said the other. "I suppose Butch jumped on you."

"Butch?" asked Grant, bewildered.

"Sure, Butch. Butch is my octopus. Raised him from a pup. Used to sit around inside the dome with me until he got too big and I had to shut him out. He still tries to sneak in on me every now and then."

Butch squatted to one side, his tentacle still clutched in the steel hand of his master's suit. His eyes seemed to glint in the deep blue water.

"Sometimes," Old Gus went on, "he gets kind of gay and I've got to trim him down to his natural size. But he's a pretty good octopus just the same."

"You mean," asked Grant, slightly horrified, "you keep the thing for a pet."

"Sure," declared Gus. "Safe enough as long as he can't get at you. Another fellow up north a ways had one and he kind of noised it around his octopus could lick anything that swam, so I took Butch and went up to see him. That, stranger, was a brawl worth seeing. But Butch had it all over that other octopus. Polished him off inside of fifteen minutes and then wouldn't give up the corpse. Lugged it around for days, taking lunches off of it."

"Sort of a tough citizen," suggested Grant.

"Butch," said Old Gus pridefully, "can be downright ornery when he takes a mind to be."

Old Gus talked as he brewed the coffee. "A man gets sort of lonesome down here once in a while," he explained, "and you like some company, even if it ain't nothing but a thing like Butch. Sharks, now, are downright friendly once you get to know them, but they ain't no account as pets. They wander too much. You never know where they are. But octopuses are home bodies. Butch lairs out in the cliff back there and comes a-humping every time he sees me."

"How long have you been here?" asked Grant.

"Only four or five years here," said Gus. "Used to live up around three hundred feet, but when they put out this improved quartz I moved down here. Like it better. But, all in all, I been living on The Bottom for nigh onto forty years. Last time I was up on the surface I got a terrible headache. Too many bright colors. Greens and blues and reds and yellows. All you get down here is blue, more of a violet really. It's restful."

The coffeepot sent out tantalizing odors. The electrolysis plant chuckled. The heat grids sang softly.

Outside the dome, Butch squatted dolefully.

"This a Snider dome?" asked Grant.

"Yep," said Gus. "Set me back a couple thousand bucks. And then I had to pay to get it hauled down here. Thought I could do it with my old tub, but it was too risky."

"I hear some of the Snider domes aren't working out too well," said Grant. "Breaking down under pressure. Maybe something wrong with their construction."

The old man lifted the coffeepot off the stove, poured coffee into the cups.

"There's been a lot of failures," he said, "but I ain't had no trouble. Don't think it's the fault of the glass at all. Something else. Something funny about it. Some of the boys around here have been talking of getting up a vigilante party."

Grant had his cup half lifted to his lips, but set it down suddenly. "Vigilante party?" he asked. "Why a vigilante party?"

Old Gus leaned across the table, lowered his voice dramatically. "Ever hear of Robber's Deep?" he asked.

"No," said Grant. "I don't believe I ever have."

The old man settled back. "A little over a half mile down," he declared. "A sort of little depression. Bad country. Too rough for tanks. Got to go on foot to reach it."

He sipped the steaming coffee noisily, wiped his whiskers with a horny hand.

Grant waited, sipping his own coffee. Butch, he saw, was swarming up the dome's curving side.

"There's been too dang many robberies," said Old Gus. "Too much helling around. This country is getting sort of civilized now and we ain't going to stand for it much longer."

"You think there's a gang of robbers down in that deep?" asked Grant.

"That's the only place they could be," said Gus. "It's bad country and hard to get around in. Lots of caves and a couple of canyons that run down to the Big Deep. Dozens of places where a gang could hide."

Gus sipped gustily at the coffee. "It used to be right peaceable down here," he mourned. "A man could find him a bed of clams and post the place and know it was his. Nobody would touch it. Or you could stake out a radium workings and know that your stakes wouldn't be pulled up. And if you found an old ship you just slapped up a notice on it saying you had found it and nobody would take so much as a single plank away. But it ain't that way no more. There's been a lot of claim jumping and clam beds have been robbed. We kind of figure we'll have to put a stop to it."

"Look," said Grant, "the *Evening Rocket* sent me out here to find out why so many domes were failing—why there were so many catastrophes on The Bottom. You tell me robbers are responsible—desperadoes of the deep. Would they go to the length of smashing a man's dome to get what little treasure he might have inside?"

Old Gus snorted. "Why not?" he asked. "Up on the surface your thugs kill a man, shoot him down in cold blood, to get the little money he might have in his pocket. Down here there are fortunes in some of the domes. Radium and pearls and priceless treasure salvaged from old wrecks."

Grant nodded. "I suppose so. But it's not only here it's happening. Domes are failing all over. On all parts of The Bottom."

"I don't know about them other places," said Old Gun brusquely, "but I know out here most of the failures ain't the fault of the glass. It's the fault of a bunch of thieving cutthroats and it keeps on we'll sure make them hard to catch."

The old man sloshed the last of the coffee down his throat and rattled the cup down on the table. "I got a bed of clams posted not very far from here and if them fellows get into that bed I'll just naturally go on the warpath all by myself."

He stopped and looked at Grant. "Say," he asked, "have you ever seen a real clam bed?"

Grant shook his head.

"If you can stay," said Old Gus, "I'll show you one tomorrow that'll make your eyes pop. Some of them five feet across, and if one old girl is open I'll show you a pearl as big as your hat. It isn't quite as perfect as it should be yet, but given a little more time it will be. The old girl is working on it and I'm watching it. But I haven't been over there for a month or so."

He shook his head. "I sure hope them Robber's Deep fellows ain't found her," he said. "If they ever touch that pearl I'm going to declare me a war right then and there."

Butch lolloped happily along ahead of them, soaring awkwardly over occasional boulders and making furtive side trips into the deep-blue darkness on either side.

"Just like a dog," said Old Gus. "He gets cantankerous at times and I have to give him a good whaling to cool him down, but he seems to like me anyhow. But to anyone but me he's meaner than poison. That's his nature and he can't help it."

They plodded on. Grant was having less difficulty working his suit.

"The clam bed," said Old Gus, "is just up this way a piece. Robber's Deep is down in that direction." He swung his arm toward the down slope, half turning his suit. He did not turn back again. "Nagle"—his voice was a husky whisper—"I don't remember ever seeing that before."

Grant turned and through the haze of the water he saw a queer formation, a shady thing rising out of the ocean bed.

"What is it?" he asked. "It looks—Damned if it don't look almost like a piece of machinery."

"I don't know," said Gus softly, "but, by the good Lord Harry, we're going to find out."

They moved forward slowly, cautiously. Grant felt an unaccountable prickling at the back of his neck—an eerie sense of danger.

Butch gamboled ahead of them. Suddenly he stopped, stood stiff-legged, almost bristling. He pranced forward a few steps and waved his tentacles. Then he became a bundle of unseemly rage, rushing about, his eyes red, his body color changing from black to pink, to violet and finally to a dull brick-red.

"Butch sure has got his dander up," said Old Gus, half fearfully.

The octopus ceased his demonstration of rage almost as suddenly as it had started and headed straight for the hazy mass before them. Old Gus broke into a sprint and Grant followed.

The towering mass was machinery, Grant saw. Two great cylinders standing close together, with a massive squat machine between them, connected to both of the cylinders by heavy pipes.

The muck and ooze had been scraped away for some distance around the cylinders and machine, probably to make way for secure anchorage, and a mighty hole had been blasted in the seabed rock.

There was no sign of life around the cylinders or the machine, but the machine was operating.

Butch reached the cylinders and whipped around them and the next instant something that looked like a merman shot out from behind the cylinders, with Butch in close pursuit.

The manlike thing flashed through the water with astonishing ease, but Butch was out for blood. With a tremendous burst of speed he drew nearer to the fleeing thing, launched his body in a great leap and closed in, tentacles flailing.

Old Gus was running now, yelling at the octopus. "Damn you, Butch; you stop that!"

But, by the time Grant reached them, it was all over. Old Gus, still furious, was prying an angry Butch from his prey, which the octopus still held in the death-grip of his tentacles.

"Someday," Old Gus was saying, "I'm going to plumb lose patience with you, Butch."

But Butch wasn't worrying much about that. His one thought at the moment was to retain the choice morsel he had picked up. He clung stubbornly, but finally Gus hauled him loose. He tried to charge in again, but Gus booted him away and at that he withdrew, squatting at the base of one of the cylinders, fairly jigging with rage.

Grant was staring down at the thing on the bare rock. "Gus," he said, "do you know what this is?"

"Danged if I do," said Gus. "I've heard of mermen and mermaids, but I never did set no stock by them. I been roaming these ocean beds for nigh forty years and I never seen one yet." He moved close, touched the body with the toe of his suit. "But," he declared, "this is the spitting image of those old pictures of them."

"That," said Grant, "is a Venusian. A native of Venus. A fish man. The boss sent me to Venus a couple years ago to find out what I could about them. He had a screwy idea they were further advanced in science than they ever let the Earth people suspect.

But I couldn't do much about it, for it would be sheer suicide for a man to venture into a Venusian sea. The seas are unstable chemically. Always with more or less acid—lots of chlorine. They stink like hell, but these fellows seem to like it. The acid and pressure and chemical changes don't seem to harm them and maybe the stink smells good to them."

"If this is a Venusian, how did he get here?" asked Gus suspiciously.

"I don't know," said Grant, "but I aim to find out. To my knowledge a Venusian has never visited Earth. They can stand almost any pressure under the water, but they don't like open air, even the Venusian air and that's half water most of the time."

"Maybe you're mistaken," suggested Gus. "Maybe this ain't a Venusian but something almost like one."

Grant shook his head behind the plate. "No, I'm not mistaken. There are too many identifying marks. Look at the gills—feathered. And the hide. Almost like steel. Really a shell—an outside skeleton."

The newsman turned around and stared at the cylinders, then shifted his gaze to the machine squatting between them. It was operating smoothly and silently. Several large blocks of stone lay in front of it, and several similar blocks protruded from a hopperlike arrangement which surmounted the machine. The dangling jaws of a crane showed how the blocks had been lifted into the hopper. To one side of the machine were a number of small jugs.

"Gus," Grant asked, "what kind of rock is this?"

The old man scooped up a couple of splinters and held them before his vision glass. The suit's spotlight caught the splinters and they blazed with sudden moving light.

"Fluorite," said Gus. "Crystals embedded all through this stuff." He flung the splinters away. "The rock itself," he said, "is old; older than hell. Probably Archean."

"You're sure about the fluorite?" asked Grant.

"Sure, it's fluorite," sputtered the old man. "The rock is lousy with it. You find lots of it on The Bottom. Lots of old rock here, and that's where you find it mostly."

Grant dismissed the subject of the rock and turned his attention to the engine and the tanks. The engine seemed simple in its operation—little more than a piston and a wheel—but it seemed without controls and it ran without visible source of power.

The hopper was a hopper and that was all. Across its throat flashed a ripple of fiery flame that ate swiftly at the block of stone, breaking it up and feeding it into the maw of the machine below.

Grant rapped against one of the tanks with his steel fist and it gave back a dead clicking sound unlike the ring of steel.

"Would you know what those tanks are made of?" he demanded of Gus.

The old man shook his head. "It's got me all bogged down," he confessed. "I seen some funny things in forty years down here, but nothing like this. A Venusian feeding rock into a machine of some sort. It just don't add up."

"It adds up to a hell of a lot more than we think," said Grant gravely.

He picked up one of the jugs and rapped it. It gave back the same clicking sound. Carefully he worked the stopper out and from the neck of the jug spouted a puff of curling, deadly-appearing greenish yellow. Swiftly he jabbed the stopper in again and stepped back quickly.

"What is that stuff?" Gus shrieked at him, his blue eyes wide behind the plate of quartz.

"Hydrofluoric acid," said Grant, a strange tenseness in his voice. "The only acid known that will attack glass!"

"Well, I be damned," said Old Gus weakly. "Well, I be damned."

"Gus," said Grant, "I won't be able to look at those clams today. I've got to get back to Deep End. I have a message to send."

Gus looked gravely at the cylinders, at the body of the Venusian. "Yes, I guess you have," he said.

"Maybe you'd like to go with me. I'll come right back again."

Gus shook his head. "Nope, I'll stick around. But you might bring me back a couple pounds of coffee and some sugar."

Out of the twilit waters came a charging black streak. It was Butch. He had made a flanking movement and now was coming in to get the dead Venusian.

His strategy succeeded. Gus rushed at him roaring, but Butch, hugging the body, squirted himself upward at a steep angle and disappeared.

Gus shook a fist after him.

"Someday," he yelped, "I'll give that danged octopus a trimming down that he'll remember."

Hart had been wrong, apparently, about the Snider glass, but he had been right, that time before, about the Venusians. For there could be no doubt of it. The Venusians were coming to Earth—might have been coming to Earth these many years, roaring down out of the sky in their ships, diving into the ocean, their natural habitat—quietly taking over Earth's oceans without making any sort of fuss.

And then Man, pressed by economic necessity, by the love of adventure, by the lure of wealth, spurred on by scientific and engineering developments, had invaded the sea himself. For centuries he had ridden on it and flown over it, and now he had walked into it, embarking upon the last great venture, invading the last frontier little old Earth had to offer.

Strange tales of flashing things that dropped into the sea—strange reports of mystery planes sighted in midocean, planes that had a strange look about them. Planes tearing upward into space or dropping like a flash into the water. For years those reports had been heard—way back in the twentieth century—even in some instances in the nineteenth century, when planes were yet a thing unheard of.

And tales much older yet—tales from antiquity—from the old days when men first pushed outward from the shore, talks of mermaids and mermen.

Could the Venusians have been coming to Earth for all these centuries? Quietly, unobtrusively dropping out of space—perhaps carrying on a lucrative trade for many years with treasures snatched from Earth's ocean beds. Perhaps even now there were many Venusian colonies planted on The Bottom. That could easily be so, for Man as yet had only started his exploitation of the sea beds. His health and tourist resorts, his sea farms and oil fields, his floral gardens and mines only fringed the continental shelves, and at no point was The Bottom thickly settled. A few depth-dippy coots like Old Gus, spending their lives on The Bottom, caught by the mystic love of its silences and weird mystery, had pushed ever deeper and deeper, but they were few. The Bottom, to all intent and purpose, was still a wilderness. In that wilderness might be many colonies of Venusians.

Grant Nagle pondered the matter as he headed his tank back into the depths from Deep End, back to Old Gus' dome.

He chuckled as he remembered the result of his visaphone call to Hart.

He could imagine Hart now—cussing up and down the office, ripping things wide open, laying down the law to Washington. By nightfall Hart would have every government submarine in the entire world combing the ocean bottoms.

Combing the ocean bottoms to ferret out Venusians and their deadly little chemical plants where they were manufacturing hydrofluoric acid.

Maybe they didn't mean anything by manufacturing the acid. Maybe it was for some perfectly innocent purpose of their own. But the fact that hydrofluoric acid was the only acid known to have an effect on glass, the fact that quartz domes had been failing all tied up too neatly to be disregarded.

After all, wouldn't that be the logical way for the Venusians to proceed if they wished to keep the oceans for themselves. If they wished to drive Earthmen from the beds of their own seas, how better might they do it than by making Earthmen fear the sea, by destroying their confidence in the quartz that made possible domes and submarines and tanks and underwater suits? Without quartz man would be practically helpless on The Bottom, for quartz was the eyes of men down here. In time to come, of course, television could be worked out so that quartz would be unnecessary, but that would be an unsatisfactory substitute—indirect sight instead of direct sight.

And if the worst came to worst, might it not be possible that the Venusians, with their chemical factories, might entirely alter the chemical content of the oceans? The material lay at hand. Fluorite for hydrogen fluoride. Most of the compounds in the oceans' waters were chlorides—simple to juggle them chemically. Vast deposits of manganese.

Grant shuddered to think of the witches' broth that well-directed chemical effort might stir up in these depths. A great job, truly—but not impossible—especially when one considered the Venusians might have developed chemical treatment, might hold knowledge of chemistry which was still a closed book to Man. That machine and the hopper and the cylinders—nothing like one would find in an Earthly chemical plant—but apparently efficient. With unlimited raw material, with many machines such as that—what might not the Venusians be able to do?

And it didn't make a bit of difference to them. In Venus they lived in seas that frothed and bubbled and stank to the high heavens—seas that seethed with continual chemical change. A few chemical changes in Earth's seas wouldn't bother them at all, but it would the people and the creatures of the Earth. All sea life would die, men would be driven from The Bottom, perhaps many sections of country lying close to the sea would become virtually uninhabitable because of the fumes.

Grant cursed at himself. "You damn fool," he said, "creating a world catastrophe when you aren't absolutely certain of any fact as yet."

No facts, of course, except that he had actually found a Venusian operating a machine which produced hydrofluoric acid. He studied his chart closely and corrected his course. He was getting close to Old Gus' dome.

Half an hour later he sighted the black, shadowy cliffs and cruised slowly in toward them.

He didn't see the dome until the tank was almost on top of it. Then he cried out in amazement, jerked the tank to a halt and flattened his face against the glass, playing the spotlight on the ruins of the dome.

Old Gus' dome had been literally blown to bits. Only a few jagged stumps of its foundation, firmly anchored to the rock beneath, still stood. The rest was hurled in shattered fragments over The Bottom!

There was no sign of Old Gus. Apparently the old man had been away when the dome had crashed or his body had been carried away.

But there was little mystery as to what had caused the dome to fall. The broad wheel marks of a large undersea tank led away from the scene of destruction. Deep footprints still made a tracery about the dome site and the interior of the dome had plainly been rifled after the dome itself had been destroyed. This had been the work of men. A shell, loaded with high explosive, driven by compressed air, had smashed the dome.

"Robber's Deep," said Grant, half to himself, staring along the direction in which the tank trail led. The tale of Robber's Deep, as he had heard it from Old Gus, had sounded like one of those tall tales for which The Bottom men were famous. Tales inspired by superstition, by loneliness, by the strange things that they saw. But maybe Robber's Deep wasn't just a tale—maybe there really was something to it after all.

Grant turned back to his waiting tank. "By Heaven," he said, "I'm going to find out!"

The tread marks were easy to follow. They led straight away, down the slope toward the Big Deep, then angled sharply to the north, still leading down.

The water grew darker, became a dirty gray with all the blue gone from it. Sparks flittered in the darkness—flashes that came and went, betraying the presence of little luminous things—sea life carrying their own lanterns. Arrow worms slid across the vision plate, like white threads. Copepods, the insects of the deep, jerked along with oarlike strokes, like motes of dust dancing in the sunlight. A shrimp, startled, turned into a miniature firecracker, hurling out luminous fluid which seemed to explode almost in Grant's face.

A swarm of fish with cheek and lateral lights flashed by the glass and a nightmare of a thing, with flame-encircled eyes, bobbing lantern barbells and silver tinsel on its body, crawled over the nose of the tank, perched there for a moment like a squatting ogre, then slipped out of sight.

The gauges were swinging over. Deeper and deeper, with the pressure rising. The grayness of the water held and the lights outside increased, like little fireflies rustling through the gloom.

What had happened to Old Gus? And why had his dome been smashed?

Those two questions pounded in Grant's brain. If Gus was still alive, where was he? Out rounding up the vigilantes he had spoken of? Hurrying back to Deep End to inform the police? Or haunting the trail of the marauders?

Grant shrugged his shoulders. Old Gus probably was dead. The old coot was depth-dippy. He would fight at the drop of the hat, no matter what the odds. Somewhere a blasted tank or a shattered suit was hidden in the ocean's mud, marking the last resting place of the old Bottom man.

But why the attack on the dome? Could Old Gus have had treasure there? It was not unlikely. He had talked of old ships loaded with treasure, he was watching a five-foot clam with a pearl as big as a man's hat. Even at the lower price of pearls due to their greater abundance now, that pearl itself would represent a small-sized fortune.

The trail led deeper and deeper, down into a darker gray, with more fireflies dancing, with monstrous shadows slipping through the water. Weird formations began to thrust themselves out of the ocean bed and the trail dipped swiftly. The track of the larger tank wound tortuously around the outcroppings.

Without a doubt they were approaching Robber's Deep. The depth gauge read slightly under two thousand feet and the pressure gauge sent a shiver of fear along Grant's spine. Exposed to that pressure for an instant, a man would be jelly—less than jelly, less than a grease spot on the floor.

The trail led into a narrow canyon, with mighty rock walls rearing up straight into the water. There was barely clearance for Grant's tank—the larger machine must have almost brushed the walls.

Suddenly the canyon debouched into a wider space, a sort of circular arena, with the walls sweeping to left and right and then closing in again narrower than ever, forming a little pocket.

Grant jerked the machine to a stop, tried frantically to spin it and retreat. For in that little arena were other tanks, a battery of them, large and small.

He had run slam-bang into a trap and as he ripped savagely at the controls he felt the cold perspiration trickling down his chest and arms.

A voice boomed in his radio receiver: "Stay where you are or we'll blast you!"

He saw the snouts of guns mounted on the tanks swiveling around to menace him. He was beaten and he knew it. He halted the tank, switched off the motor.

"Get into your suit and get out," boomed the voice in the receiver.

He was in for it now—clear up to his neck.

Out of the tank, he walked slowly across the arena floor. A man from one of the tanks came out to meet him. Neither of them spoke until they were face to face.

Then, in the dim light, Grant recognized the man in the other suit. It was the Rat!

"Nice hide-out you have here, Rat," said Grant.

The Rat leered at him. "Hellion will be glad to see you," he said. "This is a sort of unexpected visit, but he'll be glad to see you just the same." The Rat's face twisted. "He liked your message."

"Yes," said Grant, "I figured that he would."

Alcatraz on Ganymede had done something to Hellion Smith, had instilled in him a deeper, sharper cruelty, a keener cunning, a fouler bitterness. It showed in his squinted eyes, his twitching face with the jagged scar that ran from chin to temple, the thin, bloodless lips.

"Yes," he told Grant, "I have a nice place here. Convenient in a good many ways. The police would never think to hunt for me down here and if they did and we wanted to make a fight of it, we could hold them off until the crack of doom. Or if we wanted to run for it, they'd never be able to trail us through those canyons that run into the Big Deep."

"Clever," said Grant. "But you always were clever. Your only trouble was that you took a lot of chances."

"I am not taking them any more," said Hellion, but his tone still held that puzzling, light note of pleasant conversation.

"By the way," he said, "the Rat told me you remembered me. Sent your regards to me. I appreciated that."

"Here it comes," Grant told himself. Involuntarily his body tensed.

But nothing came.

Hellion waved his arm to indicate the mighty dome which nestled in another larger, deeper arena in the canyon. Through the quartz, even in the murkiness of the gray water, one could see the towering canyon walls that ran up from the ocean floor.

"Just like on the surface," said Hellion proudly. "All the comforts of home. The boys like it down here. A few things to do and a good place to loaf around. Lamps that take the place of daylight, latest electrolysis equipment, generators—everything. We have it cozy." He turned to face Grant squarely. "I wish you could stay with us a while," he said, "but I suppose you will want to be going back."

Grant gasped. "Why, yes," he said. "The chief will be expecting me."

But there was something wrong. No word or action. Nothing in the atmosphere. Nothing at all—except that Hellion Smith hated his guts. Hellion Smith wouldn't let him walk out of this place and go back to the surface.

And yet—that was what he had said: "—you will want to be going back."

"I'll walk to the lock with you," Hellion offered.

Grant held his breath, waiting for the joker. But there wasn't any joker. Hellion chatted amiably, his scarred face twitching, his eyes a-glitter, but his voice smooth and easy. Small talk about old times back in New York, gossip of the underworld, life in the Ganymedean prison.

Grant's suit stood within the lock, just as he had left it.

Hellion held out his hand.

"Come and see us again," he said. "Any time. But maybe you had better get started now." And for the first time Grant sensed a note of warning and of mockery in Hellion's voice.

"So long, Hellion," said Grant.

Still puzzled, he clambered into his suit, screwed shut the entrance port, snapped on the interior lights. Everything all right—dials intact, mechanism O.K. He snapped on the power and tested the controls. But there was something wrong. Something missing. A soft purr that should have been in his ears.

Then he knew, and as the realization struck him the strength seemed to go out of his body and a cold dew of perspiration dampened his entire body. "Hellion," he said, "my electrolysis unit has gone haywire."

Hellion stood just outside the lock, ready to slam home the port. He smiled engagingly at Grant, as if Grant might have just told him a funny joke. "Now," he said, "isn't that too bad."

"Look, Hellion," shouted Grant, "if you want to wipe me out, use your guns."

"Why, no," said Hellion. "I wouldn't think of that. This is so much neater. You have your emergency reserve of oxygen, enough for three or four hours. Maybe in that time you can figure out a way to save your neck. I'm giving you a chance, see? That's more than you gave me, you dirty little pencil pusher." He slammed the port and Grant watched it spinning home.

Water was hissing into the lock, shattered to fog by the mighty pressure, raising the pressure inside the lock to that outside the dome.

Grant stood still, waiting, mad thoughts thundering in his brain. Four hours' air at the most. Hours short of the time that would be necessary to get back to Deep End. If Old Gus' dome still stood, no problem would have existed, for he could have made the dome easily. Probably there were other domes as near, but he had no idea where they were.

There was just one thing—and he had to face it—death within his suit when his air gave out. Four hours. Plenty of time to get to Gus' dome.

His mind snagged and held, revolved around one idea. Time to get to Gus' dome. Follow the tracks left by the tanks. Scale the canyon walls and cut southward to intersect the tank tracks.

The site of the Venusian's machinery was a scant quarter mile from Gus' dome. Two hours would do it, less than two hours. Two hours to go there—two hours to come back.

He wondered grimly what a dozen jugs of hydrofluoric acid, dropped into the canyon, would do to the dome. He chuckled and the chuckle echoed ghastly inside the suit. "We go out together, Smith," he whispered.

Climbing the canyon wall had been no child's play. Several times he had nearly fallen when the mighty grip of the suit's steel hands had slipped on slimy rock. Not that such a fall would have been fatal, although it might have been.

But now Grant was near the top. Slowly, carefully, he manipulated the right arm of the suit toward a projection, hooked the fingers around it, tightened them savagely with a vicious thrust of a lever. The motors droned as the arm swung the suit, scraping along the rocky face of the looming wall. Now the left arm and the fingers hooked upon a ledge, anchored there. Grant jerked on the arm several times to make sure of the grip, then applied the power. The arm bent, mechanical muscles straining, and the suit moved upward.

Time was valuable, but he must be careful. One slip now and he would have to do it all over again—if he could, for the fall might crush him to death on the rocks below, might crack his visor, might damage the suit so it wouldn't operate.

It had taken him longer than he thought to reach the top, but there was still time enough. Time to reach the Venusians' camp and get the acid. Time to get back and hurl jug after jug out into the canyon. Time to watch the jugs settle and break on the glowing dome down on the canyon floor. Time to watch the yellow-greenish liquid creep over the quartz. Time to see the quartz walls crumple inward beneath the terrific pressure of the deep.

"A message, Hellion?" he shrieked into the watery canyon. "I'll have one for you. I'll have a dozen of them—in jugs!"

But maybe he was just kidding himself. Playing at dramatics. Jousting with windmills. Maybe that much acid wouldn't touch the dome—maybe it would take hundreds of gallons of the stuff, dumped into the canyon, before it would affect the quartz. Maybe the jugs would collapse under the pressure before he could get them down this deep. That was funny stuff they and the cylinders were made of—neither steel nor quartz, and steel and quartz were the only two materials that would stand up even at five hundred feet. In the laboratories on the surface hydrofluoric acid was kept in wax containers, but that, of course, would be just as crazy at this depth as quartz containers.

Those jugs must be made of some new material, some material unknown to Earthmen, but developed by the Venusians. The Venusians, naturally, would have developed materials of that kind—materials that were immune to acid action, could withstand tremendous pressures.

The oxygen jet, hissing warningly, roused Grant from his speculations. His eyes went to the reserve-tank pressure gauge and what he saw was like a blow between the eyes. Of the two tanks, one was empty—or almost empty, just enough for a few more minutes. The second tank was at full pressure—but something had happened to that first tank. He had counted on it carrying him almost to the Venusians' camp—on not being forced to call upon the second tank until he was ready for the return trip to the canyon's edge. Some imperfection, perhaps a faulty gauge—it didn't matter now, for the damage was done. The hissing of the jet ebbed lower and lower and Grant snapped on the second tank.

Well, that settled it.

He'd never live to get to the Venusians' camp and back to the canyon. Two hours—that was all that was left to him of life—perhaps not even that much. And that wasn't long enough.

Someone else would have to get Hellion Smith. Perhaps Old Gus, if Old Gus were still alive. Perhaps some stony-eyed veteran of the Undersea Patrol—perhaps one of the government submarines, nosing around to find other camps of the Venusian invaders.

"The last story," said Grant Nagle, staring out over the canyon, down into the depths where the dome gleamed dimly. "The last story and I won't write it."

Grant swung the right arm of the suit upward, found a handhold with his spotlight, hooked the steel fingers on it, tested their grip and geared the motors. The suit bumped and scraped against the rock as the arm levered it up a few feet.

Only a few feet more and he would reach the top of the canyon wall. What would he do then? What was there to do? What does a man do when he had just an hour or two to live?

He shifted the spotlight to find a hold for the fingers of the left arm and, as he did so, a shadowy, ghostly thing leaped over the canyon's lip and plunged out into the watery space behind him. An oblong thing, a tubelike thing, that seemed to be spinning as it fell. A thing that plunged down, straight at the dome below.

Grant twisted the periscopic lenses to watch and, as he recognized it, he sucked in his breath. That falling thing was one of the cylinders from the Venusians' camp! One of the great cylinders to which the motor had been connected! The cylinder was falling faster now, faster and faster, still spinning along its axis.

From above came a coughing hiss, as if someone had uncorked a bottle, and down toward the spinning cylinder flashed a shimmering projectile. Someone had fired an airgun!

In the split second before the projectile struck, Grant found a handhold for the left hand of the suit, clamped the steel fingers into it savagely. The concussion of the exploding projectile as it blasted against the spinning cylinder battered his suit against the wall. But the fingers held and, hanging there against the canyon rocks, he saw the cylinder split open as if a man had sliced it with a knife. Saw it spill a flood of curling greenish-yellow substance down upon the dome.

With little regard for safety, Grant swarmed up the wall those few remaining feet, pulled himself over the edge and turned to stare down into the depths.

The dome was gone—flattened out—shattered into a million shards as the acid had weakened it, allowed the pressure to get in its deadly work.

Hellion Smith was dead. So was the Rat and all the others. Except for a few, perhaps, who might be guarding the tanks.

The waters of Robber's Deep were painted a ghastly yellow—a yellow that swirled and crawled and eddied like fiendish, writhing arms.

"Who the hell are you?" asked a voice.

Grant whirled. "Gus," he cried. "Gus, you old devil, you did it!"

The suited figure stood stolidly in the gloom, a gun clutched in one hand. Behind it bulked the outline of an underwater tank.

"I kind of got my dander up," Old Gus explained. "First they knocked over my dome and that put me out of sorts, and then they took my pearl and that made me downright sore."

He turned his spotlight on Grant's vision plate. "It's Nagle," he said. "I was wondering where you were."

"It's a long story," said Grant.

"You can tell it to me in the tank," said Gus. "I got to be getting back."

"Where are you going?" asked Grant.

"I got to get Butch," said Gus. "When I went up to the Venusians' camp and got ready to haul the cylinder down here, Butch was bound to follow me. I told him the pressure would be too much for him and I tried to make him stay. But he got stubborn, so I had to stake him out."

Gus chuckled thinly. "I bet he's madder than hell by now," he said.

ETERNITY LOST

Possibly impressed by Switzerland's ability to remain neutral during World War II, Clifford Simak used Geneva as the world capitol in a number of his future-set stories—including some of the City *stories; and although he never got over to Europe, he imagines Geneva, in this story, as a place of beauty . . . which makes it all the more striking that political corruption would be exposed in such a place. And who better than an old-fashioned newspaperman would recognize, and resent, that corruption?*

Sent to John W. Campbell Jr., during the last few days of 1948, the story was accepted in less than two weeks, and was first published in the July 1949 issue of Astounding Science Fiction. *Cliff got $200 for it, and it is an ugly story.*

—dww

Mr. Reeves: The situation, as I see it, calls for well defined safeguards which would prevent continuation of life from falling under the patronage of political parties or other groups in power.

Chairman Leonard: You mean you are afraid it might become a political football?

Mr. Reeves: Not only that, sir, I am afraid that political parties might use it to continue beyond normal usefulness the lives of certain so-called elder statesmen who are needed by the party to maintain prestige and dignity in the public eye.

—From the Records of a hearing before the science subcommittee of the public policy committee of the World House of Representatives.

Senator Homer Leonard's visitors had something on their minds. They fidgeted mentally as they sat in the senator's office and drank the senator's good whiskey. They talked, quite importantly, as was their wont, but they talked around the thing they had come to say. They circled it like a hound dog circling a coon, waiting for an opening, circling the subject to catch an opportunity that might make the message sound just a bit offhanded—as if they had just thought of it in passing and had not called purposely on the senator to say it.

It was queer, the senator told himself. For he had known these two for a good while now. And they had known him equally as long. There should be nothing they should hesitate to tell him. They had, in the past, been brutally frank about many things in his political career.

It might be, he thought, more bad news from North America, but he was as well acquainted with that bad news as they. After all, he told himself philosophically, a man cannot reasonably expect to stay in office forever. The voters, from sheer boredom if nothing else, would finally reach the day when they would vote against a man who had served them faithfully and well. And the senator was candid enough to admit, at least to himself, that there had been times when he had served the voters of North America neither faithfully nor well.

Even at that, he thought, he had not been beaten yet. It was still several months until election time and there was a trick or two that he had never tried, political dodges that even at this late date might save the senatorial hide. Given the proper time and the proper place and he would win out yet. Timing, he told himself—proper timing is the thing that counts.

He sat quietly in his chair, a great hulk of a man, and for a single instant he closed his eyes to shut out the room and the sunlight in the window. Timing, he thought. Yes, timing and a feeling for the public, a finger on the public pulse, the ability to know ahead of time what the voter eventually will come to think—those were the ingredients of good strategy. To know ahead of time, to be ahead in thinking, so that in a week or month or year, the voters would say to one another: "You know, Bill, old Senator Leonard had it right. Remember what he said last week—or month or year—over there in Geneva. Yes, sir, he laid it on the line. There ain't much that gets past that old fox of a Leonard."

He opened his eyes a slit, keeping them still half closed so his visitors might think he'd only had them half closed all the time. For it was impolite and a political mistake to close one's eyes when one had visitors. They might get the idea one wasn't interested. Or they might seize the opportunity to cut one's throat.

It's because I'm getting old again, the senator told himself. Getting old and drowsy. But just as smart as ever. Yes, sir, said the senator, talking to himself, just as smart and slippery as I ever was.

He saw by the tight expressions on the faces of the two that they finally were set to tell him the thing they had come to tell. All their circling and sniffing had been of no avail. Now they had to come out with it, on the line, cold turkey.

"There had been a certain matter," said Alexander Gibbs, "which had been quite a problem for the party for a long time now. We had hoped that matters would so arrange themselves that we wouldn't need to call it to your attention, senator. But the executive committee held a meeting in New York the other night and it seemed to be the consensus that we communicate it to you."

It's bad, thought the senator, even worse than I thought it might be—for Gibbs is talking in his best double-crossing manner.

The senator gave them no help. He sat quietly in his chair and held the whiskey glass in a steady hand and did not ask what it was all about, acting as if he didn't really care.

Gibbs floundered slightly. "It's a rather personal matter, senator," he said.

"It's this life continuation business," blurted Andrew Scott.

They sat in shocked silence, all three of them, for Scott should not have said it that way. In politics, one is not blunt and forthright, but devious and slick.

"I see," the senator said finally. "The party thinks the voters would like it better if I were a normal man who would die a normal death."

Gibbs smoothed his face of shocked surprise.

"The common people resent men living beyond their normal time," he said. "Especially—"

"Especially," said the senator, "those who have done nothing to deserve it."

"I wouldn't put it exactly that way," Gibbs protested.

"Perhaps not," said the senator. "But no matter how you say it, that is what you mean."

They sat uncomfortably in the office chairs, with the bright Geneva sunlight pouring through the windows.

"I presume," said the senator, "that the party, having found I am no longer an outstanding asset, will not renew my application for life continuation. I suppose that is what you were sent to tell me."

Might as well get it over with, he told himself grimly. Now that it's out in the open, there's no sense in beating around the bush.

"That's just about it, senator," said Scott.

"That's exactly it," said Gibbs.

The senator heaved his great body from the chair, picked up the whiskey bottle, filled their glasses and his own.

"You delivered the death sentence very deftly," he told them. "It deserves a drink."

He wondered what they had thought that he would do. Plead with them, perhaps. Or storm around the office. Or denounce the party.

Puppets, he thought. Errand boys. Poor, scared errand boys.

They drank, their eyes on him, and silent laughter shook inside him from knowing that the liquor tasted very bitter in their mouths.

Chairman Leonard: *You are agreed then, Mr. Chapman, with the other witnesses, that no person should be allowed to seek continuation of life for himself, that it should be granted only upon application by someone else, that—*

Mr. Chapman: *It should be a gift of society to those persons who are in the unique position of being able to materially benefit the human race.*

Chairman Leonard: *That is very aptly stated, sir.*

—From the Records of a hearing before the science subcommittee of the public policy committee of the World House of Representatives.

The senator settled himself carefully and comfortably into a chair in the reception room of the Life Continuation Institute and unfolded his copy of the *North American Tribune.*

Column one said that system trade was normal, according to a report by the World Secretary of Commerce. The story went on at length to quote the secretary's report. Column two was headed by an impish box that said a new life form may have been found on Mars, but since the discoverer was a spaceman who had been more than ordinarily drunk, the report was being viewed with some skepticism. Under the box was a story reporting a list or boy and girl health champions selected by the state of Finland to be entered later in the year in the world health contest. The story in column three gave the latest information on the unstable love life of the world's richest woman.

Column four asked a question:

WHAT HAPPENED
TO DR. CARSON?
NO RECORD OF
REPORTED DEATH

The story, the senator saw, was by-lined Anson Lee and the senator chuckled dryly. Lee was up to something. He was always up to something, always ferreting out some fact that eventually was sure to prove embarrassing to someone. Smart as a steel trap, that Lee, but a bad man to get into one's hair.

There had been, for example, that matter of the spaceship contract.

Anson Lee, said the senator underneath his breath, is a pest. Nothing but a pest.

But Dr. Carson? Who was Dr. Carson?

The senator played a little mental game with himself, trying to remember, trying to identify the name before he read the story.

Dr. Carson?

Why, said the senator, I remember now. Long time ago. A biochemist or something of the sort. A very brilliant man. Did something with colonies of soil bacteria, breeding the things for therapeutic work.

Yes, said the senator, a very brilliant man. I remember that I met him once. Didn't understand half the things he said. But that was long ago. A hundred years or more.

A hundred years ago—maybe more than that.

Why, bless me, said the senator, he must be one of us.

The senator nodded and the paper slipped from his hands and fell upon the floor. He jerked himself erect. There I go again, he told himself. Dozing. It's old age creeping up again.

He sat in his chair, very erect and quiet, like a small scared child that won't admit it's scared, and the old, old fear came tugging at his brain. Too long, he thought. I've already waited longer than I should. Waiting for the party to renew my application and now the party won't. They've thrown me overboard. They've deserted me just when I needed them the most.

Death sentence, he had said back in the office, and that was what it was—for he couldn't last much longer. He didn't have much time. It would take a while to engineer whatever must be done. One would have to move most carefully and never tip one's hand. For there was a penalty—a terrible penalty.

The girl said to him: "Dr. Smith will see you now."

"Eh?" said the senator.

"You asked to see Dr. Dana Smith," the girl reminded him. "He will see you now."

"Thank you, miss," said the senator. "I was sitting here half dozing."

He lumbered to his feet.

"That door," said the girl.

"I know," the senator mumbled testily. "I know. I've been here many times before."

Dr. Smith was waiting.

"Have a chair, senator," he said. "Have a drink? Well, then, a cigar, maybe. What is on your mind?"

The senator took his time, getting himself adjusted to the chair. Grunting comfortably, he clipped the end off the cigar, rolled it in his mouth.

"Nothing particular on my mind," he said. "Just dropped around to pass the time of day. Have a great and abiding interest in your work here. Always have had. Associated with it from the very start."

The director nodded. "I know. You conducted the original hearings on life continuation."

The senator chuckled. "Seemed fairly simple then. There were problems, of course, and we recognized them and we tried the best we could to meet them."

"You did amazingly well," the director told him. "The code you drew up five hundred years ago has never been questioned for its fairness and the few modifications which have been necessary have dealt with minor points which no one could have anticipated."

"But it's taken too long," said the senator.

The director stiffened. "I don't understand," he said.

The senator lighted the cigar, applying his whole attention to it, flaming the end carefully so it caught even fire.

He settled himself more solidly in the chair. "It was like this," he said. "We recognized life continuation as a first step only, a rather blundering first step toward immortality. We devised the code as an interim instrument to take care of the period before immortality was available—not to a selected few, but to everyone. We viewed the few who could be given life continuation as stewards, person who would help to advance the day when the race could be granted immortality."

"That still is the concept," Dr. Smith said, coldly.

"But the people grow impatient."

"That is just too bad," Smith told him. "The people will simply have to wait."

"As a race, they may be willing to," explained the senator. "As individuals, they're not."

"I fail to see your point, senator."

"There may not be a point," said the senator. "In late years I've often debated with myself the wisdom of the whole procedure. Life continuation is a keg of dynamite if it fails of immortality. It will breed system-wide revolt if the people wait too long."

"Have you a solution, senator?"

"No," confessed the senator. "No, I'm afraid I haven't. I've often thought that it might have been better if we had taken the people into our confidence, let them know all that was going on. Kept them up with all developments. An informed people are a rational people."

The director did not answer and the senator felt the cold weight of certainty seep into his brain.

He knows, he told himself. He knows the party had decided not to ask that I be continued. He knows that I'm a dead man. He knows I'm almost through and can't help him any more—and he's crossed me out. He won't tell me a thing. Not the thing I want to know.

But he did not allow his face to change. He knew his face would not betray him. His face was too well trained.

"I know there is an answer," said the senator. "There's always been an answer to any question about immortality. You can't have it until there's living space. Living space to throw away, more than we ever think we'll need, and a fair chance to find more of it if it's ever needed."

Dr. Smith nodded. "That's the answer, senator. The only answer I can give."

He sat silent for a moment, then he said: "Let me assure you on one point, senator. When Extrasolar Research finds the living space, we'll have the immortality."

The senator heaved himself out of the chair, stood planted solidly on his feet.

"It's good to hear you say that, doctor," he said. "It is very heartening. I thank you for the time you gave me."

Out on the street, the senator thought bitterly:

They have it now. They have immortality. All they're waiting for is the living space and another hundred years will find that. Another hundred years will simply have to find it.

Another hundred years, he told himself, just one more continuation, and I would be in for good and all.

Mr. Andrews: *We must be sure there is a divorcement of life continuation from economics. A man who has money must not be allowed to purchase additional life, either through the payment of money or the pressure of influence, while another man is doomed to die a natural death simply because he happens to be poor.*

Chairman Leonard: *I don't believe that situation has ever been in question.*

Mr. Andrews: *Nevertheless, it is a matter which must be emphasized again and again. Life continuation must not be a commodity to be sold across the counter at so many dollars for each added year of life.*

> —From the Records of a hearing before the science subcommittee of the public policy committee of the World House of Representatives.

The senator sat before the chessboard and idly worked at the problem. Idly, since his mind was on other things than chess.

So they had immortality, had it and were waiting, holding it a secret until there was assurance of sufficient living space. Holding it a secret from the people and from the government and from the men and women who had spent many lifetimes working for the thing which already had been found.

For Smith had spoken, not as a man who was merely confident, but as a man who knew. When Extrasolar Research finds the living space, he'd said, we'll have immortality. Which meant they had it now. Immortality was not predictable. You would not know you'd have it; you would only know if and when you had it.

The senator moved a bishop and saw that he was wrong. He slowly pulled it back.

Living space was the key, and not living space alone, but economic living space, self-supporting in terms of food and other raw materials, but particularly in food. For if living space had been all that mattered, Man had it in Mars and Venus and the moons of Jupiter. But not one of those worlds was self-supporting. They did not solve the problem.

Living space was all they needed and in a hundred years they'd have that. Another hundred years was all that anyone would need to come into possession of the common human heritage of immortality.

Another continuation would give me that hundred years, said the senator, talking to himself. A hundred years and some to spare, for this time I'll be careful of myself. I'll lead a cleaner life. Eat sensibly and cut out liquor and tobacco and the woman-chasing.

There were ways and means, of course. There always were. And he would find them, for he knew all the dodges. After five hundred years in world government, you got to know them all. If you didn't know them, you simply didn't last.

Mentally he listed the possibilities as they occurred to him.

ONE: A person could engineer a continuation for someone else and then have that person assign the continuation to him. It would be costly, of course, but it might be done.

You'd have to find someone you could trust and maybe you couldn't find anyone you could trust that far—for life continuation was something hard to come by. Most people, once they got it, wouldn't give it back.

Although on second thought, it probably wouldn't work. For there'd be legal angles. A continuation was a gift of society to one specific person to be used by him alone. It would not be transferable. It would not be legal property. It would not be something that one owned. It could not be bought or sold, it could not be assigned.

If the person who had been granted a continuation died before he got to use it—died of natural causes, of course, of wholly natural causes that could be provable—why, maybe, then—But still it wouldn't work. Not being property, the continuation would not be part of one's estate. It could not be bequeathed. It most likely would revert to the issuing agency.

Cross that one off, the senator told himself.

TWO: He might travel to New York and talk to the party's executive secretary. After all, Gibbs and Scott were mere messengers. They had their orders to carry out the dictates of the party and that was all. Maybe if he saw someone in authority—

But, the senator scolded himself, that is wishful thinking. The party's through with me. They've pushed their continuation racket as far as they dare push it and they have wrangled about all they figure they can get. They don't dare ask for more and they need my continuation for someone else most likely—someone who's a comer; someone who has vote appeal.

And I, said the senator, am an old has-been.

Although I'm a tricky old rascal, and ornery if I have to be, and slippery as five hundred years of public life can make one.

After that long, said the senator, parenthetically, you have no more illusions, not even of yourself.

I couldn't stomach it, he decided. I couldn't live with myself if I went crawling to New York—and a thing has to be pretty bad to make me feel like that. I've never crawled before and I'm not crawling now, not even for an extra hundred years and a shot at immortality.

Cross that one off, too, said the senator.

THREE: Maybe someone could be bribed.

Of all the possibilities, that sounded the most reasonable. There always was someone who had a certain price and always someone else who could act as intermediary. Naturally, a world senator could not get mixed up directly in a deal of that sort.

It might come a little high, but what was money for? After all, he reconciled himself, he'd been a frugal man of sorts and had been able to lay away a wad against such a day as this.

The senator moved a rook and it seemed to be all right, so he left it there.

Of course, once he managed the continuation, he would have to disappear. He couldn't flaunt his triumph in the party's face. He couldn't take a chance of someone asking how he'd been continuated. He'd have to become one of the people, seek to be forgotten, live in some obscure place and keep out of the public eye.

Norton was the man to see. No matter what one wanted, Norton was the man to see. An appointment to be secured, someone to be killed, a concession on Venus or a spaceship contract—Norton did the job. All quietly and discreetly and no questions asked. That is, if you had the money. If you didn't have the money, there was no use of seeing Norton.

Otto came into the room on silent feet.

"A gentleman to see you, sir," he said.

The senator stiffened upright in his chair.

"What do you mean by sneaking up on me?" he shouted. "Always pussyfooting. Trying to startle me. After this you cough or fall over a chair or something so I'll know that you're around."

"Sorry, sir," said Otto. "There's a gentleman here. And there are those letters on the desk to read."

"I'll read the letters later," said the senator.

"Be sure you don't forget," Otto told him, stiffly.

"I never forget," said the senator. "You'd think I was getting senile, the way you keep reminding me."

"There's a gentleman to see you," Otto said patiently. "A Mr. Lee."

"Anson Lee, perhaps."

Otto sniffed. "I believe that was his name. A newspaper person, sir."

"Show him in," said the senator.

He sat stolidly in his chair and thought: Lee's found out about it. Somehow he's ferreted out the fact the party's thrown me over. And he's here to crucify me.

He may suspect, but he cannot know. He may have heard a rumor, but he can't be sure. The party would keep mum, must necessarily keep mum, since it can't openly admit its traffic in life continuation. So Lee, having heard a rumor, had come to blast it out of me, to catch me by surprise and trip me up with words.

I must not let him do it, for once the thing is known, the wolves will come in packs knee deep.

Lee was walking into the room and the senator rose and shook his hand.

"Sorry to disturb you, senator," Lee told him, "but I thought maybe you could help me."

"Anything at all," the senator said, affably. "Anything I can. Sit down, Mr. Lee."

"Perhaps you read my story in the morning paper," said Lee. "The one on Dr. Carson's disappearance."

"No," said the senator. "No, I'm afraid I—"

He rumbled to a stop, astounded.

He hadn't read the paper!

He had forgotten to read the paper!

He always read the paper. He never failed to read it. It was a solemn rite, starting at the front and reading straight through to the back, skipping only those sections which long ago he'd found not to be worth the reading.

He'd had the paper at the institute and he had been interrupted when the girl told him that Dr. Smith would see him. He had come out of the office and he'd left the paper in the reception room.

It was a terrible thing. Nothing, absolutely nothing, should so upset him that he forgot to read the paper.

"I'm afraid I didn't read the story," the senator said lamely. He simply couldn't force himself to admit that he hadn't read the paper.

"Dr. Carson," said Lee, "was a biochemist, a fairly famous one. He died ten years or so ago, according to an announcement from a little village in Spain, where he had gone to live. But I have reason to believe, senator, that he never died at all, that he may still be living."

"Hiding?" asked the senator.

"Perhaps," said Lee. "Although there seems no reason that he should. His record is entirely spotless."

"Why do you doubt he died, then?"

"Because there's no death certificate. And he's not the only one who died without benefit of certificate."

"Hm-m-m," said the senator.

"Galloway, the anthropologist, died five years ago. There's no certificate. Henderson, the agricultural expert, died six years ago. There's no certificate. There are a dozen more I know of and probably many that I don't."

"Anything in common?" asked the senator. "Any circumstances that might link these people?"

"Just one thing," said Lee. "They were all continuators."

"I see," said the senator. He clasped the arms of his chair with a fierce grip to keep his hands from shaking.

"Most interesting," he said. "Very interesting."

"I know you can't tell me anything officially," said Lee, "but I thought you might give me a fill-in, an off-the-record background. You wouldn't let me quote you, of course, but any clues you might give me, any hint at all—"

He waited hopefully.

"Because I've been close to the Life Continuation people?" asked the senator.

Lee nodded. "If there's anything to know, you know it, senator. You headed the committee that held the original hearings on life continuation. Since then you've held various other congressional posts in connection with it. Only this morning you saw Dr. Smith."

"I can't tell you anything," mumbled the senator. "I don't know anything. You see, it's a matter of policy—"

"I had hoped you would help me, senator."

"I can't," said the senator. "You'll never believe it, of course, but I really can't."

He sat silently for a moment and then he asked a question: "You say all these people you mention were continuators. You checked, of course, to see if their applications had been renewed?"

"I did," said Lee. "There are no renewals for any one of them—at least no records of renewals. Some of them were approaching death limit and they actually may be dead by now, although I doubt that any of them died at the time or place announced."

"Interesting," said the senator. "And quite a mystery, too."

Lee deliberately terminated the discussion. He gestured at the chessboard. "Are you an expert, senator?"

The senator shook his head. "The game appeals to me. I fool around with it. It's a game of logic and also a game of ethics. You are perforce a gentleman when you play it. You observe certain rules of correctness of behavior."

"Like life, senator?"

"Like life should be," said the senator. "When the odds are too terrific, you resign. You do not force your opponent to play out to the bitter end. That's ethics. When you see that you can't win, but that you have a fighting chance, you try for the next best thing—a draw. That's logic."

Lee laughed, a bit uncomfortably. "You've lived according to those rules, senator?"

"I've done my best," said the senator, trying to sound humble.

Lee rose. "I must be going, senator."

"Stay and have a drink."

Lee shook his head. "Thanks, but I have work to do."

"I owe you a drink," said the senator. "Remind me of it sometime."

For a long time after Lee left, Senator Homer Leonard sat unmoving in his chair.

Then he reached out a hand and picked up a knight to move it, but his fingers shook so that he dropped it and it clattered on the board.

Any person who gains the gift of life continuation by illegal or extralegal means, without bona fide recommendation or proper authorization through recognized channels, shall be, in effect, excommunicated from the human race. The facts of that person's guilt, once proved, shall be published by every means at humanity's command throughout the Earth and to every corner of the Earth so that all persons may know and recognize him. To further insure such recognition and identification, said convicted person must wear at all times, conspicuously displayed upon his person, a certain badge which shall advertise his guilt. While he may not be denied the ordinary basic requirements of life, such as food, adequate clothing, a minimum of shelter and medical care, he shall not be allowed to partake of or participate in any of the other refinements of civilization. He will not be allowed to purchase any item in excess of the barest necessities for the preservation of life, health and decency; he shall be barred from all endeavors and normal associations of humankind; he shall not have access to nor benefit of any library, lecture hall, amusement place or other facility, either private or public, designed for instruction, recreation or entertainment. Nor may any person, under certain penalties hereinafter set forth, knowingly converse with him or establish any human relationship whatsoever with him. He will be suffered to live out his life within the framework of the human community, but to all intent and purpose he will be denied all the privileges and obligations of a human being. And the same provisions as are listed above shall apply in full and equal force to any person or persons who shall in any way knowingly aid such a person to obtain life continuation by other than legal means.

—From the Code of Life Continuation.

"What you mean," said J. Barker Norton, "is that the party all these years has been engineering renewals of life continuation for you. Paying you off for services well rendered."

The senator nodded miserably.

"And now that you're on the verge of losing an election, they figure you aren't worth it any longer and have refused to ask for a renewal."

"In curbstone language," said the senator, "that sums it up quite neatly."

"And you come running to me," said Norton. "What in the world do you think I can do about it?"

The senator leaned forward. "Let's put it on a business basis, Norton. You and I have worked together before."

"That's right," said Norton. "Both of us cleaned up on that spaceship deal."

The senator said: "I want another hundred years and I'm willing to pay for it. I have no doubt you can arrange it for me."

"How?"

"I wouldn't know," said the senator. "I'm leaving that to you. I don't care how you do it."

Norton leaned back in his chair and made a tent out of his fingers.

"You figure I could bribe someone to recommend you. Or bribe some continuation technician to give you a renewal without authorization."

"Those are a pair of excellent ideas," agreed the senator.

"And face excommunication if I were found out," said Norton. "Thanks, senator, I'm having none of it."

The senator sat impassively, watching the face of the man across the desk.

"A hundred thousand," the senator said quietly.

Norton laughed at him.

"A half a million, then."

"Remember that excommunication, senator. It's got to be worth my while to take a chance like that."

"A million," said the senator. "And that's absolutely final."

"A million now," said Norton. "Cold cash. No receipt. No record of the transaction. Another million when and if I can deliver."

The senator rose slowly to his feet, his face a mask to hide the excitement that was stirring in him. The excitement and the naked surge of exultation. He kept his voice level.

"I'll deliver that million before the week is over."

Norton said: "I'll start looking into things."

On the street outside, the senator's step took on a jauntiness it had not known in years. He walked along briskly, flipping his cane.

Those others, Carson and Galloway and Henderson, had disappeared, exactly as he would have to disappear once he got his extra hundred years. They had arranged to have their own deaths announced and then had dropped from sight, living against the day when immortality would be a thing to be had for the simple asking.

Somewhere, somehow, they had got a new continuation, an unauthorized continuance, since a renewal was not listed in the records. Someone had arranged it for them. More than likely Norton.

But they had bungled. They had tried to cover up their tracks and had done no more than call attention to their absence.

In a thing like this, a man could not afford to blunder. A wise man, a man who took the time to think things out, would not make a blunder.

The senator pursed his flabby lips and whistled a snatch of music.

Norton was a gouger, of course. Pretending that he couldn't make arrangements, pretending he was afraid of excommunication, jacking up the price.

The senator grinned wryly. It would take almost every dime he had, but it was worth the price.

He'd have to be careful, getting together that much money. Some from one bank, some from another, collecting it piecemeal by withdrawals and by cashing bonds, floating a few judicious loans so there'd not be too many questions asked.

He bought a paper at the corner and hailed a cab. Settling back in the seat, he creased the paper down its length and started in on column one. Another health contest. This time in Australia.

Health, thought the senator, they're crazy on this health business. Health centers. Health cults. Health clinics.

He skipped the story, moved on to column two.

The head said:

SIX SENATORS
POOR BETS FOR
RE-ELECTION

The senator snorted in disgust. One of the senators, of course, would be himself.

He wadded up the paper and jammed it in his pocket.

Why should he care? Why knock himself out to retain a senate seat he could never fill? He was going to grow young again, get another chance at life. He would move to some far part of the earth and be another man.

Another man. He thought about it and it was refreshing. Dropping all the old dead wood of past association, all the ancient accumulation of responsibilities.

Norton had taken on the job. Norton would deliver.

Mr. Miller: *What I want to know is this: Where do we stop? You give this life continuation to a man and he'll want his wife and kids to have it. And his wife will want her Aunt Minnie to have it and the kids will want the family dog to have it and the dog will want—*

Chairman Leonard: *You're facetious, Mr. Miller.*

Mr. Miller: *I don't know what that big word means, mister. You guys here in Geneva talk fancy with them six-bit words and you get the people all balled up. It's time the common people got in a word of common sense.*

—From the Records of a hearing before the science subcommittee of the public policy committee of the World House of Representatives.

"Frankly," Norton told him, "it's the first time I ever ran across a thing I couldn't fix. Ask me anything else you want to, senator, and I'll rig it up for you."

The senator sat stricken. "You mean you couldn't—But, Norton, there was Dr. Carson and Galloway and Henderson. Someone took care of them."

Norton shook his head. "Not I. I never heard of them."

"But someone did," said the senator. "They disappeared—"

His voice trailed off and he slumped deeper in the chair and the truth suddenly was plain—the truth he had failed to see.

A blind spot, he told himself. A blind spot!

They had disappeared and that was all he knew. They had published their own deaths and had not died, but had disappeared.

He had assumed they had disappeared because they had got an illegal continuation. But that was sheer wishful thinking. There was no foundation for it, no fact that would support it.

There would be other reasons, he told himself, many other reasons why a man would disappear and seek to cover up his tracks with a death report.

But it had tied in so neatly!

They were continuators whose applications had not been renewed. Exactly as he was a continuator whose application would not be renewed.

They had dropped out of sight. Exactly as he would have to drop from sight once he gained another lease on life.

It had tied in so neatly—and it had been all wrong.

"I tried every way I knew," said Norton. "I canvassed every source that might advance your name for continuation and they laughed at me. It's been tried before, you see, and there's not a chance of getting it put through. Once your original sponsor drops you, you're automatically cancelled out.

"I tried to sound out technicians who might take a chance, but they're incorruptible. They get paid off in added years for loyalty and they're not taking any chance of trading years for dollars."

"I guess that settles it," the senator said wearily. "I should have known."

He heaved himself to his feet and faced Norton squarely. "You are telling me the truth," he pleaded. "You aren't just trying to jack up the price a bit."

Norton stared at him, almost unbelieving. "Jack up the price! Senator, if I had put this through, I'd have taken your last penny. Want to know how much you're worth? I can tell you within a thousand dollars."

He waved a hand at a row of filing cases ranged along the wall.

"It's all there, senator. You and all the other big shots. Complete files on every one of you. When a man comes to me with a deal like yours, I look in the files and strip him to the bone."

"I don't suppose there's any use of asking for some of my money back?"

Norton shook his head. "Not a ghost. You took your gamble, senator. You can't even prove you paid me. And, besides, you still have plenty left to last you the few years you have to live."

The senator took a step toward the door, then turned back.

"Look Norton, I can't die! Not now. Just one more continuation and I'd be—"

The look on Norton's face stopped him in his tracks. The look he'd glimpsed on other faces at other times, but only glimpsed. Now he stared at it—at the naked hatred of a man whose life is short for the man whose life is long.

"Sure, you can die," said Norton. "You're going to. You can't live forever. Who do you think you are!"

The senator reached out a hand and clutched the desk.

"But you don't understand."

"You've already lived ten times as long as I have lived," said Norton, coldly, measuring each word, "and I hate your guts for it. Get out of here, you sniveling old fool, before I throw you out."

Dr. Barton: *You may think that you would confer a boon on humanity with life continuation, but I tell you, sir, that it would be a curse. Life would lose its value and its meaning if it went on forever, and if you have life continuation now, you eventually must stumble on immortality. And when that happens, sir, you will be compelled to set up boards of review to grant the boon of death. The people, tired of life, will storm your hearing rooms to plead for death.*

Chairman Leonard: *It would banish uncertainty and fear.*

Dr. Barton: *You are talking of the fear of death. The fear of death, sir, is infantile.*

Chairman Leonard: *But there are benefits—*

Dr. Barton: *Benefits, yes. The benefit of allowing a scientist the extra years he needs to complete a piece of research; a composer an additional lifetime to complete a symphony. Once the novelty wore off, men in general would accept added life only under protest, only as a duty.*

Chairman Leonard: *You're not very practical-minded, doctor.*

Dr. Barton: *But I am. Extremely practical and down to earth. Man must have newness. Man cannot be bored and live. How much do you think there would be left to look forward to after the millionth woman, the billionth piece of pumpkin pie?*

—From the Records of the hearing before the science subcommittee of the public policy committee of the World House of Representatives.

So Norton hated him.

As all people of normal lives must hate, deep within their souls, the lucky ones whose lives went on and on.

A hatred deep and buried, most of the time buried. But sometimes breaking out, as it had broken out of Norton.

Resentment, tolerated because of the gently, skillfully fostered hope that those whose lives went on might some day make it possible that the lives of all, barring violence or accident or incurable disease, might go on as long as one would wish.

I can understand it now, thought the senator, for I am one of them. I am one of those whose lives will not continue to go on, and I have even fewer years than the most of them.

He stood before the window in the deepening dusk and saw the lights come out and the day die above the unbelievably blue waters of the far-famed lake.

Beauty came to him as he stood there watching, beauty that had gone unnoticed through all the later years. A beauty and a softness and a feeling of being one with the city lights and the last faint gleam of day above the darkening waters.

Fear? The senator admitted it.

Bitterness? Of course.

Yet, despite the fear and bitterness, the window held him with the scene it framed.

Earth and sky and water, he thought. I am one with them. Death has made me one with them. For death brings one back to the elementals, to the soil and trees, to the clouds and sky and the sun dying in the welter of its blood in the crimson west.

This is the price we pay, he thought, that the race must pay, for its life eternal—that we may not be able to assess in their true value the things that should be dearest to us; for a thing that has no ending, a thing that goes on forever, must have decreasing value.

Rationalization, he accused himself. Of course, you're rationalizing. You want another hundred years as badly as you ever did. You want a chance at immortality. But you can't have it and you trade eternal life for a sunset seen across a lake and it is well you can. It is a blessing that you can.

The senator made a rasping sound within his throat.

Behind him the telephone came to sudden life and he swung around. It chirred at him again. Feet pattered down the hall and the senator called out: "I'll get it, Otto."

He lifted the receiver. "New York calling," said the operator. "Senator Leonard, please."

"This is Leonard."

Another voice broke in. "Senator, this is Gibbs."

"Yes," said the senator. "The executioner."

"I called you," said Gibbs, "to talk about the election."

"What election?"

"The one here in North America. The one you're running in. Remember?"

"I am an old man," said the senator, "and I'm about to die. I'm not interested in elections."

Gibbs practically chattered. "But you have to be. What's the matter with you, senator? You have to do something. Make some speeches, make a statement, come home and stump the country. The party can't do it all alone. You have to do some of it yourself."

"I will do something," declared the senator. "Yes, I think that finally I'll do something."

He hung up and walked to the writing desk, snapped on the light. He got paper out of a drawer and took a pen out of his pocket.

The telephone went insane and he paid it no attention. It rang on and on and finally Otto came and answered.

"New York calling, sir," he said.

The senator shook his head and he heard Otto talking softly and the phone did not ring again.

The senator wrote:

To Whom It May Concern:

Then crossed it out.

He wrote:

A statement to the world:

And crossed it out.

He wrote:

A Statement by Senator Homer Leonard:

He crossed that out, too.

He wrote:

Five centuries ago the people of the world gave into the hands of a few trusted men and women the gift of continued life in the hope and belief that they would work to advance the day when longer life spans might be made possible for the entire population.

From time to time, life continuation has been granted additional men and women, always with the implied understanding that the gift was made under the same conditions—that the persons so favored should work against the day when each inhabitant of the entire world might enter upon a heritage of near-eternity.

Through the years some of us have carried that trust forward and have lived with it and cherished it and bent every effort toward its fulfillment.

Some of us have not.

Upon due consideration and searching examination of my own status in this regard, I have at length decided that I no longer can accept further extension of the gift.

Human dignity requires that I be able to meet my fellow man upon the street or in the byways of the world without flinching from him. This I could not do should I continue to accept a gift to which I have no claim and which is denied to other men.

The senator signed his name, neatly, carefully, without the usual flourish.

"There," he said, speaking aloud in the silence of the night-filled room, "that will hold them for a while."

Feet padded and he turned around.

"It's long past your usual bedtime, sir," said Otto.

The senator rose clumsily and his aching bones protested. Old, he thought. Growing old again. And it would be so easy to start over, to regain his youth and live another lifetime. Just the nod of someone's head, just a single pen stroke and he would be young again.

"This statement, Otto," he said. "Please give it to the press."

"Yes, sir," said Otto. He took the paper, held it gingerly.

"Tonight," said the senator.

"Tonight, sir? It is rather late."

"Nevertheless, I want to issue it tonight."

"It must be important, sir."

"It's my resignation," said the senator.

"Your resignation! From the senate, sir?"

"No," said the senator. "From life."

Mr. Michaelson: *As a churchman, I cannot think otherwise than that the proposal now before you gentlemen constitutes a perversion of God's law. It is not within the province of man to say a man may live beyond his allotted time.*

Chairman Leonard: *I might ask you this: How is one to know when a man's allotted time has come to an end? Medicine has prolonged the lives of many persons. Would you call a physician a perverter of God's law?*

Mr. Michaelson: *It has become apparent through the testimony given here that the eventual aim of continuing research is immortality. Surely you can see that physical immortality does not square with the Christian* concept. I tell you this, sir: You can't fool God and get away with it.

> —From the Records of a hearing before the science subcommittee of the public policy committee of the World House of Representatives.

Chess is a game of logic.

But likewise a game of ethics.

You do not shout and you do not whistle, nor band the pieces on the board, nor twiddle your thumbs, nor move a piece then take it back again.

When you're beaten, you admit it. You do not force your opponent to carry on the game to absurd lengths. You resign and start another game if there is time to play one. Otherwise, you just resign and you do it with all the good grace possible. You do not knock all the pieces to the floor in anger. You do not get up abruptly and stalk out of the room. You do not reach across the board and punch your opponent in the nose.

When you play chess you are, or you are supposed to be, a gentleman.

The senator lay wide-awake, staring at the ceiling.

You do not reach across the board and punch your opponent in the nose. You do not knock the pieces to the floor.

But this isn't chess, he told himself, arguing with himself. This isn't chess; this is life and death. A dying thing is not a gentleman. It does not curl up quietly and die of the hurt inflicted. It backs into a corner and it fights, it lashes back and does all the hurt it can.

And I am hurt. I am hurt to death.

And I have lashed back. I have lashed back, most horribly.

They'll not be able to walk down the street again, not ever again, those gentlemen who passed the sentence on me. For they have no more claim to continued life than I and the people now will know it. And the people will see to it that they do not get it.

I will die, but when I go down I'll pull the others with me. They'll know I pulled them down, down with me into the pit of death. That's the sweetest part of all—they'll know who pulled them down and they won't be able to say a word about it. They can't even contradict the noble things I said.

Someone in the corner said, some voice from some other time and place: *You're no gentleman, senator. You fight a dirty fight.*

Sure I do, said the senator. They fought dirty first. And politics always was a dirty game.

Remember all that fine talk you dished out to Lee the other day?

That was the other day, snapped the senator.

You'll never be able to look a chessman in the face again, said the voice in the corner.

I'll be able to look my fellow men in the face, however, said the senator.

Will you? asked the voice.

And that, of course, was the question. Would he?

I don't care, the senator cried desperately. I don't care what happens. They played a lousy trick on me. They can't get away with it. I'll fix their clocks for them. I'll—

Sure, you will, said the voice, mocking.

Go away, shrieked the senator. Go away and leave me. Let me be alone.

You are alone, said the thing in the corner. *You are more alone than any man has ever been before.*

Chairman Leonard: *You represent an insurance company, do you not, Mr. Markely? A big insurance company.*

Mr. Markely: *That is correct.*

Chairman Leonard: *And every time a person dies, it costs your company money?*

Mr. Markely: *Well, you might put it that way if you wished, although it is scarcely the case—*

Chairman Leonard: *You do have to pay out benefits on deaths, don't you?*

Mr. Markely: *Why, yes, of course we do.*

Chairman Leonard: *Then I can't understand your opposition to life continuation. If there were fewer deaths, you'd have to pay fewer benefits.*

Mr. Markely: *All very true, sir. But if people had reason to believe they would live virtually forever, they'd buy no life insurance.*

Chairman Leonard: *Oh, I see. So that's the way it is.*

—From the records of a hearing before the science subcommittee of the public policy committee of the World House of Representatives.

The senator awoke. He had not been dreaming, but it was almost as if he had awakened from a bad dream—or awakened to a bad dream—and he struggled to go back to sleep again, to gain the Nirvana of unawareness, to shut out the harsh reality of existence, to dodge the shame of knowing who and what he was.

But there was someone stirring in the room, and someone spoke to him and he sat upright in bed, stung to wakefulness by the happiness and something else that was almost worship which the voice held.

"It's wonderful, sir," said Otto. "There have been phone calls all night long. And the telegrams and radiograms still are stacking up."

The senator rubbed his eyes with pudgy fists.

"Phone calls, Otto? People sore at me?"

"Some of them were, sir. Terribly angry, sir. But not too many of them. Most of them were happy and wanted to tell you what a great thing you'd done. But I told them you were tired and I could not wake you."

"Great thing?" said the senator. "What great thing have I done?"

"Why, sir, giving up life continuation. One man said to tell you it was the greatest example of moral courage the world had ever known. He said all the common people would bless you for it. Those were his very words. He was very solemn, sir."

The senator swung his feet to the floor, sat on the edge of the bed, scratching at his ribs.

It was strange, he told himself, how a thing would turn out sometimes. A heel at bedtime and a hero in the morning.

"Don't you see, sir," said Otto, "you have made yourself one of the common people, one of the short-lived people. No one has ever done a thing like that before."

"I was one of the common people," said the senator, "long before I wrote that statement. And I didn't make myself one of them. I was forced to become one of them, much against my will."

But Otto, in his excitement, didn't seem to hear.

He rattle on: "The newspapers are full of it, sir. It's the biggest news in years. The political writers are chuckling over it. They're calling it the smartest political move that was ever pulled. They say that before you made the announcement you didn't have a chance of being re-elected senator and now, they say, you can be elected president if you just say the word."

The senator sighed. "Otto," he said, "please hand me my pants. It is cold in here."

Otto handed him his trousers. "There's a newspaperman waiting in the study, sir. I held all the others off, but this one sneaked in the back way. You know him, sir, so I let him wait. He is Mr. Lee."

"I'll see him," said the senator.

So it was a smart political move, was it? Well, maybe so, but after a day or so, even the surprised political experts would begin to wonder about the logic of a man literally giving up his life to be re-elected to a senate seat.

Of course the common herd would love it, but he had not done it for applause. Although, so long as the people insisted upon thinking of him as great and noble, it was all right to let them go on thinking so.

The senator jerked his tie straight and buttoned his coat. He went into the study and Lee was waiting for him.

"I suppose you want an interview," said the senator. "Want to know why I did this thing."

Lee shook his head. "No, senator, I have something else. Something you should know about. Remember our talk last week? About the disappearances?"

The senator nodded.

"Well, I have something else. You wouldn't tell me anything last week, but maybe now you will. I've checked, senator, and I've found this—the health winners are disappearing, too. More than eighty percent of those who participated in the finals of the last ten years have disappeared."

"I don't understand," said the senator.

"They're going somewhere," said Lee. "Something's happening to them. Something's happening to two classes of our people—the continuators and the healthiest youngsters."

"Wait a minute," gasped the senator. "Wait a minute, Mr. Lee."

He groped his way to the desk, grasped its edge and lowered himself into a chair.

"There is something wrong, senator?" asked Lee.

"Wrong?" mumbled the senator. "Yes, there must be something wrong."

"They've found living space," said Lee, triumphantly. "That's it, isn't it? They've found living space and they're sending out the pioneers."

The senator shook his head. "I don't know, Lee. I have not been informed. Check Extrasolar Research. They're the only ones who know—and they wouldn't tell you."

Lee grinned at him. "Good day, senator," he said. "Thanks so much for helping."

Dully, the senator watched him go.

Living space? Of course, that was it.

They had found living space and Extrasolar Research was sending out handpicked pioneers to prepare the way. It would take years of work and planning before the discovery could be announced. For once announced, world government must be ready to confer immortality on a mass production basis, must have ships available to carry out the hordes to the far, new worlds. A premature announcement would bring psychological and economic disruption that would make the government a shambles. So they would work very quietly, for they must work quietly.

His eyes found the little stack of letters on one corner of the desk and he remembered, with a shock of guilt, that he had meant to read them. He had promised Otto that he would and then he had forgotten.

I keep forgetting all the time, said the senator. I forget to read my paper and I forget to read my letters and I forget that some men are loyal and morally honest instead of slippery and slick. And I indulge in wishful thinking and that's the worst of all.

Continuators and health champions disappearing. Sure, they're disappearing. They're headed for new worlds and immortality.

And I . . . I . . . if only I had kept my big mouth shut—

The phone chirped and he picked it up.

"This is Sutton at Extrasolar Research," said an angry voice.

"Yes, Dr. Sutton," said the senator. "It's nice of you to call."

"I'm calling in regard to the invitation that we sent you last week," said Sutton. "In view of your statement last night, which we feel very keenly is an unjust criticism, we are withdrawing it."

"Invitation," said the senator. "Why, I didn't—"

"What I can't understand," said Sutton, "is why, with the invitation in your pocket, you should have acted as you did."

"But," said the senator, "but, doctor—"

"Good-by, senator," said Sutton.

Slowly the senator hung up. With a fumbling hand, he reached out and picked up the stack of letters.

It was the third one down. The return address was Extrasolar Research and it had been registered and sent special delivery and it was marked both PERSONAL and IMPORTANT.

The letter slipped out of the senator's trembling fingers and fluttered to the floor. He did not pick it up.

It was too late now, he knew, to do anything about it.

IMMIGRANT

The story "Immigrant" was entitled "Emigrant" when Cliff sent it to John W. Campbell Jr. in May of 1953. Campbell returned it for revision; but whatever revision was required, Cliff got it back to the editor in less than a week, and received, in just a few weeks, $700 (it's a long one). The story then appeared as the cover story in the March 1954 issue of Astounding Science Fiction *(except that someone listed the story, on the issue's cover, as "Immigration").*

The cover painting was by Kelly Freas, who, Cliff told me, had originally presented Campbell with a surrealistic silver-gray painting to be that cover. Campbell handed it back and told Kelly that it needed grass. Kelly went home furious, Cliff said, telling his wife that if John wanted grass, he'd get *grass—he was angry, but needed the money, so he spent the evening laying down, blade by tiny blade, an image of a large lawn. But later he got up in the middle of the night, looked at what he'd done, and said 'By God, it* did *need grass!'*

It got *grass, lots of grass filling the expanse of a great lawn that stretched to a distant starship, standing under a vast black sky—with a variety of children's toys abandoned on the lawn.*

The painting grabbed Cliff when he saw it, and he wrote Kelly, explaining he didn't have much money but would like the painting. Kelly wrote back to say he had a rule never to give away his work—but he would sell it for a dollar and an autographed copy of City. *Cliff went out and got the newest silver dollar he could find, then had his bank get him the oldest one it could find (which turned out to be from the 1880s); and he sent Kelly the book and, under separate cover, the dollars, explaining that a dollar was no good unless you had a second one to clink it against . . . By the time Cliff told me the story, he was able to say, with a certain pride, that the* City *volume was probably pretty valuable, and the dollars, too—so he had given Kelly value, after all.*

—dww

He was the only passenger for Kimon and those aboard the ship lionized him because he was going there.

To land him at his destination the ship went two light-years out of its way, an inconvenience for which his passage money, much as it had seemed to him when he'd paid it back on Earth, did not compensate by half.

But the captain did not grumble. It was, he told Selden Bishop, an honor to carry a passenger for Kimon.

The businessmen aboard sought him out and bought him drinks and lunches and talked expansively of the markets opening up in the new-found solar systems.

But despite their expansive talk, they looked at Bishop with half-veiled envy in their eyes and they said to him: "The man who cracks this Kimon situation is the one who'll have it big."

One by one, they contrived to corner him for private conversations, and the talk, after the first drink, always turned to billions if he ever needed backing.

Billions—while he sat there with less than twenty credits in his pocket, living in terror against the day when he might have to buy a round of drinks. For he wasn't certain that his twenty credits would stretch to a round of drinks.

The dowagers towed him off and tried to mother him; the young things lured him off and did not try to mother him. And everywhere he went, he heard the whisper behind the half-raised hand:

"To Kimon!" said the whispers. "My dear, you know what it takes to go to Kimon! An I.Q. rating that's positively fabulous and years and years of study and an examination that not one in a thousand passes."

It was like that all the way to Kimon.

II

Kimon was a galactic El Dorado, a never-never land, the country at the rainbow's foot. There were few who did not dream of going there, and there were many who aspired, but those who were chosen were a very small percentage of those who tried to make the grade and failed.

Kimon had been reached—either discovered or contacted would be the wrong word to use—more than a hundred years before by a crippled spaceship out of Earth which landed on the planet, lost and unable to go farther.

To this day no one knew for sure exactly what had happened, but it is known that in the end the crew destroyed the ship and settled down on Kimon, and wrote letters home saying they were staying.

Perhaps the delivery of those letters, more than anything else, convinced the authorities of Earth that Kimon was the kind of place the letters said it was—although later on there was other evidence which weighed as heavily in the balance.

There was, quite naturally, no mail service between Kimon and Earth, but the letters were delivered, and in a most fantastic, although when you think about it, a most logical way. They were rolled into a bundle and placed in a sort of tube, like the pneumatic tubes that are used in industry for interdepartmental communication, and the tube was delivered, quite neatly, on the desk of the World Postal chief in London. Not on the desk of a subordinate, mind you, but on the desk of the chief himself. The tube had not been there when he went to lunch; it was there when he came back, and so far as could be determined, despite a quite elaborate investigation, no one had been seen to place it there.

In time, still convinced that there had been some sort of hoax played, the postal service delivered the letters to the addresses by special messengers who in their more regular employment were operatives of the World Investigation Bureau.

The addressees were unanimous in their belief the letters were genuine, for in most cases the handwriting was recognized and in every letter there were certain matters in the context which seemed to prove that they were *bona fide*.

So each of the addressees wrote a letter in reply and these were inserted in the tube in which the original letters had arrived and the tube was placed meticulously in the exact spot where it had been found on the desk of the postal chief.

Then everyone watched and nothing happened for quite some time, but suddenly the tube was gone and no one had seen it go—it had been there one moment and not there the next.

There remained one question and that one soon was answered. In the matter of a week or two the tube reappeared again, just before the end of office hours. The postal chief had been working away, not paying much attention to what was going on, and suddenly he saw that the tube had come back again.

Once again it held letters and this time the letters were crammed with sheafs of hundred-credit notes, a gift from the marooned spacemen to their relatives, although it should be noted immediately that the spacemen themselves probably did not consider that they were marooned.

The letters acknowledged the receipt of the replies that had been sent from Earth and told more about the planet Kimon and its inhabitants.

And each letter carefully explained how they had hundred-credit notes on Kimon. The notes as they stood, the letters said, were simply counterfeits, made from bills the spacemen had in their pockets, although when Earth's fiscal experts and the Bureau of Investigation men had a look at them there was no way in which you could tell them from the real thing.

But, the letters said, the Kimonian government wished to make right the matter of counterfeiting. To back the currency the Kimonians, within the next short while, would place on deposit with the World Bank materials not only equivalent to their value, but enough additional to set up a balance against which more notes could be issued.

There was, the letters explained, no money as such on Kimon, but since Kimon was desirous of employing the men from Earth, there must be some way to pay them, so if it was all right with the World Bank and everyone else concerned . . .

The World Bank did a lot of hemming and hawing and talked about profound fiscal matters and deep economic principles, but all this talk dissolved to nothing when in the matter of a day or two several tons of carefully shielded uranium and a couple of bushels of diamonds were deposited, during the afternoon coffee hour, beside the desk of the bank's president.

With evidence of this sort, there was not much that Earth could do except accept the fact that the planet Kimon was a going concern and that the Earthmen who had landed there were going to stay, and take the entire situation at face value.

The Kimonians, the letters said, were humanoid and had parapsychic powers and had built a culture which was miles ahead of Earth or any other planet so far discovered in the galaxy.

Earth furbished up a ship, hand-picked a corps of its most persuasive diplomats, loaded down the hold with expensive gifts, and sent the whole business out to Kimon.

Within minutes after landing, the diplomats had been quite undiplomatically booted off the planet. Kimon, it appeared, had no desire to ally itself with a second-rate, barbaric planet. When it wished to establish diplomatic relationships it would say so. Earth people might come to Kimon if they wished and settle there, but not just any Earth person. To come to Kimon, the individual would have to possess not only a certain minimum I.Q., but must also have an impressive scholastic record.

And that was the way it was left.

You did not go to Kimon simply because you wished to go there; you worked to go to Kimon.

First of all, you had to have the specified I.Q. rating, and that ruled out ninety-nine per cent or better of Earth's population. Once you had passed the I.Q. test, you settled down to grueling years of study, and at the end of the years of study you wrote an examination and, once again, most of the aspirants were ruled out. Not more than one in a thousand who took the examination passed.

Year after year Earth men and women dribbled out to Kimon, settled there, prospered, wrote their letters home.

Of those who went out, none came back. Once you had lived on Kimon, you could not bear the thought of going back to Earth.

And yet, in all those years, the sum of knowledge concerning Kimon, its inhabitants and its culture, was very slight indeed. What knowledge there was, the only knowledge that there was, was compiled from the letters delivered meticulously once each week to the desk of the postal chief in London.

The letters spoke of wages and salaries a hundred times the wages and salaries that were paid on Earth, of magnificent business opportunities, of the Kimonian culture and the Kimonians themselves, but in no detail, of culture or of business or any other factor, were the letters specific.

And perhaps the recipients of the letters did not mind too much the lack of specific information, for almost every letter carried with it a sheaf of notes, all crisp and new, and very, very legal, backed by tons of uranium, bushels of diamonds, stacked bars of gold and other similar knick-knacks deposited from time to time beside the desk of the World Bank's president.

It became, in time, the ambition of every family on the Earth to send at least one relative to Kimon, for a relative on Kimon virtually spelled an assured and sufficient income for the rest of the clan for life.

Naturally, the legend of Kimon grew. Much that was said about it was untrue, of course. Kimon, the letters protested, did not have streets paved with solid gold, since there were no streets. Nor did Kimonian damsels wear gowns of diamond dust—the damsels of Kimon wore not much of anything.

But to those whose understanding went beyond streets of gold and gowns of diamonds, it was well understood that in Kimon lay possibilities vastly greater than either gold or diamonds. For here was a planet with a culture far in advance of Earth, a people who had schooled themselves or had naturally developed parapsychic powers. On Kimon one could learn the techniques that would revolutionize galactic industry and communications; on Kimon one might discover philosophy that would set mankind overnight on a new and better—and more profitable?—path.

The legend grew, interpreted by each according to his intellect and his way of thought, and grew and grew and grew . . .

Earth's government was very helpful to those who wished to go to Kimon, for government, as well as individuals, could appreciate the opportunities for the revolution of industry and the evolution of human thought. But since there had been no invitation to grant diplomatic recognition, Earth's government sat and waited, scheming, doing all it could to settle as many of its people on Kimon as was possible. But only the best, for even the densest bureaucrat recognized that on Kimon Earth must put its best foot forward.

Why the Kimonians allowed Earth to send its people was a mystery for which there was no answer. But apparently Earth was the only other planet in the galaxy which had been allowed to send its people. The Earthmen and the Kimonians, of course, both were humanoid, but this was not an adequate answer, either, for they were not the only humanoids in the galaxy. For its own comfort, Earth assumed that a certain common understanding, a similar outlook, a certain parallel evolutionary trend—with Earth a bit behind, of course—between Earth and Kimon might account for Kimon's qualified hospitality.

Be that as if may, Kimon was a galactic El Dorado, a never-never land, a place to get ahead, the place to spend your life, the country at the rainbow's end.

III

Selden Bishop stood in the parklike area where the gig had landed him, for Kimon had no spaceports, as it likewise failed to have many other things.

He stood, surrounded by his luggage, and watched the gig drive spaceward to rendezvous with the liner's orbit.

When he could see the gig no longer, he sat down on one of his bags and waited.

The park was faintly Earthlike, but the similarity was only in the abstract, for in each particular there was a subtle difference that said this was an alien planet. The trees were too slim and the flowers just a shade too loud and the grass was off a shade or two from the grass you saw on Earth. The birds, if they were birds, were more lizardlike than the birds of Earth and their feathers were put on wrong and weren't quite the color one associated with plumage. The breeze had a faint perfume upon it that was no perfume of Earth, but an alien odor that smelled as a color looked, and Bishop tried to decide, but couldn't, which color it might be.

Sitting on his bag, in the middle of the park, he tried to drum up a little enthusiasm, tried to whistle up some triumph that he finally was on Kimon, but the best that he could achieve was a thankfulness that he'd made it with the twenty still intact.

He would need a little cash to get along on until he could find a job. But, he told himself, he shouldn't have to wait too long before he found a job. The thing, of course, was not to take the first one offered him, but to shop around a little and find the one for which he was best fitted. And that, he knew, might take a little time.

Thinking of it, he wished that he had more than a twenty. He should have allowed himself a bigger margin, but that would have meant something less than the best luggage he could buy and perhaps not enough of it, off-the-rack suits instead of tailored, and all other things accordingly.

It was, he told himself, important that he made the best impression, and sitting there and thinking it over, he couldn't bring himself to regret the money he had spent to make a good impression.

Maybe he should have asked Morley for a loan. Morley would have given him anything he asked and he could have paid it back as soon as he got a job. But he had hated to ask, for to ask, he now admitted, would have detracted from his new-found importance as a man who had been selected to make the trip to Kimon. Everyone, even Morley, looked up to a man who was sent to blast for Kimon, and you couldn't go around asking for a loan or for other favors.

He remembered that last visit he had with Morley, and looking back at it now, he saw that, while Morley was his friend, that last visit had a flavor, more or less, of a diplomatic job that Morley had to carry out.

Morley had gone far and was going farther in the diplomatic service. He looked like a diplomat and he talked like one and he had a better grasp, old heads at the department said, of Sector Nineteen politics and economics than any of the other younger men. He wore a clipped mustache that had a frankly cultivated look, and his hair was always quite in place, and his body, when he walked, was like a panther walking.

They had sat in Morley's diggings and had been all comfortable and friendly, and then Morley had gotten up and paced up and down the room with his panther walk.

"We've been friends for a long, long time," said Morley. "We've been in a lot of scrapes together."

And the two of them had smiled, remembering some of the scrapes they had been in together.

"When I heard you were going out to Kimon," Morley said, "I was pleased about it naturally. I'd be pleased at anything that came your way. But I was pleased, as well, for another reason. I told myself here finally was a man who could do a job and find out what we want."

"What do you want?" Bishop had asked and, as he remembered it, he had asked it as if he might be asking whether Morley wanted Scotch or bourbon. Although, come to think of it, he never would have asked that particular question, for all the young men in the alien relations section religiously drank Scotch. But, anyhow, he asked it casually, although he sensed that there was nothing casual at all about the situation.

He could smell the scent of cloak and dagger and he caught a sudden glimpse of huge official worry, and for an instant he was a little cold and scared.

"There must be some way to crack that planet," Morley had told him, "but we haven't found it yet. So far as the Kimonians are concerned, none of the rest of us, none of the other planets, officially exist. There's not a single planet accorded diplomatic status. On Kimon there is not a single official representative of any other people. They don't seem to trade with anyone, and yet they must trade with someone, for no planet, no culture can exist in complete self-sufficiency. They must have diplomatic relations somewhere, with someone. There must be some reason, beyond the obvious one that we are an inferior culture, why they do not recognize Earth. For even in the more barbaric days of Earth there was official recognition of many governments and peoples who were cultural inferiors to the recognizing nation."

"You want me to find out all this?"

"No," said Morley. "Not all that. All we want are clues. Somewhere there is the clue that we are looking for, the hint that will tell us what the actual situation is. All we need is the opening wedge—the foot in the door. Give us that and we will do the rest."

"There have been others," Bishop told him. "Thousands of others. I'm not the only one who ever went to Kimon."

"For the last fifty years or more," said Morley, "the section has talked to all the others, before they went out, exactly as I'm talking to you now."

"And you've got nothing?"

"Nothing," said Morley. "Or almost nothing. Or nothing, anyhow, that counted or made any sense."

"They failed—"

"They failed," Morley told him, "because once on Kimon they forgot about Earth . . . well, not forgot about it, that's not entirely it. But they lost all allegiance to it. They were Kimon-blinded."

"You believe that?"

"I don't know," said Morley. "It's the best explanation that we have. The trouble is that we talk to them only once. None of them come back. We can write letters to them, certainly. We can try to jog them—indirectly, of course. But we can't ask them outright."

"Censorship?"

"Not censorship," said Morley, "although they may have that, too; but mostly telepathy. The Kimonians would know if we tried to impress anything too forcibly upon their minds. And we can't take the chance of a simple thought undoing all the work that we have done."

"But you're telling me."

"You'll forget it," Morley said. "You will have several weeks in which you can forget it—push it to the back of your mind. But not entirely—not entirely."

"I understand," Bishop told him.

"Don't get me wrong," said Morley. "It's nothing sinister. You're not to look for that. It may be just a simple thing. The way we comb our hair. There's some reason—perhaps many little ones. And we must know those reasons."

Morley had switched it off as quickly as he had begun it, had poured another round of drinks, had sat down again and talked of their school days and of the girls they'd known and of week-ends in the country.

It had been, all in all, a very pleasant evening.

But that had been weeks ago, and since then he'd scarcely remembered it and now here he was on Kimon, sitting on one of his bags in the middle of a park, waiting for a welcoming Kimonian to show up.

All the time that he'd been waiting, he had been prepared for the Kimonian's arrival. He knew what a Kimonian looked like and he should not have been surprised.

But when the native came, he was.

For the native was six foot, ten, and almost a godlike being, a sculptured humanoid who was, astonishingly, much more human than he had thought to find.

One moment he had sat alone in the little parklike glade and the next the native was standing by his side.

Bishop came to his feet and the Kimonian said, "We are glad you are here. Welcome to Kimon, sir."

The native's inflection was as precise and beautiful as his sculptured body.

"Thank you," Bishop said, and knew immediately that the two words were inadequate and that his voice was slurred and halting compared with the native's voice. And, looking at the

Kimonian, he had the feeling that by comparison, he cut a rumpled, seedy figure.

He reached into his pocket for his papers and his fingers were all thumbs, so that he fumbled for them and finally dug them out—dug is the word exactly—and handed them to the waiting being.

The Kimonian flicked them—that was it, flicked them—then he said. "Mr. Selden Bishop. Very glad to know you. Your I.Q. rating, 160, is very satisfactory. Your examination showing, if I may say so, is extraordinary. Recommendations good. Clearance from Earth in order. And I see you made good time. Very glad to have you."

"But—" said Bishop. Then he clamped his mouth tight shut. He couldn't tell this being he'd merely flicked the pages and could not possibly have read them. For, obviously, he had.

"You had a pleasant flight, Mr. Bishop?"

"A most pleasant one," said Bishop and was filled with sudden pride that he could answer so easily and urbanely.

"Your luggage," said the native, "is in splendid taste."

"Why, thank you—" then Bishop was filled with rage. What right had this person to patronize his luggage!

But the native did not appear to notice.

"You wish to go to the hotel?"

"If you please," said Bishop, speaking very tightly, holding himself in check.

"Please allow me," said the native.

Bishop blurred for just a second—a definite sense of blurring—as if the universe had gone swiftly out of focus, then he was standing, not in the parklike glade, but in a one-man-sized alcove off a hotel lobby, with his bags stacked neatly beside him.

IV

He had missed the triumph before, sitting in the glade, waiting for the native, after the gig had left him, but now it struck him, a heady, drunken triumph that surged through his body and rose in his throat to choke him.

This was Kimon! He finally was on Kimon! After all the years of study, he was here—the fabulous place he'd worked for many years to reach.

A high I.Q., they'd said behind their half-raised hands—a high I.Q. and many years of study, and a stiff examination that not more than one in every thousand passed.

He stood in the alcove, with the sense of hiding there, to give himself a moment in which to regain his breath at the splendor of what had finally come to pass, to gain the moment it would take for the unreasoning triumph to have its way with him and go.

For the triumph was something that must not be allowed to last. It was something that he must not show. It was a personal thing and as something personal it must be hidden deep.

He might be one of a thousand back on Earth, but here he stood on no more than equal footing with the ones who had come before him. Perhaps not quite on equal footing, for they would know the ropes and he had yet to learn them.

He watched them in the lobby—the lucky and the fabulous ones who had preceded him, the glittering company he had dreamed about during all the weary years—the company that he presently would join, the ones of Earth who were adjudged fit to go to Kimon.

For only the best must go—the best and smartest and the quickest. Earth must put her best foot forward, for how otherwise would Earth ever persuade Kimon that she was a sister planet?

At first the people in the lobby had been no more than a crowd, a crowd that shone and twinkled, but with that curious lack of personality which goes with a crowd. But now, as he watched, the crowd dissolved into individuals and he saw them, not as a group, but as the men and women he presently would know.

He did not see the bell captain until the native stood in front of him, and the bell captain, if anything, was taller and more handsome than the man who'd met him in the glade.

"Good evening, sir," the captain said. "Welcome to the Ritz."

Bishop started. "The Ritz? Oh, yes, I had forgotten. This place is the Ritz."

"We're glad to have you with us," said the captain. "We hope your stay will prove to be a long one."

"Certainly," said Bishop. "That is, I hope so, too."

"We had been notified," the captain said, "that you were arriving, Mr. Bishop. We took the liberty of reserving rooms for you. I trust they will be satisfactory."

"I am sure they will be," Bishop said.

As if anything on Kimon could be unsatisfactory!

"Perhaps you will want to dress," the captain said. "There still is time for dinner."

"Oh, certainly," said Bishop. "Most assuredly I will."

And wished he had not said it.

"We'll send up the bags," the captain said. "No need to register. That is taken care of. If you will permit me, sir."

V

The rooms were satisfactory. There were three of them.

Sitting in a chair, Bishop wondered how he'd ever pay for them.

Remembering the lonely twenty credits, he was seized with a momentary panic.

He'd have to get a job sooner than he planned, for the twenty credits wouldn't go too far with a layout like this one. Although he supposed if he asked for credit it would be given him.

But he recoiled from the idea of asking for credit, of being forced to admit that he was short of cash. So far he'd done everything correctly. He'd arrived aboard a liner and not a battered trader; his luggage—what had the native said?—was in splendid taste; his wardrobe was all that could be expected; and he hoped that he'd not communicated to anyone the panic and dismay he'd felt at the luxury of the suite.

He got up from the chair and prowled about the room. There was no carpeting, for the floor itself was soft and yielding, and you left momentary tracks as you walked, but they puffed back and smoothed out almost immediately.

He walked over to a window and stood looking out of it. Evening had fallen and the landscape was covered with a dusty blue—and there was nothing, absolutely nothing, but rolling countryside. There were no roads that he could see and no lights that would have told of other habitations.

Perhaps, he thought, I'm on the wrong side of the building. On the other side there may be streets and roads and homes and shops.

He turned back to the room and looked at it—the Earthlike furniture so quietly elegant that it almost shouted, the beautiful, veined marble fireplace, the shelves of books, the shine of old wood, the matchless paintings hanging on the wall, and the great cabinet that almost filled one end of the room.

He wondered what the cabinet might be. It was a beautiful thing, with an antique look about it and it had a polish—not a wax, but a polish of human hands and time.

He walked toward it.

The cabinet said, "Drink, sir?"

"I don't mind if I do," said Bishop, then stopped stock-still, realizing that the cabinet had spoken and he had answered it.

A panel opened in the cabinet and the drink was there.

"Music?" asked the cabinet.

"If you please," said Bishop.

"Type?"

"Type? Oh, I see. Something gay, but maybe just a little sadness too. Like the blue hour of twilight spreading over Paris. Who was it used that phrase? One of the old writers. Fitzgerald. I'm sure it was Fitzgerald."

The music told about the blue hour stealing over that city far away on Earth, and there was soft April rain and distant girlish laughter and the shine of the pavement in the slanting rain.

"Is there anything else you wish, sir?" asked the cabinet.

"Nothing at the moment."

"Very well, sir. You will have an hour to get dressed for dinner."

He left the room, sipping his drink as he went—and the drink had a certain touch to it.

He went into the bedroom and tested the bed, and it was satisfactorily soft. He examined the dresser and the full-length glass and peeked into the bathroom and saw that it was equipped with an automatic shaver and massager, that it had a shower and tub, an exercising machine and a number of other gadgets that he couldn't place.

And the third room.

It was almost bare by the standards of the other two. In the center of it stood a chair with great flat arms, and on each of the arms many rows of buttons.

He approached the chair cautiously, wondering what it was—what kind of trap it was. Although that was foolish, for there were no traps on Kimon. This was Kimon, the land of opportunity, where a man might make a fortune and live in luxury and rub shoulders with an intelligence and a culture that was the best yet found in the galaxy.

He bent down over the wide arms of the chair and found that each of the buttons was labeled. They were labeled "History," "Poetry," "Drama," "Sculpture," "Literature," "Painting,"

"Astronomy," "Philosophy," "Physics," "Religions" and many other things. And there were several that were labeled with words he'd never seen and that had no meaning to him.

He stood in the room and looked around at its starkness and saw for the first time that it had no windows, but was just a sort of box—a theater, he decided, or a lecture room. You sat in the chair and pressed a certain button and—

But there was no time for that. An hour to dress for dinner, the cabinet had said, and some of that hour was already gone.

The luggage was in the bedroom and he opened the bag that held his dinner clothes. The jacket was badly wrinkled.

He stood with it in his hands, staring at it. Maybe the wrinkles would hang out. Maybe—

But he knew they wouldn't.

The music stopped and the cabinet asked, "Is there something that you wish, sir?"

"Can you press a dinner jacket?"

"Surely, sir, I can."

"How soon?"

"Five minutes," said the cabinet. "Give me the trousers, too."

VI

The bell rang and he went to the door.

A man stood just outside.

"Good evening," said the man. "My name is Montague, but they call me Monty."

"Won't you come in, Monty?"

Monty came in and surveyed the room.

"Nice place," he said.

Bishop nodded. "I didn't ask for anything at all. They just gave it to me."

"Clever, these Kimonians," said Monty. "Very clever, yes."

"My name is Selden Bishop."

"Just come in?" asked Monty.

"An hour or so ago."

"All dewed up with what a great place Kimon is."

"I know nothing about it," Bishop told him. "I studied it, of course."

"I know," said Monty, looking at him slantwise. "Just being neighborly. New victim and all that, you know."

Bishop smiled because he didn't quite know what else to do.

"What's your line?" asked Monty.

"Business," said Bishop. "Administration's what I'm aiming at."

"Well, then," Monty said, "I guess that lets you out. You wouldn't be interested."

"In what?"

"In football. Or baseball. Or cricket. Not the athletic type."

"Never had the time."

"Too bad," Monty said. "You have the build for it."

The cabinet asked: "Would the gentleman like a drink?"

"If you please," said Monty.

"And another one for you, sir?"

"If you please," said Bishop.

"Go on and get dressed," said Monty. "I'll sit down and wait."

"Your jacket and trousers, sir," said the cabinet.

A door swung open and there they were, cleaned and pressed.

"I didn't know," said Bishop, "that you went in for sports out here."

"Oh, we don't," said Monty. "This is a business venture."

"Business venture?"

"Certainly. Give the Kimonians something to bet on. They might go for it. For a while, at least. You see, they can't bet—"

"I don't see why not—"

"Well, consider for a moment. They have no sports at all, you know. Wouldn't be possible. Telepathy. They'd know three moves ahead what their opponents were about to do. Telekinesis. They could move a piece or a ball or a what-have-you without touching a finger to it. They—"

"I think I see," said Bishop.

"So we plan to get up some teams and put on exhibition matches. Drum up as much enthusiasm as we can. They'll come out in droves to see it. Pay admission. Place bets. We, of course, will play the bookies and rake off our commissions. It will be a good thing while it lasts."

"It won't last, of course."

Monty gave Bishop a long look.

"You catch on fast," he said. "You'll get along."

"Drinks, gentlemen," the cabinet said.

Bishop got the drinks, gave one of them to his visitor.

"You better let me put you down," said Monty. "Might as well rake in what you can. You don't need to know too much about it."

"All right," Bishop told him agreeably. "Go ahead and put me down."

"You haven't got much money," Monty said.

"How did you know that?"

"You're scared about this room," said Monty.

"Telepathy?" asked Bishop.

"You pick it up," said Monty. "Just the fringes of it. You'll never be as good as they are. Never. But you pick things up from time to time—a sort of sense that seeps into you. After you've been here long enough."

"I had hoped that no one noticed."

"A lot of them will notice, Bishop. Can't help but notice, the way you're broadcasting. But don't let it worry you. We are all friends. Banded against the common enemy, you might say. If you need a loan—"

"Not yet," said Bishop. "I'll let you know."

"Me," said Monty. "Me or anyone. We are all friends. We got to be."

"Thanks."

"Not at all. Now you go ahead and dress. I'll sit and wait for you. I'll bear you down with me. Everyone's waiting to meet you."

"That's good to know," said Bishop. "I felt quite a stranger."

"Oh, my, no," said Monty. "No need to. Not many come, you know. They'll all want to know of Earth."

He rolled the glass between his fingers.

"How about Earth?" he asked.

"How about—"

"Yes, it is still there, of course. How is it getting on? What's the news?"

VII

He had not seen the hotel before. He had caught a confused glimpse of it from the alcove off the lobby, with his luggage stacked up beside him, before the bell captain had showed up and whisked him to his rooms.

But now he saw that it was a strangely substantial fairyland, with fountains and hidden fountain music, with the spidery tracery of rainbows serving as groins and arches, with shimmery columns of glass that caught and reflected and duplicated many times the entire construction of the lobby so that one was at once caught up in the illusion that here was a place that went on and on forever, and at the same time you could cordon off a section of it in your mind as an intimate corner for a group of friends.

It was illusion and substantiality, beauty and a sense of home—it was, Bishop suspected, all things to all men and what you wished to make it. A place of utter magic that divorced one from the world and the crudities of the world, with a gaiety that was not brittle and a sentimentality that stopped short of being cheap, and that transmitted a sense of well-being and of self-importance from the very fact of being a part of such a place.

There was no such place on Earth, there could be no such place on Earth, for Bishop suspected that something more than human planning, more than human architectural skill, had gone into its building. You walked in an enchantment and you talked with magic and you felt the sparkle and the shine of the place live within your brain.

"It gets you," Monty said. "I always watch the faces of the newcomers when they first walk in it."

"It wears off after a time," said Bishop, not believing it.

Monty shook his head. "My friend, it does not wear off. It doesn't surprise you quite so much, but it stays with you all the time. A human does not live long enough for a place like this to wear thin and commonplace."

He had eaten dinner in the dining room, which was old and solemn, with an ancient other-worldness and a hushed, tiptoe atmosphere, with Kimonian waiters at your elbow, ready to recommend a certain dish or a vintage as one that you should try.

Monty had coffee while he ate and there had been others who had come drifting past to stop a moment and welcome him and ask him of Earth, always using a studied casualness, always with a hunger in their eyes that belied the casualness.

"They make you feel at home," said Monty, "and they mean it. They are glad when a new one comes."

He did feel at home—more at home than he had ever felt in his life before, as if already he was beginning to fit in. He had not expected to fit in so quickly and he was slightly astonished at it—for here were all the people he had dreamed of being with, and he finally was with them. You could feel the magnetic force of them, the personal magnetism that had made them great, great enough to be Kimon-worthy, and looking at them he wondered which of them he would get to know, which would be his friends.

He was relieved when he found that he was not expected to pay for his dinner or his drinks, but simply sign a chit, and once he'd caught onto that, everything seemed brighter, for the dinner of itself would have taken quite a hole out of the twenty nestling in his pocket.

With dinner over and with Monty gone somewhere into the crowd, he found himself in the bar, sitting on a stool and nursing a drink that the Kimonian bartender had recommended as being something special.

The girl came out of nowhere and floated up to the stool beside him and she said:

"What's that you're drinking, friend?"

"I don't know," said Bishop. He made a thumb toward the man behind the bar. "Ask him to make you one."

The bartender heard and got busy with the bottles and the shaker.

"You're fresh from Earth," said the girl.

"Fresh is the word," said Bishop.

"It's not so bad," she said. "That is, if you don't think about it."

"I won't think about it," Bishop promised. "I won't think of anything."

"Of course, you do get used to it," she said. "After a while you don't mind the faint amusement. You think, what the hell, let them laugh all they want to so long as I have it good. But the day will come—"

"What are you talking about?" asked Bishop. "Here's your drink. Dip your muzzle into that and—"

"The day will come when we are old to them, when we don't amuse them any longer. When we become passé. We can't keep thinking up new tricks. Take my painting, for example—"

"See here," said Bishop. "You're talking way above my head."

"See me a week from now," she said. "The name's Maxine. Just ask to see Maxine. A week from now, we can talk together. So long, Buster."

She floated off the stool and suddenly was gone.

She hadn't touched her drink.

VIII

He went up to his rooms and stood for a long time at a window, staring out into the featureless landscape lighted by a moon.

Wonder thundered in his brain, the wonder and the newness and the many questions, the breathlessness of finally being here, of slowly coming to a full realization of the fact that he was here, that he was one of the glittering, fabulous company he had dreamed about for years.

The long grim years peeled off him, the years of books and study, the years of determined driving, the hungry, anxious, grueling years when he had lived a monkish life, mortifying body and soul to drive his intellect.

The years fell off and he felt the newness of himself as well as the newness of the scene. A cleanness and a newness and the sudden glory.

The cabinet finally spoke to him.

"Why don't you try the live-it, sir?"

Bishop swung sharply around.

"You mean—?"

"The third room," said the cabinet. "You'll find it most amusing."

"The live-it!"

"That's right," said the cabinet. "You pick it and you live it."

Which sounded like something out of the Alice books.

"It's safe," said the cabinet. "It's perfectly safe. You can come back any time you wish."

"Thank you," said Bishop.

He went into the room and sat down in the chair and studied the buttons on the arms.

History?

Might as well, he told himself. He knew a bit of history. He'd been interested in it and had taken several courses and done a lot of supplemental reading.

He punched the "History" button.

A panel in the wall before the chair lit up and a face appeared—the face of a Kimonian, the bronzed and golden face, the classic beauty of the race.

Aren't any of them homely? Bishop wondered. None of them ugly or crippled, like the rest of humanity?

"What type of history, sir?" the face in the screen asked him.

"Type?"

"Galactic, Kimonian, Earth—almost any place you wish."

"Earth, please," said Bishop.

"Specifications?"

"England," said Bishop. "October 14, 1066. A place called Senlac."

And he was there.

He was no longer in the room with its single chair and its four bare walls, but he stood upon a hill in sunny autumn weather with the gold and red of trees and the blueness of the haze and the shouts of men.

He stood rooted in the grass that blew upon the hillside and saw that the grass had turned to hay with its age and sunshine—and out beyond the grass and hill, grouped down on the plain, was a ragged line of horsemen, with the sun upon their helmets and flashing on their shields, with the leopard banners curling in the wind.

It was October 14th and it was Saturday and on the hill stood Harold's hosts behind their locked shield wall, and before the sun had set new forces would have been put in motion to shape the course of empire.

Taillefer, he thought. Taillefer will ride in the fore of William's charge, singing the *"Chanson de Roland"* and wheeling his sword into the air so that it becomes a wheel of fire to lead the others on.

The Normans charged and there was no Taillefer. There was no one who wheeled his sword into the air, there was no singing. There was merely shouting and the hoarse crying of men riding to their death.

The horsemen were charging directly at him and he wheeled and tried to run, but he could not outrun them and they were upon him. He saw the flash of polished hoofs and the cruel steel of the shoes upon the hoofs, the glinting lance point, the swaying, jouncing scabbard, the red and green and yellow of the cloaks, the dullness of the armor, the open roaring mouths of men—and they were upon him. And passing through him and over him as if he were not there.

He stopped stock-still, heart hammering in his chest, and, as if from somewhere far off, he felt the wind of the charging horses that were running all around him.

Up the hill there were hoarse cries of "Ut! Ut!" and the high, sharp ring of steel. Dust was rising all around him and somewhere off to the left a dying horse was screaming. Out of the dust a man came running down the hill. He staggered and fell and got up and ran again and Bishop could see that blood poured out of the ripped armor and washed down across the metal, spraying the dead, sere grass as he ran down the hill.

The horses came back again, some of them riderless, running with their necks outstretched, with the reins flying in the wind, with foam dashing from their mouths.

One man sagged in the saddle and fell off, but his foot caught in the stirrup and his horse, shying, dragged him sideways.

Up on top of the hill the Saxon square was cheering and through the settling dust he saw the heap of bodies that lay outside the shield wall.

Let me out of here! Bishop was screaming to himself. *How do I get out of here! Let me out—*

He was out, back in the room again, with its single chair and the four blank walls.

He sat there quietly and he thought: *There was no Taillefer.*

No one who rode and sang and tossed the sword in the air.

The tale of Taillefer was no more than the imagination of some copyist who had improved upon the tale to while away his time.

But men had died. They had run down the hill, staggering with their wounds, and died. They had fallen from their horses and been dragged to death by their frightened mounts. They had come crawling down the hill, with minutes left of life and with a whimper in their throats.

He stood up and his hands were shaking. He walked unsteadily into the next room.

"You are going to bed, sir?" asked the cabinet.

"I think I will," said Bishop.

"Very good, then, sir. I'll lock up and put out."

"That's very good of you."

"Routine, sir," said the cabinet. "Is there anything you wish?"

"Not a thing," said Bishop. "Good night."

"Good night," said the cabinet.

IX

In the morning he went to the employment agency which he found in one corner of the hotel lobby.

There was no one around but a Kimonian girl, a tall, statuesque blonde, but with a grace to put to shame the most petite of humans. A woman, Bishop thought, jerked out of some classic Grecian myth, a blonde goddess come to life and beauty. She didn't wear the flowing Grecian robe, but she could have. She wore, truth to tell, but little, and was all the better for it.

"You are new," she said.

He nodded.

"Wait, I know," she said. She looked at him. "Selden Bishop, age twenty-nine Earth years, I.Q., 160."

"Yes, ma'm," he said.

She made him feel as if he should bow and scrape.

"Business administration, I understand," she said.

He nodded bleakly.

"Please sit down, Mr. Bishop, and we will talk this over."

He sat down and he was thinking: It isn't right for a beautiful girl to be so big and husky. Nor so competent.

"You'd like to get started doing something," said the girl.

"That's the thought I had."

"You specialized in business administration. I'm afraid there aren't many openings in that particular field."

"I wouldn't expect too much to start with," Bishop told her with what he felt was a becoming modesty and a realistic outlook. "Almost anything at all, until I can prove my value."

"You'd have to start at the very bottom. And it would take years of training. Not in method only, but in attitude and philosophy."

"I wouldn't—"

He hesitated. He had meant to say that he wouldn't mind. But he would mind. He would mind a lot.

"But I spent years," he said. "I know—"

"Kimonian business?"

"Is it so much different?"

"You know all about contracts, I suppose."

"Certainly I do."

"There is no such thing as a contract on all of Kimon."

"But—"

"There is no need of any."

"Integrity?"

"That, and other things as well."

"Other things?"

"You wouldn't understand."

"Try me."

"It would be useless, Mr. Bishop. New concepts entirely so far as you're concerned. Of behavior. Of motives. On Earth, profit is the motive—"

"Isn't it here?"

"In part. A very small part."

"The other motives—"

"Cultural development for one. Can you imagine an urge to cultural development as powerful as the profit motive?"

Bishop was honest about it. "No, I can't," he said.

"Here," she said, "it is the more powerful of the two. But that's not all. Money is another thing. We have no actual money. No coin that changes hands."

"But there is money. Credit notes."

"For the convenience of your race alone," she said. "We created your money values and your evidence of wealth so that we could hire your services and pay you—and I might add that we pay you well. We have gone through all the motions. The currency that we create is as valid as anywhere else in the galaxy. It's backed by deposits in Earth's banks and it is legal tender so far as you're concerned. But Kimonians themselves do not employ money."

Bishop floundered. "I can't understand," he said.

"Of course you can't," she said. "It's an entirely new departure for you. Your culture is so constituted that there must be a certain physical assurance of each person's wealth and worth. Here we do not need that physical assurance. Here each person carries in his head the simple bookkeeping of his worth and debts. It is there for him to know. It is there for his friends and business associates to see at any time they wish."

"It isn't business, then," said Bishop. "Not business as I think of it."

"Exactly," said the girl.

"But I am trained for business, I spent—"

"Years and years of study. But on Earth's methods of business, not on Kimon's."

"But there are businessmen here. Hundreds of them."

"Are there?" she asked.

She was smiling at him. Not a superior smile, nor a taunting one—just smiling at him.

"What you need," she said, "is contact with Kimonians. A chance to get to know your way around. An opportunity to appreciate our point of view and get the hang of how we do things."

"That sounds all right," said Bishop. "How do I go about it?"

"There have been instances," said the girl, "when Earth people sold their services as companions."

"I don't think I'd care much for that. It sounds . . . well, like baby sitting or reading to old ladies or . . ."

"Can you play an instrument or sing?"

Bishop shook his head.

"Paint? Draw? Dance?"

He couldn't do any of them.

"Box, perhaps," she said. "Physical combat. That is popular at times, if it's not overdone."

"You mean prize fighting?"

"I think that is one way you describe it."

"No, I can't," said Bishop.

"That doesn't leave much," she said as she picked up some papers.

"Transportation?" he asked.

"Transportation is a personal matter."

And of course it was, he told himself. With telekinesis you could transport yourself or anything you might have a mind to move—without mechanical aid.

"Communications," he said weakly. "I suppose that is the same?"

She nodded.

With telepathy, it would be.

"You know about transportation and communications, Mr. Bishop?"

"Earth variety," said Bishop. "No good here, I gather."

"None at all," she said. "Although we might arrange a lecture tour. Some of us would help you put your material together."

Bishop shook his head. "I can't talk," he said.

She got up.

"I'll check around," she said. "Drop in again. We'll find something that you'll fit."

"Thanks," he said and went back to the lobby.

X

He went for a walk.

There were no roads or paths.

There was nothing.

The hotel stood on the plain and there was nothing else.

No buildings around it. No village. No roads. Nothing.

It stood there, huge and ornate and lonely, like a misplaced thing.

It stood stark against the skyline, for there were no other buildings to blend into it and soften it and it looked like something that someone in a hurry had dumped down and left.

He struck out across the plain toward some trees that he thought must mark a watercourse and he wondered why there were no paths or roads, but suddenly he knew why there were no paths or roads.

He thought about the years he had spent cramming business administration into his brain and he remembered the huge book of excerpts from the letters written home from Kimon hinting at big business deals, at responsible positions.

And the thought struck him that there was one thing in common in all of the excerpts in the book—that the deals and positions were always hinted at, that no one had ever told exactly what he did.

Why did they do it? he asked himself. Why did they fool us all?

Although, of course, there might be more to it than he knew. He had been on Kimon for somewhat less than a full day's time. I'll look around, the Grecian blonde had said—I'll look around, we'll find something that you fit.

He went on across the plain and reached the line of trees and found the stream. It was a prairie stream, a broad, sluggish flow of crystal water between two grassy banks. Lying on his stomach to peer into the depths, he saw the flash of fishes far below him.

He took off his shoes and dangled his feet in the water and kicked a little to make the water splash, and he thought:

They know all about us. They know about our life and culture. They know about the leopard banners and how Senlac must have looked on Saturday, October 14, 1066, with the hosts of England massed upon the hilltop and the hosts of William on the plain below.

They know what makes us tick and they let us come and because they let us come, there must be some value in us.

What had the girl said, the girl who had floated to the stool and then left with her drink still standing and untouched. Faint amusement, she had said. You get used to it, she had said. If you don't think too much about it, you get used to it.

See me in a week, she had said. In a week you and I can talk. And she had called him Buster.

Well, maybe she had a right to call him that. He had been starry-eyed and a sort of eager beaver. And probably ignorant-smug.

They know about us and how do they know about us?

Senlac might have been staged, but he didn't think so—there was a strange, grim reality about it that got under your skin, a crawling sort of feeling that told you it was true, that that was how it had happened and had been. That there had been no Taillefer and that a man had died with his guts dragging in the grass and that the Englishmen had cried "Ut! Ut!" which might have meant almost anything at all or nothing just as well, but probably had meant "Out."

He sat there, cold and lonely, wondering how they did it. How they had made it possible for a man to punch a button and live a scene long dead, to see the death of men who had long been dust mingled with the earth.

There was no way to know, of course.

There was no use to guess.

Technical information, Morley Reed had said, that would revolutionize our entire economic pattern.

He remembered Morley pacing up and down the room and saying: "We must find out about them. We must find out."

And there was a way to find out.

There was a splendid way.

He took his feet out of the water and dried them with handfuls of grass. He put his shoes back on and walked back to the hotel sitting by itself.

The blond goddess was still at her desk in the Employment Bureau.

"About that baby-sitting job," he said.

She looked startled for a moment—terribly, almost childishly startled; but her face slid swiftly back to its goddess-mask.

"Yes, Mr. Bishop."

"I've thought it over," he said. "If you have that kind of job I'll take it."

XI

He lay in bed, sleepless, for a long time that night and took stock of himself and of the situation and he came to a decision that it might not be as bad as he thought it was.

There were jobs to be had, apparently. The Kimonians even seemed anxious that you should get a job. And even if it weren't the kind of work a man might want, or the kind that he was fitted for, it at least would be a start. From that first foothold a man could go up—a clever man, that is. And all the men and women, all the Earthians on Kimon, certainly were clever. If they weren't clever, they wouldn't be there to start with.

All of them seemed to be getting along. He had not seen either Monty or Maxine that evening but he had talked to others and all of them seemed to be satisfied—or at least keeping up the appearance of being satisfied. If there were general dissatisfaction, Bishop told himself, there wouldn't even be the appearance of being satisfied, for there is nothing that an Earthian likes better than some quiet and mutual griping. And he had heard none of it—none of it at all.

He had heard some more talk about the starting of the athletic teams and had talked to several men who had been enthusiastic about it as a source of revenue.

He had talked to another man named Thomas who was a gardening expert at one of the big Kimonian estates and the man had talked for an hour or more on the growing of exotic flowers. There had been a little man named Williams who had sat in the bar beside him and had told him enthusiastically of his commission to write a book of ballads based on Kimonian history and another man named Jackson who was executing a piece of statuary for one of the native families.

If a man could get a satisfactory job, Bishop thought, life could be pleasant here on Kimon.

Take the rooms he had. Beautiful appointments, much better than he could expect at home. A willing cabinet-robot who dished up drinks and sandwiches, who pressed clothes, turned out and locked up, and anticipated your no-more-than-half-formed wish. And the room—the room with the four blank walls and the single chair with the buttons on its arm. There, in that room, was instruction and entertainment and adventure. He had made a bad choice in picking the battle of Hastings for his first test of it, he knew now. But there were other places, other times, other more pleasant and less bloody incidents that one could experience.

It was experience, too—and not merely seeing. He had really been walking on the hilltop. He had tried to dodge the charging horses, although there'd been no reason to, for apparently, even in the midst of a happening, you stood by some special dispensation as a thing apart, as an interested but unreachable observer.

And there were, he told himself, many happenings that would be worth observing. One could live out the entire history of mankind, from the prehistoric dawnings to the day before yesterday—and not only the history of mankind, but the history of other things as well, for there had been other categories of experience offered—Kimonian and Galactic—in addition to Earth.

Some day, he thought, I will walk with Shakespeare. Some day I'll sail with Columbus. Or travel with Prester John and find the truth about him.

For it was truth. You could sense the truth.

And how the truth?

That he could not know.

But it all boiled down to the fact that while conditions might be strange, one still could make a life of it.

And conditions would be strange, for this was an alien land and one that was immeasurably in advance of Earth in culture and in its technology. Here there was no need of artificial communications nor of mechanical transportation. Here there was no need of contracts; since the mere fact of telepathy would reveal one man to another, there'd be no need of contracts.

You have to adapt, Bishop told himself.

You have to adapt to play the Kimon game, for they were the ones who would set the rules. Unbidden he had entered their planet and they had let him stay and, staying, it followed that he must conform.

"You are restless, sir," said the cabinet from the other room.

"Not restless," Bishop said. "Just thinking."

"I can supply you with a sedative. A very mild and pleasant sedative."

"Not a sedative," said Bishop.

"Then, perhaps," the cabinet said, "you would permit me to sing you a lullaby."

"By all means," said Bishop. "A lullaby is just the thing I need."

So the cabinet sang him a lullaby and after a time Bishop went to sleep.

XII

The Kimonian goddess at the Employment Bureau told him next morning that there was a job for him.

"A new family," she said.

Bishop wondered if he should be glad that it was a new family or if it would have been better if it had been an old one.

"They've never had a human before," she said.

"It's fine of them," said Bishop, "to finally take one in."

"The salary," said the goddess, "is one hundred credits a day."

"One hundred—"

"You will only work during days," she said. "I'll teleport you there each morning and in the evening they'll teleport you back."

Bishop gulped. "One hundred—What am I to do?"

"A companion," said the goddess. "But you needn't worry. We'll keep an eye on them and if they mistreat you—"

"Mistreat me?"

"Work you too hard or—"

"Miss," said Bishop, "for a hundred bucks a day I'd—"

She cut him short. "You will take the job?"

"Most gladly," Bishop said.

"Permit me—" The universe came unstuck, then slapped back together.

He was standing in an alcove and in front of him was a woodland glen with a waterfall and from where he stood he could smell the cool, mossy freshness of the tumbling water. There were ferns and trees, huge trees like the gnarled oaks the illustrators like to draw to illustrate King Arthur and Robin Hood and other tales of very early Britain—the kind of oaks from which the Druids had cut the mistletoe.

A path ran along the stream and up the incline down which the waterfall came tumbling and there was a blowing wind that carried music and perfume.

A girl came down the path and she was Kimonian, but she didn't seem as tall as the others he had seen and there was something a little less goddesslike about her.

He caught his breath and watched her and for a moment he forgot that she was Kimonian and thought of her only as a pretty girl who walked a woodland path. She was beautiful, he told himself—she was lovely.

She saw him and clapped her hands.

"You must be he," she said.

He stepped out of the cubicle.

"We have been waiting for you," she told him. "We hoped there'd be no delay, that they'd send you right along."

"My name," said Bishop, "is Selden Bishop and I was told—"

"Of course you are the one," she said. "You needn't even tell me. It's lying in your mind."

She waved an arm about her.

"How do you like your house?" she asked.

"House?"

"Of course, silly. This. Naturally, it's only the living-room. Our bedrooms are up in the mountains. But we changed this just yesterday. Everyone worked so hard at it. I do hope you like it. Because, you see, it is from your planet. We thought it might make you feel at home."

"House," he said again.

She reached out a hand and laid it on his arm.

"You're all upset," she said. "You don't begin to understand."

Bishop shook his head. "I just arrived the other day."

"But you do like it?"

"Of course I do," said Bishop. "It's something out of the old Arthurian legend. You'd expect to see Lancelot or Guinevere or some of the others riding through the woods."

"You know the stories?"

"Of course I know the stories. I read my Tennyson."

"And you will tell them to us."

He looked at her, a little startled.

"You mean you want to hear them?"

"Why, yes, of course we do. What did we get you for?"

And that was it, of course.

What had they got him for?

"You want me to begin right now?"

"Not now," she said. "There are the others you must meet. My name is Elaine. That's not exactly it, of course. It is something else, but Elaine is as close as you'll ever come to saying it."

"I could try the other name. I'm proficient at the languages."

"Elaine is good enough," she said carelessly. "Come along."

He fell in behind her on the path and followed up the incline.

And as he walked along, he saw that it was indeed a house—that the trees were pillars holding up an artificial sky that somehow failed to look very artificial and that the aisles between the trees ended in great windows which looked out on the barren plain.

But the grass and flowers, the moss and ferns, were real and he had a feeling that the trees must be real as well.

"It doesn't matter if they're real or not," said Elaine. "You couldn't tell the difference."

They came to the top of the incline into a parklike place, where the grass was cut so closely and looked so velvety that he wondered for a moment if it were really grass.

"It is," Elaine told him.

"You catch everything I think," he said. "Isn't—?"

"Everything," said Elaine.

"Then I mustn't think."

"Oh, but we want you to," she told him. "That is part of it."

"Part of what you got me for?"

"Exactly," said the girl.

In the middle of the parklike area was a sort of pagoda, a flimsy thing that seemed to be made out of light and shadow rather than anything with substance, and around it were half a dozen people.

They were laughing and chatting and the sound of them was like the sound of music—very happy, but at the same time sophisticated, music.

"There they are," cried Elaine.

"Come along," she said.

She ran and her running was like flying and his breath caught in his throat at the slimness and the grace of her.

He ran after her and there was no grace in his running. He could feel the heaviness of it. It was a gambol rather than a run, an awkward lope in comparison to the running of Elaine.

Like a dog, he thought. Like an overgrown puppy trying to keep up, falling over his own feet, with its tongue hanging out and panting.

He tried to run more gracefully and he tried to erase the thinking from his mind.

Mustn't think. Mustn't think at all. They catch everything. They will laugh at you.

They *were* laughing at him.

He could feel their laughter, the silent, gracious amusement that was racing in their minds.

She reached the group and waited.

"Hurry up," she called and while her words were kindly, he could feel the amusement in the words.

He hurried. He pounded down upon them. He arrived somewhat out of breath. He felt winded and sweaty and extremely uncouth.

"This is the one they sent us," said Elaine. "His name is Bishop. Is that not a lovely name?"

They watched him, nodding gravely.

"He will tell us stories," said Elaine. "He knows the stories that go with a place like this."

They were looking kindly at him, but he could sense the covert amusement, growing by the moment.

She said to Bishop: "This is Paul. And that one over there is Jim. Betty. Jane. George. And the one on the end is Mary."

"You understand," said Jim, "those are not our names."

"They are approximations," said Elaine. "The best that I could do."

"They are as close," said Jane, "as he can pronounce them."

"If you'd only give me a chance," said Bishop, then stopped short.

That was what they wanted. They wanted him to protest and squirm. They wanted him to be uncomfortable.

"But of course we don't," said Elaine.

Mustn't think. Must try to keep from thinking. They catch everything.

"Let's all sit down," said Betty. "Bishop will tell us stories."

"Perhaps," Jim said to him, "you will describe your life on Earth. I should be quite interested."

"I understand you have a game called chess," said George.

"We can't play games, of course. You know why we can't. But I'd be very interested in discussing with you the technique and philosophy of chess."

"One at a time," said Elaine. "First he will tell us stories."

They sat down on the grass, in a ragged circle.

All of them were looking at him, waiting for him to start.

"I don't quite know where to start," he said.

"Why, that's obvious," said Betty. "You start at the beginning."

"Quite right," said Bishop.

He took a deep breath.

"Once, long ago, in the island of Britain, there was a great king, whose name was Arthur—"

"Yclept," said Jim.

"You've read the stories?"

"The word was in your mind."

"It's an old word, an archaic word. In some versions of the tales—"

"I should be most interested sometime to discuss the word with you," said Jim.

"Go on with your story," said Elaine.

He took another deep breath.

"Once, long ago, in the island of Britain, there was a great king whose name was Arthur. His queen was Guinevere and Lancelot was his staunchest knight—"

He found the writer in the desk in the living room and pulled it out. He sat down to write a letter.

He typed the salutation:

Dear Morley:

He got up and began pacing up and down the room.

What would he tell him?

What could he tell him?

That he had safely arrived and he had a job?

That the job paid a hundred credits a day—ten times more than a man in his position could earn at any Earth job?

He went back to the writer again.

He wrote:

Just a note to let you know that I arrived here safely and already have a job. Not too good a job, perhaps, but it pays a hundred a day and that's better than I could have done on Earth.

He got up and walked again.

There had to be more than that. More than just a paragraph.

He sweated as he walked.

What could he tell him?

He went back to the writer again:

In order to learn the conditions and the customs more quickly have taken a job which will keep me in touch with the Kimonians. I find them to be a fine people, but sometimes a little hard to understand. I have no doubt that before too long I shall get to understand them and have a genuine liking for them.

He pushed back his chair and stared at what he'd written.

It was, he told himself, like any one of a thousand other letters he had read.

He pictured in his mind those other thousand people, sitting down to write their first letter from Kimon, searching in their mind for the polite little fables, for the slightly colored lie, for the balm that would salve their pride. Hunting for the words that would not reveal the entire truth:

I have a job of entertaining and amusing a certain family. I tell them stories and let them laugh at me. I do this because I will not admit that the fable of Kimon is a booby trap and that I've fallen into it—

No, it would never do to write like that.

Nor to write:

I'm sticking on in spite of them. So long as I make a hundred a day, they can laugh as much as they want to laugh. I'm staying here and cleaning up no matter what—

Back home he was one of a thousand. Back home they talked of him in whispers because he made the grade.

And the businessmen on board the ship, saying to him: "The one who cracks this Kimon business is the one who'll have it big," and talking in terms of billions if he ever needed backing.

He remembered Morley pacing up and down the room. A foot in the door, he'd said: "Some way to crack them. Some way to understand them. Some little thing—no big thing, but some little thing. Anything at all except the deadpan face that Kimon turns toward us."

Somehow he had to finish the letter. He couldn't leave it hanging and he had to write it.

He turned back to the writer:

I'll write you later at a greater length. At the moment I'm rushed.

He frowned at it.

But whatever he wrote, it would be wrong. This was no worse than any of another dozen things that he might write.

Must rush off to a conference.

Have an appointment with a client.

Some papers to go through.

All of them were wrong.

What was a man to do?

He wrote:

Think of you often. Write me when you can.

Morley would write him. An enthusiastic letter, a letter with a fine shade of envy tingeing it, the letter of a man who wanted to be, but couldn't be, on Kimon.

For everyone wanted to go to Kimon. That was the hell of it.

You couldn't tell the truth, when everyone would give their good right arm to go.

You couldn't tell the truth when you were a hero and the truth would turn you into a galactic heel.

And the letters from home, the prideful letters, the envious letters, the letters happy with the thought you were doing so well—all of these would be only further chains to bind you to Kimon and to the Kimon lie.

He said to the cabinet, "How about a drink?"

"Yes, sir," said the cabinet. "Coming right up, sir."

"A long one," said Bishop. "And a strong one."

"Long and strong it is, sir."

XIV

He met her in the bar.

"Why, if it isn't Buster!" she said, as though they met there often.

He sat on the stool beside her.

"That week is almost up," he said.

She nodded. "We've been watching you. You're standing up real well."

"You tried to tell me."

"Forget it," said the girl. "Just a mistake of mine. It's a waste of time telling any of them. But you looked intelligent and not quite dry behind the ears. I took pity on you."

She looked at him over the rim of her glass.

"I shouldn't have," she said.

"I should have listened."

"They never do," said Maxine.

"There's another thing," he said. "Why hasn't it leaked out? Oh, sure, I have written letters, too. I didn't admit what it was like. Neither did you. Nor the man next to you. But someone, in all the years we've been here—"

"We are all alike," she said. "Alike as peas in the pod. We are the anointed, the hand-picked, stubborn, vanity-stricken, scared. All of us got here. In spite of hell and high water we got here. We let nothing stand in our way and we made it. We beat the others out. They're waiting back there on Earth—the ones that we beat out. They'll never be quite the same again. Don't you understand it? They had pride, too, and it was hurt. There's nothing they would like better than to know what it's really like. That's what all of us think of when we sit down to write a letter. We think of the belly laughs by those other thousands. The quiet smirks. We think of ourselves skulking, making ourselves small so no one will notice us—"

She balled a fist and rapped against his shirt front.

"That's the answer, Buster. That's why we never write the truth. That's why we don't go back."

"But it's been going on for years. For almost a hundred years. In all that time someone should have cracked—"

"And lost all this?" she asked. "Lost the easy living. The good drinking. The fellowship of lost souls. And the hope. Don't forget that. Always the hope that Kimon can be cracked."

"Can it?"

"I don't know. But if I were you, Buster, I wouldn't count on it."

"But it's no kind of life for decent—"

"Don't say it. We aren't decent people. We are scared and weak, every one of us. And with good reason."

"But the life—"

"You don't live a decent life, if that was what you were about to say. There's no stability in us. Children? A few of us have children and it's not so bad for the children as it is for us, because they know nothing else. A child who is born a slave is better off, mentally, than a man who once knew freedom."

"We aren't slaves," said Bishop.

"Of course not," Maxine said. "We can leave any time we want to. All we got to do is walk up to a native and say, 'I want to go back to Earth.' That's all you need to do. Any single one of them could send you back—swish—just as they send the letters, just like they whisk you to your work or to your room."

"But no one has gone back."

"Of course no one has," she said.

They sat there, sipping at their drinks.

"Remember what I told you," she said. "Don't think. That's the way to beat it. Never think about it. You got it good. You never had it so good. Soft living. Easy living. Nothing to worry about. They best kind of life there is."

"Sure," said Bishop. "Sure, that's the way to do it."

She slanted her eyes at him.

"You're catching on," she said.

They had another round.

Over in the corner a group had got together and was doing some impromptu singing. A couple were quarreling a stool or two away.

"It's too noisy in this place," Maxine said. "Want to see my paintings?"

"Your paintings?"

"The way I make a living. They are pretty bad, but no one knows the difference."

"I'd like to see them."

"Grab hold then."

"Grab—"

"My mind, you know. Nothing physical about it. No use riding elevators."

He gaped at her.

"You pick it up," said Maxine. "You never get too good. But you pick up a trick or two."

"But how do I go about it?"

"Just let loose," she said. "Dangle. Mentally, that is. Try to reach out to me. Don't try to help. You can't."

He dangled and reached out, wondering if he was doing it the way it should be done.

The universe collapsed and then came back together.

They were standing in another room.

"That was a silly thing for me to do," Maxine said. "Some day I'll slip a cog and get stuck in a wall or something."

Bishop drew a deep breath.

"Monty could read me just a little," he said. "Said you picked it up—just at the fringes."

"You never get too good," said Maxine. "Humans aren't . . . well, aren't ripe for it, I guess. It takes millennia to develop it."

He looked around him and whistled.

"Quite a place," he said.

It was all of that.

It didn't seem to be a room at all, although it had furniture. The walls were hazed in distance and to the west were mountains peaked with snow, and to the east a very sylvan river and there were flowers and flowering bushes everywhere, growing from the floor. A deep blue dusk filled the room and somewhere off in the distance there was an orchestra.

A cabinet-voice said, "Anything, madam?"

"Drinks," said Maxine. "Not too strong. We've been hitting the bottle."

"Not too strong," said the cabinet. "Just a moment, madam."

"Illusion," Maxine said. "Every bit of it. But a nice illusion. Want a beach? It's waiting for you if you just think of it. Or a polar cap. Or a desert. Or an old chateau. It's waiting in the wings."

"Your painting must pay off," he said.

"Not my painting. My irritation. Better start getting irritated, Buster. Get down in the dumps. Start thinking about suicide. That's a sure-fire way to do it. Presto, you're kicked upstairs to a better suite of rooms. Anything to keep you happy."

"You mean the Kimonians automatically shift you?"

"Sure. You're a sucker to stay down there where you are."

"I like my layout," he told her. "But this—"

She laughed at him. "You'll catch on," she said.

The drinks arrived.

“Sit down,” Maxine said. “Want a moon?”

There was a moon.

“Could have two or three,” she said, “but that would be overdoing it. One moon seems more like Earth. Seems more comfortable.”

“There must be a limit somewhere,” Bishop said. “They can’t keep on kicking you upstairs indefinitely. There must come a time when even the Kimonians can’t come up with anything that is new and novel.”

“You wouldn’t live long enough,” she told him, “for that to come about. That’s the way with all you new ones. You underestimate the Kimonians. You think of them as people, as Earth people who know just a little more. They aren’t that, at all. They’re alien. They’re as alien as a spider-man despite their human form. They conform to keep contact with us.”

“But why do they want to keep contact with us? Why—”

“Buster,” she said. “That’s the question that we never ask. That’s the one that can drive you crazy.”

XV

He had told them about the human custom of going out on picnics and the idea was one that they had never thought of, so they adopted it with childish delight.

They had picked a wild place, a tumbled mountain area filled with deep ravines, clothed in flowers and trees and with a mountain brook with water that was as clear as glass and as cold as ice.

They had played games and romped. They had swum and sunbathed and they had listened to his stories, sitting in a circle, needling him and interrupting him, picking arguments.

But he had laughed at them, not openly, but deep inside

himself, for he knew now that they meant no harm, but merely sought amusement.

Weeks before he had been insulted and outraged and humiliated, but as the days went on he had adapted to it—had forced himself to adapt. If they wished a clown, then he would be a clown. If he were court fool, with bells and parti-colored garments, then he must wear the colors well and keep the bells ringing merrily.

There was occasional maliciousness in them, and some cruelty, but no lasting harm. And you could get along with them, he told himself, if you just knew how to do it.

When evening came they had built a fire and had sat around it and had talked and laughed and joked, for once leaving him alone. Elaine and Betty had been nervous. Jim had laughed at them for their nervousness.

"No animal will come near a fire," he said.

"There are animals?" Bishop had asked.

"A few," said Jim. "Not many of them left."

He had lain there, staring at the fire, listening to their voices, glad that for once they were leaving him alone. Like a dog must feel, he thought. Like a pup hiding in a corner from a gang of rowdy children who are always mauling it.

He watched the fire and remembered other days—outings in the country and walking trips when they had built a fire and lain around it, staring at the sky, seeing the old, familiar skies of Earth.

And here again was another fire.

And here, again, a picnic.

The fire was Earth and so was the picnic—for the people of Kimon did not know of picnics. They did not know of picnics and there might be many other things of which they likewise did not know. Many other things, perhaps. Barbaric, folkish things.

Don't look for the big things, Morley had said that night. Watch for the little things, for the little clues.

They liked Maxine's paintings because they were primitives. Primitives, perhaps, but likewise not very good. Could it be that paintings also had been something the Kimonians had not known until the Earthmen came?

Were there, after all, chinks in the Kimonian armor? Little chinks like picnics and paintings and many other little things for which they valued the visitors from Earth?

Somewhere in those chinks might be the answer that he sought for Morley.

He lay and thought, forgetting to shield his mind, forgetting that he should not think because his thoughts lay open to them.

Their voices had faded away and there was a solemn nighttime quiet. Soon, he thought, we'll all be going back—they to their homes and I to the hotel. How far away, he wondered. Half a world or less? And yet they'd be there in the instant of a thought.

Someone, he thought, should put more wood on the fire.

He roused himself to do it, standing up.

And it was not until then that he saw he was alone.

He stood there, trying to quiet his terror.

They had gone away and left him.

They had forgotten him.

But that couldn't be. They'd simply slipped off in the dark. Up to some prank, perhaps. Trying to scare him. Talking about the animals and then slipping out of sight while he lay dreaming at the fire. Waiting now, just outside the circle of the firelight, watching him, drinking in his thoughts, reveling in his terror.

He found wood and put it on the fire. It caught and blazed.

He sat down nonchalantly, but he found that his shoulders were hunched instinctively, that the terror of aloneness in an alien world still sat by the fire beside him.

Now, for the first time, he realized the alienness of Kimon. It had not seemed alien before except for those few minutes he had waited in the park after the gig had landed him, and even then it had not been as alien as an alien planet should be, because he knew that he was being met, that there would be someone along to take care of him.

That was it, he thought. Someone to take care of me. We're taken care of—well and lavishly. We're sheltered and guarded and pampered—that was it, *pampered.* And for what reason?

Any minute now they'd tire of their game and come back into the circle of the firelight.

Maybe, he told himself, I should give them their money's worth. Maybe I should act scared, maybe I should shout out for them to come and get me, maybe I should glance around out into the darkness, as if I were afraid of those animals that they talked about. They hadn't talked too much, of course. They were too clever for that, far too clever. Just a passing remark about existent animals, then on to something else. Not stressing it, not laying it on too thick. Not overdoing it. Just planting a suggestion that there were animals one could be afraid of.

He sat and waited, no as scared as he had been before, having rationalized away the fear that he first had felt. Like an Earth campfire, he thought. Except it isn't Earth. Except it's an alien planet.

There was a rustle in the bushes.

They'll be coming now, he thought. They've figured out that it didn't work. They'll be coming back.

The bushes rustled again and there was the sound of a dislodged stone.

He did not stir.

They can't scare me, he thought.

They can't scare—

He felt the breath upon his neck and leaped into the air, spinning as he leaped, stumbling as he came down, almost falling in the fire, then on his feet and scurrying to put the fire between him and the thing that had breathed upon his neck.

He crouched across the fire from it and saw the teeth in the gaping jaws. It raised its head and slashed, as if in pantomime, and he could hear the clicking of the teeth as they came together and the little moaning rumble that came from the massive throat.

A wild thought came to him: It's not an animal at all. This is just part of the gag. Something they dreamed up. If they can build a house like an English wood, use it for a day or two, then cause it to disappear as something for which they would have no further use, surely it would be a second's work to dream up an animal.

The animal padded forward and he thought: Animals should be afraid of fire. All animals are afraid of fire. It won't get me if I stay near the fire.

He stooped and grabbed a brand.

Animals are afraid of fire.

But this one wasn't.

It padded round the fire. It stretched out its neck and sniffed.

It wasn't in any hurry, for it was sure of him.

Sweat broke out on him and ran down his sides.

The animal came with a smooth rush, whipping around the fire.

He leaped, clearing the fire, to gain the other side of it. The animal checked itself, spun around to face him.

It put its muzzle to the ground and arched its back. It lashed its tail. It rumbled.

He was frightened now, cold with a fright that could not be laughed off.

It might be an animal.

It must be an animal.

No gag at all, but an animal.

He paced back toward the fire. He danced on his toes, ready to run, to dodge, to fight if he had to fight. But against this thing that faced him across the fire, he knew, there was no fighting chance. And yet, if it came to fighting, he could do no less than fight.

The animal charged.

He ran.

He slipped and fell and rolled into the fire.

A hand reached down and jerked him from the fire, flung him to one side, and a voice cried out, a cry of rage and warning.

Then the universe collapsed and he felt himself flying apart and, as suddenly, he was together once again.

He lay upon a floor and he scrambled to his feet. His hand was burned and he felt the pain of it. His clothes were smoldering and he beat them out with his uninjured hand.

A voice said, "I'm sorry, sir. This should not have happened."

The man was tall, much taller than the Kimonians he had seen before. Nine feet, perhaps. And yet not nine feet, actually. Not anywhere near nine feet. He was no taller, probably, than the taller men of Earth. It was the way he stood that made him seem so tall, the way he stood and looked and the way his voice sounded.

And the first Kimonian, Bishop thought, who had ever shown age. For there was a silvering of the temple hairs and his face was lined, like the faces of hunters or of sailors may be lined from squinting into far distances.

They stood facing one another in a room which, when Bishop looked at it, took his breath away. There was no describing it, no way to describe it—you felt as well as saw it. It was a part of you and a part of the universe and a part of everything you'd ever known or dreamed. It seemed to thrust extensions out into unguessed time and space and it had a sense of life and the touch of comfort and the feel of home.

Yet, when he looked again, he sensed a simplicity that did not square with his first impressions. Basic simplicities that tied in with the simple business of living out one's life, as if the room and the folks who lived within its walls were somehow integrated, as if the room were trying its best not to be a room, but to be a part of life, so much a part of life that it could pass unnoticed.

"I was against it from the first," said the Kimonian. "Now I know that I was right. But the children wanted you—"

"The children?"

"Certainly. I am Elaine's father."

He didn't say Elaine, however. He said the other name—the name that Elaine had said no Earthman could pronounce.

"Your hand?" asked the man.

"It's all right," said Bishop. "Only burned a little."

And it was as if he had not spoken, as if he had not said the words—but another man, a man who stood off to one side and spoke the words for him.

He could not have moved if he'd been paid a million.

"This is something," said the Kimonian, "that must be recompensed. We'll talk about it later."

"Please, sir," said the man who talked for Bishop. "Please, sir, just one thing. Send me to my hotel."

He felt the swiftness of the other's understanding—the compassion and the pity.

"Of course," said the tall man. "With your permission, sir."

XVI

Once there were some children (human children, naturally) who had wanted a dog—a little playful puppy. But their father said they could not have a dog because they would not know how to treat him. But they wanted him so badly and begged their father so that he finally brought them home a dog, a cunning little puppy, a little butterball, with a paunchy belly and four wobbly legs and melting eyes, filled with the innocence of puppyhood.

The children did not treat him as badly as you might have imagined that they would. They were cruel, as all children are.

They roughed and tumbled him; they pulled his ears and tail; they teased him. But the pup was full of fun. He liked to play and no matter what they did he came back for more. Because, undoubtedly, he felt very smug in this business of associating with the clever human race, a race so far ahead of dogs in culture and intelligence that there was no comparison at all.

But one day the children went on a picnic and when the day was over they were very tired, and forgetful, as children are very apt to be. so they went off and left the puppy.

That wasn't a bad thing, really. For children will be forgetful, no matter what you do, and the pup was nothing but a dog.

The cabinet said, "You are very late, sir."

"Yes," said Bishop, dully.

"You hurt somewhere, sir. I can sense the hurt."

"My hand," said Bishop. "I burned it in a fire."

A panel popped open in the cabinet.

"Put it in there," said the cabinet. "I'll fix it in a jiffy."

Bishop thrust his hand into the opening. He felt fingerlike appendages going over it, very gentle and soothing.

"It's not a bad burn, sir," said the cabinet, "but I imagine it is painful."

Playthings, Bishop thought.

This hotel is a dollhouse—or a doghouse.

It is a shack, a tacked-together shack like the boys of Earth build out of packing cases and bits of board and paint crude, mystic signs upon.

Compared to that room back there it is no more than a hovel, although come to think of it, a very gaudy hovel.

Fit for humans, good enough for humans, but a hovel just the same.

And we? he thought.

And we?

The pets of children. The puppy dogs of Kimon.

Imported puppy dogs.

"I beg your pardon, sir," said the cabinet. "You are not puppy dogs."

"What's that?"

"You will pardon me, sir. I should not have spoken out. But I wouldn't have wanted you to think—"

"If we aren't pets, what are we?"

"You will excuse me, sir. It was a slip, I quite assure you. I should not have—"

"You never do a thing," said Bishop bitterly, "without having it all figured out. You or any of them. For you are one of them. You spoke because they wanted you to speak."

"I can assure you that's not so."

"You would deny it, naturally," said Bishop. "Go ahead and do your job. You haven't told me all they wanted you to tell me. Go ahead and finish."

"It's immaterial to me what you think," the cabinet told him. "But if you thought of yourselves as playmates . . ."

"That's a hot one," Bishop said.

"Infinitely better," said the cabinet, "than thinking of yourself as a puppy dog."

"So that's what they want me to think."

"They don't care," the cabinet said. "It is all up to you. It was a mere suggestion, sir."

So, all right, it was a mere suggestion.

So, all right, they were playmates and not pets at all.

The kids of Kimon inviting the dirty, ragged, runny-nosed urchins from across the tracks to play with them.

Better to be an invited kid, perhaps, than an imported dog.

But even so, it was the children of Kimon who had engineered it all—who had set up the rules for those who wished to come to Kimon, who had built the hotel, had operated it and furnished it with the progressively more luxurious and more enticing rooms, who had found the so-called jobs for humans, who had arranged the printing of the credits.

And if that were so, then it meant that not merely the people of Earth, but the government of Earth, had negotiated, or had attempted to negotiate with the children of another race. And that would be the mark of the difference, he thought, the difference between us.

Although, he told himself, that might not be entirely right.

Maybe he *had* been wrong in thinking, in the first flush of his bitterness, that he was a pet.

Maybe he *was* a playmate, an adult Earthman downgraded to the status of a child—and a stupid child, at that. Maybe, if he had been wrong on the pet angle, he was wrong in the belief, as well, that it had been the children of Kimon who had arranged the immigration of the Earth folk.

And if it hadn't been simply a childish matter of asking in some kids from across the tracks, if the adults of Kimon had had a hand in it, what was the setup then? A school project, a certain phase of progressive education? Or a sort of summer camp project, designed to give the deserving, but underprivileged, Earthman a vacation away from the squalor of their native planet? Or simply a safe way in which the children of Kimon might amuse and occupy themselves, be kept from underfoot?

We should have guessed it long ago, Bishop told himself. But even if some of us might have entertained the thought, that we were either pet or playmate, we would have pushed it far away from us, would have refused to recognize it, for our pride is too tender and too raw for a thought like that.

"There you are, sir," said the cabinet. "Almost as good as new. Tomorrow you can take the dressing off."

He stood before the cabinet without answering. He withdrew his hand and let it fall to his side, like so much dead weight.

Without asking if he wanted it, the cabinet produced a drink.

"I made it long and strong," said the cabinet. "I thought you needed it."

"Thank you," Bishop said.

He took the drink and stood there with it, not touching it, not wanting to touch it until he'd finished out the thought.

And the thought would not finish out.

There was something wrong. Something that didn't track.

Our pride is too raw and tender—

There was something there, some extra words that badly needed saying.

"There is something wrong, sir."

"Nothing wrong," said Bishop.

"But your drink."

"I'll get around to it."

The Normans had sat their horses on that Saturday afternoon, with the leopard banners curling in the breeze, with the pennons on their lances fluttering, with the sun upon their armor and the scabbards clinking as the horses pranced. They had charged, as history said they had, and they were beaten back. That was entirely right, for it had not been until late afternoon that the Saxon wall was broken and the final fight around the dragon standard had not taken place until it was nearly dark.

But there had been no Taillefer, riding in the fore to throw up his sword and sing.

On that history had been wrong.

A couple of centuries later, more than likely, some copyist had whiled away a monotonous afternoon by writing into the prosaic story of the battle the romance and the glitter of the charge of Taillefer. Writing it in protest against the four blank walls, against his Spartan food, against the daily dullness when spring was in the air and a man should be in the fields or woods instead of shut indoors, hunched with his quills and inkpots.

And that is the way it is with us, thought Bishop. We write the half-truth and the half-lie in our letters home. We conceal a truth or we obscure a fact or we add a line or two that, if not a downright lie, is certainly misleading.

We do not face up to facts, he thought. We gloss over the man crawling in the grass, with his torn-out guts snagging on the brambles. We write in the Taillefer.

And if we only did it in our letters, it would not be so bad. But we do it to ourselves. We protect our pride by lying to ourselves. We shield our dignity by deliberate indignation.

"Here," he said to the cabinet, "have a drink on me."

He set the glass, still full, on the top of the cabinet.

The cabinet gurgled in surprise.

"I do not drink," it said.

"Then take it back and put it in the bottle."

"I can't do that," said the cabinet, horrified. "It's already mixed."

"Separate it, then."

"It can't be separated," wailed the cabinet. "You surely don't expect me—"

There was a little swish and Maxine stood in the center of the room.

She smiled at Bishop.

"What goes on?" she asked.

The cabinet wailed at her. "He wants me to unmix a drink. He wants me to separate it, the liquor from the mix. He knows I can't do that."

"My, my," she said. "I thought you could do anything."

"I can't unravel a drink," the cabinet said primly. "Why don't you take it off my hands?"

"That's a good idea," said the girl. She walked forward and picked up the drink.

"What's wrong with you?" she asked Bishop. "Turning chicken on us?"

"I just don't want a drink," said Bishop. "Hasn't a man got a right to—"

"Of course," she said. "Of course you have."

She sipped the drink, looking at him above the rim.

"What happened to your hand?"

"Burned it."

"You're old enough not to play with fire."

"You're old enough not to come barging into a room this way," Bishop told her. "One of these days you'll reassemble yourself in the precise spot where someone else is standing."

She giggled. "That would be fun," she said. "Think of you and I—"

"It would be a mess," said Bishop.

"Invite me to sit down," said Maxine. "Let's act civilized and social."

"Sure, sit down," said Bishop.

She picked out a couch.

"I'm interested in this business of teleporting yourself," said Bishop. "I've asked you before, but you never told me—"

"It just came to me," she said.

"But you can't teleport. Humans aren't parapsychic—"

"Some day, Buster, you'll blow a fuse. You get so steamed up."

He went across the room and sat down beside her.

"Sure, I get steamed up," he said. "But—"

"What now?"

"Have you ever thought . . . well, have you ever tried to work at it? Like moving something else, some object—other than yourself?"

"No, I never have."

"Why not?"

"Look, Buster. I drop in to have a drink with you and to forget myself. I didn't come primed for a long technical discussion. I couldn't anyway. I just don't understand. There's so much we don't understand."

She looked at him and there was something very much like fright brimming in her eyes.

"You pretend that you don't mind," she said. "But you do

mind. You wear yourself out pretending that you don't mind at all."

"Then let's quit pretending," Bishop said. "Let's admit—"

She had lifted the glass to drink and now, suddenly it slipped out of her hand.

"Oh—"

The glass halted before it struck the floor. It hovered for a moment, then it slowly rose. She reached out and grasped it.

And then it slipped again from her suddenly shaking hand. This time it hit the floor and spilled.

"Try it again," said Bishop.

She said, "I never tried. I don't know how it happened. I just didn't want to drop it, that was all. I wished I hadn't dropped it and then—"

"But the second time—"

"You fool," she screamed. "I tell you I didn't try. I wasn't putting on an exhibition for you. I tell you that I don't know what happened."

"But you did it. It was a start."

"A start?"

"You caught the glass before it hit the floor. You teleported it back into your hand."

"Look, Buster," she said grimly, "quit kidding yourself. They're watching all the time. They play little tricks like that. Anything for a laugh."

She rose, laughing at him, but there was a strangeness in her laughing.

"You don't give yourself a chance," he told her. "You are so horribly afraid of being laughed at. You got to be a wise guy."

"Thanks for the drink," she said.

"But Maxine—"

"Come up and see me sometime."

"Maxine! Wait!"

But she was gone.

XVII

Watch for the clues, Morley had said, pacing up and down the room. Send us back the clues and we will do the rest. A foot in the door is all we expect from you. Give us a foot inside the door and that is all we need.

Clues, he had said.

Not fact, but clues.

And perhaps he had said clues instead of facts because he had been blinded like all the rest of them. Like the copyist who could not face up to the fact of battle without chivalry. Like those who wrote the letters home from Kimon. Like Maxine, who said quit kidding yourself, Buster, they're watching all the time, they play little tricks like this.

And here were facts.

Facts he should send home to Morley.

Except he couldn't send them.

Facts that he was ashamed to send.

You couldn't write:

We are pets. The children house and feed us. They throw sticks for us to chase. They like to hear us bark—

He sweated as he thought of it.

Or the kinder fact:

We are playmates—

You couldn't write that, either. You simply couldn't write it.

And yet, he said, the facts are there—the truth is there. And you must admit it. You must admit the fact. And you must admit the truth.

If not for Morley, if not for Earth, if not for fellow man, then you must admit it for yourself.

For a man may fool his friends, he may deceive the world—but he must be truthful with himself. Let's forget the bitterness, he told himself—the bitterness and hurt. Let's forget the pride.

Let us look for facts.

The Kimonians are a race more culturally advanced than we are, which means, in other words, that they are farther along the road of evolution, farther from the ape. And what does it take to advance along the evolutionary road beyond the high tide of my own race of Earth?

Not mere intelligence alone, for that is not enough.

What then would it take to make the next major stride in evolution?

Perhaps philosophy rather than intelligence—a seeking for a way to put to better use the intelligence that one already had, a greater understanding and a more adequate appreciation of human values in relation to the universe.

And if the Kimonians had that greater understanding, if they had won their way through better understanding to closer brotherhood with the galaxy, then it would be inconceivable that they'd take the members of another intelligent race to serve as puppy dogs for children. Or even as playmates for their children, unless in the fact of playing with their children there be some greater value, not to their child alone, but to the child of Earth, than the happiness and wonder of such association. They would be alive to the psychic damage that might be done because of such a practice, would not for a moment run the danger of that damage happening unless out of it might come some improvement or some change.

He sat and thought of it and it seemed right, for even on his native planet history showed increasing concern with social values as the culture improved.

And something else.

Parapsychic powers must not come too soon in human evolution, for they could be used disastrously by a culture that was not equipped, emotionally and intellectually, to handle them. No culture which had not reached an adult stage could have parapsychic powers, for they were nothing to be fooled around with by an adolescent culture.

In that respect at least, Bishop told himself, the Kimonians are the adults and we are the adolescents. In comparison with the Kimonians, we have no right to consider ourselves any more than children.

It was hard to take.

He gagged on it.

Swallow it, he told himself. Swallow it.

The cabinet said, “It is late, sir. You must be getting tired.”

“You want me to go to bed?”

“It’s a suggestion, sir.”

“All right,” he said.

He rose and started for the bedroom, smiling to himself.

Sent off to bed, he thought—just as a child is sent.

And going.

Not saying: “I’ll go when I am ready.”

Not standing on your adult dignity.

Not throwing a tantrum, not beating your heels upon the floor and howling.

Going off to bed—like a child when it’s told to go.

Maybe that’s the way, he thought. Maybe that’s the answer. Maybe that’s the *only* answer.

He swung around.

“Cabinet.”

“What is it, sir?”

“Nothing,” Bishop said. “Nothing at all . . . that is. Thanks for fixing up my hand.”

“That’s quite all right,” said the cabinet. “Good night.”

Maybe that’s the answer.

To act like a child.

And what does a child do?

He goes to bed when he is told.

He minds his elders.

He goes to school.

He—Wait a minute!

He goes to school!

He goes to school because there is a lot to learn. He goes to kindergarten so that he can get into first grade and he goes to high school so that he can go to college. He realizes there is a lot to learn, that before he takes his place in the adult world it must be learned and that he has to work to learn.

But I went to school, Bishop told himself. I went for years and years. I studied hard and I passed an examination that a thousand others failed to pass. I qualified for Kimon.

But just suppose.

You went to kindergarten to qualify for first grade.

You went to high school to qualify for college.

You went to Earth to qualify for Kimon.

You might have a doctorate on Earth, but still be no more than a kindergarten youngster when you got to Kimon.

Monty knew a bit of telepathy and so did some of the others. Maxine could teleport herself and she had made the glass stop before it hit the floor. Perhaps the others could, too.

And they'd just picked it up.

Although just telepathy or stopping a glass from hitting the floor would not be all of it. There'd be much more of it. Much more to the culture of Kimon than the parapsychic arts.

Maybe we are ready, he thought. Maybe we're almost finished with our adolescence. Maybe we are on the verge of being ready for an adult culture. Could that be why the Kimonians let us in, the only ones in the galaxy they are willing to let in?

His brain reeled with the thought.

On Earth only one of every thousand passed the examination that sent them on to Kimon. Maybe here on Kimon only another one in every thousand would be qualified to absorb the culture that Kimon offered them.

But before you could even start to absorb the culture, before you could start to learn, before you ever went to school, you'd have to admit that you didn't know. You'd have to admit that you were a child. You couldn't go on having tantrums. You couldn't be a wise guy. You couldn't keep on polishing up false pride to hold as a shield between you and the culture that waited for your understanding.

Morley, Bishop said, I may have the answer—the answer that you're awaiting back on Earth.

But I can't tell it to you. It's something that can't be told. It's a thing that each one must find out for himself.

And the pity of it is that Earth is not readily equipped to find it out. It is not a lesson that is often taught on Earth.

Armies and guns could not storm the citadel of Kimonian culture, for you simply could not fight a war with a parapsychic people. Earth aggressiveness and business cunning likewise would fail to crack the dead-pan face of Kimon.

There is only one way, Morley, Bishop said, talking to his friend. There is only one thing that will crack this planet and that is humility.

And Earthmen are not humble creatures.

Long ago they forgot the meaning of humility.

But here it's different.

Here you have to be different.

You start out by saying, I don't know.

Then you say, I want to know.

Then you say, I'll work hard to learn.

Maybe, Bishop thought, that's why they brought us here, so that the one of us in every thousand who has a chance of learning would get that chance to learn. Maybe they are watching, hoping that there may be more than one in every thousand. Maybe they are more anxious for us to learn than we are to learn. For they may be lonely in a galaxy where there are no others like them.

Could it be that the ones at this hotel were the failures, the ones who had never tried, or who might have tried and could not pass.

And the others—the one out of every thousand—where were they?

He could not even guess.

There were no answers.

It was all superstition.

It was a premise built upon a pipedream—built on wishful thinking.

He'd wake up in the morning and know that it was wrong.

He'd go down to the bar and have a drink with Maxine or with Monty and laugh at himself for the things that he'd dreamed up.

School, he'd told himself. But it wouldn't be a school—at least not the kind of school he'd ever known before.

I wish it could be so, he thought.

The cabinet said, "You'd better get on to bed, sir."

"I suppose I should," said Bishop. "It's been a long, hard day."

"You'll want to get up early," said the cabinet, "so you aren't late to school."

CLIFFORD D. SIMAK, during his fifty-five-year career, produced some of the most iconic science fiction stories ever written. Born in 1904 on a farm in southwestern Wisconsin, Simak got a job at a small-town newspaper in 1929 and eventually became news editor of the *Minneapolis Star-Tribune*, writing fiction in his spare time.

Simak was best known for the book *City*, a reaction to the horrors of World War II, and for his novel *Way Station*. In 1953 *City* was awarded the International Fantasy Award, and in following years, Simak won three Hugo Awards and a Nebula Award. In 1977 he became the third Grand Master of the Science Fiction and Fantasy Writers of America, and before his death in 1988, he was named one of three inaugural winners of the Horror Writers Association's Bram Stoker Award for Lifetime Achievement.

DAVID W. WIXON was a close friend of Clifford D. Simak's. As Simak's health declined, Wixon, already familiar with science fiction publishing, began more and more to handle such things as his friend's business correspondence and contract matters. Named literary executor of the estate after Simak's death, Wixon began a long-term project to secure the rights to all of Simak's stories and find a way to make them available to readers who, given the fifty-five-year span of Simak's writing career, might never have gotten the chance to enjoy all of his short fiction. Along the way, Wixon also read the author's surviving journals and rejected manuscripts, which made him uniquely able to provide Simak's readers with interesting and thought-provoking commentary that sheds new light on the work and thought of a great writer.

THE COMPLETE SHORT FICTION OF CLIFFORD D. SIMAK

FROM OPEN ROAD MEDIA

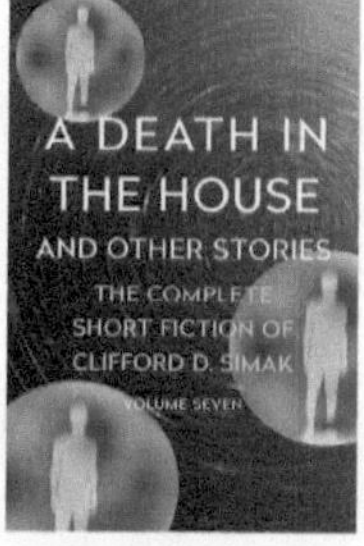

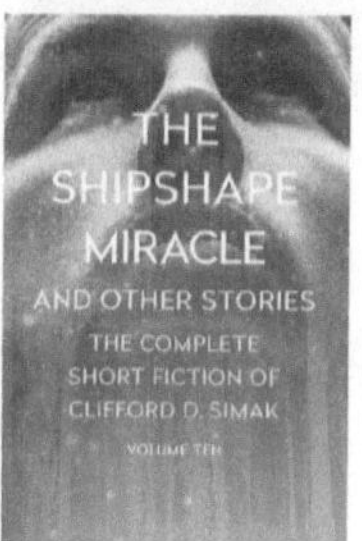

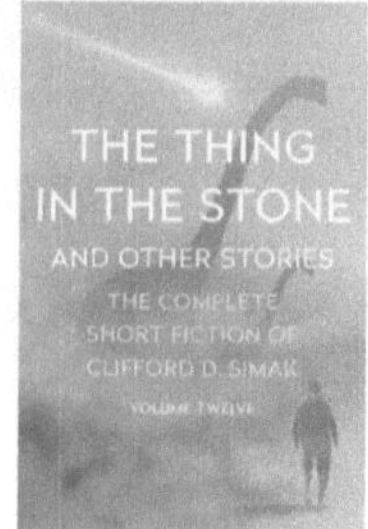

Find a full list of our authors and titles at www.openroadmedia.com

FOLLOW US

@OpenRoadMedia

www.ingramcontent.com/pod-product-compliance
Lightning Source LLC
Chambersburg PA
CBHW060416030726
47495CB00003B/606

* 9 7 8 1 5 0 4 0 7 3 9 3 6 *

EARLY BIRD BOOKS

FRESH DEALS, DELIVERED DAILY

Love to read?
Love great sales?

Get fantastic deals on bestselling ebooks delivered to your inbox every day!

Sign up today at
earlybirdbooks.com/book